Praise for the Seaside Knitters Mysteries

"Comforting. . . . Goldenbaum has created an idyllic world in which good friends, good works, and discussing the passing of time and changes in the community are as important as solving crimes." —*Publishers Weekly*

"*Murder Wears Mittens* is not another crime mystery like any other mystery. Sally Goldenbaum's characters feel for one another. It is a brilliantly written crime mystery, full of suspense and human warmth. Sally Goldenbaum knows how to monopolize your attention with her characters and writing style." —*The Washington Book Review*

"The Seaside Knitters go all out to solve another murder. . . . This one keeps you guessing a bit longer than usual and features such caring sleuths you can't help but like them." —*Kirkus Reviews*

"An intriguing murder . . . Izzy and her fellow Seaside Knitters feel an obligation to find the truth. . . . Happily, a sock pattern is appended." —*Booklist*

"The Seaside Knitters are a wonderful group of friends who care about each other, and readers will care about them, too."
—Nancy Pickard, *New York Times* bestselling author

"A quirky and colorful yarn."
—*Women's World* magazine (Book Club Pick of the Week)

"Another spectacular book from Sally Goldenbaum. . . . A mystery filled with cozy characters in a charming small town that will have you a little sad when it ends and anxious for your next visit." —*Escape with Dollycas*

"One of the best in the series and I can't wait to see where we go next in this delightfully endearing series." —*Dru's Musings*

Books by Sally Goldenbaum

The Seaside Knitters Society mysteries

Murder Wears Mittens

How to Knit a Murder

A Murderous Tangle

A Crime of a Different Stripe

The Queen Bees Quilt Shop mysteries

A Patchwork of Clues

A Thread of Darkness

A Bias for Murder

A Crime of a Different Stripe

Sally Goldenbaum

www.kensingtonbooks.com

KENSINGTON BOOKS are published by

Kensington Publishing Corp.
119 West 40th Street
New York, NY 10018

All Kensington titles, imprints, and distributed lines are available at special quantity discounts for bulk purchases for sales promotion, premiums, fund-raising, educational, or institutional use.

Special book excerpts or customized printings can also be created to fit specific needs. For details, write or phone the office of the Kensington Sales Manager: Attn.: Sales Department. Kensington Publishing Corp., 119 West 40th Street, New York, NY 10018. Phone: 1-800-221-2647.

First Kensington Hardcover Edition: November 2020

ISBN-13: 978-1-4967-2939-2 (ebook)

ISBN-13: 978-1-4967-2938-5

First Kensington Trade Paperback Edition: November 2021

10 9 8 7 6 5 4 3 2 1

Printed in the United States of America

A Crime of a Different Stripe Cast

The Seaside Knitters

Birdie Favazza (Bernadette): Sea Harbor's wealthy, wise octogenarian
Cass Halloran (Catherine Mary Theresa): Co-owner of the Halloran Lobster Company; married to Danny Brandley, mystery writer
Izzy Perry (Isabel Chambers Perry): Former attorney, owner of the Sea Harbor Yarn Studio; married to Sam Perry, award-winning photographer; toddler daughter, Abby
Nell Endicott: Retired nonprofit director; married to Ben Endicott, retired lawyer and family business owner

Family, Friends, and Townsfolk

Abigail Kathleen Perry: Izzy and Sam's daughter
Annabelle Palazola: Owner of the Sweet Petunia Restaurant
Archie and Harriet Brandley: Owners of the Sea Harbor Bookstore; Danny Brandley's parents
Beatrice Scaglia: Mayor of Sea Harbor
Charlotte Simpson: Harrison Grant's office assistant
Deb Carpenter: College student and an Art Haven caretaker
Don Wooten: Owner of the Ocean's Edge Restaurant
Eddie Porter: Student and Art Haven caretaker; Detective Tommy Porter's brother
Elena Costa: Marco Costa's twenty-two-year-old bride
Ella and Harold Sampson: Birdie's housekeeper and groundskeeper/driver
Frank Ames: Businessman
Gus McGlucken: Owner of McGlucken's Hardware Store

Harmony Fairchild: Yoga instructor
Harrison Grant: New York photographer
Harry and Margaret Garozzo: Owners of Garozzo's Deli
Libby: Waitress at Garozzo's Deli
Jake Risso: Owner of the Gull Tavern
Jane and Ham Brewster: Artists and founders of the Canary Cove Art Colony
Jerry Thompson: Police chief
Liz Santos: Manager of the Sea Harbor Yacht Club
Mae Anderson: Manager of the Sea Harbor Yarn Studio
Marco Costa: Lobsterman; Elena Costa's husband
Martina Silva: Rico Silva's wife
Mary Halloran: Cass and Pete's mother
Mary Pisano: Newspaper columnist; owner of Ravenswood B and B
Pete Halloran: Cass's brother; co-owner of the Halloran Lobster Company
Rico Silva: Sea Harbor resident; dog, Frodo
Tegan Johnson: Town veterinarian
Tommy Porter: Police detective

A Crime of a Different Stripe

Prologue

At first, Izzy Perry was puzzled when her husband, Sam, hesitated to invite the well-known photographer Harrison Grant to deliver the debut lectures for Sea Harbor's fall art series. He was charming, charismatic, and would draw a crowd.

But the fact was, Sam did invite him, and that invitation would change all their lives, at least for a period of time.

Murder could do that.

Chapter 1

Harrison Grant stood against the deck railing, watching the waves pummel the shore below, a narrow stretch of beach diminishing with each surge of tide. A gigantic moon played along the curve of the waves, nearly dipping into them. Mesmerizing. *Otherworldly*, he thought.

Although the ocean spray wasn't cold tonight, it was needle sharp, uncomfortable enough to finally drive him back inside, where a fire at one end of the Beauport Hotel bar helped dispel the damp. He found an empty chair at the bar and resumed watching the drama playing out beyond the windows.

He had nearly forgotten the power of the sea.

Unrelenting. Frighteningly beautiful and unpredictable. Destructive and majestic.

Like life.

"A drink, sir?"

It wasn't until the bartender asked again, this time leaning slightly toward him, one elbow on the bar and a silky tendril of blond hair falling over her cheek, that her words worked their way into his thoughts. She held a bottle of fine Scotch in one hand, a glass in the other, as if she knew he was that kind of man—the kind who drank fine liquor and was referred to as "sir."

He looked up at the young woman, into intent, quizzical eyes.

She was smiling. And even though the hotel bar was crowded, with hands waving, demanding service, the woman stayed still, waiting.

Harrison returned the smile. A nod. He held the woman's face in focus for a minute as she filled his glass. Without conscious thought, he framed her image in his mind's eye—the long line of her nose, the low light falling over the curve of smooth cheekbones. A small dimple in one cheek. He felt the familiar weight of an invisible Canon EOS resting in his hand. As elemental as his own fingers.

A sudden mix of feelings swept over him. He took a quick breath.

"Sir, are you okay?"

He wrapped his fingers around the glass. "I am fine. As fine as this Scotch, my fair lady. Thank you." He lifted his glass, as if to make a toast.

The woman behind the polished bar didn't move away. She pulled her brows together, her eyes focused on the handsome silver-haired man in front of her. Her head tilted to one side, as if seeking another angle, while absently wiping a damp spot on the bar with a rag. "Have I seen you before?" she finally asked. "I have, haven't I?"

"I suppose that's always a possibility in this small world of ours. But no. I don't think we've met. I've never been in this hotel before. It looks new. A beautiful place. Gloucester needed one in this area."

"I don't mean seeing you *here*. Somewhere else. Bigger. Like a TV show? Late night, *Jimmy Kimmel* maybe? Or in a movie? Lots of movies have been filmed on Cape Ann. Adam Sandler's here a lot. Served him myself. Maybe I saw you on a set around town. Are you someone I should know?"

Harrison chuckled. "No, sorry." A strand of hair fell across his forehead, and he pushed it back. It happened often enough that Harrison took it in stride. He'd never been in a movie, never doubled for George Clooney or Richard Gere or some British actor in an older film that the young woman might have seen her parents watching. And if she'd been around when he was last in the area, she would have been playing with dolls, and certainly wouldn't remember people like himself.

But the fact that the young woman *could* have seen a photo of him wasn't lost on Harrison, either. Not likely, he suspected, but possible if she read magazines featuring famous people. He'd photographed plenty of them, and sometimes a sidebar of the photographer was attached to the article. His name mentioned. Or maybe the society pages—*Vanity Fair*, the *NYT*, "Page Six." As his professional reputation had grown, so, too, had his personal notoriety, and with that had come coveted invitations. "H. Grant is right up there with Annie Leibovitz," a generous critic had once penned.

"Somewhere," the bartender persisted. "I know it."

A couple sitting nearby called for beers and martinis, forcing the reluctant bartender away. She glanced back once, seemingly unconvinced that the man at the bar with the strong cleft chin, thick hair, and deep-set eyes wasn't someone she could tell her friends about when she got off her shift. She caught his eye, and her smile grew mischievous. Flirtatious.

For a brief moment, Harrison considered his response. Not a consideration, really, but a familiar impulse. Possibly there'd be a phone number on his check. But a deep breath put the night, the journey, back in perspective and the old habits at bay.

He took a drink of Scotch and looked again toward the ocean. Flames from the outdoor firepit were dramatic against the now-dark sky, a huge autumn moon holding it all together.

He let himself sink into the scene, the din in the crowded room forming a cocoon around him, blocking out, for that moment at least, the past or the future.

Finally, one drink later, he stood and stretched, trying to release the kinks in his back. A photographer's plague. He was tired. Perhaps a walk would help everything. The kinks, the mind, the spirit. He'd come to Cape Ann early, and sitting in a safe, comfortable hotel suite wasn't the reason. What he needed was thinking time, and not for next week's lecture series at the small art colony. The lectures could write themselves. But his life couldn't. He needed to write that himself page by page. Finally. Time to deal with mistakes, with life. With death. All those lofty things.

Harrison walked over to the windows, nursing the last of his drink, the hours ahead playing out against the night.

The invitation from Sam Perry had come out of the blue. A gift from the gods. Or the devil, maybe. Who knew? Sometimes he found it hard to differentiate. What he did know was that he had planned to come to Cape Ann, anyway. It was on his list. His last stop. But fate, in the person of this former student, had set things in motion, bringing him to the island a few weeks earlier than planned. Fate sometimes took away the need to make decisions. A relief.

A lecture series for the Canary Cove Art Colony. In the art association's new magnificent old house on a cliff. He didn't deserve it, but he'd accepted the invitation almost immediately.

Although he and Sam Perry hadn't kept in touch personally, they would run into each other at events occasionally. He'd see the younger man's name in the press, an award here, a lecture there. A new photography book.

He remembered Sam clearly from that long-ago workshop, back when Harrison himself was inflating his worth to anyone who would listen. Teaching workshops at prestigious locations brought him attention and contacts and something else he needed way back then—money to live on. An additional bonus was that now and then he'd have a student like Sam Perry. Harrison recognized the young man's talent immediately. A fledgling photographer who had that innate gift—the eye, the ability to see things through a camera lens that were invisible to ordinary people. Perry had that talent in spades. Harrison knew it. And used it. And, as he suspected would happen, Perry had done just fine in spite of his instructor's interference. And somehow, that made whatever he did okay, although the old Harrison Grant wouldn't have cared either way.

He looked down at his watch, a despicable habit he couldn't shake.

No messages. He shrugged. No one was expecting him for a couple of days. There was no reason to let the lecture organizers know he had arrived in Cape Ann early. Or anyone else. He had no obligations before Friday. It gave him time.

He put some bills on the bar and anchored them with his glass. He'd be back home soon, wherever that might be. New York for starters, Paris maybe. He liked this new sense of freedom, for however long it lasted. Cleansing the soul had done even more for him than he'd anticipated. A feeling that he could fly.

Harrison took off his jacket and swung it over one shoulder. He made his way through the bar toward the crowded lobby. It was still early. Maybe he'd take a walk along the water, revisit the beauty of the harbor. See if his memory was triggered by the streets. Think it all through.

He glanced back at the bar. The bartender looked over the top of a customer's head and nodded her thanks for the oversized tip he'd left. He nodded back, then turned his thoughts to the rest of his evening. The old address, which certainly would be useless after all these years. He'd given up rights to the place.

The bar and the hotel lobby melted into one another, a sea of activity. Harrison stood between the two, looking over a maze of faces. At one end of the lobby was another fireplace, where cheery flames cast light and shadows across a wide circle of chatting groups, their faces blending together like in an impressionistic painting. People sat or stood, laughing, greeting, hugging farewell. Harrison stood quietly, enveloped in the lives of others.

Finally, he looked once more through the bar's wall of glass, toward the dark night. An unexpected chill ran through him, causing his shoulders to twitch.

Nerves?

No. He was known for many things, but nerves weren't one of them.

Yet the chill lingered. Harrison Grant was an intuitive man. Perceptive. Important traits for a photographer, he would tell his students. *It's what's behind the face, the eyes, that your lens needs to capture. It's what your eye and your camera can see, and what others miss.*

But this night, as a giant moon hovered over the ocean and the town, the photographer chose to ignore the sensation that all wasn't right. He chose not to look into the crowd. But if he had, the source of the strange slither up his back might have been made clear. His keen eye would surely have spotted the lone figure near the fireplace, would have framed it in his mind's eye.

A heart-stopping portrait of a shadowy face. Piercing eyes staring into his imaginary camera lens.

Staring at Harrison Grant.

Chapter 2

The hostess showed Izzy and Cass to the window table in the Franklin Cape Ann, leaving Danny behind, chatting with a friend on the other side of the cozy restaurant.

Cass sighed, shrugging free of a large, worn military-style jacket.

"You can double that sigh," Izzy said. "But the reception's almost ready."

Cass nodded. "But for the record, I'm not much of a party planner. This was it."

"I never wanted you helping with this. You know that. The last thing you need to be doing right now is carrying things, moving chairs around, standing on ladders. Jeez, Cass." The irritation in Izzy's voice was masking what she really felt. *Concern.* Cass looked tired and uncomfortable. She seemed to deny the fact that pregnancy could affect one's life in a multitude of ways. But when Izzy and Nell had offered to plan the lecture series opening reception, there had been no keeping Cass out.

Cass lifted one hand to stop Izzy's words. "You're right. No more ladders. But I'm not an invalid, Iz. And I'm not about to let people make me feel that way."

Izzy's voice softened. "I know." What she also knew was that Cass was stubborn and refused to let up on anything. Including the stress and work involved in running a lobster business.

"But, hey, wipe away the concern, Iz. I'm relaxing. I'm even getting into that yoga, which you tell me cures all ills. It's good." She looped the heavy jacket across her arm.

"Harmony Fairchild's class, right? Yes, she's great. One of my customers says taking her class is like going to church. Does your little fisherman's wife like it?"

"The fisherman is big and bulky. It's the wife who's little. Her name, as you well know, is Elena."

Before Cass could expand on her yoga partner, Danny Brandley walked over to the table, carrying a basket of warm bread and the restaurant's lemony hummus.

"Stole this from the waitress. I told her my pregnant wife might start eating silverware soon if she didn't have sustenance."

He noticed the trace of a frown on Cass's face and attempted a tease to lessen it, pointing to the jacket she was holding. "Hey, isn't that mine?" He set the bread on the table and took the jacket from Cass's hands, then shook it out dramatically in front of Izzy. "Mine, Iz. The woman has taken everything I own. My jacket. My sweats. My pj's. The last straw was my *Wicked Tuna* shirt."

Izzy laughed.

Cass shook her head. "It's your baby, too, buddy. This is the only jacket that fits. And little Hal here was cold." She patted the baby bump, which had ballooned into a mountain over the months, and sat down, arranging her unfamiliar body as comfortably as she could on the chair.

"What if little Hal is a gal?" Izzy looked with unabashed affection at Cass's transformed figure. Baby Hal was somehow already a part of their lives, already loved by this group of friends.

"Halloran Brandley. Hallie for short. Or Allie."

"Or Loran. Or Brandley Brandley," Danny said, shrugging out of his jacket.

Baby responded with a kick.

Danny sat down, staring at the slight movement in awe, then leaned in and said in a hushed tone, "Okay, no Brandley Brandley." He stole one more glance at Cass's now-quiet profile, then looked over at the empty chair. "So where's our driver?"

"Good question." Izzy looked out the window at Gloucester's lively Main Street, packed tonight with cars and a parade of people out and about. "He's probably still looking for a parking place. Kinda crazy for the middle of the week."

"That's good. We will be lost in the crowd, strangers in a strange land," Cass said.

It was Danny who had suggested dinner in Gloucester, a short drive from Sea Harbor. He knew his wife's emotions up close. Putting a few miles between them and the town in which Cass had been born and raised and knew nearly every person who lived there would lessen the chances of well-intentioned teasing. Or that was the hope.

"One more comment about it being triplets or late or early or next year and I think I might say things I'd regret," Cass had complained.

Or you might cry, Izzy had thought. She remembered feeling the same emotions not that long ago, when Abigail Kathleen Perry had stubbornly refused to enter the world on schedule. In birth classes they didn't teach one fully about how to handle dancing hormones. And right now Cass was dealing with all that—and pretending she wasn't. Cass needed to feel safe these days. And loved.

They sat in the front window of the dimly lit, cozy Franklin Cape Ann restaurant, the sounds of laughter, conversation, and the smells of fine food circling around them like a finely knit blanket. The basket of warm bread and the hummus took the edge off their hunger. Danny ordered a bottle of wine and hot tea for Cass.

And then they saw Sam, his eyes peering through the window at them, his nose flattened, his phone held up in his hand.

Izzy waved him in.

The smell of the sea clung to Sam as he strode over to the table. He tugged off his jacket and dropped down next to Izzy, then stared at the now-empty breadbasket. "Did I miss dinner, too?"

"Almost. What took you so long?" Izzy asked.

"No place to park. I ended up at the Beauport Hotel parking lot. You'd think this was the last night of good weather. The whole town is out."

Danny glanced out the window. "Maybe a concert down at the Harbor Loop."

"Nope, I think it's the weather. The moon, the ocean. Huge waves tonight, even in the harbor. And the light on the water is amazing." Sam set his phone on the table.

Izzy picked it up. An image of a magnificent moon filled the small screen. She held it up for Danny and Cass to see. "We've been stood up for a photo op. It's the story of my life."

Sam took his phone back. "You're lucky I didn't have my Canon along. I'd still be down there. The moon is mesmerizing. It's almost eerie, like it's playing games with the tide. Teasing it, whipping it into a frenzy." He paused, glancing out the window, then back, as if he didn't want the moon to hear. "But it's strange, too. Ominous."

"Ominous, like spooky?" Cass asked. She craned her neck to see around Izzy and out the front window.

Sam shrugged. He sat back in his chair when the waiter brought hot tea and a bottle of wine to the table, then ordered a plate of appetizers.

"The moon can do that," Izzy said. "Clouds drift in front of it, and you can read all sorts of things in the moon's face. Sometimes on warm summer nights, Sam and I lie on the beach with Abby, looking up into the galaxy. Abby can already point out the Dippers, Mars. And she thinks the moon man looks a little like Uncle Ben."

"There's no Uncle Ben in this one. It's a mysterious face, one that seems to be driving the tide crazy. A harbinger maybe."

"Of what?" Izzy asked.

"Murder?" Danny suggested, his brows lifting up into the mop of brown hair that fell over his forehead, a few stray strands touching the rim of his glasses.

"Enough, Brandley," Cass said, resisting the temptation to brush his hair off his forehead, like his mother always did. She shifted in her chair. "This is what happens when Danny's in the middle of writing a new mystery. Even the moon becomes a suspect. And, hey, sometimes the old moon man did it. But don't tell that to Abby. I don't want my goddaughter scared of the solar system." Cass tried to tilt sideways and plant a kiss on Danny's cheek, but her lopsided figure got in the way.

Danny leaned over and gave her a hug. "See why I love this lady? She understands writers. Murder. Moons. All those things. What can I say? She gets me."

Sam and Izzy chuckled, not yet used to the open affection that seemed to have developed along with Cass's pregnancy. But liking it. Pregnancy was nicely rubbing off some of their dear friend's callouses.

The waiter showed up and filled the table with platters of

mussels and Thai spring rolls. While Izzy passed around small plates, Sam turned his head toward the window again and squinted, his brow creased.

"That moon has you in a spell, Perry," Cass said. "You do know that it's over two hundred thousand miles away, right? It's not going to get you. Not tonight, anyway. What's up with you?"

Sam turned back and shrugged, but a slight furrow in his forehead remained. He reached for the wine bottle and poured it slowly, as if trying to figure out his own thoughts. When he spoke, the furrow had smoothed out slightly. "When I was a kid spending summers at the Kansas ranch, being crazy and wild with Izzy's brothers, drinking cans of beer behind the barn, I'd look up and imagine the moon was following us. I feel like that tonight." He looked at Izzy, a half smile creasing his face. "It's weird how strong that memory is."

Izzy listened, trying to reach back into Sam's memory, remembering when Sam had been her brothers' friend, not hers. He'd been someone to be ignored, a pest or a tease, along with her bratty brothers. She had had her own world back then, one that hadn't included any boys. Sam hadn't been quite as bad as her brothers, Charlie and Jack, but he'd still been a boy. Back then, Izzy had much preferred horses and riding alone along the wooded edge of the Chambers family ranch. Her thoughts had been focused on Ella, her favorite mare, and the newest Nancy Drew book she'd begun. The fact that Sam had had his own world then, too, had never occurred to her. And here they both were in Massachusetts. No ranch, but each other. A baby. An ocean. And then a moon.

Somehow Sam's thoughts seemed more immediate tonight. Closer to Cape Ann than to Kansas.

"I don't think it's just the moon tonight," she said to Danny and Cass, then looked at Sam, her brows lifted.

Sam was quiet. He motioned to the waiter for another basket of bread.

"So what, then?" Cass asked in that way friends could do, ignoring quiet Sam and instead asking his wife.

"It's about his old teacher—inviting him to be the guest of honor at the Art Haven weekend reception and the lecture series."

"The infamous Harrison Grant," Danny said. "I met him once, in the old days, when I wrote news features about real people, and not made-up ones about people being killed or brilliantly solving murders. When's he coming? Soon, right?"

"Not for a couple days, just in time for the reception," Izzy answered. "Sam is on duty to pick him up Friday morning, so he'll have time to settle in at the grand Art Haven building, check out the town maybe, and get ready for the event."

Cass folded her hands over her loose top. "Grant is a big wheel in photography circles, even I know that. Some digital portraits of the rich and famous. Some arty stuff. He'll be a draw, that's for sure." She looked at Sam. "And the cocktail party, thanks to all of us unpaid helpers, is going to be great. And those words come from me, someone who hates cocktail parties. So if you're worried your famous teacher is going to be embarr—"

Sam stopped her words. "I'm not worried. I thought there might be better choices, that's all. But Jane Brewster wanted this guy. She's the boss, founder of our whole art world. I knew Grant. So I invited him. End of story."

"That's all true," Izzy said. "I can vouch for that. He invited Grant because Jane asked him to, and who can say no to Jane? Mother Earth incarnate. And Sam's a pushover, we all know that. He wouldn't turn her down."

That was a given. Everyone knew and loved Jane and Ham Brewster. Not only were they Izzy's aunt and uncle's close friends, but they had cofounded the Canary Cove Art Colony and were Mom and Pop to any artist in need. If Jane thought Harrison Grant's presence would benefit the art colony and her artists and the town, Sam would do as she asked. They all would.

Danny took his glasses off and rubbed them absently with a napkin, his broad forehead creased in thought. "But, Sam, here's what I don't get—"

The waiter approached to take their orders, interrupting Danny's sentence.

Sam's relief at the interruption wasn't lost on any of them.

But even the young waiter's description of pan-seared salmon in a lemony basil sauce, the restaurant's famous hanger steak and hand-cut frites in truffle butter, scampi, and braised short ribs couldn't move Danny away from his question. As soon as the waiter had taken their orders and walked away, Danny picked up the conversation

"I'm curious why you didn't agree with Jane's choice. Who would have been better? Why is Grant a bad choice?"

Sam shrugged, reaching for the last spring roll.

Izzy spoke up, replying to Danny, but with her eyes focused on her husband. "I've been wondering the same thing. I see the man's photo in *Vanity Fair*, places like that. He seems to end up on their party page. But that doesn't disqualify him."

Sam listened, tracing invisible circles on the table with his fork. Finally, he looked up. "I think you're all making too much out of this. I don't even know the guy that well. I took a semester workshop from him. That's how we met. It was a coup to get into his workshop, even back then. And he was a good teacher—I'll give him that. He pushed me to do better. Gave me lots of feedback—not always kindly, but always helpful. Some people in the workshop weren't so lucky. Anyway, the guy was arrogant. Ambitious, huge ego." He shrugged. "Not my kind of guy."

"That's true of a lot of talented people," Cass said. "Not any of the talented ones at this table, for sure, but lots of other people."

"Maybe I thought he'd embarrass Jane, the program. The guy used to like his drinks. I have a feeling about him. Unfair, maybe. People can change, I suppose."

"But you gave in," Danny said. "Why?"

"Like Izzy said, Jane wanted him. And what fledgling photographer wouldn't want to learn from the guy? He's made quite a name for himself. And besides—" Sam paused and finished off his glass of wine, then poured another.

"Besides what?" Cass asked.

"Grant hobnobs with the rich and famous—the beautiful people, the best galleries, the best . . . everything. Not communities like ours. When Jane insisted, I finally agreed to give it a try because I realized he'd probably turn down the invitation anyway. It would be beneath him. Then I'd help Jane find someone else."

"So much for my prescient husband," Izzy said, still sorting through Sam's comments, which, frankly, made little practical sense to her.

Cass leaned as far forward in her chair as she could, then put her elbows on the table. "Okay, Perry, so do I have this right? A well-known photographer with a world-class ego has accepted an invitation to participate in our art colony's lecture series and even grace us with his presence at a cocktail party—a good thing because many of the folks who are coming have money and will buy art, helping our starving, talented artists. But you were sure he wouldn't accept your gracious invitation, because we're not good enough for him. And you're not crazy about him. Then, to top it off, the whole situation is causing the moon to do weird things. Am I right so far?"

Even Sam managed a laugh at Cass's dramatic spiel. And

soon the arrival of steaks in a port wine sauce, grilled salmon for Izzy, and a fresh basket of warm bread moved the group on to a discussion of a new health food store in Sea Harbor, a Patriot's score, and Danny's new murder mystery and reading, happening soon at the Bookstore of Gloucester—topics that seemed to ease the look in Sam Perry's eyes.

But Izzy saw something else. Something that had nothing to do with the moon that had chased Sam across her family's Kansas ranch. Something else was chasing Sam.

Something he couldn't explain, he'd told her earlier. "Not now," he'd said.

And maybe not ever.

They stayed at the Franklin longer than planned, but the evening had accomplished its goal. By the time they'd finished off the warmed fruit cobbler and taken care of the bill, the mood was mellow, any sharp edges of real life gone.

"I feel totally lolled," Cass said.

"Lolled?" Sam laughed. "What the heck is that?"

"Hey, you forget I live with a writer. Lolled. Lazed. Floppy. Warm and lovey and immune to the rest of the world. It's just the four of us and this little babe here. Life is good."

Danny chuckled, holding out his worn jacket for his wife. "There's nothing better in this world than a totally lolled Cass Halloran," he said. "I'm a happy camper."

As the music in the background pulsed a little louder, the speakers belting out David Bowie singing about "Modern Love," Sam headed toward the door, the others following. He pushed it open against a sudden strong wind coming up off the harbor.

"Geesh," Sam said. The weather had changed during their dinner, the moon still holding court in a deep sky, but strong gusts of wind whipped up debris from the street, flattening a can against the curb, slapping a flyer against Cass's legs as she stepped out the door.

"We can't afford to have Cass blow away before this baby comes," Sam said, grabbing the scarf that had escaped from Izzy's neck. "You guys hang out with David Bowie while I bring the car around."

No one argued. They stepped back inside as Sam headed out, his sandy hair whipped back as he eyed the same moon that had stunned him earlier. He headed toward the parking lot, weaving his way in between cars and people heading home.

Sam turned down a lit alleyway between the shops, a shortcut to the lot, the wind calmer between the buildings. At the far side he paused before crossing the busy street, fiddling in his pocket for his keys. He looked around and noticed a new coffee shop that had recently opened, the kind Danny liked to write in. He found the name above the door and made a note to pass it along. And then he stopped.

Although the coffee shop was closed, lights on the second floor indicated apartments or maybe condos. An entrance was below, the glass door open. A tall man stood in front of it, his arms loose at his sides. Inside, a woman with dark hair was silhouetted against the hall light behind her. She was tall and stood steady, holding the door partly open with her body, as she talked to the well-dressed older man.

The collar of the man's jacket was turned up, and his body shadowed hers.

Perhaps it was the woman's still stance, one shoulder pressed against the door, or the moonlight glancing off the glass that caught his attention. Sam wasn't sure. It was a sort of noir scenario that captured his photographer's eye, and he stared, then squinted, bringing the scene into focus.

Finally, the man turned, and the hall light outlined his profile, his silvery hair. The long, prominent nose, strong cheekbones. And eyes that, even from a distance, were intense.

Sam knew he was too far away to see the man's eyes. But he remembered.

His mouth dropped open; his keys fell to the gravel.

Harrison Grant stood tall and imposing. He lifted a hand, grabbed the edge of the door above the woman's shoulder, helping hold it open against the wind. Although the gusts were blowing the woman's hair across her cheeks, Grant's haircut defied the wind, every hair in place.

Sam stared. He squinted to be sure it wasn't a trick of the light or his thoughts of the past week playing games with him. Grant wasn't expected for a couple of days.

But it was Harrison Grant. The stance, the profile. Sam had seen that same profile for the length of an entire workshop. And over the years since, at random exhibits and passing encounters. Not to mention in magazine photographs and the large publicity photo on flyers now plastered all over Sea Harbor, announcing his arrival. The face hadn't changed much over those years.

At first, the woman he was talking to didn't move. But finally, she took a step back, one hand lifted in the air, her head moving slowly from side to side.

Was she afraid? Sam started to walk across the parking area that separated him from the door to the building. But he realized almost immediately that the woman wasn't frightened. She was talking, too, and her body language was calm. Composed. Finally, the man removed his hand from the door, and the woman stepped back into the hallway and turned away before disappearing into the shadows. The door closed, the wind pushing it solidly in place, and the man began to walk away.

Sam watched for a minute, then backtracked and leaned down to pick up his keys. When he straightened back up, Harrison Grant was gone. Sam scanned the busy street and finally spotted the imposing figure stopping cars with an outstretched hand. He walked briskly across Rogers Street. His head was high and tilted slightly as he walked, as if he was carrying on a conversation with the moon above.

Sam glanced back at the entrance to the building.

Standing behind the door, so close to the glass that he could nearly see her features, was the dark-haired woman who had been talking to Grant. Her palms were pressed against the door now; her eyes focused on the retreating figure of the tall, distinguished man, who was heading across a parking lot toward the Beauport Hotel.

Chapter 3

The Canary Cove Art Haven—the old Bianchi estate—was transformed. Inside and out. The arts association had envisioned it as providing a true haven for creating art, along with spaces for education, lectures, and meetings. For art shows. And for cocktail parties.

Nell stood next to Izzy at the open French doors and looked out at the flagstone patio. It was as wide as the house. Flat and smooth and welcoming, filled with chaises and comfortable outdoor furniture, a small bar. Everything was perfect—the breeze coming up off the water, the autumn night air, softened by the lit firepit in the center of the patio. Pear-shaped ceramic pots filled with gold and red and yellow mums marked the wide steps leading down to a terraced lawn. Low lights took over, casting shadows across the steep steps winding down to the narrow beach. Above it all, a nearly full moon held everything in its place.

Nell looked up at the canopy of stars filling the black sky and the amazing moon. "I wonder if this is the same moon you told me about. The one Sam photographed the other night. It's beautiful."

Izzy leaned lightly into her aunt's side, her head back as she followed Nell's gaze. "I'm not sure what's been going on with Sam, Aunt Nell. He stayed out on our deck for a long time when we got home from dinner the other night, his binoculars in his hand. It's not like him to worry about things. I wonder if he's afraid Harrison Grant won't show up tonight and it will embarrass Jane. Or he might be rude to people. Apparently, he can be a bit of a rogue."

"I know the thought of the photographer coming as the guest of honor has been making Sam uncomfortable these past couple weeks. But I didn't see that this morning when Sam drove him over."

"You were here?"

"I was helping Jane with some last-minute things when Sam dropped him off. Sam seemed to be his old self, or almost, anyway. And Harrison Grant surprised both Jane and me. He was pleasant and gracious. A perfect gentleman, and he seemed truly happy to be here. We chatted while they brought in his belongings. I'll be curious what you think after you meet him."

"That's interesting. We've been going in different directions today, and I haven't had a chance to talk to Sam. I don't know what his thing is, then. Maybe nothing."

"I suppose we've all had bad feelings once or twice about someone. Something just doesn't feel right. Sam obviously knows the man better than I do from my ten-minute introduction. And Sam is thoughtful and perceptive. We probably shouldn't ignore those feelings entirely."

Izzy nodded. "I get those feelings. But usually when you feel that way about someone, there's a reason for it. Something you can articulate. Sam doesn't seem to have much to say, other than mentioning some character traits. If there's more, he's not talking about it."

"I'm not sure a reason is always necessary," Nell said. But knowing Sam Perry as she did, she suspected that in his case, Izzy was right. If Sam didn't want to talk about it, there was a reason for that, too. "Well, we'll get through tonight," she said. "Hopefully, it will be a financial success for the art association. And the lecture series will begin with great applause next week. Even Sam admits Harrison Grant is a good teacher. He'll do a good job. And then he'll be gone."

Izzy grinned. "I hope your calm vibe calmed my husband."

"If it didn't, this lovely reception will. It'll be a beautiful party, Izzy. The place looks perfect."

Izzy agreed. "Lots of help from lots of people."

"Even the weatherman."

Izzy looked up at the sky again, a satisfied smile on her face.

Nell watched her niece as an ocean breeze came across the patio, ruffling Izzy's hair. She and Izzy often teased each other about which of them was the taller of the two. But tonight it was clearly Izzy who walked away with the prize. A pair of silver stilettos made her inches taller than Nell and nearly as tall as Sam. And Nell happily smiled up at her niece's lovely features. Wavy hair, loose with dark and light blond streaks, fell to her shoulders. "Haphazard hair," Sam often teased as he tamed it with his fingers. Izzy wasn't concerned about her hair or her appearance, or even the smudge of paint her daughter, Abby, had left on the back of her hand. Or how people sometimes stopped, looked, smiled at her for no reason. Just as Nell was doing now, smiling, loving her sister's daughter, who was as dear to her as any child of her own could be.

Movement behind her interrupted her reverie, as did two comfortable arms circling Izzy and her as one. Startled for a moment, they both turned into the warm embrace of Jane Brewster, whose smile filled a lined and lovely face. "It's wonderful, all of it. Thank you, thank you, thank you for helping make it so. Have I told you both how much I love you?"

"Not yet. Not tonight, anyway," Izzy said. "Yesterday, about seventeen times."

Jane laughed. "Well, I do. It's the truth. Having the reception was rather last minute, and you helped pull it off. And beautifully."

"You should," Izzy said. "Love us, I mean. But I think it all worked. We'll have to have lots of parties here now that we know we can throw one together in a couple weeks."

Jane's full laugh elicited smiles from several artists carrying pitchers of water and tea to the patio. Inside, the strains of violin strings being tuned filtered through the air. Jane spread her arms wide, a lacy black shawl floating out in an arc. "It's just perfect. All of it."

In the far corner, the violinist joined the rest of the quartet, who were busy arranging chairs and stands and sheet music. The spacious room, once a sedate formal living room large enough to hold crowds, had been transformed when the art colony became the new owner of the old mansion. The imported silk wallpaper was gone, and the fifteen-foot walls were now painted artist white, with paintings and photographs, fabric and woven art adding brilliant color. Chandeliers had been replaced with art lights, which highlighted the ever-changing exhibits. Comfortable groupings of furniture—slipcovered sofas and chairs—filled the area, and some had been pushed aside tonight to accommodate the crowd. Ficus trees, tall and full and glimmering with tiny lights, stood beside sculptures of mermaids and fanciful sea urchins and anchors. Everywhere one felt the power of the sea, the inspiration for the art.

The Bianchi estate had recently been given to the Canary Cove Arts Association by a generous artist. With the help of the artist community and the Brewsters' friends, it had been transformed into a comfortable, airy, and arty place, now called the Canary Cove Art Haven. Located in an elegant neighborhood a few miles away from the real Canary Cove Art Colony, the spacious estate was quickly becoming a place to get away, some of the artists had said. Tucked away on its three floors were bedrooms for visiting teachers and artists, a caretaker suite, lecture rooms, gallery space, and lounges for discussion and quiet time. A computer room, small studios, and a kitchen outfitted for a gourmet chef took up the rest of the house. And everywhere one looked was beauty and comfort and inspiration. The place was haunted, some said, but in the finest way. Many Cape Ann artists claimed to have seen Winslow Homer himself floating around the patio on dark nights, arguing with Fitz Hugh Lane or Edward Hopper about who was the better Cape Ann master.

"Sometimes I have to pinch myself to believe that we have this place," Jane said, looking around the room. "People are truly good."

Jane herself would top that list, Nell thought. Her friend had rescued many young artists and given them a place to be, a place to belong. The Bianchi estate was simply icing on the cake.

"And the evening event itself will be good, maybe great," Izzy said. "Hopefully, it will help with the electric bill."

Jane laughed, though Izzy spoke the truth. "And bless your dear Sam for helping with this, Izzy. Frankly, in my opinion, he's more talented than Mr. Grant. Sam's photographs speak to me. For all his acclaim and reputation, sometimes Grant's photography is a little too far off the grid—but no matter, it was nice of Sam to put up with my pleading. I knew he'd have a better chance of getting him here than unknown aging hippies from Berkeley, like Ham and me."

"Birdie and I went to one of his shows. Some of his portraits are beautiful," Nell said. "And others, well . . . interesting."

"*Interesting.*" Jane laughed. "Usually, that's art talk for 'I don't much like it.'"

Nell chuckled. "Maybe I'm too traditional. Some of his photographs took ordinary faces to places I'm sure the subjects never intended."

"Well, Picasso didn't shy away from that. But it's true that digital photography has changed the profession," Jane said.

"Agreed. But no matter, Janie. I think he was a good choice to get your series off and running. I'm looking forward to everything. Tonight and the lecture series. For once, I think our dear friend Sam is wrong. Harrison Grant was nothing but gracious when we met him this morning."

"I agree. But that's Sam being Sam. Overly cautious. And even Sam says he's a good teacher. And he certainly is a draw."

Jane checked her watch, then looked around the room as the caterers scurried around with last-minute preparations. She waved to several young women walking in with trays of tiny lobster rolls and bowls of sauces, and to an electrician hurrying out to the patio to check the heaters. "Oh my," she murmured as the tinkling of a broken glass sounded in the distance, and the next minute Jane was off, her long skirt swishing behind her, her thick gray ponytail moving between her shoulder blades, and her artist hands flying in all directions.

A minute later, Izzy was gone, too—out to the patio for a final check on the portable bar. On cords and patio lights.

Nell checked her phone. She wondered how Harrison had spent the rest of the day. And Sam? He'd be fine. He hadn't driven Harrison Grant into the Annisquam River on the way over from the Beauport Hotel, so that was good.

Tall, strong Sam, with a spirit that belied his full laugh and the sounds he made when watching a Patriots' game. The man who had taught his toddler daughter to walk around anthills, never over them. A man who would never hurt a fly. Or an ant. She leaned lightly against the edge of the French doors, thinking back to the day Sam Perry had come to Sea Harbor, and then realized with a start that the circumstance back then hadn't been totally unlike the one this weekend.

Jane Brewster had brought Sam to town to give a photography lecture at Canary Cove. The evening after the welcome reception, she and her husband, Ham, had brought him along to Friday night dinner on the Endicott deck. It was there, to everyone's surprise, including Sam's—and *especially* Izzy's—

that Sam found the sister of Jack Chambers, his Kansas childhood friend. Izzy Chambers.

And Izzy found a grown-up Sam, right there in Sea Harbor, in her aunt and uncle's living room.

Sam Perry never left.

Ironic, Nell thought now and wondered briefly if history would repeat itself and Jane would bring a couple together tonight as unintentionally as she had those years before. Would Harrison Grant meet someone? Would one of the talented Canary Cove artists end up remembering tonight for more than the lobster rolls and wine, more than the cool breeze and laughter?

In the distance, the screeching sound of a microphone being tested drew Nell out of her whimsy.

She caught sight of Izzy and Cass out on the patio, checking extension cords and lighting the gaslights. Last-minute checks.

She took in a deep breath and looked into the perfect night.

A perfect moon.

Nell looked up at its face, wondering what Sam Perry had seen there.

Surely this lovely moon man she was looking at portended no evil.

She simply wouldn't have it.

Chapter 4

"Is this your first time in Sea Harbor?"

Harrison Grant rubbed his chin, his blue eyes keen and clear. His forehead was slightly furrowed, as if the question carried great weight.

"Here? Yes," he finally said, one finger touching the silk ascot tie tucked into his shirt. The word *yes* echoed so loud in his head that he almost imagined someone hearing it, staring at him, wondering, remembering. Judging.

Liar. And why had he said it?

Somehow it had just come out that way.

He looked down at the lined face of a woman long past his age. The kind of face that should be immortalized in a photograph. It held wisdom and beauty and kindness. Goodness too.

She was smiling with her eyes, not correcting him or condemning him. Simply listening.

Too old to hear my thoughts, he decided.

"I've seen you before, Mr. Grant," Birdie Favazza said, leaning back to look at the man's long face, his strong chin, and clear eyes. "Although I certainly don't expect you to remember."

Harrison Grant looked down, and his blue eyes peered into her own. *She is eighty if a day*, he thought, then mentally calculated his own age. Then. Now. Her voice was strong for such a small old person. It matched her remarkable face.

The woman continued. "I attended an exhibit at the Harvard Club in Boston some years ago. You spoke to us and presented a slideshow of your photographs. I believe the club gave you some award that day. You had quite a bevy of fans surrounding you."

"I remember that day," he said, his shoulders relaxing beneath the Italian suit.

"I enjoyed it, as did my friend. We've also heard about you from a dear friend who lives here now, a former student of yours."

"Sam Perry, I suspect. He drove me over this morning."

Sam Perry. Somehow, it didn't surprise him that his former student would be a friend of this woman. She was an unusual woman, he thought, although he had nothing other than her presence by which to make such a judgment. But he knew he was right.

"Sam is a lovely man. A photographer himself, although you are surely aware of that."

Harrison nodded. "Perry was one of those rare students whom you know will move on to success. Innate talent, a unique way of viewing his subjects." Harrison remembered that the one thing he had thought might stop Perry from being renowned was his personality. He was too nice. No ruthless gene. But somehow, Perry hadn't needed that edge to succeed. He'd managed to get the attention he deserved. Not the kind of attention Harrison had acquired, but it had served Sam Perry well. And he was glad for him.

"Yes, Sam is talented," the woman was saying. "And now that we have a mutual friend, an introduction might be in order.

My name is Birdie Favazza. Welcome to our town." She held out a small hand.

Harrison took it, the skin on the back translucent and smooth as silk. It nearly disappeared in his own. The small woman had been standing in the back hallway when he came out of the restroom. It was a quiet corner, away from the crowd. Perhaps he was becoming slightly paranoid, but it seemed she might have been waiting there for him.

"I'm happy to meet you, Ms. Favazza," he said. "It's good to meet a friend of Sam Perry's. I've followed him through the years. He's done well."

Harrison had wondered about seeing Perry again, but his former student held a spot on this rocky road he was traveling. Seeing him was important. When he had gotten into Perry's car at the hotel, the younger man had been reserved. Polite but distant. He had warmed somewhat by the time they reached the art estate. It wasn't enough time to share their lives, personal things, the past, but Harrison had gained a little patience in recent months. There'd be time to talk to Sam Perry later. And he would make sure he did. He owed the man that much. If not a whole lot more.

"We're happy you came to us, Mr. Grant. And please call me Birdie."

The woman's head remained tilted back as she looked up at him. Her face was kind and welcoming, and her eyes were remarkably clear. Like a fine camera lens looking directly into his own eyes. He wondered what she was seeing and instinctively moved a few inches back.

A hand on his arm broke the connection between them, and Harrison turned away from Birdie's look.

Jane Brewster, his hostess, stood beside him, the plump, comfortable art colony founder who had welcomed him in a most gracious way when he'd arrived at the house that morning.

"Our Birdie, as you've probably realized, is Sea Harbor's

beloved matriarch." Jane wrapped one arm around Birdie's shoulders. "She is wise beyond words, someone you will want to get to know better while you're here. But for now, I have a houseful of people who want to meet you, so I am going to steal you away."

"Of course." He smiled at Birdie, nodding his head in a gallant gesture.

Jane Brewster's interruption was a relief. His hostess was a gracious chatterer. Birdie Favazza was an observer.

And Harrison wasn't at all sure what she was seeing.

Izzy looked around the crowded house, trying to find Cass. She knew she was overly solicitous of her friend, but that was simply the way it was. Cass would have to live with it.

She moved out to the patio. It was filled with happy people and lively conversations. Lobster rolls were being passed around, and drinks served from the portable outdoor bar. People were everywhere, exploring the grounds, walking down the steps to the sea.

Izzy stopped at the top of the steps and looked down toward the ocean beach. She spotted a short figure, partially hidden behind a couple walking up the steps. A small person, alone. When the couple stepped aside, the figure became more defined. *No*, she thought. It couldn't be her Rico, the cranky neighbor from down the street. Izzy had become acquainted with old Rico during her runs along the beach. He was as eccentric as they came, but there was something about him that endeared him to her. Nell, Birdie, and Cass felt the same, and although Rico wasn't very good at socializing, he'd relaxed a little in the past couple of years. At least around the four of them.

As she strained to see more clearly, the lumpy figure pivoted, turning in the other direction. His back to the house, he stood still, looking out to sea.

Maybe, hopefully, he had noticed the smooth, safe steps he was standing on. They were a sharp contrast to Rico's own dangerous decaying beach steps, which Izzy suspected would hurt someone someday. Her warnings to Rico had fallen on deaf ears.

But, of course, he wouldn't have come over to look at steps. In fact, a party, an elegant reception, would be the last place on earth Rico would be. So why was he here?

Several people moved in front of her then, blocking Rico from sight. Izzy walked around them, then down a few steps, and looked again. But all she saw now was a couple walking up from the beach. There wasn't another person in sight. She shook her head. A mirage. She must be more tired than she thought.

She turned and walked back up, tottering slightly, as she realized that even these well-cared-for steps weren't made for a crazy woman, one seeing things that weren't there, especially while wearing stilettos.

Finally, she spotted Cass sitting on a sofa in a remote, shadowy corner of the patio, the only place slightly removed from guests and drinks and voices. A large heater intended to offset the evening chill was right next to her. The flow of warm air and a voluminous knit shawl were wound around her like a blanket.

Izzy dropped down beside her on the sofa and slipped off her shoes. She rested her head back against the cushions. "How're you doing, Cass? Have you been out here long?"

"Fine. And not long. I'm staying out of the fray. When I was being social earlier, the crowds seemed to part for me. I took full advantage of it, of course. It must be how the queen feels. But then it became weird, so I retreated."

"Did you give them the royal wave?"

Cass chuckled, but Izzy could see tiredness in her eyes. Tired for two.

"I'm glad you found this spot. But what a night, right? Total success is my guess."

"Looks like it from my hidden roost. Everyone wants a glimpse of the man of the hour. He was out here a while ago. You missed him."

"I talked to him earlier. Did you meet him?"

"Now that you ask, yes, I did," Cass said. "And I have to hand it to the guy. In my limited experience, most men shy away from pregnant women. I don't know if they think it's contagious or what. But Harrison Grant wasn't like that. He was very nice. He asked about me, what I did, and seemed genuinely interested in our lobster business. He had a sense of humor, too. I wasn't expecting to, but I like him."

"Well, that's good, I guess."

"But, of course, all good things end. Somehow, a pregnant lady doesn't hold the appeal of some of these gorgeous, fit women around here. Deb what's-her-name saw us talking and joined us, and before you could say, 'When is the baby due?' she and Harry—I think I'll call him that—were off getting wine or whatever."

"Deb who?"

"You know. Eddie Porter's suite mate. The two of them are the caretakers here."

Izzy nodded. "Oh, sure, of course I know Eddie. Tommy's baby brother. He and a couple buddies of his are out in front, parking cars."

"Well, Deb's the other caretaker. I think tonight she was caretaking the guest of honor."

"Now I know who you're talking about. Deb. Yes. Mostly, I've seen her in running pants and tees. She runs a lot on the beach. She's strong. Fast. So, she's Eddie's friend?"

Everyone in town knew Eddie's family. Including his older brother, Tommy Porter, who was the first in the family to go to college, then graduated from the police academy, and now was employed as a detective in his hometown. Choosing not to leave his roots made Tommy even more lovable.

Eddie, the youngest Porter, had had a more difficult time in getting his life together. It was nice of Jane to give him the job.

"Jane thought hiring a policeman's brother as caretaker was a good thing, I guess. Anyway, Eddie and this girl he met at his college get free room and board for living here and making sure things are locked up. I think Deb makes breakfast for guests, who sometimes stay here. A nice gig," Cass said.

Izzy nodded, looking around at the crowd and trying to spot Harrison Grant with the fit caretaker. The runner. They seemed to have disappeared.

"So, tell me, Iz," Cass said, drawing her friend's attention back to the conversation. "Did you have any idea what a handsome dude Sam had invited to our town? Magazine photos don't do the guy justice. 'Silver fox'—those are the words I'm hearing from the crowd."

Izzy laughed. "Not the words Sam used."

"Speaking of Sam, how was the ride over from the hotel this morning?"

"He said it was fine. You know Sam. He's good at keeping his feelings to himself. I got the feeling he felt better about Harrison after seeing him again, though."

A group of women moved close to the heater, unaware of the two women hunkering down on the sofa in the shadowy corner. Bits of their conversation drifted back to Izzy and Cass—comments about the high quality of the art for sale, the gorgeous estate, the lobster rolls, the evening, and the moon. But the conversation always seemed to boomerang back to Harrison Grant. His looks, his photography, his reputation. His looks.

Cass lifted one brow and grinned at Izzy as the words *silver fox* floated back to them. "Told you so," she said.

Izzy laughed. Sam's discomfort about the man had seeped

into her, but meeting Harrison Grant had been disarming. He'd been gracious and friendly—and had said nice things about Sam, about the beauty of Cape Ann. He had even seemed interested in *her*, asking why she had stopped practicing law to open a yarn shop. He had seemed intrigued about it and had talked about the benefits of changing the direction of your life midstream to do something you loved. The conversation wasn't at all what she had expected. He had been the perfect gentleman—personable and seemingly sincere. Words she wouldn't ordinarily use to describe a stranger, especially this one.

"The dude is quite a dresser, too," Cass said. "Did you notice? I haven't seen a striped ascot like that since my mother took me to see *My Fair Lady*."

Izzy'd noticed it, too. Silky and perfectly looped and tucked beneath the open collar of his shirt—which was also perfect. Yes, Harrison Grant knew how to dress. But yet he wasn't a dandy. On him, it all looked natural and at home. And Cass was right; magazine photos didn't do the man justice.

And now she was wondering if Sam had also done him an *injustice*. She looked over toward the patio doors, then pointed through the crowd and waved. "Speaking of silver foxes, there's my uncle Ben."

Ben spotted Izzy's waving arm and wove his way through the crowd to the patio sofa.

"I figured I'd find you two hiding out somewhere." He laughed, pointing at Izzy's shoes on the ground. "I wondered how long you'd last in those."

"So how are things going inside?" Cass asked. "Packed, I'm sure. Even the kitchen had people in it when I wandered in. I wonder how many fire regs we're breaking."

"Don't know about that. But you're right. It's a good crowd."

"Are Jane and Ham happy with everything?" Izzy asked. "How about our guest? Is he safe from Sam's deadly looks?"

"As best I can tell, all's well. Jane and Ham are consummate hosts. Jane remembers the names of people she barely knows, and she's introduced Harrison Grant to every big arts donor on the North Shore. As for Sam, he's fine, too."

"Hmm," Izzy said.

"So is Jane exhausted?" Cass asked.

"Yes. Even Grant seemed to realize that. He suggested a while ago that Jane take some time for herself and let him wander around alone. He enjoys that kind of thing, he said, talking with guests, local artists. Checking out the house and art."

"That was considerate," Cass said.

"Jane thought so. She headed upstairs to relax for a while before the formal introductions." Ben checked his watch. "But that was a while ago. It's almost that time."

A bell ringing from inside followed Ben's words. Soon people on the crowded patio began making their way through the French doors and into the even more crowded living room area.

"I suppose we should follow," Cass said.

"I think that's the plan," Ben said, reaching out to help Cass to her feet.

"You are as gallant as the silver fox," Cass said, grasping his hands and rising from the sofa.

Ben chuckled. "I heard our fair mayor Beatrice Scaglia murmur those exact words after she met Grant. Beatrice seems quite taken with the man."

Izzy reluctantly slipped her feet back into the stilettos. She followed Ben and Cass across the patio.

Inside, guests jostled for space to see the front of the room, where the microphone was set up.

Ben looked over heads and spotted Danny and Sam near the wide arch leading to the front door.

"Thata way," Ben said, pointing to the foyer. Cass and Izzy followed, then detoured off to the ladies' room.

Ben walked over to the two men. "Where's Nell?" he asked, looking around.

"She stepped outside to check on something. She thought she heard a crash."

Ben looked through one of the small windows flanking the wide front door. "I don't see anything."

"I told her Eddie Porter was out there, keeping an eye on the cars and late-arriving or early-leaving guests. But you know Nell. She needed to check."

A few minutes later Nell came back in, a concerned look on her face.

"Is everything okay?" Ben asked in a low voice.

"Probably. Eddie tripped over a yard statue. One of those small stone gnomes the Bianchis must have left behind when the house was sold."

"Is he okay?" Ben asked.

"He's fine. The gnome didn't fare so well, though. We can talk about it later." She looked up and smiled as Cass and Izzy walked toward them.

Cass moved to Danny's side. "My savior," she said. "You found the perfect spot. There's more air here. Less perfume. Less bodies. This guy thanks you, too." She patted her belly.

Danny looped one arm around her shoulders and looked around at the others. "Can you believe my girl made it through the evening so far?"

In truth, Izzy wondered more about Danny making it through the evening. Seeing Cass on the patio ledge arranging a string of lights earlier had nearly done him in. She patted Danny's shoulder. "She's a wonder woman through and through."

"For sure," Cass laughed. "But on to less important things. Where's the man of the hour?"

"Over there, I think." Izzy pointed at the back of a tall silver-haired man standing near the living room windows, admiring two framed photographs hanging on the wall.

Before Cass could focus and get in another stare or two, a

group of people moved toward the windows, blocking the man from her sight.

At the far end of the room, the string quartet played its final chord and Jane stepped over to the microphone. She smiled out at the packed room, waiting for silence to wash over the crowd.

After welcoming everyone and thanking the sponsors, Jane gave a brief description of the Canary Cove Arts Association and the lecture series they were sponsoring this year. "A first for us," she said. "An *auspicious* first. And hopefully, it won't be the last." She paused briefly when polite applause followed her words, and then moved on to the introduction that the guests were waiting for, that of Harrison Grant.

Jane began with what were the highlights of Grant's career—his beginnings, his awards, the notable magazine covers, and the reviews of his peers and art critiques. And then she moved on to officially introduce Harrison Grant.

"Although many of you have already met him tonight," Jane said, "it is my great pleasure to welcome him officially to the Canary Cove Art Colony's lecture series. Harrison Grant . . ." She smiled at the crowd, one arm stretched out, welcoming and gracious.

A palpable thrum filled the air as the crowd spread out to make room for the photographer to take center stage.

Izzy and Cass looked over to the windows where they'd seen the tall, handsome photographer. The man was still there and was now turning and looking around at the crowd. His eyes lit on Izzy and Cass, and he smiled and waved.

"Oops," Izzy said softly. "Wrong fox." She waved back at Don Wooten, a friend and the owner of the Ocean's Edge Restaurant.

The shuffle of bodies and the expectant murmur spread through the audience as heads turned and craned to see the photographer. Some guests stepped back, forming a makeshift path to the microphone.

"The parting of the sea," Cass joked.

At the front of the room, Jane stood patiently, her eyes warm, the same comfortable smile that she'd used to welcome the guests still in place. Beside her, her husband, Ham, shifted from one foot to the other, scratching his white beard and looking over heads, scanning the crowd.

Jane picked up the microphone and repeated the welcome, her cheeks flushed.

And then she did it again.

And again.

And again.

But Harrison Grant was gone.

Chapter 5

The entire Perry family, in an assortment of dress, showed up at Ben and Nell's early Saturday morning. Little Abby was still in the unicorn pajamas Nell had given her for her birthday, Sam wore old jeans and a Harvard sweatshirt, and Izzy, hoping for a beach run with her dog, had on running pants and a sweatshirt. The evening's events had messed up sleep, and she desperately needed a run along the shore before heading to her yarn shop.

Abby and Red, the Perrys' aging golden retriever, ran into the family room together. Abby's curls bounced as she hugged Ben and Nell, then raced over to the toy chest in the corner. Almost always, there'd be a new surprise toy tucked away somewhere, and it would take Abby ten seconds to find it. She settled on the floor, with the dog beside her, rummaged around, and squealed, cuddling the new superhero doll she'd found hidden under a race car. She soon settled into a fantasy of her own making, ignoring the flurry of comments and questions flying around the kitchen island not far away.

"So, he never came back?" Izzy asked. She pulled out a stool at the wide butcher-block island.

Ben filled coffee mugs and passed them around. "It looks that way."

Sam was silent, looking down into his coffee mug.

Nell watched him as he forked a strand of wayward hair off his forehead. His face spoke volumes. A kind of regret, maybe, for inviting Grant, for being involved in the man's participation in any way. But there was anger there, too, and it seemed to overwhelm the regret, especially on the face of one of the least angry men she knew. Sam didn't wear anger well.

The perfect evening at the Canary Cove Art Haven had certainly not gone as planned. The crowd had been patient, happy with the lobster rolls and wine passed around by artists serving as waiters. The guest of honor's delay hadn't seemed to diminish people's enjoyment. In fact, it had caused some light banter in the room. "An Oscar moment," someone had called it, as many had assumed Harrison Grant was in the men's room, missing his moment. But when minutes passed, and then some more, and he still hadn't appeared, Jane managed the awkwardness by announcing a slight change in the schedule. With a wave of her hand, she urged guests over to the bar and out to the patio for a view of the moon and announced that dessert would be served presently.

"We'll be back on schedule soon," she said with a smile. "The evening is young. Enjoy, everyone."

And people did. At least the guests who shouldered no responsibility for the guest of honor. But for others, such as Ben, Danny, and Sam, the dessert would have to wait. Within minutes they followed Ham Brewster's lead and fanned out to search the house and grounds. Maybe the guy had gotten hurt somewhere or had even dozed off. He'd enjoyed a few drinks, Ham had observed. The estate was large, and people had been wandering everywhere, curious to see how the Bianchi estate had changed in the hands of the Canary Cove artists. Harrison could be anywhere. Maybe he was just enjoying the art and the beauty of the place and had forgotten the time, the role he'd been asked to play.

"We were the secret search posse that failed," Sam said now, then drained his orange juice. "Maybe it was a good thing we didn't find him. I might have strangled the guy."

"Eddie Porter and a buddy were out front, helping valet cars," Nell said. "Eddie saw him a few times, but he didn't see him get in a car. People were coming and going, he said."

"He was gone. That was clear," Ben said, his tone puzzled. "We checked everywhere, inside and out. Even the boathouse."

"Boathouse?" Nell frowned.

Sam shrugged. "Who knows? Grant has always been a ladies' man."

"He did have a fan base last night. A lot of them were young and gorgeous," Izzy said. "But, well, I mean, he's . . ."

"Old?" Ben said with a laugh.

Izzy blushed. "I just meant that, well, he's here on business, right? The guest of honor. A professional. It seems a little far-fetched that he'd go off with one of the guests."

But none of them knew what "far-fetched" might mean for a man they barely knew, and the topic was dropped.

"Ben and I stayed late with Jane and Ham last night," Nell said. "The two caretakers—Eddie and Deb—were there, but Jane wanted to be there herself when Harrison came back, just to be sure his room was comfortable, that he had what he needed. The perfect hostess. But she finally gave up, and we all left."

"Has anyone talked to the Brewsters today?" Izzy asked.

"I talked to Jane just before you came in. She was up at dawn, thinking about Harrison, hoping his key had worked, that the bed was comfortable. She knew Deb Carpenter would be up, so she called her. She said there'd been no sign of him."

"So he had an all-nighter," Sam said. His voice was low. A growl more than a comment.

"Jane isn't judging him. Maybe we shouldn't, either," Nell said.

Sam was quiet.

"He had a responsibility to be there last night," Izzy said. "A commitment. He knew that's why so many people came to the event."

"Maybe. But the lecture series doesn't start until Monday, so there's no reason he has to be here for the whole weekend," Nell said. "Maybe he went into Boston." She looked over at Sam. "He lived there for a while, right? He probably has contacts."

"He didn't have a car," Sam said.

"Commuter train, Uber," Ben said.

Reasonable.

But it didn't sit comfortably with any of them.

"Ham will go over this afternoon, and everything will be fine," Nell said. "In fairness to Harrison, he might not have known the schedule. Or had a phone call that pulled him away. Who knows?"

"Aunt Nell, we *all* know." Izzy's voice was firm. "At the very least, Harrison Grant was rude. And it completely erases any of that old-world kind of gallant manners he was spreading around, like he was actually a good guy. A gentleman. And interested in what others had to say. I believed that about him. I . . . I actually liked him." She cast a look at Sam, then added, "I was wrong."

Ben leaned down and took a bacon and cheese frittata out of the oven and set it on a hot pad. The smell of garlic and basil and oregano rose up with the steam and filled the kitchen with kinder thoughts.

Sam's face, along with his mood, relaxed with the sight of the food. He walked over to Nell's side, then held plates while she spooned up the rich cheesy eggs.

"It's not your fault, Sam," Nell said softly, then waited for a smile from him, but when it came, she knew it was more for the frittata than anything she had said.

Sam moved off to retrieve his daughter and her new superhero doll she'd found in the toy corner, while Izzy spooned eggs into Abby's bowl and pulled over her booster chair. Glasses and one sippy cup of orange juice were passed around the island, while Ben refreshed coffee mugs.

As sunlight poured through the kitchen windows and sweet Abby entertained her adoring audience with silly songs and giggles, uncomfortable and unkind thoughts of a silver-haired photographer began to fade.

But not entirely.

Chapter 6

Izzy ran through the neighborhood streets with Red at her side, her head lifted into the breeze. She could run through this neighborhood in her sleep. Old trees and old houses greatly cared for and loved and passed along from generation to generation.

Houses in her aunt and uncle's Sandswept Lane neighborhood had once been mostly summer homes, cottages that came alive every June, as boards were taken off windows, and sheets pulled off furniture. The houses would swell with families who came together every summer. But over the decades, home after home had been winterized and updated, and vacationing families had become permanent residents of Sea Harbor. Grown children had come back to raise families. Others, like her aunt and uncle, had eventually retired from stressful Boston careers and had settled into a quieter life by the sea.

And for that, Izzy was forever grateful. They were her surrogate family, as she had settled far from her parents' Kansas home. She'd fallen in love with the town and the large, airy house that had welcomed her on college and law school vacations.

Izzy loved it all. But most of all, she loved the people in it, who had embraced her when she closed one chapter in her life to begin another—leaving a Boylston Street law firm, an ex-boyfriend, and a cramped apartment above a deli in the Back Bay to open her very own Sea Harbor yarn shop. Uncle Ben and Aunt Nell had encouraged her. Loved her. Helped her build a new life.

Red pulled back on the leash to sniff at a neighbor's carefully raked pile of leaves, pushed his nose into it, and scattered the leaves. While he rummaged, Izzy glanced through windows as the neighborhood woke up. Kids in pajamas flicking on television sets or computers. A front door opening, and a neighbor in a robe picking up the newspaper, then waving at Izzy and Red before disappearing back inside.

Welcoming homes, as if the wreathes that decorated the doors no matter the season wore smiles, inviting one inside.

Izzy headed down the street, Red beside her, and rounded the corner to the narrow beach road. Ahead was the water, the packed sand, and the sound of the tide coming in.

Mindfulness.

Running did that, cleaned out her head, brought back her focus. Or maybe it was the ocean, the waves, the rhythm of nature.

She headed toward Paley's Beach, a small stretch of sand not far from her aunt and uncle's home. The peaceful area lacked the energy of Cape Ann's Good Harbor Beach but was perfect for those seeking a less populated place. The "mothers' beach," as some called it, was defined by a gentle curve of land that held its swimmers in a safe embrace. The sand was smooth, and even the waves slowed down a bit, gently washing onto the shore. Today the beach was almost empty, except for a few dog walkers, who were probably relieved that swimmers and tourists were gone for the season and the dogs once again could run free.

Red trotted happily along, old hips slowing him down some, but his head held high to catch the breeze and his eyes focused on a colony of gulls foraging for food at the edge of the shore. Once the tourists left, the birds had the beach to themselves, but also gone were the remnants of pizza and chips and peanut butter sandwiches that they had feasted on all summer. Today they were diving for fish, ignoring Red completely.

Izzy breathed deeply, trying to concentrate on the moment and clear her thoughts of the past evening's events. She hadn't admitted it completely to Sam, but she had found Harrison Grant appealing when she was introduced to him. She looked forward to getting to know him better, maybe having him to dinner while he was here. Somehow, it seemed like an irrational sort of betrayal to do so. But he'd been gracious and polite, gentlemanly, in a non-flirtatious way. He'd leaned his head in, blocking out the voices behind them, and listened in what had seemed to be a sincere way, as if her words mattered. It was as if this man cared about her life. About his former student's life, too. He had spoken about her husband with respect and admiration and had mentioned that he was looking forward to talking with him during his time in Sea Harbor.

For most of the evening, Harrison Grant's behavior had actually caused her to silently question Sam's reaction to the man.

But all of that had been lost when he had left the Brewsters in the lurch by disappearing without a word to anyone.

Yet something was not right. But she had no idea what it was.

She looked down the beach to the rise of the land, to where the beach narrowed to a ribbon, winding around the boulders until it was out of sight. Beyond that point, the beach was private, the property of the fine old estates that occupied the hill above. It was the Cliffside neighborhood, where they'd all gathered less than twenty-four hours before. The Canary Cove Arts Association's new home. THE CANARY COVE ART HAVEN: A COMMUNITY ARTS AND EDUCATION CENTER the brochures and the elegant sign outside the house called it. Though no one doubted that many in town would call it the Bianchi place forever.

She wondered briefly if Harrison had come back. Maybe he was sitting in the dining room right this minute, enjoying a breakfast that one of the young caretakers had prepared for him. Or, more likely, he was sprawled out in his room, recovering from whatever he'd enjoyed all those hours before.

It was Red, tugging on the leash, who finally pulled her thoughts back to the moment. Izzy looked over and spotted the object of his attention—a lone man walking slowly down Cliffside Drive, the main road that ran through the Cliffside neighborhood.

His shoulders were hunched, his stride purposeful as he made his way toward the beach. A scruffy beard and matching eyebrows defined the man's weathered face. The rest of his head was hairless. Beside him, a shaggy dog bearing a striking resemblance to his master matched the old man's gait, his eyes focused on Red.

Izzy stopped moving and tried to bring him into clear focus. To see if he matched what she imagined she'd seen the night before at the reception. Then she tossed the thought aside. What she'd seen at the party was nothing but a blurry mirage.

"Hey, Rico," she called out. "You're up early today." She waved, but only Frodo, the dog, responded, immediately pulling his master in their direction and waving his tail in the air.

By then Rico had turned off the road and begun walking along the beach, his head turned toward the waves building in the distance. It wasn't until his suddenly animated dog began pulling on the leash, jerking his arm, that he looked over at Izzy and Red.

Instead of waving, Rico glared at the woman and the dog, but his own dog refused to be still. Begrudgingly, Rico let Frodo continue to pull him in their direction.

Some thought old Rico was crazy. Others considered him weird or senile. He had a foul smell about him, a fact Izzy wouldn't deny. But she didn't agree with any of those other assessments. And neither did Nell, Birdie, or Cass, who often walked along Paley's Beach with her. The man had warmed to Birdie readily, as people did, once even accepting a hug from her when she saw him on Harbor Road and there was no one around to see. Birdie also had convinced him that occasionally sitting on a bench with her in the village green was a good thing. But most often, it was he and Izzy who met on the beach during his daily walk and her regular run.

The women knew there was more to Rico Silva than superficial impressions indicated.

He didn't tolerate people he considered fools—which in his mind included a large number of townsfolk. Nor did he hesitate to chastise them, a character trait that had helped cement his reputation. But those things didn't make him senile, in the Seaside Knitters' united opinion. Rico was also smart, they'd learned. And kind to dogs and kids. His dog, Frodo—a sweeter, gentler soul than his master—seemed to balance the man nicely, and Frodo's friendship with Red had created an odd bond between his master and Izzy.

Little by little, Rico had allowed the four women into his life—or at least to linger along the fringes.

He sometimes talked with them about his former business. How he had amassed millions of dollars from a patent for some obscure sailboat part. Part of his fortune had been poured into a Cliffside Drive mansion for his new young bride.

What he didn't talk about, but what was common lore, was that his wife, Martina, had left him—and the town—not long after they married and moved into the estate he'd built for her.

The home had twelve bedrooms, some people said, and according to children who had hurried past the house on Halloween, a ghost lived in each one of them. Mostly ugly, mean ghosts, they claimed.

Izzy thought differently, and she and Sam had made it a point of taking Abby and Red up to his door last Halloween to show off Abby's Snoopy costume. Frodo had come with Rico to the door and had licked Snoopy's paw, and Rico had dropped a brown banana in Abby's felted pumpkin.

Izzy wasn't even sure how old Rico was. She strongly suspected his emotional age was what gave him the title "old," and it exceeded his biological age by some years. Maybe a dozen.

"Hey, Rico," she called out happily. "Today's a first. You listened to me."

Rico ignored her.

Izzy persisted, repeating her words, but she could see he wasn't listening or didn't care.

Cliffside road was a safer walk to the beach than the precarious steps behind Rico's house. His home was just two houses down from the new artists' place, but the hill seemed steeper behind his estate than behind some others in the Cliffside neighborhood. But it didn't matter to Rico. No matter the weather, he and Frodo trudged down his crooked, uneven, unrepaired steps, then walked along the private stretch of sand until it led around the bend and opened to the public children's beach. Rico and Frodo had a routine they rarely seemed to deviate from. After a walk along the beach, they'd make their way into town, man and dog. Often, Izzy would spot him later on at Coffee's on Harbor Road, where he'd wait with Frodo until Jake Risso opened his tavern farther down the street.

Today, finally, Rico has deviated from this path and followed Izzy's advice about the steps. She let go of Red's leash, and he immediately flew toward his canine friend, throwing sand behind him, his tail slapping the wind.

Rico stood still, his small eyes watching the frolicking dogs. Finally, he began walking toward Izzy, a scowl on his face.

At first, Izzy thought something was wrong, but then she reminded herself that Rico always scowled.

The man stopped a few feet away, the scowl deepening. "Why are you here, missy? You should go home. Scat. It's not a day for running."

Rico often began talking to her in a way that made her think she had missed the first paragraph. He lifted one hand, and she saw that it was shaking. Nell had noticed the shaking a couple of weeks earlier, when they'd met up with Rico, and she'd mentioned it could be a sign of Parkinson's.

Izzy looked more closely at his face. "Are you okay, Rico?"

Rico responded by stepping closer and shaking a finger in Izzy's face, his own face contorted into a maze of tan wrinkles. "Where're the girls? Why are you alone today? Don't be foolish."

"Rico, I come here alone plenty of times. Cass and Nell are busy doing other things. And I'm not a fool." She kept her voice calm, seeing the consternation on his face. Then she smiled and attempted to lighten his mood. "But, Rico, speaking of foolish, I'm glad you finally took my advice and didn't try maneuvering down those rickety old steps of yours. The street is safer. Your steps could kill a person, and I don't want it to be you."

To emphasize her words, Izzy looked beyond the man toward the curve in the land at the ocean's edge, the mound of boulders banking the hill, beyond which steps meandered down the hill behind Rico's house. Although that part of the beach was private, reserved for homeowners, Izzy and Cass and most runners in town ran along the narrow beach, loving the privacy of it, the glimpses of the grand old estates, and the friendly residents, who didn't seem to mind their invasive presence.

All the properties along the bluff had steps leading down to the ocean, the way to the residents small private beach and docks and sailboats. Some homeowners had built wide wooden staircases; others had installed low lights and smooth granite, like those behind the Art Haven home.

But Rico's were narrow, unlit, old, and precarious. The reason for this was not a secret.

The story was often passed around in Jake's tavern, where well-intentioned regulars had offered to give Rico a hand. When his wife disappeared, Rico had stopped paying attention to the estate, had let the house and garden go, and his property had grown thick with trees, scrub bushes, and weeds, and coyote paths had marked the woods. The back steps especially had suffered from neglect, and their condition got worse with each nor'easter that pummeled the shore. Now the stone stairway was a ragged and crumbly path of granite.

It was *deadly*, as Izzy often told him.

Rico stopped wagging his finger, his scowl cemented on his face, and his fingers formed a fist, which he dropped to his side.

Izzy looked down at the mound his fingers had formed, at the veins protruding across the back of his hand. His hands and wrists were large for his frame and eerily strong. Like a boxer's might be, she imagined. She wondered about his growing up, if he'd been that tough kid on the block who could easily fend for himself among the big guys.

His small dark eyes were staring back toward the houses on the hill.

She looked up at his face again. His jaw was tight. "Do you feel okay, Rico? You seem a little . . . I don't know. Under the weather maybe? Sam had the flu not too long ago. How about Red and I walk back up the road with you and Frodo? Walk you home?"

Rico's weathered face seem to close in on itself, and Izzy wondered if she'd gone too far. She'd never been inside Rico's house, and she suspected he wouldn't want there to be a first time. The closest she'd gotten was the front door. But he didn't look well today. Slightly pale, if that was possible given his weathered face.

Even Frodo seemed concerned, abandoning his race for Red's tail and returning to his master's side. He sat obediently and stared up at Rico.

"Rico?" Izzy said.

The vibration of her cell phone interrupted, and she took a step back, then turned away from Rico as she pulled the phone from her belt. She saw that it wasn't an important call, and turned off the phone.

"Okay, now," she began, turning back to Rico. But he and Frodo were already a few yards away, moving down the beach toward town. Beside her, Red whined.

Izzy called Rico's name.

He turned around. Just long enough to deepen his scowl. And to call out just loud enough for her and Red to hear.

"You go home, missy. Now."

"Hey, Rico, wait a minute—" She started to walk toward him.

But both Rico and Frodo turned away abruptly and sped up. Without looking back, Rico gave a swift wave of his hand, a clear "Don't follow me" message. He said something to Frodo, patted his head, and the two continued off toward town, as if they had someplace important to be.

Someplace away from Izzy Perry.

Izzy stood still, watching the pair disappear down the beach. Sometimes Rico didn't make sense. She'd seen it before, these odd comments laced with non sequiturs. But in the end, when she'd reflected on them later, they had almost always made sense.

But she wasn't sure about today, about his wanting her to go home, as if a powerful nor'easter were coming her way on a bright sunny day.

She made a mental note to talk to Aunt Nell about it. They'd recently helped a friend with memory problems. Maybe there was more to learn about Rico's behavior. She turned back to Red, whose tail was once again in full swing as he pointed his whole body toward the far end of the beach.

Izzy happily agreed. "You're right. We still have a run to finish. You're not bad for an old dog, Red" she said.

They ran together along the smooth sand, toward the boulders and the PRIVACY sign posted at the beginning of the private beach. Izzy picked up her pace as Red rounded the curve.

At low tide the private beach was wide enough for sunbathing in summer, walking and running all year round. And today it was free of everyone. Izzy looked up the bluff as far as she could see. The estate homes loomed tall, some with castle-like towers, all with magnificent views. The terraces and guesthouses were tucked into the estates' wooded areas, protected from ocean winds by tall blue stem and turkey grasses, bushes, and live oaks, gnarled and twisted from nor'easters.

Izzy slowed and thought again of Rico. He seemed far more comfortable sitting at the bar in Jake Risso's tavern than living in this elegant neighborhood. His home was between two others just as big, just as expensive, but only Rico's was in disarray. She cupped her hand above her eyes and squinted to see where his property began. He had pointed it out to her several times, making no excuses for the rotted trees and the tangled brush that barely hid what was once a proper terrace. She could see messy seaweed and ocean debris cluttering the shore and suspected it marked the beginning of his property line. She wondered what the neighbors thought about the mess that identified Rico's land.

Red stopped short a few yards from Rico's property, suddenly alert, interrupting her thoughts.

Izzy looked back toward Paley's Cove, wondering if Rico

had come back, had followed them along the shore. He'd been acting peculiar. Well, slightly more than usual, maybe. She strained to see down the beach to the boulders.

But Red had other ideas. Without warning, he lurched ahead, pulling the leash free of Izzy's hand and sending her toppling to the ground.

"Red," Izzy yelled out, getting up and brushing the sand from her tights. But the dog had already slowed down. He had turned into a clearing on Rico's property, Izzy realized. Red's tail was the only thing visible behind the bushes as he moved away from the water. "No, Red," Izzy called, running toward him to keep him from going up the crumbly steps.

But Red had stopped. She could see his tail drop low, sweeping the ground as a deep growl rolled down the sand from her gentle dog. The sound was oddly mournful, shattering the morning quiet.

Breathless, Izzy reached Red and crouched down beside him, her eyes intent, looking for the cause of his growl. Her fingers lifted his paw, then gently moved through his coat as she looked for signs of injury.

But Red wasn't looking at his master or responding to her soft pats and probes. He was staring ahead, beyond a tangled bush, to the crumbly granite steps that led up to Rico Silva's home.

Finally, Izzy pulled her eyes away from Red and followed his look.

She gasped. One hand shot to her mouth, and with the other, she instinctively grabbed Red's collar, holding it tight.

What she saw first was a striped ascot, perfectly tied and peeking out from the open collar of a pristine white shirt. Rakish and distinctive.

Only then did she pull back and focus on the scene in front of her.

Splayed across the granite steps, as if pausing for a rest or a quiet moment in the sun, a long, elegant figure lay still, staring up at the morning sky.

A small pool of red, brilliant in the sunlight, had spread across the steps, seeped into the granite crumbles. The steps that would surely kill someone someday.

They finally had.

Chapter 7

For minutes, Izzy stood still, staring back into the lifeless eyes, the body already stiffening.

There was the face she had looked at the night before. It looked almost perfect. As if any minute he would sit up and continue their conversation, ask about her yarn shop, her life before as a lawyer, a topic that had seemed to interest him.

But Harrison Grant wasn't moving or talking or smiling in the way that had intrigued so many of the guests.

Izzy stepped back, shook away her shock, and pressed 911 into her phone, then gave precise directions to Cliffside Drive and to the steps behind the house.

And then she called Sam.

He would still be at her aunt and uncle's, talking sailboat repairs with Uncle Ben. Aunt Nell would be reading books to Abby or walking through the leaves with her in the backyard, maybe making a pile to jump in. And that would all change with her phone call. The day would change.

She knew Sam and Uncle Ben would be at her side in minutes. Even before an ambulance or the police appeared.

And they did just that.

Sam held her close, wishing he were the one, and not Izzy, who had stumbled upon a dead man, wishing he could take over the image in her mind that would take days to fade.

Izzy looked up the steps, at the granite crumbles on the side. And she thought of Rico. She'd warned him about the steps. A wave of sorrow passed through her. For Rico. And for Harrison Grant.

She and Sam stayed at the scene long enough for the police and the ambulance to arrive, for Ben to direct the medics around the house and down the steep hill. Long enough for Izzy to give her account of finding the body.

Then she, Red, and Sam left, leaving Uncle Ben and Harrison Grant behind.

Chapter 8

Cass wiped her forehead with one arm, then grimaced as she maneuvered her body into the cat pose. She looked over at Elena, her yoga partner, whose head was already facing down, her knees wide and her pregnant belly low. Cass swore Elena was smiling.

Danny had tried to coax Cass out of taking the yoga class. It was on Saturday mornings. A time to sleep in, to snuggle next to him. To savor the eggs he'd have ready for them both later. And some Saturdays, just because Danny was Danny, he'd ride his bike down to Polly's Bakery and return with chocolate croissants.

But Elena needed someone, something, Cass sensed. Driving her to a yoga class might help. Cass's fishing crew were family, and that included spouses and kids and sometimes grandparents. Many of the men had been fishing since they were young—it was all they knew. Living with a pregnant wife was an alien experience for many of the husbands.

Cass had known Elena's husband, Marco, since he was a kid. He was one of those kids who had hung out at the fishermen's wharf. She was aware even then that his father had worked too hard in the fisheries to be very present in his son's life. Marco was usually getting into some kind of kid trouble with his buddies. Cass had been a grown-up teenager back then and often helped her own dad on his boats, and she'd looked with disdain on the "brats," as the older kids called the younger ones. Marco had been a scruffy kid, and he'd been fishing since he was born. He'd turned into a good fisherman by the time he was ready to get a job. Cass and her brother, Pete, had hired him readily. But Cass suspected now that he had no idea what to do with a pregnant wife, no idea what her needs were.

Cass knew those needs. She knew young Elena needed support. She saw it in her shy manner, her eyes. The young woman was clearly overjoyed that she was going to have a baby, but she had little knowledge of what that meant.

"So where's her mother?" Izzy had asked Cass after meeting Elena a few weeks earlier. "She's just a kid. It's her mother who should be making sure she's taking vitamins, seeing a doctor, and—"

"Absolutely," Cass had said. "But there isn't one that I know of."

"Anywhere?"

"I don't think so. She doesn't talk much about things like that."

"Older sisters? Family?"

"Not that I know of. But, anyway, the big galoot who fathered this baby doesn't quite get it. I think his 'husband of a pregnant wife' skills are on a par with his Portuguese knitting expertise."

Izzy had laughed and given her friend a hug. Cass was turning motherly on all of them.

When Cass had offered rides to Elena, the younger woman gratefully accepted. Cass knew Marco's rusted-out Chevy truck ran only occasionally and always smelled of dead fish. Elena, who was always neat and immaculately groomed, her thick dark hair shiny, reminded Cass of lilacs, and she would fare much better in the shiny new SUV Danny had deemed necessary to purchase once he found out Cass was pregnant.

In the beginning the rides were to doctor's appointments, but soon the subject of exercise classes came up.

Elena had shyly suggested to Cass that they take a water aerobics class at the YMCA, something that had made Cass visibly shudder, her body instantly cold. She was quite sure there wasn't a bathing suit in all of Sea Harbor that would cover her body sufficiently. Not to mention what she would look like in it.

But tiny Elena loved the sight of her own growing figure, the way her formfitting Lycra tops beautifully outlined every curve.

Cass admired her own "growing baby" figure, too, but only in front of the full-sized mirror in her bedroom. A bedroom and a public swimming pool were two different ducks, and so Cass had encouraged Elena's second choice. Baggy pants and a yoga mat seemed the better part of valor for her. In the end, when it came to pregnant mom classes, the down dog and child's poses had won out.

Elena had taken the initiative and found the class, although not really, she'd confessed. She had met the teacher in Market Basket, of all places. The woman had come up to Elena and talked to her as if they already knew each other, Elena said. The friendly type. She'd told Elena that she had to take the class. That she would love it.

The choice turned out to be a good one, better than Cass had expected. Harmony Fairchild, the instructor, came recommended by Izzy and some of her friends, too. Although Cass hadn't warmed up to her as much as Elena had, she was a good teacher. And after just a couple of classes, Cass could feel the effects, the stretching of her muscles. Today she felt it more than usual. Soothing and calming.

She'd slept fitfully the night before, not able to find a comfortable position, shifting pillows to all sides of her body. Danny, too, had been on edge, and they had both been up before the sun. It was the way the evening had been turned on its head, with Sam, Danny, and Ben searching the Art Haven grounds, as if Harrison Grant might be hiding from them. But grown men didn't play hide-and-seek. They left. And that was what he'd done, that man who had fooled all of them last night with his unexpectedly friendly and interesting persona.

All of them but Sam.

Cass wondered briefly when Harrison Grant had finally come back to the Art Haven house. Early this morning? What excuse had he given Jane and Ham? She and Danny had left the reception earlier than the others, once the search had failed to find the photographer. But at the time, most of the guests had seemed happy. The dessert may have been more appealing than listening to a short speech, and most people who wanted to meet the photographer had already done so by then. The evening had had its art successes, with small SOLD tags attached to many of thc works of art.

She'd check in with Izzy later to see how the evening ended. For now, she'd empty her mind, embrace the quiet, and smile into the cat pose. Yoga was already calming her down.

Next to Cass, Elena moved gracefully, breathing slowly. And then, suddenly, she stopped, the curve of her back stiffening. "Wow!" she said, the sound bouncing off her mat. Elena rarely made a sound, and the single word seemed as loud as a foghorn.

Cass's brows shot up. "Wow? What's that mean? Are you okay?"

Elena's palms were planted on the floor, her fingers spread out. "My baby is doing somersaults again. Rolling like a beach ball." Her face was radiant.

From the front of the the room, the instructor's soft voice was coaxing the small group of pregnant women into another pose.

"Are you okay back there?" Harmony Fairchild asked,

straightening her tall figure and looking over the low bodies to Cass and Elena.

Cass winced as her own body protested being moved too quickly. "We're fine. Just a little baby gymnastics event going on back here, that's all," she said.

The women around them chuckled.

The two women got back to concentrating on not concentrating.

Elena brought her chin down to her chest, then exhaled as she rounded her narrow back. Slowly, perfectly.

Cass stopped her own pose, sat back on her legs, and watched Elena as she slipped back into her pose, admiring the younger woman's grace. The shy, reticent young woman she'd first met was emerging from a cocoon a smart and wise and lovely person. Or perhaps she hadn't emerged at all, but Cass simply hadn't looked hard enough.

Elena snuck a look at Cass and smiled at her, then went back to her breathing and her perfect pose.

"All right, ladies," the yoga instructor said a short while later, "it's time to grab your pillows and folded blankets. We will now move into a modified Savasana. Please move to your sides with your pillows and blankets supporting you. Breathe deeply and slowly as you relax each part of your body."

It was Cass's favorite pose. She did as directed and felt her body loosen, relax as she concentrated on her toes, her feet her ankles.

But suddenly, before the magic of the soothing exercise moved to her upper body, the blare of sirens pierced the quiet room, shattering her calm.

Cass froze.

The sounds of emergency vehicles had always startled her, then left her with an uncomfortable feeling in the pit of her stomach, the kind fishermen's families lived with. Sudden thoughts of the Harbor Patrol responding to a boat on fire, an accident in the outer harbor, lost fishermen, all created a visceral reaction. It didn't matter that such alarms almost always meant a cat was stuck in a tree or someone was locked out of a house. Especially on a lazy Saturday morning.

Cass breathed slowly, deeply.

"Finally," the woman next to her whispered. "My favorite."

Cass looked over. "Sorry, what did you say?"

Another siren blared, then faded as the vehicle moved away from the nearby fire station.

Cass glanced at the woman next to her. Her eyes were closed, her face serene. "The pose," the woman said softly. "Savasana. Total relaxation. Do you know why it's called that?"

Cass wasn't sure she wanted to know.

"They call it the corpse pose," the woman said.

A short while later, Cass and Elena rolled up their mats, gathered their pillows, and made their way toward the front of the room.

Cass smiled at a pleasant-looking man standing in the doorway. Harmony spotted him at the same time. She waved and motioned for him to come in. Then she looked over at Cass and Elena and asked them if they could wait a minute. She had a favor to ask.

The man walked in and leaned against a small desk, camera in his hand, as Harmony explained to Elena and Cass that she was working on a new marketing brochure. Then she turned to the gentleman in the room and introduced him.

"Frank is helping me with it. He's a wonderful photographer," she said.

What she needed, she explained, was photographs of pregnant students. And she wondered if Cass and Elena would agree to have their photos taken for it.

Cass laughed. Then she immediately declined. "I know what cameras do to bodies, and this one can't afford another ten pounds without toppling over. Now, Elena here . . ." She held out her hand toward a blushing Elena. "Elena is beautiful and peaceful looking. Every pregnant woman on the North Shore will want to be in your class so they can look exactly like her."

Harmony chuckled and smiled warmly at Elena, accepting Cass's refusal easily. "Well, Elena, what do you think? We'd respect your privacy, of course. There's no need to put names in the brochure. And the photos would be only for my use. We wouldn't release them to any third party. This would all be on the up-and-up."

Elena listened, smiled, and didn't seem to have any objections to the idea. "Sure. I'll be happy to if it'll help you and your class, your business. But I don't want to hold Cass up . . ." She looked at Cass, then Harmony.

"Frank is very fast. It won't take long at all."

"No problem," Cass said. "I'm not in a hurry."

The photographer stood up straight and smiled. "Thanks," he said.

Cass watched as the man snapped away, first taking one or two photos of Elena on her mat, in a peaceful pose, her back straight. He ended the brief session with several close-ups of Elena.

In no time Harmony and Frank thanked them both, then went back to talking business as Cass and Elena headed down the hall and into the bright sunshine.

"That was interesting," Cass said. "You were great, Elena. I wondered, though, why the guy didn't come ten minutes sooner so he could take shots of the whole class. All those different shapes and stages of pregnancy." Then she stopped, thought about it, and joked, "But what do I know? I turned the guy down. Besides, my only experience putting a brochure together is photographing lobsters. And, believe me, that's a whole different kettle of fish."

Elena laughed, and they crossed the street, then walked

through the small corner park on Harbor Road. Cass, still nervous about driving a perfect, dent-free car, had parked in the alley between her in-laws' bookstore and Izzy's yarn shop. A safe spot for now, at least until she got that first deadly dent. Then she'd be able to relax.

As they reached the curb, a noisy truck belching fumes and smoke sped down the street in front of them.

Elena took a step back, nearly hiding behind Cass.

Cass recognized the truck and the square-faced, unshaven man driving it. Marco Costa was speeding down Harbor Road. A man was next to him, his window open and his head held back in laughter. She looked at Elena. "What is with him? He's going to kill someone, driving like that. Geesh."

Elena looked after the truck.

"He's supposed to be helping Pete repair some traps," Cass said. "Where do you suppose he's going?"

Elena was silent.

"Elena, please tell me he doesn't chase fire trucks or police cars."

Elena smiled, a soft smile that didn't have anything to do with fire trucks. "Maybe. I don't know where he's going," she said simply, "but he's a good man. A very sweet man. He has a side you don't see, Cass. He's very lovable."

"Who was with him?"

"Eddie Porter. His good friend. They're both good guys who have little boys hiding inside them." With a smile still on her face, she stepped off the curb and began to cross the street, her small but pregnant body stopping cars as she walked.

Cass followed, glancing down Harbor Road again, but Marco's truck and the fumes had disappeared around the bend. She couldn't—wouldn't—begin to judge Marco's goodness. But a sweet man? She stumbled up the opposite curb, trying to get a mental picture of Marco Costa as a very sweet man.

Early morning shoppers were already crowding the sidewalks, the sunny day having drawn them out. They knew that a sunny day could give way to a nor'easter in less time than it took to buy groceries. Her in-laws' store, the Sea Harbor Bookstore, had its blinds pulled up, the window filled with best-selling books. Cass waved toward the glass in case Harriet or Archie Brandley was looking out.

They reached Izzy's shop and paused in front of the display window. Today the display was a backyard scene filled with the colors of autumn. Strands of thick worsted-weight yarn dripped from the branches of a tree, and below the pretend tree, loose strands of gold and crimson, magenta and brown yarn were tangled into soft and inviting piles of leaves.

But what seemed to catch Elena's eye was a clothesline attached to two branches of the tree. Cass could hear her breathing, as if she was gazing at something overwhelmingly beautiful. Hanging from the line were five tiny baby sweaters, knit in the brightest of the autumn colors, hanging side by side.

Cass followed her gaze. "Do you knit?"

Elena shook her head. "My mother had arthritis and didn't do those kinds of crafts. She was wonderful at other things, though. We spent a lot of time cooking together. But I've always wanted to learn how to knit."

Cass watched the expression on her face. She was mesmerized by the simple window display. By the tiny sweaters. Elena's face reflected pure, unexpected joy.

Cass had never asked Elena much about her background, not wanting to pry, but Elena had offered hints of her upbringing here and there, enough hints that Cass knew she'd been raised in a loving, happy home. Older parents. Somewhere in rural Pennsylvania, Cass thought she'd said.

But Cass didn't know much more, except that Elena had simply appeared on the dock one day with Marco, and he'd introduced her to Cass and Pete and the fishermen who worked for the Halloran Company as "his woman," an expression that had made Cass cringe and chew her employee out later. He had never said it again.

Cass had assigned Pete the task of finding out more information about Elena from Marco. Sometimes the men forgot Pete was part owner of the company and talked freely around him when they were out on the boats, untangling buoy lines or hauling traps.

Marco hadn't given Pete a straight answer about Elena's age, and Cass had wondered if he knew it. She'd worried that Elena might be underage, so she had asked her outright. "Twenty-two," Elena had told her proudly, much to Cass's relief. But even though she was older than Cass had guessed, Elena seemed young in ways that had little to do with the year of her birth. Young in "life," maybe. Or, as Izzy suggested after meeting her, maybe she was simply uncomplicated.

"You have to learn to knit if you're having a baby," Cass said. "It's a must. Izzy owns this shop, and she'll teach you. Your baby needs one of those little sweaters to get through the wicked winter ahead."

"I'd love to knit for my baby," Elena said, and then went back to admiring the piles of soft yarn and the sweaters, the wonder of knitting and babies lighting her large dark eyes.

Cass took a moment to pat down her backpack and find her phone. Texts had been coming in since they'd left the YMCA. Plans for tonight, probably. Izzy had talked about a girls' night to help her with a new project.

She pulled out her cell and checked the screen.

And then she frowned.

Five texts from Izzy and a voice-mail message. And not one of them told her anything. Except that Izzy was going to send out a search party if Cass didn't text her back soon.

Cass started to tap in a message, explaining that she was with Elena Costa and that neither of them had been kidnapped. But then her thumbs stopped moving. Izzy knew she had yoga this morning. Five texts without a real message meant more than "Where are you?"

Five texts meant something was *wrong*, and it was one of those wrongs you didn't confide in a text message.

She called, and Izzy answered on the first ring.

Chapter 9

For most of Sea Harbor, the chilly day, softened by a bright sun, rolled out as many autumn Saturdays did. People donned jackets and fleeces and hats and moved outdoors, hiking at Ravenswood Park, running errands, hanging with friends, or enjoying long gossipy lunches at Garozzo's deli. And then, later, once the sun had set and the air had turned colder, they moved comfortably into evening plans.

Unless they had come face-to-face with a dead man.

"It's surreal," Izzy said. "I feel helpless, like we should all be doing something, but I don't know what that something is . . ." She slipped off her shoes and folded her legs beneath her, a puddle of yarn already in her lap. Izzy had suggested the get-together with Birdie, Nell and Cass days before. They'd meet in Birdie's cozy den for a few hours on a late Saturday afternoon to help Izzy flesh out a new idea she had. A yarn-shop event.

But those were plans made before an Art Haven reception had turned everything on its head. Before a famous photographer's life had abruptly ended. Before Izzy had found a dead man at the bottom of crumbling steps.

It was Birdie who had taken matters into her own hands and insisted they meet as planned. It had taken only a brief flurry of texts from her to assure Nell, Izzy, and Cass that they were all expected at her home at four o'clock.

There is nothing we can do, my dears. Harrison has no family in Sea Harbor to comfort, no friends or relatives to whom we can bring soup or solace, she had explained. **I will see you soon.**

So they would meet as scheduled to plan a happy event. A community baby shower.

Izzy had wanted to give Cass a wild, wonderful one, but Cass had adamantly refused. "That kind of attention would make me go into early labor," she had insisted.

A part of Izzy had figured Cass was probably right. It was definitely not her thing. But a new baby was coming into their own small world, and Izzy had not been able to let it go without doing something.

It was Mae Anderson, her shop manager, who had come up with the idea, having recently volunteered at a children's hospital. And it was Izzy, Birdie, and Nell who had run with it. Cass would simply have to come along. The baby shower wouldn't be for *her*, after all. They'd have a baby shower for the universe, or at least part of it. An afternoon of knitting, chatting, and eating, with baskets of fine baby yarn on the tables, plenty of cider and sandwiches, a warm fire, and townspeople coming together to share finished or half-finished baby knitting projects and to knit up new ones—winter warmth for the babies of expectant daughters or sisters or friends or neighbors, and for all the Children's Hospital babies in need of warm hats or blankets or booties. And there were plenty, Mae had assured them. Babies needed warmth.

And somehow Harrison Grant's accident had added its own layer of incentive to the baby-shower planning. Another reason to be together. To sort through the tangle of emotions each of them had experienced over the past day. To release them, perhaps, and turn their thoughts from death to life.

Nell sat next to Izzy on the love seat in Birdie's second-floor den. She fiddled with the pad of paper she'd brought to jot down ideas they came up with for invitations and knitting patterns and food. She couldn't shake the regret she'd felt all day that she hadn't gone for that morning run with her niece. That she hadn't been the one to find Harrison Grant. Logically, she knew she couldn't have done a single thing that would have changed anything. But she was deeply sorry Izzy had been all alone when she'd come face-to-face with death. With the open, unseeing eyes of a man they had so recently been with.

"The image will fade, Izzy," she said.

"I'm okay, Aunt Nell. Honestly, I am." But Izzy didn't pull away when Nell wrapped an arm around her. "We spoke so poorly of him this morning at breakfast. And all the while he was lying on those cold, decaying steps. I . . . I can't shake it. I feel this uncontrollable need to mourn him. But I don't know him well enough to really be sad. But I *am* sad." She shook her head, trying to straighten out her thoughts. "I'm sad for Jane, I guess. For the arts association that sponsored the evening. For all of us who were involved in some way. But that seems so selfish . . ." Izzy finally gave up. The thoughts went unfinished, not holding together. Unraveling.

The day had turned chilly as clouds moved in, and Birdie's groundsman had started a fire for them in the den fireplace. Birdie moved over to it now and blew the flames to life with a leather bellows. The fire leapt and crackled, warming the room, which sat high above the harbor and the town. "Feelings are difficult to handle when you barely know the person. It's a different kind of grieving."

"I understand what Izzy is saying, though. Somehow, I feel a connection to him," Nell said. "We brought Harrison Grant here. All of us did. Jane and Ham. Sam."

And he would probably be alive if he hadn't come, if they'd listened to Sam. The words that went unsaid.

It was one of those what-ifs or "if onlys," which weren't

helpful in any way and defied common sense and the rules of logic. The four intelligent women in the room knew that. But it didn't matter. Emotions often looked logic in the face and stuck out their tongues, banishing it soundly.

"I don't think word of the accident has spread around town," Izzy said. "There wasn't any talk in the shop. Mae usually knows things before they happen, but she hadn't heard a word. I suppose it'll be different tomorrow, when it hits the news." She fingered the cashmere sweater she was making for baby Brandley. A tiny sea-green cable wound up each side.

A sudden thought came to her, and along with it concern. *Rico Silva.* The poor man. Did he even know someone had died on his steps? He had left the house early that morning and had probably ended up at Jake Risso's Gull Tavern until the wee hours. Jake stayed open as long as the town ordinance allowed on weekends. And then she thought again and realized how fractured her thoughts were. Rico lived on the property where a man had died. A neighbor, the police, someone would have contacted him as soon as possible. Certainly, he'd been told about Harrison Grant's untimely death.

"I don't think most people will pay much attention to someone they didn't know having an accident," Cass was saying. "My fishing crew never heard of Harrison Grant. And if they heard a rumor about a guy falling down some steps after a party and dying, they'd figure he'd had too much to drink. It'd be an old story. A shame, maybe. And then they'd go about their day."

"But there's another group of people who *did* know him, and many who met him last night," Birdie said. "The fact that he died in our town will get attention. Maybe not from fishermen, but from others. At least for a day or two."

"He seemed healthy, but you never know, I guess," Cass said.

"True," Birdie said, mulling over the thought. She had settled into Sonny Favazza's old leather chair. No one else ever sat in it, not wanting to disturb the scent of Birdie's late husband's cherry pipe tobacco, which Birdie breathed in and still savored all these many years later. "And I don't think he was drinking heavily. As far as I could tell, he was handling his drinks with discretion, like a man who was used to receptions and cocktail parties at which he was a notable guest."

They all agreed that their conversations with Harrison had been unexpectedly warm and friendly and definitely not dulled by alcohol.

"The steps are treacherous," Izzy said. She remembered the warning she'd given to old Rico Silva many times. *Those steps are going to kill someone someday.* Her terrible prediction had come to life.

"I wonder if he was lying down there the whole time the men were out looking for him?" Cass said.

"Ben wondered about that, too. He stayed at the scene for a while after Sam took Izzy back to the house. He wanted to answer any questions Jerry Thompson might have had . . . ," Nell began.

"The police chief came?" Cass asked. "Why?"

"The police check out unusual accidents, like when someone wasn't sick, when there wasn't any obvious reason for it," Izzy said.

"The medical examiner confirmed that Harrison had been dead for some time. Hours, she said, but they will have a more exact time frame soon." Nell looked over at Izzy.

Izzy's forehead was wrinkled, the image she'd seen appearing again and again in her mind's eye. "Lawyers sometimes know forensics only remotely. But it was clear to me that he'd been dead for hours."

"Geesh. Not a pleasant way to die. Give me a soft bed, nice dreams of my Danny." Cass fumbled around in her large bag for a pattern and a knit hat she was working on. She usually knit simple, bulky hats for bigheaded fishermen, and her bright yellow baby bonnet reflected her habit of knitting "large." It was now nearly toddler size and growing.

"Chief Thompson said his skull was damaged by the fall, but that's about all Ben knew," Nell said. "Jerry said he'd be in touch if there were any questions."

Jerry Thompson was one of Ben's closest friends. When it came to official business, both men respected the other's boundaries. But they were always there for each other to sort through thoughts and facts, whether it be a baseball game gone awry or more serious matters of life and death.

"Ben filled the chief in on some of the reception details. He said Jerry was curious why Grant had ended up a few houses away from the Art Haven home."

"I wondered that myself," Izzy said.

The thought had come to the others, too. The estates in the Cliffside neighborhood were large, and they seemed self-contained, with bushes and trees, lovely gardens, low stone walls, and patios separating one property from the next.

"It wouldn't be hard to do, though why he was over there is more curious maybe," Cass said. "Lucky Bianchi was hanging out with my brother today, and Pete said they were talking about it. Remember, the Art Haven house was Lucky's family home. He said that when he was a kid, there were always ways to sneak out to a buddy's house one or two or three houses down along the cliff. They'd make their own trails through the back wooded area. Over the years they were practically sidewalks."

Nell thought about their own backyard, which backed up to hillside woods that led down to the beach road. Over the generations Endicott kids and neighbors had made a trail through the woods to rival any the US Forest Service maintained.

"People were wandering around everywhere last night, Harrison included," Izzy said. "Some walked down to the shore. I can easily imagine someone climbing up the wrong steps on their way back up to the house."

Birdie agreed. "It happens in my neighborhood." Living on a hilly five-acre estate, Birdie looked out at the same ocean as the Cliffside homes, but on the other end of town. Her grounds were just as wooded and well maintained, and her property also had wide granite steps that wound down to the sea. "My groundsman Harold finds lost souls around my place often, especially when there's a party at the estate next door to me. He takes them under his wing and leads them back to the party or calls an Uber and sends them on their way. Even with our outdoor lights, it's sometimes difficult to see where you're going."

Ella Sampson, Harold's wife and Birdie's housekeeper and cook, came into the room, carrying a tray of napkins and a platter of warm nibbles. She set them down on a side table and explained, with a note of pride, that she was experimenting with her cooking. "I'm not about to let my culinary skills turn wrinkly and thin like this face and body," she said. Then she added that her mah-jongg group was getting competitive in terms of who brought the most innovative appetizers. She was not about to let them get the better of her.

One knobby finger pointed to the platter. "Figs, melted blue cheese, and pear crostini." Ella said the words slowly, as if it was for the first time. Then she added, "Harold refuses to taste them. He's down there eating my mac 'n' cheese."

Cass looked over at the unfamiliar dark chunks dotting the warm slices of a baguette. She frowned. Ella's lobster mac 'n' cheese was one of her favorite dishes, and her husband, Harold, was down there in the kitchen, in pasta and cheese heaven. And she wasn't. "Figs?" she said, drawing out the word.

"Figs," Ella shot back, giving her a dismissive look. She looked around at the others. "I knew you ladies would be willing to give them a try."

"And you were pretty sure we wouldn't sue you if we got sick, right?" Cass asked, her brows lifted, her voice teasing.

Ella humphed, hiding a smile behind the sound, and headed out the door. Then she stopped and stepped back into the den.

She looked over at Birdie. "Some poor fellow fell down the steps at that fancy event you went to last night. Did you know that? Harold said they found him this morning, dead as can be. Not a good way to end such a lovely event. Or a life, I suspect."

Before Birdie could respond, Ella was gone, her sensible shoes silent as she made her way down the winding steps to her kitchen.

"I guess the news is out, after all," Cass said.

"It seems so. Harold probably heard it while getting the Lincoln cleaned today," Birdie said. "Or it's something he heard on his police radio. But if we can judge by Ella's reaction, you may be right, Cass, that this isn't going to cause much of a stir." She got up and walked over to the rosewood bookcase and its hidden bar and refrigerator, then pulled out a can of Cass's favorite seltzer and uncorked a bottle of wine.

"I hope you're right, especially for Jane and Ham's sake," Nell said. She took the glass of wine Birdie offered her.

"And Sam's," Izzy said quietly. *Sam.* His emotions seemed to have been hijacked—anger when Harrison had disappeared. Sadness for the art founders that he'd brought the man to town. Then . . . then what? The man was now dead. Sam had tossed and turned the night before. And the news today that Harrison Grant was dead had thrown him into an unusual silence. Not like Sam at all.

She got up and walked over to the window, looking down at the quiet town below. The sun's late afternoon rays lit a parade of boats coming into the harbor. Crowds moved along the pier and Harbor Road, into restaurants and stores. An image of old Rico and Frodo sitting down there near the window of Jake's bar flitted across her mind. And then a stark image of a man dead at the bottom of Rico's steps.

A sudden chill ran through Izzy, and she wrapped her arms around herself. Had Rico seen Harrison Grant? Had he, too, come face to face with death?

"Izzy?" Nell looked across the room.

Izzy turned and forced a smile to her face. She picked up Ella's platter from the table and brought it back to the group, passing it around.

Cass did her part, pulling out her phone and searching for a playlist to lighten the mood. Talk had lingered too long on the dead for all of them. Soon she had Lady Gaga's infectious rhythm filling the den, singing eh-eh's and ye-ha's, which didn't make sense but filled the room nicely. She turned it up louder.

Harrison Grant's fall was unfortunate and would certainly sadden his family and friends. But life moved on.

The wine and crostini and crackling fire began to work their magic on the four friends, and the skeins of soft yarn beckoned them.

Izzy pulled a pile of baby patterns from a file folder and spread the patterns out on the coffee table, then urged them to pick out some that they could pass out in the store. As Cass's music filled the room, Izzy looked around at the fire-warmed faces of her dearest friends. Planning a happy event.

But even the pile of baby-soft yellow cashmere yarn beside her couldn't stop the flow of images fast-forwarding across her mind.

Harrison Grant, his strong handsome face leaning in. Listening, talking to her.

Then hours later, deep-set blue eyes staring, unseeing, at a beautiful morning sky.

And steps so crumbly they were sure to kill someone someday.

Izzy and Nell stood together at the den windows two hours later, watching the fiery bands of an autumn sunset sink into the ocean. Behind them, Birdie and Cass helped Ella pick up the remains of their planning—empty glasses and napkins, scraps of yarn and paper.

"Beautiful," Nell said. "A good omen, maybe. It's been a long day. Tomorrow will be better."

Izzy was silent, her eyes focused on the harbor. Streetlights flickered on, cars vied for parking spots, and workers at the popular Ocean's Edge Restaurant were outside, cleaning off the front walk, preparing for a crowd of Saturday night diners. "Birdie can watch the world go by from up here," she said softly, more to herself than to Nell.

But Nell listened and heard. They all knew that Birdie occasionally did exactly that, sometimes with the help of Sonny Favazza's powerful telescope, which was mounted on a walnut stand in the center of one of the windows. Birdie had been known to spot fires before the fire department did, and to keep secret young couples rendezvous beneath the pier.

Izzy pointed beyond Harbor Road, to where the land formed a V, the Canary Cove Art Colony in one direction, Paley's Cove beach and the Cliffside neighborhood in the other. "I can see all the way to the other end of the shore from here. It's pretty remarkable."

Nell followed her gaze and traced the bend of the shore, the lights of houses and streets marking the way, the dark area of the beach, then the hilly rise of the street and the house lights flickering through the trees on Cliffside Drive. "It is. Seeing nearly a whole town from one window. But we can't see the shore side of the Cliffside mansions, the private beach at the bottom of the hill. That's where your mind is, isn't it, Izzy? That stretch of beach hidden in darkness . . ."

As they talked, they were both looking into the darkening night, not at one another. An easier way to talk sometimes: to select your words and to protect the messages that came from your eyes and face. A kind of distance, even between two women who loved each other profoundly.

"It's a brutal image," Nell said quietly.

Izzy nodded.

"But there's something else, isn't there?"

Izzy didn't answer at first. It was something that had come to her off and on that day. And each time, she had brushed it away. Not wanting to give it any importance. Which, she told herself, she was quite sure it didn't have. Finally, she turned slightly, met Nell's eyes. "Before Red and I found Harrison, when we were walking on the beach, I ran into our Rico, and he was—"

The loud chiming of *The Four Seasons* startled the room into silence. Ella rushed out of the den and down the stairs, as if the house were on fire.

Birdie chuckled. "It's just the doorbell. Nothing like a little Vivaldi to wake us up."

She headed to the hallway, but before she made it to the top of the staircase, Ben Endicott was rounding the second landing. He met her at the top and greeted her with a hug. "Sam's on his way."

"Well, now," Birdie said, motioning toward the den, "it isn't every Saturday night that two handsome men come a-calling."

Nell watched from the den doorway. *And it's slightly odd*, she thought. Not that they hadn't all spent many happy hours in Birdie's house with a multitude of friends and neighbors, but she and Ben had agreed earlier that he'd text her after the game and they'd figure out their evening. Maybe order takeout from the new Thai place near the beach. Or have dinner at the Ocean's Edge with anyone who wanted to go.

Ben greeted his wife and Izzy and Cass. He looked around the room, as if its comfort was suddenly important—the warmth of the fire, the familiar rosewood bookcase, the Winslow Homer painting of the sea on the walls. "I've always loved this den, Birdie. It makes me feel like I know Sonny Favazza."

"Of course it does," Birdie said.

"I think he and I would have been friends."

Birdie seemed to delight in the thought.

Sonny was Birdie's first love—and more. Ben knew that, and so did anyone who had ever known Bernadette Favazza. Although she had married twice since Sonny's early death, he was the forever love of her life. They had lived and loved fully in the few years they had together before Sonny's untimely illness. Birdie often said that the magnificent home that Sonny had built for her held his spirit—that he was everywhere. She felt him in her bed, in this den, at the kitchen table, and in the Lincoln Town Car, which Harold kept in pristine condition and proudly drove in his stead. She talked with Sonny often and would love him always.

As if reading her thoughts, Ben walked over and embraced the small woman, nearly burying her in his arms.

Birdie hugged him right back.

The thud of steps being taken two at time announced Sam's arrival. He walked on in and gave Izzy a hug. Then continued to hold her close.

She pulled away finally and looked into his face. And then she said carefully, "You haven't been at the game, have you, Sam?"

Sam looked over her shoulder at the lights blinking along the harbor, then back at her face. "What? So I don't smell like beer and peanuts?" But his voice lacked laughter and told her that she wasn't wrong.

Ben had already headed to Birdie's bar and poured more drinks and glasses of water for everyone. "That fire looks inviting. How about we sit and let it warm our souls? Regroup?" He motioned toward the circle of chairs that a short while before had held skeins of brightly colored yarn, knitting patterns, and talk of baby showers.

No one questioned that they hadn't "grouped" in the first place. Instead, they joined Cass, who was now enveloped in an overstuffed chair near the fire. Ben sat down in a chair next to her, took a drink of whiskey, then leaned forward, his elbows on his knees, and looked around at the group, then over at Izzy, who was still standing behind the circle of comfortable chairs.

"Izzy?" Ben said.

But she turned away and walked slowly to the windows. She

stood still for a minute, as if frozen by the lights, the boats coming in. The night falling around them. Finally, she turned and walked back toward the circle of chairs, then stopped and rested her hands on the back of the couch.

Ben gestured in vain at an empty chair, then took a breath and sat straighter, about to speak. But before he had a chance to tell them why he and Sam had stopped by, to admit that no, they hadn't been at TD Garden . . . before he could explain that instead, they had gotten a call from Jerry Thompson and had headed back home and then up to the Cliffside neighborhood, to the Art Haven home to meet with the police chief and Jane and Ham Brewster . . . before Ben could explain why they'd abandoned their courtside seats, Izzy, interrupting, told Birdie, Nell, and Cass why Ben and Sam had come by.

"Harrison Grant was murdered."

Chapter 10

Nell and Birdie walked along old Canary Cove Road toward the Brewsters' modest art gallery late Sunday morning.

The road matched the whole art colony—an old road between old summer cottages crowded together on either side of the street. Instead of vacationers, the structures now housed art galleries, studios, lofts, a few small shops, and the Artist's Palate Bar & Grill. Narrow alleys broke up the line of colorfully painted galleries, a glimpse of the ocean at the other end. The art colony itself was a startling contrast to its new mansion up on Cliffside Drive, but the low-key creative spirit was the same wherever the art community gathered.

The Brewster's gallery looked much like the others. There was nothing about it that indicated Jane and Ham were responsible for the colony's existence. It didn't reveal that the couple had scraped together savings and grants and had depended on the largesse of friends to make the colony a reality.

And there was nothing about the cheerful, inviting Canary Cove Art Colony that indicated that a pall was creeping its way through the streets of Sea Harbor and would soon infect its creative center.

"It's still quiet here," Birdie said, looking above some of the shops at the small loft apartments, where drawn shades indicated sleeping artists. Here and there newspapers had been thrown against gallery doors and lay unopened. "Artists sleep in, I guess."

"Or maybe they are still recovering from Friday night," Nell said.

When they reached the gallery, Ham was standing out front, a wrinkled copy of the *Sea Harbor Gazette* in one hand, the other stroking his full white beard, as if he were deep in thought.

Ham spotted Nell and Birdie as they drew close, and scrunched the newspaper in one large fist. He hugged them both.

"Jane's got coffee on. Glad you could make it over. Come on in." He turned and held the door open.

Out of habit, Nell first bent down and patted the Brewsters' welcoming large brass frog, its head shiny from the many hands that had rubbed it smooth for good luck. It seemed especially appropriate today, although if asked, Nell would be unable to explain what kind of good luck she was hoping for.

Ham caught the movement and smiled. "Not a bad idea, Nellie." He closed the door behind them and flipped the OPEN sign to CLOSED.

"Closed?" Birdie asked.

"Just for this Sunday. At least I hope so."

"Is it Sunday?" Nell said, her smile small. "The arts reception seems so long ago. Weeks. Not so close that we can reach out and touch it."

"Murder has a way of coloring everything, even time," Birdie said.

Murder. Hearing it said out loud sent shivers through Nell and made her realize that of course Ham and Jane would close the gallery today. Instead of art lovers wandering the narrow streets, there'd be curiosity seekers, people wanting the scoop on what had really gone on Friday night at the Canary Cove Art Haven.

She glanced at the newspaper in Ham's hand.

At the sound of voices, Jane walked out of a smaller room behind the main gallery space. Van Gogh poppies on her caftan seemed to sway with her generous body as she walked. "Dears," she said, embracing Birdie, then Nell. Her face was pale, her eyes tired, but the soft smile that was always in place, always offering a welcome, greeted them.

"Can this week sprout any uglier tentacles?" she asked, beckoning Birdie and Nell to follow her to the gallery's cozy room in the back.

Nell glanced into a side gallery as they walked. Its white walls and strategically placed lights highlighted the works of several new artists. She made a mental note to come back later to look. But without Ben. He had purchased so many Canary Cove artists' works that Nell feared they'd need to build more walls in their home.

They walked down a short hallway and into a sunny room—the lounge, Jane called it—that spanned the back of the building. An old library desk, filled with stacks of papers and a clutter of photographs and pencils, and an occasional smudge of paint, occupied one of the shorter walls. The room had a comfortable sitting area, surrounded by windows that looked out on a small garden and the Brewsters' house beyond it. Ham had built a wall of bookcases for art books, small pieces of Jane's pottery, and a built-in refrigerator. Nell knew that all of it—the garden, this lounge, and their cottage—was intended to welcome and comfort many artists trying to find their place in the world, to help them determine their artistic direction, their special gifts. The Brewster's lounge in particular was where artists found listening ears and wise counsel.

And sometimes friends did, too.

Ham settled himself into a wide overstuffed chair and spread the newspaper out on the coffee table. He looked at it intently for a minute, then lifted his head, a frown deepening the wrinkles on his face. "Does Mary Pisano still have anything to say about this newspaper her family owns? It's spewing such—"

"Ham, shush," said Jane, cutting off his colorful words before they filled the air.

Ham pointed to a headline, then slipped on his glasses and read it out loud. "Fancy artist event ends in tragedy when famed photographer brutally murdered." He looked up from the paper. "Fancy? Didn't know we were going for fancy."

Ham's attempt to lighten his own mood brought a smile from the others. The weekend events had colored his usual demeanor—funny, kind, gentle. The murder would cast a shadow over the entire artist community, but what Ham Brewster was most concerned about, what caused the deep sadness on his face, was the distress it was already causing his wife. An event planned to showcase their Canary Cove artists, to bring people into their magnificent new center, to honor their guest had ended in murder.

Birdie and Nell had both read the headlines and the articles accompanying them when they'd gotten up that morning. Like many Sea Harbor residents, they preferred to hold the newspaper in their hands and read it out loud as a way to digest the news, not read it on a computer or hear it through earbuds. But Sunday's paper usually featured little news. It primarily contained photos of weekend sports and social events. Today the headlines were different.

"Well, the intent of headlines is to make you want to know more," Jane said, searching for something reasonable about the headline. "I suppose this does that. Maybe. At least tries to. Some young reporter wanting to stand out from the others."

"I think it's the photo that catches most people's attention," Birdie said. "It's a very handsome shot of Harrison Grant." She put on her glasses and leaned over the paper. It was a photo from the party. Plenty of people had had their phones out, and the paper's society editor and photographer had made an appearance, too. But the photos of who was there and what they were wearing had given way to one large photo. Of a murdered man.

Although it was a newspaper photo, slightly grainy, it was striking. Harrison was standing out on the Art Haven patio, a drink in one hand, and the other holding a napkin or maybe a piece of cheese. Or was it a trick of the light? His silvery hair was in place, smooth and wavy, an occasional dark streak highlighting the silver. Light from the flash reflected off his open-collared shirt, a contrast to the tanned skin beneath, his perfectly knotted striped ascot in place. His expression was intent as he listened to what someone outside the frame of the photo was saying to him. His eyes were focused. It was a look of interest, even compassion, if one was trying to read into it.

The picture was spread over two columns and was probably an object of admiration for many readers, even when considering the man would be dead hours after it was taken. But the one article attempting to capture the dead man was an empty one, except for some paragraphs about Harrison's work, awards the reporter had found. Things that revealed little about what was beneath the suit and the striped ascot. No associates were mentioned, no family or friends.

Nor were any details about the murder included. Ben had told them those details would be out soon. The medical examiner had spotted it immediately. A deep gash on Harrison's head, with slivers of granite in the wound, but an examination of the steps revealed the gash didn't result from him falling down the stairs. Someone had hit him. Hard.

Jane urged Birdie and Nell to sit and then poured coffee from a pot that stayed brewing all day.

"You're exhausted," Nell said, watching Jane sink into a chair next to Ham. "I know there were lots of questions last night."

"There was a lot to remember, even though it had happened so recently. The police needed to get the timing straight—when we first saw Harrison, what he'd done during the day, when we last saw him, when the guests came together in the living room for introductions." She took in a quick breath.

"The chief wanted to reach Sam, too, since he'd been Harrison's first contact in town, and he might be able to help the police work out some kind of a timeline," Ham said. "Sam is kind of front and center in all this."

"It was bad timing in terms of Sam and Ben's evening plans, I'm afraid," Jane said with regret. "Jerry reached Sam just as they were about to walk into a basketball game."

Ben had been the driver, Nell knew, so of course he would have gone along with Sam. And she also knew the Brewsters had to have been relieved to have Ben in the room with them, a close friend who heard the same conversation, and someone with whom they could discuss it later.

Nell reached over and patted Jane's hand. "There will be plenty more basketball games, Janie. Way too many, maybe."

Ham chuckled. "Well, both Ben and Sam were a big help to the police. Ben keeps things orderly. And he sometimes hears things others don't."

"Was Sam able to help put the events of the day in sequence?" Nell asked.

"Yes, although I don't know if the details are ones that will help. But Jerry reminded us over and over that it's sometimes all about details that seem insignificant," Jane said.

"They started with Harrison Grant's arrival in Sea Harbor Friday morning," Ham said.

Jane looked over at Nell. "We were there at the house when they arrived, Nell. All of us helped him settle in. He was happy to be on his own for a while, and we were relieved. There was a lot going on the Art Haven house that day."

Nell nodded. It was a cruel irony, she thought. Sam and Izzy both being involved in the death of this man whom Sam had never wanted to come to Sea Harbor in the first place. Life had its sad twists.

"The medical examiner updated the time of death to sometime after ten and before three the next morning. The body had been there awhile before Izzy found him," Ham said.

"We were probably still at the house when he was killed," Nell said, thinking back over the evening.

As were some of the other guests. *The sign of a good party*, they had thought at the time. In spite of the guest of honor's absence, people hadn't wanted to leave. Some had danced. Music had played. People were happy.

"The police searched his suite at the house, but there wasn't anything unusual there. A suitcase, lecture notes, expensive cameras, things like that. I'd almost forgotten the fellow was to start a photography series this week," Ham said.

Jane refreshed their coffee and carried over a plate of fresh cannoli. "One of the caretakers went for an early run Saturday morning, but she didn't notice anything unusual in the neighborhood. The sun was barely up, and most of the town was still asleep," she said.

"Speaking of early morning runs, how's our Izzy doing?" Ham asked.

"You know Izzy," Nell said. "She's resourceful and takes care of herself. She'll find a way to exorcise any demons that come along. But as you'd imagine, it was awful finding someone dead the way she did. Knowing that he was murdered adds another tragic layer to the ordeal." She thought back to her niece's pale face the evening before. The image of coming upon Harrison Grant's body was still so vivid in her memory that Izzy didn't need to hear Ben's grizzly news that it wasn't the crumbly steps that had killed Harrison Grant, after all. She knew.

Nell had checked on her niece earlier. Sam answered and said she was busy making pancakes for Abby. She was singing some silly song with her daughter. Everything was going to be okay, he'd said.

But it wasn't okay yet. And as Sam had said, the police would need to talk to Izzy again. To go over it all again. The person who found a murder victim was important to the police in lots of ways. There'd be more questions: Had she touched anything? Heard anyone nearby? Questions to nudge her memory, to dredge up that one thing hidden in the shadows of her mind. That one thing she had seen or heard that might lead them to something that would help the case. That would lead to a murderer.

"I knew Sam was worried about Izzy last night while we were talking with the police. He seemed ready to flee, anxious to be with her," Jane said. "I guess we're all worried about each other."

"That's what we do," Birdie said. "Worry, love, lift up."

A rattling at the gallery's front door pulled Ham from his chair.

"It might be one of the artists," Ham said, getting up. "This has shaken up Canary Cove. We're not used to reporters on our turf, but a few were already checking us out this morning."

"They're just doing their job," Jane said. "But we don't have anything much to say to them. Chief Thompson suggested we send everyone to the police if they have questions."

Minutes later Ham returned, followed by Eddie Porter and a young woman in a Salem State T-shirt and running tights. Nell had met her at the big house. She was tall, with platinum-blond hair pulled back in a ponytail, which emphasized high cheekbones, arched eyebrows, wide-set deep blue eyes. It was one of those faces that, if the features were examined separately, might not be considered pretty—the nose a bit too long, the chin too pointed. But when all the parts were put together, the face was arresting, beautiful even. Like a fine work of art.

"You all know Eddie, Detective Tommy Porter's younger brother," Ham said, although he knew everyone did.

Nell smiled at Eddie, and he offered one back, having relaxed slightly when he saw her. But still seemed nervous. The Porters lived a few houses from Ben and Nell, and Eddie had shoveled their driveway when he was younger. He'd spent plenty of time in the Endicotts' warm kitchen, eating cookies and drinking hot chocolate. But the last time she'd seen Eddie hadn't been quite as comfortable.

She could tell Eddie was thinking of Friday night, too. The night Harrison Grant disappeared. As Jane had been attempting to introduce the photographer from the microphone inside Art Haven, Nell had found her young neighbor staring at a shattered statue of a gnome outside the front door. He'd been red-faced and had barely met her eyes. He'd tripped over it, he confessed, then had cursed at his clumsiness. Nell had smiled to relieve his embarrassment, letting the matter go but suspecting the gnome's demise had been more forcefully enacted.

"And this is our other caretaker," Ham said. "Deb Carpenter. Marathon runner and breakfast chef for our visiting artists."

Deb nodded at Nell. "We've met." She glanced at Birdie and acknowledged the introduction with a slight smile.

"Deb and I go to Salem State together," Eddie said. There was a trace of pride in his voice, as if somehow, he was responsible for the attractive woman at his side. He was clearly proud to be in Deb's company. Or to have her in his.

"You were nice to help us bring in Mr. Grant's things," Nell said to Deb. She realized as she spoke the damage traumatic events did to memory. That was two days ago. But the events since that morning surely had filled weeks.

"Deb's really smart," Eddie said. "She's studying to be an athletic trainer. You know, like, she'll get a job with the Patriots or something."

Deb didn't seem to be listening to Eddie. In fact, she didn't seem to be enjoying being there with any of them. She looked around the room, then walked over to the windows and checked out the yard and the house in the distance. "Nice yard," she said to no one in particular.

Jane had filled two more coffee mugs and motioned for them to sit. "I'm glad you stopped by. It's not been an easy weekend for you. I'm so sorry for that."

"The police were back at the house today," Eddie said, sitting down next to Nell.

Jane and Ham nodded. Chief Thompson had called and told them some of the officers would be going there to do a few routine things. "Checking out some loose ends," he had said.

Eddie continued. "I talked to them. Deb was out running, but I took care of it. They poked around some, even though the guy didn't, well, you know . . . He didn't get killed at the Artists Haven. I told them that . . ." He gave an embarrassed laugh and shrugged. "But, sure, they already knew that."

"They need to cover everything, turn over every stone," Ham said. He smiled at Eddie, trying to put him at ease.

"I get that. Yeah. My brother says the same thing." Eddie fidgeted, his fingers tapping the arm of the chair. "You know Tommy, right? Well, sure you do. He's a detective now. Chief Thompson says he's doing a great job. My folks are really proud."

Nell smiled. She knew that Tommy, the oldest of the Porter kids, was the pride and joy of the Porter family, the first to go to college and now a police detective. And she also knew it was sometimes difficult for Eddie, the only other boy in the family. "Your mom tells me you're doing fine, too. Coaching a kids' football team?"

Eddie blushed. "Yeah. Salem State doesn't have football. But it's fun teaching the kids at the high school." His fingers began fidgeting again.

"Did the police have any questions as they looked around?" Ham asked.

"Well, not really. At least not for me. They kind of canvassed the house and wandered around the yard. But that's kind of why we stopped by." He looked over at Deb. She was still standing at the windows, her back to them. Then he looked back at the others. "We didn't want to be bothering you, but I thought we should come by."

"You're never bothering us, Eddie. You've been a help to us during this difficult time," Jane said. "Did something the police do bother you?"

Eddie straightened in the chair and shoved one hand in his pocket, then pulled out a set of keys. "Nah. It's not that. It's just that we don't want to be responsible for these, so I thought we should bring them back to you, and I wasn't sure if you'd be by today."

Deb had turned slightly and was glaring at him.

Jane took the keys from Eddie. She frowned at them, fingering the small charm of an artist's palette on the key ring.

Eddie went on. "I just, well, I didn't think we should keep them. Silly, maybe, since we're caretakers, right? But they kind of give me the creeps. And I didn't know if you'd want the police to have them or what, but I figured they shouldn't just be lying around the place."

Nell watched Jane, and she knew exactly where her friend was going inside her head, what she was thinking.

"These are the keys to Harrison Grant's room," Jane said to Eddie.

"I figured they were," Eddie said. "I don't know why they freaked me out. But—"

"Where did you find them?"

"I dunno," he said. He looked over at Deb, who had turned back to the window, intent on something in the yard and not on the conversation behind her. "In the kitchen. Or wherever," Eddie said.

Nell was remembering exactly when Jane had pulled out the

keys to the guest suite. Sam and Harrison had arrived at the house. Maybe Deb had been there, too. Nell had been helping Jane with some last-minute details and had stayed around, curious to meet the photographer in person.

They met Sam and Harrison in the foyer, where Sam introduced Nell and Jane. Sam was carrying Harrison's suitcase and some photography equipment, and Jane handed him the keys. Then she joked to Harrison that they were an honest crew, but with all the activity going on in the Art Haven that weekend, would he please keep the guest suite locked when he wasn't in it? There'd be many people in and out of the house that day and evening, she said.

The Winslow Homer print they hung in the suite to make it feel special for Grant was another reason, although Jane didn't go into it.

Harrison wholeheartedly agreed with Jane. He had some equipment of his own he'd like protected, he said, and he joked that his Hasselblad and Canon cameras had cost more than his first home. He kept his keys locked on his belt, he said, and slapped the slight bulge beneath his shirt, where the room keys would find a home.

Nell remembered less about where he was keeping his keys and more about the surprising cost of photographic equipment. Her camera, a part of her new iPhone, suddenly seemed like a tremendous bargain.

Eddie looked around the room, then back to the group. Then he got up from the chair, uncomfortable with the silence. "So, it's okay that we brought them over? And didn't give them to the cops? We had the master key to let them in. There didn't seem to be a reason. It's just a set of keys. Right?" He shook his head. "Deb was right maybe. She thought it was silly to come all the way over here and bother you guys."

"It's not silly. It's fine, Eddie," Jane said.

And it was fine, too, that Eddie wasn't connecting the dots, like the others in the room were doing. Nell looked at his flushed face. Eddie had always gone overboard by trying to please people. To do the right thing.

They all knew Harrison Grant had used the keys on Friday; he'd been in and out of the house several times that day, then later, when he had got ready for the evening event. If he had intended to go back to his room Friday night—or ever—the key ring would have been on his person. Secured on his belt, as he'd told Nell and Jane earlier on Friday.

And the keys wouldn't have been lying on the kitchen counter or just around, or wherever Eddie Porter had found them.

Chapter 11

Nell stood at the stove, stirring the thick, fragrant soup.

Cooking comforted her, and the moments spent salting and stirring, sprinkling herbs and tasting the broth brought a mindfulness. She needed these Zen moments today. The repetitive magic of stirring, the husky voice of Norah Jones in the background. Nell breathed in the aromas of wine and cream, thyme and chives that were carried into the room on the billowing steam from the pot. They filled not only her spirit but her kitchen and the living area beyond it.

The day had turned unseasonably cold once the sun had disappeared, a typical New England October day. Ben had texted from a yacht club meeting that he was stopping off for bread and wine and wood for a fire on his way home. Could Nell perform her soup magic? They hadn't seen each other since early morning coffee. An evening at home, just the two of them, a fire and soup, would be the perfect ending to his day, he said.

And Nell's, too. She looked over at Ben now. He was at the other end of the spacious living area, kneeling on one knee in front of the fireplace grate, his long back curved, an elbow on his knee as he gazed into the flames. His body was still, and firelight haloed his silvery hair.

Zen moments didn't belong to her alone, Nell thought. Ben was better at it than she was, somehow managing to put aside sadness or ugliness or meanness more easily. Filling himself with emotions that suited him better. She smiled at his back, then turned back to the stove and filled their bowls with supper.

They sat on either side of the fire, listening to easy jazz playing in the background, branches slapping against the side of the house, and the sound of the wind through the maples, tugging leaves to the ground. Comforted by the creamy richness of the butternut squash soup and the warmth of the fire, they ate in comfortable silence.

Ben was the first to interrupt the quiet. He knew, in spite of the peaceful setting, that Nell's thoughts wouldn't be far from his own. "There are lots of 'whys' in this case."

"Did you see Jerry today?"

Ben nodded. "Just briefly. 'It's the lull before the storm,' he said. The police are trying hard to collect as much information as they can before the town gets more involved in the fray."

"But sometimes new leads come out once everyone becomes alert and pays attention to things around them."

"True." Ben wiped the bottom of his soup bowl with a crust of bread. "But they're working on other things . . . like the guest list. Narrowing all that down. Scouring the neighborhood. Jerry says they've about ruled out as suspects the people who came from the city. It wasn't as large a group as we had thought and apparently Eddie kept pretty good track of the cars and who left when."

Nell was still. She took a sip of wine, then set the glass down, her expression serious. "But it doesn't make sense that it would be someone from around here. Grant wasn't from here—"

"Murder doesn't make sense, Nellie." Ben moved to the fire, knelt down, and added a log to the flames.

Calling it a murder was too new. Nell wasn't ready to take that step, to think that someone on Cape Ann, someone she might know, would have murdered Harrison Grant, a man almost no one knew.

"There's another thing that Tommy Porter is looking into that might be important," Ben said, sitting back down. "It's what Harrison did earlier on Friday," Ben said.

"Friday? Sam picked him up in the morning."

"Right. But according to Sam, Harrison mentioned on the ride over that he wanted to settle into his room and maybe explore the town, get to know it," Ben said.

"That makes sense." Nell smiled sadly, remembering Sam's protestations that Harrison might not come, because the town wouldn't interest him. Where had Sam gone so wrong in his thoughts about Harrison Grant?

"Since he was going to be here for a couple weeks teaching the course, getting the lay of the land was a good idea. Sam offered to show him around."

"Sam?"

"I know. But remember, Sam spoke a little more kindly about the guy after he picked him up and had that time in the car with him. It didn't matter, though. He turned Sam down. Said he'd like to wander around by himself."

"Wander around where?"

"That's what the police are looking into."

"Hmm."

Ben looked over at Nell. He was used to his wife's "hmms" and knew that the thoughts behind the sound were sometimes too unformed to share. But often proved to be insightful ones. "So, " he began, "tell me how Jane and Ham were when you saw them today."

"They're more concerned about the artists wanting their lives to go back to normal. But we had an interesting visitor while Birdie and I were there. Two, actually. Eddie Porter came by and—"

The doorbell chime scattered her words.

Ben frowned.

Nell read her husband's thoughts. Sunday evenings usually offered a quiet time together to share thoughts or days or simply to be together. And a ringing doorbell meant that it wasn't friends who were on the front door stoop. Friends walked right on in.

While Ben went to the door, Nell collected the dishes and took them to the kitchen sink.

A minute later Ben returned, with Eddie Porter following him. "Speaking of Eddie, look who's here—"

"Well, Eddie, hi," Nell said, walking back across the room. "I don't see you for weeks and then twice in one day. This is a treat."

Eddie shifted, looking around the room. Finally his gaze settled on the fire.

Nell followed his gaze and motioned toward a chair near the fireplace. "Ben and I were enjoying the fire. There's a hint of winter in the air. Come on in and join us."

Eddie shrugged out of his jacket and dropped it on a chair, then followed Nell and sank into a leather chair near the fire.

"Wow. This is nice. It's always comfy in here." Eddie looked up as Ben walked over with glasses and a bottle of wine. "How about a drink, Eddie?"

Eddie glanced at the glass as if he had never seen one before. "Nah, but thanks, Mr. E." He leaned forward in the chair, his legs bent, elbows on his knees, and one shoe tapping the floor. "I shouldn't have barged in like this, but I was heading over to my folks and I saw your lights on, so . . ." His voice drifted off. He looked down at his feet, then out the French doors to the deck. Nell wondered what he was seeing. Or thinking. Although his parents lived close by, Eddie Porter hadn't been in their home for a long time. Not since he had moved to Maine after high school and worked various jobs for a while. "Finding himself," his mother had said. But Eddie had finally come back home and enrolled in college.

Nell watched the expressions moving across his face, but she was having trouble reading them. Longing for times past, perhaps. Eddie looked troubled.

Norah Jones was still singing and playing in the background, and her soft piano chords helped to fill in the awkward silence. Eventually, Ben poked at the fire to bring it back to life, then suggested to Eddie that he get him a beer.

Eddie's brows shot up, and his look suggested that maybe two or three would be even better.

Ben was back in seconds with a couple of beers and a plate of brownies he set on the coffee table within easy reach.

Eddie guzzled half the bottle, then set it down on the table and murmured a thanks. "Guess I was thirsty," he said, a crooked smile easing the tension in his face.

Nell held up her wineglass to Ben for a refill, thinking from Eddie's posture that the three of them might be sitting there for a while. "It was good to see you at the Brewsters' today," she said, watching Eddie devour one of the buttermilk brownies she'd made that afternoon. Two bites and it was gone. He guzzled down the rest of his beer.

"Jane and Ham, they're good guys. But I shouldn't have gone over there. I mean, what was I thinking . . . ?" He picked up his second brownie, his words muffled as he chewed.

Nell leaned closer to hear.

"I shouldn't have bothered them, that's all," he said. "Shouldn't have done it. Like Deb said, we're supposed to be their employees. Trusted caretakers. Take-charge people. Not . . . well, whatever we were. Whatever I was."

Nell was puzzled. And Ben was completely confused. He looked over at Nell.

"Eddie and his friend Deb stopped by the gallery this morning while we were there," Nell said, taking a stab at bringing the conversation back to something she understood. "Jane and Ham mentioned how relieved they are to have dependable caretakers in that big house. Especially now."

"Right," Eddie said. He looked longingly at the second beer, then gave in and took a swig. "That's what I mean. Deb said the same thing. The Brewsters trust us. We should take care of things. Not go bothering them for no reason."

"Deb didn't want you to go over to the gallery this morning?" Nell asked.

"Want? She was wicked mad. Still is. Said it was silly, and a bunch of other things."

"Why? Having keys floating around isn't a good thing."

Eddie pushed himself out of the chair. Instead of answering the question, he picked up his empty beer bottles and took them to the kitchen, then came back and managed a smile. "Anyway, Mrs. E, I saw your lights and just wanted to apologize for interrupting you and the Brewsters. Got in big trouble for it. So sorry."

"Eddie—" Nell said. She and Ben were both standing now, trying to follow both Eddie and his words, which seemed scattered. None of them fitting together well.

But Eddie was moving toward the front door, still speaking as he walked. "Thanks for the beer and the brownies, Mrs. E. You're a great cook. I had almost forgot about those cookies and brownies you used to make."

"Eddie, your jacket," Nell said, pointing to the chair where he'd dropped it.

Eddie came back and grabbed the jacket from the chair. He shook his head. "Sorry. Long day." He pushed his arms through the sleeves and shrugged the jacket over his broad shoulders.

"Are you okay, Ed?" Ben asked. He walked over to Eddie.

"Fine as fine," Eddie said and headed back toward the door.

Nell frowned, then a thought came to her, and she hurried after him. Her voice was pleasant but firm. "Eddie, wait," she said. "You might be able to help us with something." She reached him as he was turning the doorknob.

Eddie paused, holding the door open a crack.

"I just need one minute of your time."

Eddie shook his head. "I know. It was dumb to make a fuss over a set of keys."

"It's not about the keys, Eddie. Were you in class last Friday, or were you up at the house?"

Eddie looked slightly relieved but still on guard. "I don't have classes on Friday. I can go fishing if I want. But Friday I stuck around the estate, helping out. I saw you over there, from a distance, though. I was out back, trimming some bushes on those trails that go off . . ."

Nell nodded. "That was nice of you. It all looked beautiful that night. Did you meet Mr. Grant when he got in that morning?"

Eddie's shoulders relaxed. "Sure. He came down to the kitchen for coffee after checking out his suite. He was real friendly."

"What did you talk about?"

"Nothing much. He asked questions about the neighborhood, who lived around here, the town, mostly, and what Deb and I were studying."

"Did he go out while you were there?"

"Out?"

"You know, to explore the area, maybe."

Eddie nodded.

"Where did he go?"

"I showed him around the grounds, down to the beach, all those places people want to see."

"That was nice of you. Did he stay around the house for the rest of the day, then? He would have had a few hours before the reception."

Eddie shrugged. "He wanted to take a walk. He went around the neighborhood for a while. Said he wanted to see the homes around here."

Eddie opened the door wider and took a step outside. A gust of wind blew in, and Nell put her hand on the side of the open door, holding it steady.

"So that was it? What about the afternoon? Maybe he went up and took a nap before the reception?" Nell smiled, trying to relieve Eddie's apparent nervousness. He looked ready to flee. "That's probably what Ben would have done. Receptions can be tiring if you're the guest of honor."

Eddie's voice was strained. "Maybe. After he came back he walked through the kitchen, got a soft drink. And then he left again. So I don't know what else he did, where he went, what he saw."

"Left?"

Eddie started walking away, as if he hadn't heard the question. Then he stopped and turned halfway around. A scowl marred his strong features. His hand was curled into a fist. "Yeah, he left. To explore, I guess."

"Without a car?"

"He had a car. Mine. Deb took my keys, my car. And they left. Together."

This time Eddie left, too, hurrying down the front walk without a backward glance.

Chapter 12

Nell hurried down Harbor Road, her collar pulled up against the wind. Helping Izzy in her yarn shop today had been an easy thing to say yes to. Mae, Izzy's manager, had a doctor's appointment, Izzy's part-time college helpers were all in class, and Mondays were crazy days. Izzy was desperate.

The Monday drop-in knitting group would be coming in, Izzy had said, and she'd just gotten in a new shipment of yarn and needles, so she had to take inventory. Plus, she had a week's worth of planning to do.

Not to mention news of a murder winding its way through the town.

Most of all, Nell had decided, Izzy needed family today. Double-shot lattes might help, too. So she detoured down to Coffee's, the local coffee shop, for fortification.

Talk of the murder on Cliffside Drive was already taking shape in the coffee shop. Nell could feel it as she walked toward the counter to place her order. It was that eerie, expectant vibe that something was happening, but no one knew quite how to place it in a normal Sea Harbor Monday morning.

Yesterday's Sea Harbor paper had given few details of the tragedy, except for the blaring headline. And few read the Sunday paper, anyway, preferring the weightier Sunday *Boston Globe* or the *New York Times*. But today's *Sea Harbor Times* would be more detailed, since reporters had had a full day to dig up whatever they could find about Harrison Grant.

Nell placed her order and moved to the end of the counter. She noticed scattered copies of the local paper on several tables, open and stained with coffee. Here and there people sat in front of laptops or held cell phones, catching Twitter feeds and sharing them from table to table. Names and conjectures were thrown out in the air, the words vying with the sounds of the espresso machine.

Minutes later Nell's name was called, and she collected her lattes, then hurried toward the door. This early hour wasn't her usual time at Coffee's, and she was relieved not to have to stop and talk to anyone, substituting a quick wave to a few casual acquaintances. She'd be able to make a quick escape.

At least she thought she would.

"So what do you know, Nell?" Tall, scrawny Gus McGlucken, owner of the Harbor Road hardware store bearing his name, came up alongside Nell and stopped her just inside the door. His words were abbreviated, but Nell and Gus had been friends for enough years that unnecessary details could be eliminated. Nell knew what Gus meant. And Gus knew she knew.

"Not much more than you know, Gus," Nell said. And she knew that might be the truth. Harbor Road shop owners sometimes were the first to find out the particulars of news reports. Gus was a good man, but Nell knew he rarely missed a conversation that had any spice to it.

"It's a terrible thing," Gus said, his expression thoughtful. "But none of us knew him, you know. That's the thing."

The "him" didn't need a name.

But Nell wasn't sure what "That's the thing" meant. "You mean, the town isn't emotionally involved, as they might otherwise be?"

"Not sure that's what I mean, Nell. The town *is* involved. Talk to the folks in here, and you'll see that. Someone was murdered right here in Sea Harbor. A murder requires a murderer."

Nell looked beyond Gus's slightly bent frame at the faces around the coffee shop. Concern. And over in a booth she spotted a couple of young moms with toddlers sitting on booster seats. And there she saw fear. Gus was right.

"I understand what you're saying. I met Harrison Grant, talked with him. Now he's dead, and that tragedy—that a man who was healthy and active three days ago is no longer living—that's what has occupied my thoughts. But if you didn't know him . . ."

Gus was nodding and picked up the thought. "That's it, Nellie. Most of us never set eyes on the man. Now, we're not bad people around here, but his death means little to us. It's the thought that there's someone walking around our town that would kill someone—that's what's going on here."

Of course it was. That much Nell did know. And she knew the police had been working around the clock to figure it out.

"So he was famous, some are saying," Gus said.

"He was a very talented photographer," Nell said. "The profession has lost a fine talent." Nell surprised herself. She was picturing the Harrison she had met briefly, not the one Sam had prepared them for. A pleasant enough person. And certainly a talented one.

Gus's mind seemed to be on things other than talent. "And the fella was murdered at the Art Haven reception? What's that about?" Gus shook his head, as if releasing other thoughts, conversations that might have been percolating before Nell had arrived. *Artists. Long hair. Sculptures that didn't always look as they should.*

Sea Harbor loved and supported the Canary Cove Art Colony and all its traditional watercolorists and creators of mermaid and fishermen statues, artistic tributes to fishermen and their families. But sometimes artists wandered in that old timers didn't know, and art crept in that was different, not understood by everyone. And in times of stress, understanding could shrink in the time it took to read a headline.

Gus glanced down at a photo on the front page of a stray newspaper on an empty table near the door. Nell looked down, too. It was a photograph Harrison Grant had taken, not one of his usual award-winning portraits, but a distorted image, the facial features rearranged through the magic of digital tools. A nose here, lips there. It looked more like a Picasso than an actual woman's face.

Nell knew Grant had experimented with different techniques. She frowned at the stained photo, a donut crumb resting beside it. She looked back at Gus and smiled. "Art is in the eye of the beholder, right?"

Gus chuckled. "You got me there, Nellie. And these old eyes don't especially like it. But no matter, it's Jane and Ham I worry about, not so much this goofy photograph. They're good people, those two. Don't deserve this trouble on their watch, that's for sure."

"Jane will be fine. You know how she is. A rock. And a compassionate one. She's terribly sad that a man lost his life here in Sea Harbor. That's what gets forgotten in all this. It's a horrible tragedy."

"Any ideas of who did it? Can't be anyone from around here."

Nell had known the question was coming. She pushed the

door open with her hip and shrugged, letting Gus know that she didn't know a thing. Or have a single idea.

And that was the truth.

Gus took the hint and held the door open for her to leave, chuckling a bit as he sent his good friend on her way.

Chapter 13

The Sea Harbor Yarn Studio hadn't yet opened its doors to customers when Nell arrived. Izzy was busy cutting open boxes in the shop's large main room and finishing up a display.

The smell of the lattes and the sight of her aunt stopped her midstream. In an instant she had uncurled her long body from the floor and rushed over, relieving Nell of the two cups. "You're amazing, Aunt Nell. A lifesaver."

Lifesaver. If only.

The word *lifesaver* hung in the air for a minute. Ben and the others had all gone out hunting for Harrison Grant Friday night. If they had found him, would they have been lifesavers? Or had he already been dead? Could anyone have saved his life? Nell tried to shake off the feeling the single word had engendered. Her conversation with Gus was clouding her thoughts.

She replaced the emotion with a hug for Izzy, a longer one than usual. Izzy didn't resist. It was a day that welcomed hugs.

Nell took a deep breath, shrugged out of her coat, and walked over to the checkout counter. She looked at the new card reader and notepad computer Izzy had installed for purchases. She liked change, but sometimes, like when she was facing notepads and unfamiliar computer software, she yearned for plain old cash registers that clinked and jangled. One thing she knew for sure: her years as the director of a Boston public health nonprofit hadn't prepared her for the intricacies of recording yarn and needle sales.

"Okay, Iz, what's all this?"

"Don't worry, Aunt Nell. Mae should be back by noon," Izzy said. She was back in the middle of the room, her latte and an antique baby cradle on a tall table. As Izzy worked, the cradle filled up with skeins of baby-soft alpaca and silk and cashmere yarn. Topping off the bed of yarn were tiny knit animals—lambs and goats, bears and camels and donkeys—all looking like they were romping around on hills of baby yarn.

Nell stopped fiddling with the card reader for a minute and admired the brilliant array of colors: lavender and bright yellows, reds and greens, and blues in every shade of the sea. "It's a gorgeous display, Izzy. Perfect."

"Baby clothes are all colors these days. Look at these—purple, orange, avocado, sage . . ."

"It sounds like my vegetable garden."

"Unisex colors." Izzy grinned, adjusting the cradle on the round table.

The infant bed sat on a low table in the center of the room, a focus for customers as they wandered around the room, exploring floor-to-ceiling cubbies filled with yarn, an array of mannequins modeling sweaters and bulky scarves, crocheted hats and coats.

Two smaller rooms spun off the shop's main room. The Fleece and Fiber Room had a window overlooking the sea and was decorated with framed photos and paintings of sheep, alpacas, cashmere goats, and llamas. Books on weaving and animal fibers filled a small bookcase, and a giant basket of leftover yarns stood in the corner, welcoming takers. Izzy had painted three rocking chairs and redone the hardwood floor, covering it with a thick rag rug. A sign in the room welcomed knitters to come sit and knit for a while or read or simply *be*. And more than a few of her regulars found it a comfortable place for a short nap on a busy day.

The Magic Room was the other small room, filled with toys and children's books, soft rugs and beanbag chairs. It was a safe place that welcomed small bodies while moms took a class or received help with dropped stitches or complicated lace patterns.

And the third opening, a wide archway painted bright blue like the sky, framed three steps that led down to the heart of Izzy's shop: the back room with its corner fireplace and cozy chairs, a wall of built-in bookshelves and an old library table that Izzy and Nell had found at a flea market. On the back wall a cushioned window seat had bay windows that opened up to the sea and provided a favorite snoozing place for Purl, the shop's calico cat. The cozy room hosted classes and was a place for friends and strangers to gather and chat while their fingers shaped elaborate sweaters and cowls and socks. A place sacred to the Seaside Knitters on Thursday night.

Today all the rooms were quiet and empty, save for Nell and Izzy. But soon, they knew, the shop would be filled with people wanting to RSVP for the community baby shower, needing to purchase patterns or needles and yarn, or wishing to settle in the back room with coffee, needles, yarn, and gossip. For Izzy, Monday was also a key day for people who had messed up a pattern over the weekend and were in serious need of help.

Not to mention that this Monday would carry an added layer of energy, as shoppers would carry into the shop news of a murder—and the need for information to ease their minds.

Izzy put the last knit reindeer on the piles of yarn and looked over at her aunt. "Do you think about him, Aunt Nell?"

"Harrison Grant?"

Izzy nodded. "I can't shake it. Somehow . . . I don't know . . . somehow being the one to find him has made me feel a connection to him. The kind that is requiring something of me, and I don't know what it is. It's what we talked about the other night. It's sadness, but it's not."

"We're sad, Izzy," Nell said. But Izzy was right that it was a different kind of sadness. Sad that this kind of notoriety had been brought to Sea Harbor and especially to the Canary Cove Art Colony. Sad that soon people they knew would be questioned, asked to think so hard it might hurt, to try to dredge out of memory something that might help the police. Family, friends. Nell felt a sudden chill so strong, she wrapped her sweater tight.

Just then, the bell above the door rang, too loud, too intrusive in the quiet shop harboring sobering thoughts.

Beatrice Scaglia rushed in, clearly upset. The mayor was dressed as she always was, in a tailored suit of fine wool and heels too tall for comfort, her bottle-black hair coiffed.

"Nell, I'm glad you're here," she said, waving to Izzy and dropping her black purse next to the checkout counter. "This is outrageous, horrible for our town."

Nell set the iPad aside. "Yes. It's all those things." Nell had seen Beatrice briefly at the Friday reception. She was the ultimate politician at such events and always appeared looking years younger than her nearly sixty years. She knew exactly whom to greet and what to say, whom to compliment, whom to gush over, whom to avoid. Her actions, although sometimes seeming self-aggrandizing, were usually geared to what would benefit the town but also, as most were aware, to benefit herself.

And Nell also knew that Beatrice Scaglia, even when she could be irritating and officious, loved Sea Harbor. And when the town was in distress, so was the mayor, who assumed it was her responsibility to fix it.

"I know this is hard on you, Beatrice," Nell began.

Beatrice waved away her words. "The town needs me to make it better. And that means finding the fool who did this. I just came from a meeting with Chief Thompson."

Nell winced, imagining Beatrice's meeting with Jerry. She could almost hear the mayor's expression of dismay that the murderer hadn't yet been caught. It should have happened before the news was out. Or before it even happened. The mayor didn't like surprises.

"This all happened at Rico Silva's house. You know that, don't you?"

Nell nodded. Everyone knew that. Especially Rico Silva.

Rico had told the police he was home that night. In bed, he'd said. The music from the reception had kept him awake. In fact, he'd called in a complaint about it. And then he'd finally gone to sleep.

"The police are working hard on this, checking everything out," Nell said.

Beatrice took a deep breath, her small chest visibly moving beneath the suit jacket. "Yes, of course they are. It's just never fast enough, is it? You are good for me, Nell. You calm me."

Nell's brows lifted in surprise. Beatrice wasn't one to give compliments, or to be so easily pacified.

Beatrice didn't miss Nell's look. "I know what you're wondering," she said. "It's yoga."

Nell frowned. Beatrice sometimes spoke in her own code. But Nell could usually figure out what she was saying. Today she wasn't sure.

"Yoga. That's why I'm more easily calmed. I'm taking yoga classes from a woman named Harmony. We actually had yoga in a hidden cove one day. The 'lost cove,' she called it, and I believe it was exactly that. Hard to find. Not that you'd want to. It wasn't my thing, really. I prefer a floor. But Harmony said it had some spiritual something or other."

Izzy walked over. "Are you talking about Harmony Fairchild?" Izzy asked. "She's good. And I know the place, Beatrice. She held a birthday yoga class there one morning. And you're right. She talked a lot about the special spiritual vibes it held. She said it was a place of beginnings and endings, of new life. It got a little heavy for me, but it seemed to mean a lot to Harmony. And it was a beautiful morning, though."

"The vibes didn't seem to like me," Beatrice said. "Or the sand in my tights."

Izzy chuckled. Then she asked, "Are you here to knit? The Monday morning drop-ins will be here soon."

Even Beatrice managed a smile at the question.

The mayor had finally acknowledged that they all knew her secret, that their mayor had never formed a single knit or purl stitch in her life. But they also knew that she paid her way into the knitting groups by purchasing expensive needles and yarn every time she came into the store, which she would then hold in her lap while she sat with the knitting groups in the back room, listening and recording in her head bits and pieces of relevant conversation and complaints and ideas from attentive moms. The topics ranged widely, but Beatrice filtered out the ones she needed to attend to, discussions about school buses running late, stop signs not working, council members not listening to the moms' issues, sporadic communication between the mayor's office, the school administration, and parents. So often did Beatrice show up that the knitting moms stopped noticing her and talked freely. The group became Beatrice's private focus group.

When the mayor would leave the shop, the needles and yarn got stored neatly in her basement; the town gossip and concerns, the suggestions and comments and complaints went with her to city hall.

She would learn to knit in time, she had often said, though the words sounded hollower with each new purchase she made and shelved away. In the meantime, Beatrice was one of the best-informed mayors Sea Harbor had ever had.

"I can't stay long today," Beatrice said. "But I need to take everyone's pulse about this ghastly murder. People shouldn't be blasé about it."

"Why do you think people would be indifferent about it?" Nell asked. "A man has been murdered. That's hardly a trivial matter."

For a minute Beatrice didn't answer. It was as if she didn't know the answer but was figuring it out in that moment.

"Here's why," she finally said. "If people weren't at the party, what happened that night might as well have happened in Siberia. It didn't touch their lives in any way. But the truth is, it did affect them. All of us. It does. And they need to be aware of that. A murder occurred right here in Sea Harbor. And it may have absolutely nothing to do with the Art Haven reception or its guests or a neighborhood that is rather exclusive. But it happened, and we need it to go away."

Nell and Izzy were quiet, listening. They weren't quite sure Beatrice knew where she was going with her declaration. But it seemed worth listening to.

Beatrice took a deep breath, and then she went on, more quietly, as if speaking to a confessor. "I went to the reception that night simply to see Harrison Grant," she said. "I knew I had seen him before, but I'm not sure where. Maybe at a talk. And I wanted to talk to him—not because he was so charismatic, which he was, or good looking and well known, which he was, but for some other reason, which I can't explain. I'm trying to look more closely into people's eyes these days. To be more mindful. And his eyes seemed to be telling me something Friday night.

"We talked for a while, just the two of us. We talked about our town, the people in it. He was sincerely interested in who lived here and what they did. And later, when I wasn't talking to him, I watched him, at first because I was trying to remember when or where I'd seen him before, but mostly because he intrigued me in a way that made me slightly uncomfortable. I sometimes watch other people that way, to try to figure out what they're thinking. He moved around the crowd, and then I saw him standing in a shadow, next to a potted tree on the patio. He was looking around the crowd, as if he were looking for someone. Just before I left, I saw him sitting on one of those garden benches that look over the water. All by himself." Beatrice paused.

The shop door began opening and closing as customers drifted in, and before long they called Izzy away from Nell and Beatrice. People seeking advice on yarn weights and needles and plans for the baby shower. Others heading down the back steps with their knitting in hand.

Nell and Beatrice stood alone and unnoticed in the midst of the traffic. Nell was quiet, waiting for Beatrice to finish.

Finally, Beatrice smiled as if slightly embarrassed by her ramblings. She looked at Nell intently. "I'm not crazy, Nell, and I don't usually feel this way about someone I don't know. But this man had more on his mind Friday night than giving photography lectures in Sea Harbor. Harrison Grant was looking for something here. And I wonder if he found it."

Before Nell could respond, Beatrice picked up her knitting bag and walked away, following the women down to the back room.

Chapter 14

Monday was Cass's day off, and it usually began at Coffee's, where she hid at a corner table, sat with her feet up on an extra chair and her back to the rest of the shop—and read mysteries while eating blueberry muffins and drinking Americanos.

But pregnancy had changed Cass's life significantly, and Monday morning Americanos had been replaced with visits to Lily Virgilio's ob-gyn clinic.

Cass brought her SUV to a stop in front of the small house Marco and Elena Costa shared near the fishing docks. She paused for a minute, catching her bearings. Sleep had come only grudgingly the night before, her mind filled with images of a dead man lying on a shallow beach. A *murdered* dead man.

It was only after Danny's back rub that she had finally drifted off.

The Costas lived in a neighborhood of small houses, many owned by fishermen and their families as had the generations before them. Most of Cass and Pete's employees lived in the area. But the Costa home stood out. Not bigger or smaller or of a different style. But special.

Cass looked at it and smiled. It had been transformed in the short time Elena had lived in it with Marco. She was some kind of woodland spirit, an elf, Cass decided. Otherworldly. She had transformed the small house from a run-down bachelor cottage to a welcoming home. Marco had had little interest in keeping his house in shape, but Elena had changed all that.

She had rid the yard of debris, and all summer long she had tended a small garden in front of the house, replacing the rocky soil with fresh compost. Peonies, coral bells, zinnias, and sweet-smelling lavender lived and bloomed alongside a colorful bed of annuals. Black-eyed Susans lined the edge of the walkway as the summer season moved into fall. Elena had told Cass she had planted them in honor of Cass's black eyes and generous spirit.

Cass had laughed at that. *Generous?* But somehow this small elf-like woman had made her feel that way. Or maybe it was baby Brandley growing within her. Her fishing crew had recently teased her about going soft, which had only made her scowl and chastise them for being late. But they'd laughed. And then she had, too.

Cass rolled down the passenger window and let the sea breeze in, then looked around the yard, through the windows of Elena's house. It wasn't just the garden that set the Costa home apart; the house was no longer the depressing, unkempt structure it had once been. The windows were clean, new siding was in place, and a large autumn wreath hung from a bright yellow door. The home was a warm and loving place. Cass hoped it was that way behind the bright yellow door.

Elena appeared in the doorway, waving happily, and hurried out to the car.

"Your garden is gorgeous," Cass said as Elena slid into the front seat.

"My farming roots," Elena said. "I was raised on a farm in Pennsylvania. My parents loved the earth. We had so many vegetables. I'm planting some in the back to make my Marco healthier."

Cass pulled away from the curb, listening. This was more personal information than Elena had offered in all their weeks together. "Have they come to see what you've done?"

Still smiling, Elena said, "No. My mother and father were much older than my friends' parents. They died before I came east and met Marco. But they would have been proud of my garden. And they would have loved him. I am sure of that."

Cass smiled and wondered, not for the first time, how Marco Costa had gotten so lucky. And just as quickly she rid herself of the thought. Elena seemed to be crazy about her husband. Who was she to say?

Everyone couldn't be Danny Brandley, after all.

The doctor's office was crowded when Cass and Elena walked in. Dr. Lily Virgilio took care of nearly every woman in Sea Harbor.

"Hey, Cass," Chelsey Onnan called out from behind the desk. "'Bout time you got here." As she had most young millennials in Sea Harbor, Cass had once babysat for the receptionist—a fact Chelsey and others seemed to enjoy reminding her of.

Cass waved back and informed Chelsey that she was *early*. But she refrained from explaining that it was because of her companion, who was now sitting quietly and reading a magazine about giving babies their baths. Elena was always prompt, never wanting to inconvenience anyone.

Cass sat down and looked around the comfortable room. Lily Virgilio had begun collecting local art when she opened the clinic, and after half a dozen years, the walls were filled with the spirit of the ocean—framed paintings of Cape Ann's heritage—churning waves, stately schooners and humble dories, and the weathered faces of brave fishermen.

Couches and chairs were positioned discreetly, grouped around the room and designed to provide some sense of privacy. Tall plants divided the areas and made it harder to see everyone. But this didn't prevent Cass from looking around at the fresh young faces—and feeling a little bit like the mother of some of them.

She paused on a familiar face of a woman sitting near the waiting-room juice bar, but the woman wore large sunglasses, her head lowered, and her face shadowed by a Red Sox cap, and Cass couldn't really tell who it was. But the woman stood out, even in a room filled with pregnant women. She sat unnaturally still, almost like a statue, her eyes lowered, but without a book or a magazine, at least not that Cass could see. She wondered if she was pregnant, feeling a vague connection since the woman was even older than she. *Several years older*, she thought as she looked again. But the woman's face was so calm that it was hard to tell. She had the kind of demeanor and face that probably never contorted in anger or shouted at fishermen, keeping it smooth and peaceful.

It wasn't until Elena's name was called that the woman across the room looked up. She took her dark glasses off and watched Elena as she followed the nurse through the door to the examining rooms, the door silently closing behind her.

Oh geesh, Cass thought, finally recognizing her. *Harmony, of course.*

At that moment, their eyes met, and the woman smiled and waved, then rose from her chair, more like a dancer than a possibly pregnant patient in the ob-gyn office. She walked around the group of chairs to where Cass was sitting and pointed to Elena's vacated chair. "Hey, may I?"

"Of course. Sure," Cass said. "I almost didn't recognize you without hearing your calming instructions to move my hands forward into the puppy dog pose."

Harmony laughed, but in a controlled way. No wrinkles forming.

Amazing, Cass thought. *So that's the secret.*

"Dr. Virgilio is a great doctor," Harmony said. "You're in good hands."

"Agreed," Cass said, then tried to ask delicately, "Are you and Lily friends? A patient?"

Harmony laughed. "Well, definitely not a pregnant one. I suppose it would be possible these days, but I'm fifty-five and not pregnant. I don't live in Sea Harbor either. I have a condo a few miles away, but I've known Lily for a while. She took a class as I was getting started, and I liked her. I come in for annual checkups, menopause, all those sorts of exciting things. That's all."

"Oh, of course. She treats all female parts. When one gets pregnant, it seems to slant your world and I almost forgot."

"Well, you're certainly in great condition. If Lily is prescribing vitamins for you, I would like some, please."

The yoga instructor wore jeans and a sweatshirt today, her athletic form clearly hidden. But after that first yoga class, both Cass and Elena had remarked on the instructor's strong physique. She was a large woman, but when her body was defined in seamless pants and a yoga bra, Harmony presented a beautiful figure. Imposing and graceful. *A nice combo*, Cass thought.

"Elena is doing well in the class," Harmony said, glancing toward the closed door. "Are you related?"

"To Elena? No. Her husband works for me, so we've teamed up with this pregnancy thing."

"She's married, right? A fisherman, I think she said."

Cass nodded. "I know, she looks young. She *is* young. But not nearly as young as she looks."

Harmony looked back at the door. "She looks like she's sixteen."

"I thought so, too. But she turned twenty-two recently."

"Twenty-two," Harmony repeated. She seemed happy to

hear Elena's age. Almost relieved. She looked out the window for a minute, her brows furrowed in thought, then brought her attention back to Cass. "She's young looking for twenty-two, for sure. And beautiful. She took to yoga like a pro. Almost as if she were born to it."

"Which reminds me," Cass said. "How's the brochure coming?"

"Brochure?"

"The one Elena's photo will be in. I'd like to see it. I could pass it along to my crew."

For a minute Harmony looked flustered; then she regained her calm composure. "Oh, that. Having some trouble with the printer, but I'm in no rush. It'll work out. She was a perfect fit, though, don't you think?"

"I do. And it's amazing, because I think your class is her first. She has that kind of body that intuits cat-cow and pigeon and dolphin poses. I don't know how she does it. Dolphins and pigeons? I was raised by a fisherman, and I don't understand those poses. What gives there?"

Harmony smiled. "I had to learn it, too, believe me. It wasn't in my genes."

"Hah. Look at you. I bet you practiced yoga in utero."

This time Harmony laughed out loud, and Cass saw a hint of wrinkles. She also noticed a bold silver stripe of hair, a contrast to Harmony's full head of dark brown hair. Without thinking, Cass lifted a hand to her own temple, where she knew wisps of white were trying to make an appearance.

"I came late to yoga," Harmony said. "It was my salvation."

Cass didn't respond. Harmony's words had the tone of a confession, and she wasn't sure what to do with them or what was coming next. She barely knew the woman, and confessions from near strangers weren't really her thing.

But then Harmony's body language lightened, and she changed the subject, turning the discussion to Cass. To her life.

But later, when she replayed the conversation with Danny, Cass realized that the yoga instructor hadn't really been interested in her life at all. Cass had been only a springboard. It had been all about Elena Costa.

Were you born in Sea Harbor, Cass? And then, *Is Elena a lifelong Sea Harbor resident, too? Where was she born?*

What is it like to run a lobster company? And then, *How long has Elena's husband worked for you?*

Have you ever lived anyplace other than Sea Harbor? Then, *Where did Elena live before coming to Sea Harbor?*

So you have family here? Then, *Does Elena have family here?*

When did you and your husband get married? And then, *How long has Elena been married?*

Harmony Fairchild was nice enough and a good yoga instructor, but she truly hadn't been at all interested in getting to know Cass Halloran.

When Cass had turned the conversation around and tried to get to know the yoga instructor better, she'd discovered Harmony Fairchild wasn't even interested in talking about herself.

Elena Costa, down a long hallway, in one of the clinic's examining rooms, had held the waiting-room spotlight. It was Elena who had been up front and center.

Chapter 15

The library board meeting was held at the Sea Harbor Yacht Club, and Birdie and Nell walked out of the club's conference room happy that they'd attended. Sea Harbor had a wonderful old library, but the building clearly needed its own offices and meeting rooms, and the board had finally agreed on plans to make that happen. The fact that they had to move their meetings around to places like the yacht club only added to the wisdom of the decision.

"It's good to be thinking into the future," Birdie said as they headed toward the club's entrance.

"Rather than feeling like life's at a standstill," Nell said. "I feel that way, too."

The cloud of murder lingered over everything, like a nor'easter that had stalled over the town and refused to move. Planning on enlarging the library was a welcome relief.

Nell checked her watch, then glanced into the club lounge. Soft music was playing, but the bar area was almost empty as waiters and staff scurried around the dining room instead, preparing for the evening buffet.

"Yes," Birdie said, reading Nell's thought. "Let's treat ourselves to a moment of quiet."

They found a spot in the corner, near glass doors that overlooked the patio and the manicured beach beyond. A scattering of sailboats could be seen in the distance, bobbing on the quiet sea.

"Even the sailboats are at a standstill," Birdie mused.

They ordered wine spritzers, then settled into the leather seats.

Nell waved at Tommy Porter, who was standing at the bar by himself.

Tommy hesitated for a minute, then walked over to them, a cup of coffee in his hand.

"What's up with that weary look, Tommy?" Birdie said. "Would you like to join us?"

The young detective looked around, then pulled out a chair. "It's been a long day."

The two women nodded, knowing if their own days were long, for the police, they were endless.

Although Nell wanted to, asking for a progress update seemed out of place, a little like people asking Cass if there was any update on the baby's arrival.

"I just talked to Izzy," Tommy said. "We need to talk to her and Sam again tomorrow. It's hard when it's friends you're beating up with this investigation. I went over the events of the evening again today with Jane and Ham, looking for that one thing someone saw and forgot to mention. Or forgot they saw it and then remembered. It's those little things. The crumbs."

"Eddie was at the event that night. I know this is on his mind. Have you talked to him?" Nell asked.

"My brother? Yeah. Well, actually, I didn't. One of the other guys talked to him and also to the other caretaker. Deb Carpenter. It seemed better that way. Sibling stuff, y'know?"

Nell knew. She and Caroline, Izzy's mother, had had a sometimes conflicted relationship when they were growing up. The good thing was that age and maturity had a nice way of smoothing out sibling relationships. "Is Deb Carpenter Eddie's girlfriend?" Nell asked.

Tommy shrugged. "I think he'd like her to be. Have you met her?"

Nell nodded.

"She's hard to miss." Tommy took a drink of coffee, then set down his cup. "Frankly, I think Deb is kind of a cold fish. But that's just my personal opinion."

Tommy didn't expand, and Nell held back from relating her own encounters with the two caretakers over the past few days. Eddie's love life didn't seem relevant to much of anything in the middle of a murder investigation.

"Have you found any family of Harrison's?" Nell asked.

"His parents died years ago. No siblings. No close friends that we've found, although it seems there was always a woman somewhere in his life. But they changed monthly. Daily sometimes. He was a loner, it seems. We're still looking into it, though. He did have an assistant in New York. A woman who'd been with him for a long time. She's coming up to talk to us."

"He told me he hadn't been to Sea Harbor before," Birdie said. "But there was something about the way he said it that made me think he wasn't telling the truth."

Tommy frowned. "Oh?"

Their wine arrived, and Birdie took a sip before answering. Then she said, "Harrison Grant had one of those faces that has trouble being quiet. Or maybe it was his eyes. I actually hadn't given our brief exchange much thought until now. Our conversation was short—and guarded."

"Guarded?" Tommy asked.

"For some reason, Harrison seemed reluctant to say that he had been here before. I'm not sure why. His mouth said no, but his eyes said yes."

"Is that it?"

Birdie nodded. "As I remember it, yes. Jane came by about that time and whisked him off before I could contradict him."

"Accuse him of lying?" Nell asked, smiling at her friend.

Tommy allowed a smile, too, then pushed back his chair and stood. "That's interesting. Thanks, Birdie. So far no one has mentioned seeing him around here before. But then, we're a vacation destination, so lots of people have been here. Seems like half the world sometimes. Have you ever met anyone from Boston who hasn't been to Cape Ann? But, anyway, I will plug this in. You just never know."

Nell watched as Tommy her neighbor, who, as a thoughtful young boy, used to help her bring in the groceries, disappeared, and Tommy the detective came into being. He was momentarily on unofficial duty, recording the information. And as nonchalant as he seemed, she knew he would check into it. "The crumbs," he had said.

He checked his watch and smiled at both of them. "Off to the salt mines. But seeing you two is always a bright spot in my day."

They watched him walk away, young, confident. And a very good man. Nell wondered if his niceness got in the way of his thinking of people he knew as possible suspects.

"Little brother Eddie has a lot to live up to," Birdie said.

Nell agreed, and she told Birdie about Eddie's surprise visit the night before.

"That's odd. What do you suppose was really on his mind?"

"I think he simply needed to unload his feelings. He probably meant it when he said he saw the lights and just stopped in. Unlike his brother, Eddie doesn't seem to think ahead, doesn't weigh consequences easily. Once he got inside our house, he wasn't sure why he'd come or what to say. I think he was jealous of his friend going off with Harrison Grant that day, and he needed to unload on someone. I had been with both of them that morning, so maybe he thought I'd understand what he was feeling. His emotions were probably tangled up, since his jealousy was directed toward a man who was now dead."

"Murdered," Birdie said, which certainly added gravity to Eddie's story.

And motive for murder, if one was stretching out the connections.

But Eddie Porter was not a murderer. The thought settled on both women at the same time, followed by the realization that murderers were never murderers.

Until they were.

They finished their spritzers just as the bar began filling up with people getting off work, coming in to rehash the day, meet a friend, to have a drink before dinner.

Birdie and Nell stood and collected their bags and left the lounge. They reached the wide marble lobby just as Liz Palazola Santos was walking down the hallway from her office.

"Birdie, Nell, hi. I didn't know you were here or I'd have come out sooner." The tall, club manager, dressed in a shapely red suit, hugged them both. "You two are my comfort pills. I have a few minutes before the dinner crowd comes in. Can you come visit for a minute, fill me in on your lives?"

"For a minute," Birdie agreed. "You are a busy woman, and we are on our way home."

They followed Liz into her tasteful office and settled into two chairs facing Liz's desk. The entire club had become more tasteful since Liz was promoted to a management role. In her forties now, Liz had been working at the club since she was a teenager, literally working her way up, from lifeguard to waitress to hostess. And now manager. And Liz had excelled in each incarnation.

"Tell me how your mother is," Birdie asked.

Annabelle Palazola worked harder and longer hours than any of them. The Sweet Petunia Restaurant in Canary Cove was her fifth child, she often said, and thanks to its success, she had been able to raise four children alone after Liz's father died at sea. And all had become successful adults, but Liz alone had an unnatural beauty to go along with her intelligence. After graduating from NYU in business, she'd worked for a short time in publishing, then decided to head back to where she'd grown up, to be close to family and to finally settle down.

She smiled across the desk at them, her platinum hair shiny and a flawless complexion making her look ten years younger. She was as comfortable in her position as she was in her body. Competent and self-assured.

"Mom's fine. But all of us are worried about this murder hanging over everyone's heads. I saw Tommy Porter come in earlier," she said. "He looked haggard. It's a tough week. People are on edge."

"I suppose there's plenty of talk floating around here," Birdie said.

"Plenty. The Cliffside neighborhood isn't that far from here. But it's also because some of the club members were at the reception that night. Many talked to the man. And everyone else is simply trying to come to grips with the fact that someone had enough hate in their heart to kill him."

Hate. Birdie mulled over the word.

"Why else would someone kill?" Liz asked.

"Jealousy. Or to keep someone from revealing a secret," Nell offered.

"Revenge, maybe," Birdie said.

"Revenge, even jealousy, is hard to separate from hate," Liz said.

They agreed those emotions certainly could lead to hate. Emotions became tangled, difficult to pull apart sometimes.

"So who hated Grant?" Liz said. She shook her head as she said the dead man's name.

Nell caught Liz's look. It was one of disgust. "Did you know him, Liz?"

Liz was quiet for a moment. She glanced out the window, into the darkening night, before answering.

Then she said, "I didn't really know him. But yes, we had met."

"Of course. You worked in marketing? Publishing? While you were in New York?" Nell said.

"New York? No, I met Harrison Grant right here in Sea Harbor."

Birdie's white brows lifted.

Before Liz could continue, the restaurant hostess came to the door to tell Liz she was needed in the dining room. And Stu, the bartender, had a question, too. Liz stood up and motioned to them that she'd be out in a minute.

Liz's story came out quickly, short sentences and not many embellishments. Then she confirmed what Birdie had thought was the case. Harrison wasn't completely new to Sea Harbor.

"I was a kid. It was a long time ago. Maybe twenty years? I was in school but waitressed here in the summer. He came in one night. We get a lot of people doing that. People who aren't members just coming in for a drink. None of us knew who he was, but he had killer looks. Lots of the beach staff, waitresses were flirting with him. He would have been what? Maybe about the age I am now? I was a kid in my twenties then. But I remember him because when I got off work that night, he cornered me in the parking lot."

"What?" Nell's voice echoed in the small room.

"I was unlocking my car and he spread his arms on either side of me, put his hands on the car so I couldn't much move. He scared me. He acted like he thought he was doing me a favor, that I'd jump at the chance. I didn't."

"What happened?" Birdie asked.

"Just as I was ready to knee my way out of the situation, one of the bartenders came out and hollered good night to me. Grant was lucky. He stepped away quickly before I could ruin his manhood. I had a few choice words for him, got in my car, and left. I think I may have run over his foot." Liz started to walk toward the door.

"Did you see him again?" Birdie asked.

Liz paused and then looked back. "A couple times. But only from a distance. I think he originally came to town on business, photographing something. Nothing big. Apparently, he ended up having an affair with a woman who lived somewhere around here. Married maybe, or so the staff rumors said. I'm not sure how long it lasted. He wasn't a big deal back then, and I wouldn't even know this much about him except for the fact that he came on to me that night. I had to check his bar tab to find out his name. Over the years I would see the name here and there in magazines, but I didn't really think about him again until I saw the flyers that said he was giving the photography lecture series at Canary Cove. People change. I gave him the benefit of the doubt and hoped he might be one of them."

Stu, the bartender, appeared at her side, his face as red as Liz's jacket. "Soda gun busted in the bar," he said. "Ruined some lady's dress. I think she's the mayor."

Liz waved at them once, rolled her eyes, then rushed down the hall toward the bar, leaving Birdie, Nell, and images of a forty-something Harrison Grant in her wake.

Chapter 16

Cass had come over unannounced and had offered to babysit for Abby that night. "I need the practice," she told Izzy.

"You're aware that babies don't come out like that, aren't you?" Izzy asked.

"I know that."

They sat at Izzy's kitchen counter, watching Abby slathering paint on an easel and paint set Cass had given her goddaughter.

"She's into impressionism," Izzy said.

"And very good at it."

Abby giggled and waved her brush at them.

"And you know I don't need a sitter tonight, right?"

"Abby needs me tonight," Cass said. "I could feel it. Her dad's gone. I'm filling in. Where is he, by the way?"

Izzy sighed. "He's taking over Harrison Grant's lecture series."

Cass's eyes widened in surprise. "That's nice of him."

"It's one thing he could do to make life easier for Jane and Ham right now. And according to Jane, enrollment even went up a little, proving her point that my Sam is every bit as talented as the rich and famous."

"We all knew that. But why is Sam's car out front?"

"Because it doesn't start. It's very dead. So Sam picked up a rental. The only one they had was an orange convertible."

Cass hooted.

"Shelby Pickard is on his way over to tow Sam's away and hopefully work some magic on it."

The sound of a vehicle pulling up to the house caused Abby to twist around quickly and lose control of a brush thick with bright orange paint. It landed with a splash on the floor.

Izzy grimaced as Abby started to cry. She scooped her up and soothed her, then suggested to Cass that she was the giver of the paint set. Would she please grab the paper towels?

Still cuddling Abby, Izzy grabbed Sam's keys from the counter and headed for the front door.

But it wasn't Shelby Pickard who stood on the step.

"Auntie Nell," Abby squealed, her face lit with smiles, the tears gone, and her short arms reaching for Nell.

Nell cuddled Abby close, breathing in the sweet smell of baby shampoo, and walked on in. Behind her, Birdie stepped inside. She gave Izzy a hug.

Izzy closed the door and walked back into the kitchen, suddenly warm with friends.

Birdie chuckled at the look on Izzy's face. "Well, now, didn't anyone tell you there was a party tonight at the Perrys'?" She held up a bag of cookies and walked over to where Cass was laboriously wiping orange paint from the floor. "You'll have to share these with Abby, Cass. Now, let me help you with that. Orange isn't a good color for Izzy's floor. Yellow would be my choice."

She put the cookies on the counter, filled a bucket with warm water, then held on to the edge of a stool and lowered herself down beside Cass.

"You do know that neither of us will ever get up from here, don't you?" Cass asked.

Birdie nodded and smiled. "Our first campout together, Catherine."

Soon the paint-splattered area was clean, and with Nell's help, Birdie and Cass made it up off the floor. Cass went off to treat Abby to a bedtime story, while Izzy, Nell, and Birdie settled in the family room, in front of a fire, a pizza ordered and hopefully coming soon.

Once Cass rejoined them, Birdie explained the impromptu visit by saying there really wasn't a good explanation. Except that she and Nell had just come from the yacht club, where they had discovered Harrison Grant wasn't a complete stranger to Sea Harbor after all. And the discovery had made them realize they needed to be together. When they had seen Cass's car at Izzy's, the Perry house had won the coin toss. There were things they should talk about. People they were concerned about.

And, as Birdie said, keeping those concerns bottled up in individual heads wasn't productive. They needed to pool them in one big pot. In a few short sentences, she told them what they'd learned.

Izzy poked at the fire until embers glowed on the grate. She was thinking about Harrison Grant. His visits to Sea Harbor. And other worries she hadn't yet shared with them. "Twenty years ago—that's long before Nell and I lived here," she said.

"I was finishing up a couple of classes in Boston," Cass said. "But I came home a lot. I don't think I heard the name Harrison Grant back then. Or if I did, it didn't fit in my world and I got rid of it."

"Not to mention there was no Facebook or Instagram," Izzy added.

"I was here, of course," Birdie said. "But I doubt if I had heard about things like someone from out of town having an affair in Sea Harbor. Especially since Harrison Grant wasn't well known back then. My circle wouldn't have been interested. Although I must admit, at my age, twenty years ago was practically yesterday. It seems to me that there would be people around here who might remember that."

"Like the woman who had the affair," Cass said.

"Of course," Nell said, surprised she hadn't made the connection immediately. "And if she'd been hurt somehow by Harrison Grant, rejected, maybe, or if her marriage had been made to suffer, she would certainly have a motive to kill him."

"Or the husband, whoever he may be," Cass said.

The thought sent a chill through Nell, and she realized that subconsciously she had been thinking, like so many others in Sea Harbor, that the person who killed Harrison Grant was someone from out of town. Especially since no one in Sea Harbor really knew the man, and therefore, no one would have any reason to kill him. They were strangers to townsfolk, both the dead man and the murderer. But maybe they weren't.

"But why did Harrison lie about being on Cape Ann?" Birdie wondered out loud. "He could simply have said, 'Yes, a few years ago.' I wouldn't have pursued it further. And certainly wouldn't have asked if he'd come here back then to have an affair."

Cass laughed.

The doorbell rang, and Izzy rushed to the front of the house before it rang again and woke up Abby.

She took the pizza and set it on the hall table, then paid the delivery boy and started to close the door. But just then a tow truck rumbled down the street and pulled into the spot vacated by Mario's Pizza car.

Shelby Pickard lumbered up the front walkway. "Sorry I'm late, Izzy. Had an emergency stop."

"An accident?"

"Sort of. I was headed over here and spotted old man Rico and Frodo walking in the dark. Rico was a little tipsy, and some guy on a Harley got too close and clipped the dog."

"Oh, no." Izzy's hand went to her mouth. Frodo was Rico's life.

"I checked the dog out, then got them both in my truck and took them on home. I think Frodo will be okay. He wasn't nearly as wobbly as Rico."

"Sometimes mechanics are called on to fix more than cars, I guess. You're a good man, Shelby Pickard."

"And a tired one. Let me get that car out of here so I can go to bed." He took the keys and promised to call her in the morning with his expert diagnosis. Then he urged her back inside so he could be about his business.

Izzy walked slowly inside, thoughts on a man and his dog. A scruffy, sweet mutt that had become Red's best friend.

Nell had already cleared off the coffee table and found plates and napkins. Birdie uncorked a bottle of wine, which, Izzy figured, she must have had in her knitting bag, and Cass retrieved a can of Abby's cranberry juice from the refrigerator.

Izzy curled up next to the fire and told them about Rico and his dog.

"I had almost forgotten about Rico in all this tragedy," Nell said. "That poor man. He doesn't accommodate people easily. And they, him. I'm sure reporters have been beating on his door."

"I'm sure they have. And the police, as well. It was Rico's house. His steps. His property that Harrison found his way to," Birdie said. "It's still a puzzle to me how Harrison got over to the Silva place."

"Not *how*, really," Izzy said. "You could just walk down the sidewalk and into the backyard. It's the *why* that confuses me.

Why go into a stranger's backyard?" She knew she was shifting the emphasis slightly. Putting it back on a man who could no longer answer their wonderings. But somehow concentrating on logistics was easier than her vague wonderings about the Rico Silva she had seen the morning after. Seemingly disoriented.

And for the first time she could remember, avoiding his crumbling steps.

Birdie followed up on Izzy's question. "Why, and with whom?" She had carefully wiped her hands and then had pulled out a tiny yellow piece of knitting that was turning into a bootie.

"If he was having a conversation with someone and needed privacy, he could have found a spot right there at the Art Haven estate," Cass said. "All those rooms inside, or down on the beach, in the boathouse. That estate has more getaway spots than my high school stadium."

"The beach steps," Izzy said suddenly.

"Not the steps. There's not much privacy there." Cass looked at Izzy curiously. The former lawyer in the group usually had clever answers.

"No, I'm not talking about the privacy issue. I'm talking about something else that happened that night. I was looking around for you, Cass. And I looked down toward the beach. And just like you mentioned, a few people were coming up those beach steps. But then . . ." She stumbled on the last words, then frowned.

"Then what?" Cass asked.

Izzy hesitated. She reached for a piece of pizza. "Then nothing. My mind must have been playing tricks on me, that's all. I shouldn't have brought it up. It doesn't make any kind of logical sense."

"What doesn't?" Cass persisted.

Izzy took a drink of wine. "For a minute that night, I thought

I saw Rico Silva on the Art Haven steps, coming up behind a couple."

"I can't imagine that, Izzy," Nell said. "You're right. Besides, Rico would have stood out in that crowd and been noticed. People would have talked about it. But what's more definite is the fact that he hates crowds."

Izzy nodded. "And he doesn't go anywhere without Frodo. It had to be my imagination. I shouldn't have said anything."

"Tommy Porter told Nell and me that Rico was upset about the noise that night," Birdie said. "So that might have given him a reason to go over—"

"But he called the police about it," Nell said. "A much more likely scenario than showing up himself."

They all agreed, then remained silent as pieces of pizza disappeared. Izzy refilled wineglasses and brought out a pitcher of water. Thoughts were knit together, then pulled apart. Then looped together again.

"But forget about Rico on the steps for a minute. The fact is that he *was* home that night," Birdie said. She was working her stitches to the rhythm of her voice—exact, quick, fitting together with precision. "And his house is close enough to the Art Haven for him to have been bothered by the noise from the party. His hearing must be decent, maybe better than mine, and mine is pretty good. He was closer than anyone else to the exact spot where it happened, well, except for the two people standing at the top of his crumbling steps."

She paused for a second, both her fingers and her words. And then she said, "Someone was murdered in Rico's backyard. That's the truth. Someone hit Grant forcefully enough to send him tumbling down those awful steps. That would certainly make noise."

Birdie knew from experience that she spoke the truth, having spent many hours looking out her window or telescope at the hint of noise or activity along the harbor, no matter the time of night that the sounds had beckoned her. If Rico could hear music two houses away, wouldn't it be likely he could hear a man being murdered in his backyard?

Rico Silva. A man many people in Sea Harbor would happily put behind bars to remove the shroud that was slowly enveloping their town.

A man small in stature, but with a mighty fist.

Chapter 17

Izzy supposed it was because of Red, who placed two paws on her quilt early the next morning and began licking her face. He and Frodo probably had some sort of dog telepathy going on. But either way, Izzy woke up with a wet face and a clear idea of how her day would unwind.

She made bacon and pancakes shaped like little turtles for Abby, and listened to Sam talk about how much he had enjoyed giving his lecture the night before. It had been a full house, with talented people, and he decided he was liking the gig more than he had imagined. Izzy told him about her day, about her friends coming over, informed him that they had a compassionate and very kind auto mechanic, and that Sam should probably keep his rental car for at least another day or two.

And then she told him that on her way to the shop, she was going to stop at Rico's house and demand to see Frodo. To make sure he was okay.

What they didn't talk about was the fact that Rico would never let her in.

Sam was pretty sure of it. But he knew better than to argue

with Izzy when her mind was made up, so he kissed his wife soundly and told a giggling Abby that he was going to take her to day care in his fancy rented car. An orange convertible. They'd bundle up, put the top down, and pretend they were riding in a pumpkin in a parade, waving good morning to everyone in town.

The electric wrought-iron gate, which the previous owners had always kept closed and which was opened with codes, was one of the many things that Rico had let go. One side of the double gate hung at a peculiar angle on its hinges; the other side was wide open.

Izzy pulled into the driveway, parked in front of the garage, and sat there for a minute, thinking. The discussion about Rico the night before, her own comments included, had disturbed her. Rico's house. Rico's steps. They knew everyone connected in any way to a murdered man needed attention. But it seemed misplaced, and motives were as important as proximity, surely.

She wasn't sure why she had held back from telling Nell, Birdie, and Cass about seeing Rico the morning she found Harrison Grant's body. His behavior that day had been odd. But the more she thought about it, twisting it this way and that, the more she was convinced that had it been an ordinary day. She wouldn't think much about the way he had acted. Rico was Rico. Some days he was almost talkative; some days not. She shouldn't be picking that morning apart, wondering why that day, of all days, he'd walked down to the beach via the road instead of the steps. After all, she'd been begging him to do that for months. The steps were hard for Frodo, too. And the fact that Rico didn't always talk in complete paragraphs early in the morning wasn't unusual. Sometimes she didn't, either.

But the thing that convinced her she was simply imagining unusual behavior on that day was the fact that she liked Rico. He was eccentric, but that wasn't bad. And beneath his eccentricities, he was a good man. Kind, even. She'd seen it in his eyes and in the way he was with Frodo and with the little kids on the beach. Catching their beach balls when the wind tossed them away, chasing gulls to prevent them from eating the kids' snacks. She'd even seen him pick up a crying baby from a blanket one day when the mom was off chasing a runaway toddler down the beach. He hadn't looked comfortable, but he'd done it. Rico had compassion.

Surely he hadn't known there was a dead man lying at the bottom of his steps. And not gone for help. Not told anyone. Surely not.

With that thought in her head, she headed for the front door of Rico's large home.

It took several knocks, then standing back far enough so Rico could see who it was if he was peering through a window. She wasn't sure if that would make a difference, but she gave it a try. In the distance, she heard Frodo barking.

Finally, the door opened an inch or two. Izzy stepped closer and slipped her boot into the opening.

"Whatta you want?" Rico asked.

"I came to see how Frodo is doing. Shelby Pickard told me he was injured last night."

Rico spewed forth some choice comments about motorcycles and their drivers, then told her Frodo was fine.

"He's not beside you at the door. He's not fine."

Rico growled.

Izzy smiled at Rico's hand, which was cupped around the door's edge, holding it in place—and keeping Izzy in hers.

"Please let me in, Rico," she said quietly. "I love Frodo. Let's just make sure he's okay. I won't steal anything. I just want to see your pup."

Rico was silent, but he hadn't tried to push her foot out of the door opening or threatened to call the police.

"Think of it this way, Rico. If Frodo gets an infection, you won't have anyone to walk with. Except maybe me. How awful would that be?" Then she spoke more softly." But the thing is, if he gets an infection that sweet pup will be in pain."

With that, Rico opened the door, his face somber, although Izzy detected a slight loosening of facial muscles, almost as if there was a smile hidden somewhere on that face.

"He's back here," Rico said. "Though I don't know what makes you an expert."

"*Love*, Rico. And not you. I love dogs."

Rico moved fast, and Izzy followed closely, hurrying to keep up with him. She tried to sneak a look at the surroundings as they moved, at the winding staircase and what seemed to be many doors opening off the foyer. It was a house she could easily lose her way in, and she concentrated on Rico's back as they walked down a long hall leading to the back of the house. As curious as she was, getting lost in Rico Silva's house wasn't a thought she relished.

In the corner of the large kitchen, lying on a dog bed, Frodo lifted his head and slapped his tail against the cushion, welcoming Izzy. The bed had been placed in a pool of sunshine, a bowl of water had been pushed up close, and a food dish was nearby.

Izzy walked across the room and squatted down beside him. She petted him gently beneath his chin, talking softly. She noticed absently that Frodo was clean, his coat brushed, a stark contrast to the clutter on the counter, the half-empty cans and soiled dish towels nearby. Frodo was well cared for by his master.

"Look at his rear end," Rico growled. He was standing behind her, watching and guarding. "That's where the fool hit him."

Izzy did and saw the laceration on his hip immediately. She touched it gently and felt Frodo cringe. But he didn't twist his head, and he made no attempt to nip her hand away.

She could also see that Rico had cleaned the wound and applied an antiseptic. She was surprised, and then she wasn't.

She felt some swelling beneath her fingers and could see that, in spite of the ointment, some festering was happening at the laceration's edges. It was the same kind of wound Red had gotten last summer, when he'd lost his balance and fallen down a concrete step, scraping his hip. The vet's antibiotic had done wonders.

She looked up at Rico. "What would you think about getting him to the vet and—"

"No."

Izzy kept her voice calm. "Frodo is going to be fine, but this wound might need some help to make that happen, Rico."

"What makes you an expert on my dog?"

Rico began to pace the room as Izzy talked, explaining to him what had happened to Red, how quickly he had been healed with antibiotics. How the vet had said infections were dangerous in all dogs, but especially in old dogs, like her Red and his Frodo.

She watched him circle the room, go around the kitchen table, which was piled high with papers and open cereal boxes, then walk over to large glass doors leading out to an empty patio. And walk some more.

Izzy let him pace and took stock of the rest of the large kitchen. A crack in a window, a shutter outside the sink windows hanging crookedly. But if cleaned and loved, it would be a perfect family kitchen.

A door near Frodo's bed was open, and Izzy could see that it belonged to a small room, originally the servants' quarters, she guessed. She got up and glanced inside the room while Rico was staring out the back windows, coming to his senses, Izzy hoped.

An unmade bed stood in the middle of the room. Sheets were tousled, half on the floor. The drapes were still pulled shut, and dark shadows fell across the floor.

She turned her back on the loneliness she saw inside the room.

This is where he lives, she thought. *He and Frodo. In these two rooms.*

Rico finally stopped pacing. "The vet can come here," he said, then walked across the room to where Frodo lay.

The new town veterinarian was a distant cousin of Cass's. She was young, eager to expand her practice. And she was kind. She would come.

"I will ask," Izzy said.

Rico had lowered himself to the floor beside the dog. With a gentleness that astounded Izzy, he rubbed his fingers beneath the dog's chin, then scratched him lightly. Frodo tilted his head back, his tongue out, and his eyes loving Rico.

Izzy walked across the room and rummaged around the kitchen table for paper and a pencil.

She found a black marker, then took out her phone, called the vet, explained the situation, and arranged a time for her to do a house call.

"It's all set, Rico," she called across the room. "I'll leave the veterinarian's information on the table."

Rico nodded. "You can let yourself out."

Izzy shrugged. She did like this man, but he sure made it difficult sometimes. As she pushed aside some papers to make room for the information she had written down, she moved a few bills, newspapers. A familiar flyer.

And then she looked again. The flyer was the announcement of a new lecture series at the Canary Cove Art Colony. Famed photographer Harrison Grant would be coming to Sea Harbor to deliver the first lecture series. And at the bottom, highlighted in yellow and circled, was information about the reception tickets and directions to the new Art Haven center on Cliffside Drive. Just two doors down from Rico's house.

Harrison Grant's publicity photo was large and prominent on the flyer.

But Izzy knew it was Harrison Grant only because she had distributed some of the flyers herself to help Jane out, and she had posted one in her shop. The photo on the flyer on Rico's kitchen table was gone, completely destroyed with careful, deliberate strokes of a black marking pen.

Chapter 18

Mae reported that Izzy hadn't come in yet. Something about a man and a dog. She held her cell phone between her pointed chin and thin shoulder.

"Hah. I've heard that one before," Cass said. Then she told Mae why she was calling. A favor. "Is there any space left in the Wednesday beginners' knitting class meeting that afternoon?" Cass knew the class was always full. But Mae liked her.

"This pregnancy is making you way too humble, Cass," Mae chuckled. "We all know you're not a great knitter, but as best I know, you've finally figured out how to cast on."

"Hey, watch it, Mae," Cass said. "I'm pretty darn good. I am, without question, the master knitter of fishermen hats, as you well know."

"Wait a minute, Cass. I have a customer."

Cass listened while Mae talked to a customer about why vicuña yarn was so expensive. Then she came back to her phone and listened while Cass explained why she was calling. It was for Elena Costa. A young fisherman's wife who didn't know how to knit. Not at all. And then Cass dropped the bomb that she knew would compel Mae to find Elena a place in the class no matter if the waiting list was all the way down Harbor Road and back. "And she's pregnant, Mae."

Mae's voice moved up enough decibels that Cass had to hold the phone away from her ear. "That's absolutely abhorrent," she said. "Utterly shameful. What were her mother and grandmother thinking? We will find her a spot if it means sitting on someone's lap."

Cass could hear the buzz in the back room as she and Elena walked through Izzy's front door. Mae immediately took a liking to the young woman, as if she alone had rescued the young woman from the unwashed shame of being a non-knitter. She handed Elena a beginners' kit before ushering her away from Cass and over to the table in the center of the room. Elena's dark eyes soaked in the sight of the baby cradle filled with mountains of yarn and tiny knit animals.

"Izzy's here, rushing around somewhere," Mae called over to Cass, then guided Elena on to cubby after cubby of sweet, soft yarns.

Izzy came up the stairs, her attempt at a ponytail failing. Strands of dark and light blond hair flew out of her scrunchie as she walked over to Cass.

"You look bothered," Cass said. "Everything okay?"

"It's been a day."

"And there's a few more hours of it to come."

Izzy nodded, setting a loose pile of orders down on the checkout desk. "I had a late start this morning and haven't caught up yet." She paused and looked at Cass. Opened her mouth, then closed it again. Cass looked like she was about to walk out, and Izzy had a class starting in minutes. As much as she wanted to talk to Cass about how her day had started, she couldn't. Not now, not in the middle of a yarn shop teeming with people. Before she could share it and lessen the load, she needed the time and space to process Rico Silva's damage to the photo on the flyer. And to believe in the deepest recesses of her being that that was all Rico had damaged when it came to Harrison Grant.

"It looks like Mae is taking good care of Elena," Cass said, nodding to the two women on the other side of the shop.

Izzy looked across the room. Elena's whole face was smiling, lighting up the shop, as Mae introduced her to the world of knitting, to the amazing yarns they carried, and showed off the baby clothes on display that she herself had knit for grandnieces and nephews.

Izzy smiled back without intention or thought. The woman's joy was contagious. A wonderful reprieve today. "She's lovely, Cass. Pregnancy surely agrees with her. She's even more beautiful than when I met her a few weeks ago."

Elena wore tights today, along with a stretchy knit tunic that covered her baby bump like a second skin.

Cass looked down at her extra-large ALL THE NEWS THAT'S FIT TO PRINT sweatshirt, which someone had given Danny when he was a reporter. It surrounded her like a tight gray blanket. "I'm kinda cute, too, right?"

Izzy laughed and hugged her friend.

Cass pulled out her keys. "I'm off to pick up some new buoys. My exciting life just never stops." She waved to Elena, then hurried out as a new wave of shoppers came in.

Izzy gathered up her supplies for the class and looked again at Elena. She was dutifully following Mae around the displays of yarn, seemingly entranced by what she saw. She was beautiful, yes. But there was something else there, Izzy thought. Elena Costa looked tranquil. Peaceful.

A line of customers called Mae back to the checkout counter, and Izzy took charge of Elena, leading her down to the back room. "This room is a special place for knitters," she said with a smile.

As soon as Elena walked down into the knitting room, she spotted Purl near the window, and before Izzy could show her around, she had walked over to the window seat and begun talking to the shop calico as if she had just discovered a long-lost friend. Purl seemed to be talking back, and Elena soon joined her on the cushioned window seat.

Izzy watched Purl situate herself on the nearly lapless Elena and saw the pregnant woman shift her body until there was plenty of room for needles, yarn, and a sweet, warm cat.

A few minutes later Birdie and Nell, helpers in the beginners' class, came in, pulled off jackets, and greeted customers. Then Nell checked in with Izzy, while Birdie looked around for the woman Mae had told her about. She had yet to meet Cass's new friend.

Elena. A pretty name, Birdie thought.

She spotted her immediately, sitting with sweet Purl on the window seat. A bath of afternoon sunlight fell through the bay window, lighting the pair and turning them into an ethereal-looking painting. Birdie smiled, in spite of suspecting she was no longer Purl's favorite lap.

On the other side of the room, Izzy welcomed the class and introduced Birdie and Nell. And then she did what she always did at the beginning of the class: she held up a short garter-stitch scarf and promised them that they'd be making one themselves in the time it might take to do their holiday shopping. "Online," she added, her encouraging smile lighting up faces with anticipation. And in the next lesson they would move to a stockinette scarf.

Even Beatrice Scaglia, who had slipped into the room without being noticed, smiled, her new yarn and needles in hand, as she surveyed the group.

Birdie and Nell moved around the room as Izzy talked, leaning down to point out a missed cast-on or twisted yarn, guiding fingers as they worked the yarn. They soothed frustrations and encouraged tiny advances.

All the while Elena sat on the window seat with Purl, listening, her fingers magically following directions, her row of cast-ons leading to a row of knit stitches, then a second and third and fourth row.

"You are a natural at this," Birdie said, finding room on the window seat beside Elena and Purl.

Elena smiled. Purl tilted her head to the side for Birdie to scratch.

Birdie explained her relationship to Cass, to Izzie, to Nell. "Now, who are *you*, Elena Costa? How did you happen upon Sea Harbor?"

Elena smiled, at ease with the questions from this comforting, safe woman. Birdie's voice was warm, her eyes welcoming, and Elena talked comfortably with her. She explained how she, an au pair working in Boston, had met Marco Costa, her Gloucester fisherman husband.

"The family I worked for was vacationing in Annisquam, near here. And one pretty day I was walking the children down near the water, and there was Marco, coming along the river in a big boat, delivering lobsters. Imagine. *Lobsters*!" Her face opened in delight. And then she blushed. "And I fell in love with this big, not so pretty man."

Birdie had known Marco Costa since he was a scrappy kid who got in trouble on the docks, causing his poor parents grief. His grandmother was a friend of Birdie's, and she'd spent many bridge sessions holding the grandmother's hand as she fretted about her grandson. It was clear that Elena saw something different in Marco Costa.

Birdie was happy about that.

With the knitting class deep into their first rows of the garter stitch, Nell walked over to talk to Elena, curious about Cass's friend, who seemed to be holding Birdie captive. And Mae, too, had seemed ready to adopt the young mother-to-be. In minutes, Nell understood why. She pulled over a chair and admired Elena's knitting, listening to the woman talk softly about the magic of turning simple loops of yarn into sweaters and hats and scarves.

"Isn't it a miracle?" Elena asked, looking from Birdie to Nell, her large eyes lighting up as one hand rested on her belly. "Just like babies."

The tap of heels announced Beatrice Scaglia's presence, and Nell looked up into the mayor's carefully made-up face. She suspected that the mayor had realized the class of new knitters was not very talkative, was not exchanging news or rumors, their concentration directed instead to the foreign way of using their fingers and holding strands of yarn.

Beatrice noticed Elena and frowned. "And who are you, young lady?" Her question was not that different from Birdie's, but from Beatrice, it held a note of interrogation.

Elena blushed, but before Birdie could step in with introductions, Beatrice had turned away and moved on to another topic—Eddie Porter's girlfriend.

"I spoke to the chief about her today," Beatrice said. "Deb something. They are caretakers, you know, she and Eddie. They were there at the artists' reception. Did you see them? I saw her—Deb something—that night, flirting her way through the crowd, her eyes on Harrison Grant."

Elena concentrated on her knitting, her head lowered.

"I also told Jerry he should talk to that fool Rico Silva about those steps of his."

"Why?" Birdie asked softly, hoping Beatrice would follow her example and lower her voice. "I'm sure the chief is in touch with Rico. And it wasn't the steps that killed Harrison Grant."

Birdie glanced at Nell. They both held their breath, wondering what else Beatrice would say about the man she openly disliked.

But Beatrice moved on to yet another bone she had to pick with Rico Silva.

"The *Gloucester Times* did an article on his property, you know. They showed all the weeds, the mess behind Rico's house. They even photographed the horrible steps. And in the nicest neighborhood in town. People come here to vacation. We can't have them forming negative images about our town."

Izzy had brought the class to a close and walked over as people stuffed knitting in bags and looked for their purses. She had heard Rico's name being tossed around and stood quietly on the edge of the conversation.

Beatrice went on. "I sent Eddie Porter and a friend over to Silva's a couple weeks ago. Said I'd pay them myself if they'd clean the place up."

"You sent them to Rico's?" Birdie said.

"I did. Who knows? Maybe I could have saved the photographer's life if old Rico hadn't called the police and accused them of trespassing." She looked around at them, Birdie, Nell, and Izzy, but ignored the quiet newcomer on the window seat. "I worked it all out with the police, of course. Had the guys do a little community service work at Rico's, which satisfied the police and which Rico finally agreed to. Two problems solved. The place is looking a tiny bit better." She looked around, waved to a councilwoman leaving the class, then sighed.

"It's simply too much," she said, the frustration in her voice now tempered with despair as she shifted topics again. "If someone doesn't put a murderer behind bars—and find a way to clean up Rico's property—I will do it myself. I swear I will."

She seemed to put the two issues on a parallel plane, and before anyone could bring that to her attention, she spun around and headed up the stairs, the tapping of her heels louder than usual, and the slam of the outside door that followed even louder.

Izzy looked over at Elena. She was looking after the mayor, a strange look on her face.

"It's all right," Izzy said. "That's the mayor. She's having a bad day, is all."

"She was talking about my Marco with Eddie. He said it was nothing when the police called our house. Just a mistake." She looked sad, her eyes filling with tears.

"It was a mistake," Nell said. "It was actually the mayor's fault. It's nothing to be concerned about. Everyone is nervous about this murder," Nell said.

"The man who fell down the steps?" Elena asked.

"Yes."

"Marco said he was a stranger. No one knew him."

"That seems to be true," Nell said. "At least no one knew him well."

"Then why would someone kill him?"

Birdie patted Elena's hand and nodded.

And *that* seemed to be the question.

A short while later, once everyone had gone, Birdie and Nell began picking up yarn remnants, empty coffee cups, and scattered papers.

"I don't think Beatrice is well," Birdie said. "She has high blood pressure, and the last thing she should be worried about is a murderer in her town."

"Or Rico Silva's messy property. It's causing her distress," Nell said. "He seems to be very much on her mind."

Izzy was organizing a pile of patterns. Rico's name seemed to be everywhere. She picked up several needles from the floor and tossed them in a basket.

Cleanup after a class was a familiar routine, and in short order the room was neat again. They could hear Mae up in the front room, flipping the CLOSED sign against the door and putting things in the safe.

"You look tired, Izzy," Nell said. "Everything okay?"

"Fine. Just tired." She gave her aunt a hug. "I could fall asleep standing here, and I still have the grocery store and dinner ahead of me."

A ruckus at the front door disturbed her thoughts, and they all walked up to see Mae peering out the front door, then unlocking it.

Shelby Pickard walked in, carrying a plastic storage box.

"Is Sam's car in there?" Izzy said, looking at the box.

Shelby laughed, a gruff sound. He greeted the others and walked farther into the store.

"I need a few more days with the car," he explained. "Sam is stuck with that pumpkin for a few more days."

"Abby loves it."

"I figured as much. That's why I told Sam it was the only car I could loan him." He chuckled at his ploy, then walked over to Mae's desk and set the box down beside it. "Anyhoo, I found this here thing in the trunk of Sam's car and thought I'd drop it by in case either of you needed it. When I spotted the light and your car out front, I decided to save a little gas and leave it here. So there you have it." He tipped an imaginary hat and was out the door.

Shelby was gone before Izzy could tell him the box was most likely full of sandy old beach toys and he could have thrown it in the trash. Smelly toys by now. She looked at it and wrinkled her nose at the thought, then pushed it closer to the counter with her foot.

"Ladies?" she said, motioning toward the door.

"What about the box?" Nell looked back at the counter.

"I'll ask Mae to get rid of it in the morning."

Nell frowned at the unopened box. Then pushed away the niggling feeling it had created.

An unsolved murder was turning even old beach toys into suspicious objects.

It was time to go home.

Chapter 19

"Did you get Harmony's email?" Elena asked Cass. Her earbuds were in place, and she held a shiny new iPhone in her hand. At Cass's suggestion, Marco had bought Elena a new cell phone, one that worked.

"I did. I'm on my way."

In minutes Cass showed up in front of Elena's house, and the two drove off to the Y. Harmony Fairchild had sent around an email announcing an extra prenatal yoga class—a weekday class for some who weren't comfortable with the Saturday schedule. Free for the takers, her email had said. Namaste.

Cass knew she should have stayed at work—the new boat was having a computer problem—but Pete had offered to handle it. And the yoga classes were good for her. Even Danny had agreed that they seemed to make her more comfortable. And calm. And peaceful. And nice to her husband. And . . .

Cass had finally stopped Danny's litany of niceness by removing his glasses and showing him how nice she could be. And it wasn't all because of yoga.

Beside her in the car, Elena rested back against the seat and told Cass about knitting. About being enchanted by the feel of the yarn, about the pure magic of turning it into something soft and warm for her baby. And then she'd make a hat for Marco, she said, loving the one she'd found in her closet, the one that Cass had made for Marco years before.

Cass refrained from telling her that it had taken her months to make her first hat. Instead, she said, "So how's Marco doing?" Nell had told her about Elena's revelation that the mayor had somehow put Marco in an awkward position. A humorous event, some of them thought, knowing the mayor had made it all right. But apparently, an embarrassing one for Elena.

Elena rolled her head to the side and told Cass about the Marco she loved. "Marco bought a book on being a dad," she said softly.

Cass smiled, her eyes on the road. She knew about the book but would never fess up to it. She had bought it and put it in Marco's locker down at the dock, where he'd be sure to see it. And she had hoped he would take it home. And her higher, but more tenuous hope had been that he would read it.

"I told him he didn't need a book. He would pick up his beautiful baby, and he would instantly fall in love. Just like he did with me." Elena smiled softly, one hand moving instinctively to her belly.

Cass smiled.

Elena went on. "But last night, after dinner, I walked up behind Marco and looked over his big, strong shoulder. And guess what he was reading? It was the chapter on how important dads were in their sweet baby's life. And in the mom's life, too. And I was so happy."

Cass was, too.

A short while later they walked into the small yoga room, which looked much bigger today since only a few women had taken Harmony up on her generous offer.

The instructor stood at the front of the room, looking around at the three people spreading out their mats.

Cass called over a hello, and Harmony looked up, and then her face opened into a smile. She waved back at Cass, then noticed Elena, and the smile grew, as if Cass had just given her a present.

"Up here," Harmony said, pointing to empty spaces in front of her. "Let's be closer."

They stretched out their mats and settled down to the soft yoga music, Tibetan and crystal bowls playing in the background as a few others joined the group.

At first, the music Harmony played had made Cass uncomfortable. "All those oms," she had told Izzy. But the sounds had changed in her ears, her head, as they had begun to resonate inside her. She even found them soothing now. She closed her eyes and relaxed to the pleasing sound of a flute. And many slow, soothing oms.

When she opened her eyes a few minutes later, Harmony was sitting cross-legged on the floor, her back straight, her hands on her knees in a perfect . . . what? Cass tried to remember. *Sukhasana? Siddhasana?* But the words didn't come easily to her, and what attracted her more than the words she tended to tangle, even more than Harmony's position, was the look on the instructor's face as she talked to Elena.

Once or twice, Cass had seen un-yoga-like expressions flit across the yoga teacher's face—stern, even sad looks—but they'd quickly disappear when Harmony began the class, her body, strong and somewhat muscular, moving like a dancer's into perfect poses.

Elena was talking softly now, as was her way, and Harmony was listening, smiling. Then she nodded and talked back to Elena.

There was something about the connection between the two that Cass found interesting. An invisible tie, maybe, even though they were decades apart in age. Like her friendship with Birdie. Nell. And Izzy, the youngest in their circle. Age was irrelevant.

She smiled at the thought, then wondered if Harmony had forgotten about the rest of them. But she hadn't, and in minutes they were happily sinking into cat and dog poses, their unborn babies happy, too.

When the class ended a short while later, Harmony invited Cass and Elena to join her for a drink at the juice bar. Even after the modified poses, they were all sweating and needed hydration.

"Coconut water is my favorite," Harmony said as they walked down the hall to the small bar with its three stools, all tucked into a corner of the Y's lobby. "Great at replenishing electrolytes."

Harmony took the last stool and swiveled it sideways. "So I can see you both," she said.

Elena hopped up on the middle stool, with Cass at the other end of the threesome.

While Harmony advised Elena on the drinks, Cass looked over, watching her.

Harmony was taller than she was, about Izzy's height, Cass surmised. She had pulled her dark hair back into a ponytail for class, and today, as always, she wore a blue tank top and black tights. She had thrown a denim work shirt over the tank top as they left the studio. Harmony was ordinary looking, her face showing more wear than one would expect on a fifty-five-year-old. But when she was leading them through a yoga routine, her face changed, taking on a calming and pleasant look. *Fascinating*, Cass thought. And she wondered if her own inner state showed so openly on her face.

"How long have you been practicing yoga, Harmony," Elena asked after they had ordered their drinks.

Harmony chuckled. "I'm a Johnny-come-lately to yoga, at

least compared to many. Seven, eight years maybe? Elena, you look like you've been doing it longer than I have."

"No, no," Elena blushed. "But I love it. It helps me focus. You're a great teacher."

Harmony seemed inordinately pleased at the compliment. "Yoga does that. It makes you peaceful. And it does so much more. It truly did save my life once."

Cass listened more carefully, leaning in. Harmony's voice had turned soft and personal.

"I had some difficult years a while ago. I was angry at life, at anyone who happened to cross my path. I used to drink too much. I had trouble keeping a job . . ." Harmony laughed, a self-deprecating sound. "But anyway . . ." She glanced over at Cass. "You asked once about my getting into yoga. It was during that low point in my life. I took a class one day because it was nasty outside, I was feeling sorry for myself, and a woman I worked with had given me a free pass. It warmed me up and made me feel less sorry for myself. And then I took a second class. And somehow, week by week, I began to feel cleaned out."

"Cleaned out?" Elena said.

"Of anger. Distrust."

"So yoga transformed you, sort of?" Cass said.

Harmony looked at her, as if it were a trick question. Then she said with a short laugh, "Never. There isn't any such thing, except maybe under a makeup artist's fingers. Not in this life, I don't think. But yoga seems to keep me on a good path most of the time. I like life better than I did. And myself, too. But that's way too much about me."

Harmony seemed embarrassed that she had gotten so personal. It surprised Cass, too, but Elena had sat quietly, listening intently.

Her parents raised her well, Cass thought. Then she swallowed a laugh, realizing that was something usually said by older people. Like her mother, to be exact. She'd heard it many times.

She wondered more about Harmony Fairchild than Elena. Her name came up frequently whenever yoga was talked about and people liked her. She'd held yoga events for friends who were sick—and even a special yoga on the beach to celebrate Izzy's birthday last year. It had been on a remote part of the beach, a private little cove. Harmony had said it was where she was most at home.

But Cass wondered more about the kind of anger that would drive a woman to become a yoga guru. *And a generous guru*, she thought as she watched Harmony pick up the tab for their coconut drinks.

Chapter 20

"Let's not skip our Thursday nights together, like we did last week," Birdie said. "It disturbs my equilibrium."

They all felt that disturbance and had come together earlier than usual on this Thursday, showing up as Mae was shooing out the last customer of the day. Hungry for Nell's supper and togetherness.

Birdie looked around the back room, as if greeting an old friend. She shrugged off the alpaca and lambswool shawl she had knit on Thursday nights during the last long winter and hung it over a chair. "Time is disturbed. It feels like a long time since we've had this room to ourselves, just the four of us, for our knitting and wine. Shutting out the rest of the world. A normal night."

A normal night.

Nell, Izzy, and Cass listened to Birdie's words. Except it wasn't normal. They each had brought a burden with them, one that needed the kind of release friendship would bring. Between eating and knitting and sips of wine and water, they could share their concerns. And maybe lighten their load.

Cass stood at the table, hovering over Nell's hot plate and inhaling the aromas floating up from a covered casserole. "I smell mushrooms. And wine. Nutmeg?"

"I don't know how you do it, Cass," Nell said. "For someone who can't boil water, you do a magnificent job with food smells. But who can smell wine in a casserole?"

"Me. Because you rarely cook anything without it."

Nell chuckled. "And you're right about the nutmeg. It has other good things, too, but the true comfort comes from the portobello mushrooms and buttery sauce over the noodles. It's my cookbook friend Ina Garten's comforting casserole. Tonight seemed like a good night to try it."

The Thursday night routine was a well-rehearsed dance—its familiar steps bringing their own kind of comfort. The back room was a special place on these nights, the walls holding close the women's friendship, their secrets shared, their tears and laughter. Each year added a layer of richness, a closer melting together of lives.

Nell's supper dish was always plentiful; Birdie's wine, always crisp. And dessert from Harry Garozzo's deli or the new Italian bakery on the corner was always sweet and most often filled with chocolate.

Friendship. Bamboo needles and soft chairs. Laps filled with yarn.

Nell filled their plates with generous helpings of the casserole, Birdie poured the wine and soft drinks, and Cass fiddled with her phone, looking for music.

Nell noticed her niece was quieter than usual, letting those around her take charge. She'd tried to call Izzy that afternoon, but she hadn't picked up. So she had tried the store phone, just once. Midday. For no reason other than that Izzy had been on her mind.

Mae had said she'd stepped out for a bit.

Nell hadn't left a message then, and Izzy hadn't called back.

"Izzy, is everything okay?" she asked now.

Before Izzy could respond, Cass's music kicked in, pouring out of the speakers and filling the room. Marvin Gaye and Tammi Terrell were suddenly in the midst of knitting night, belting out "Ain't No Mountain High Enough."

On the other side of the table, Cass's body began moving.

"Can't sit still with this one," she said, her whole being moving with the singers' voices. She danced her way to a chair near the fireplace, balancing her larger body and her full plate, as she sang along in full throttle.

Birdie chuckled at Cass and settled into her own chair near the fire. She took a forkful of the mushroom casserole and declared it one of Ina and Nell's best, knowing that Nell always added her own touch, even when using a master chef's recipe. She motioned for Nell and Izzy to sit, too, and took a sip of her wine. "It's true, you know, what our friend Marvin says." Her eyes were soft and touched with concern. But her kind face, as always, held resolve and optimism at once. "We've climbed many mountains together. None of them have been too high."

Birdie's message was clear, but so were the real feelings lying in wait in the room, right beneath Marvin Gaye's voice.

It had been almost a week. A man was dead. A man who hadn't been buried or mourned, and who wasn't even much cared for in their town. But in the long run those things didn't matter. Murder had cast its own poison, and it was rumbling through the town and contaminating people on its way. Sucking them in.

"Tommy Porter stopped in the shop today." Izzy curled her long legs up beneath her and spoke slowly. "He hasn't slept much, I don't think. He asked if I would walk over to the park across the street with him. To talk about a couple things. So I did." She looked over at Nell, and her look explained why she hadn't taken her aunt's call.

"What kind of things?" Nell asked. But she knew before Izzy spoke that the topics weren't pleasant.

Izzy took a long breath, then followed it with an equally long drink of wine. "He began his questions with my Sunday run, wondering if I might have missed something, maybe remembered some detail in the past couple of days."

"What? Like a murderer hiding in the sand?" Cass said.

"We need to give him a break. It wasn't easy for him, Cass."

They all liked Tommy and knew him well. He was the kind of man mothers wanted their sons to be. But it was difficult when he put on his police hat and had to question friends in ways that seemed intrusive.

"What else was he wondering about?" Birdie asked. She finished the last of her mushrooms and noodles and set her plate on the coffee table.

"He asked me some things that it pained him to ask, I could tell. The questions were personal. He wanted to know how well I knew Grant. Did I like him? What had we talked about at the reception Friday night? How much time had I spent with him there? Who else did he talk to? And what about Sam? Did he know Grant well? Was he happy that he managed to get such a well-known guy to participate in the lecture series?" Izzy tried to smile. "He probably knew the answers to all those questions about Sam already but thought maybe I'd say something that would add something new."

Nell felt herself stiffen. Or, in policeman's mode, was he questioning Izzy's veracity? "Sam's feelings don't seem relevant," she said. But of course they were. Nell knew that. If Sam were some stranger they were talking about, someone who had expressed dislike for a murdered man, they would unquestionably be relevant questions. But it wasn't a stranger they were talking about. It was Sam Perry. And that changed everything.

"How did the police know to ask that question? Sam certainly didn't broadcast his feelings about Harrison. He wouldn't do that," Nell said.

"Jane told me the police talked to the secretary at the Canary Cove arts council office. She's young, kind of a drama queen, Jane said, and also an eavesdropper. She helped with preparations for Grant's coming, things like organizing his schedule, scheduling his suite over at the Art Haven estate. She was also around the Canary Cove office when Sam and Jane met a few times to talk about the lecture series. Times when Sam was resisting inviting him."

"I've met the young woman," Nell said. "Yes, I can imagine her interview with the police."

"She probably overheard Sam's arguments," Izzy said. "Maybe even heard him using some choice words. I don't know. According to Jane, the secretary is not very discreet, and she likes attention. She told the police that Sam didn't want Harrison Grant to come to town or to be involved in the lecture series. She told the police that Sam hated him."

"Hated him? Oh, goodness," Birdie said. "Don't people understand that words matter? You don't say someone hates another lightly. Maybe you don't say it ever."

"And you don't make it up," Nell said.

Izzy pushed her plate aside and opted for another glass of wine. "Of course, the woman had no idea why Sam 'hated' him, so I guess that's why the question came to me."

"This is all crazy. The chief knows Sam well," Cass said. "Why didn't the police just ask him?"

"That's in the works. They asked Sam to come in tomorrow to clear up some things. He's calm about it, as Sam would be, and not worried."

But Izzy was; they could all tell that. Or maybe disturbed. Either way, the fact that Sam would even be questioned about hating someone made no sense, and probably not even to the chief of police. The thought of him doing anything aggressive or even unseemly was also ridiculous to anyone who knew him.

"I should probably be the one going in to talk to the police," Izzy said.

"Why?" Nell and Cass spoke at the same time.

"Because of Rico."

"Rico?" Birdie said. "The more I think about him, Izzy, the more I think Rico couldn't have killed Harrison. The fact that he was home the night Grant was killed doesn't add up to murder. Not even if it happened in his backyard. Not without a lot more to add to it. For starters, there doesn't seem to be any connection between Rico and the photographer. The police surely know that."

"But there *is* more," Izzy said. Her voice was sad. "I don't know what the connection would be, but I'm beginning to think there might be one." In a few words, feeling like she was being disloyal to a friend, Izzy described her visit to Rico's house the day before. Checking Frodo, calling the vet, then finding the flyer about the Art Haven reception. "Frodo will be okay. But the flyer won't. It was marked up horribly," she said. "Harrison Grant's face was pretty much obliterated."

Birdie got up and began clearing the dishes, a sign she was troubled and needed to think. Although Izzy saw Rico most frequently, and Nell and Cass saw him occasionally, it was Birdie who sometimes found him sitting on a bench down near the pier, Birdie with whom he sometimes talked in a personal way. Sometimes touching on his sadness. His life. Never in a concrete way, but the sadness was there.

The others used the next few minutes to wipe their hands clean and pull out knitting needles with unfinished baby hats and sweaters attached. To refill wineglasses and fill water glasses. All the while imagining a marked-up flyer and a man they cared about.

Cass fumbled with a dropped stitch on the baby bonnet she was knitting, one that was now almost big enough to fit one of her fishermen. She finally broke the silence, bringing their thoughts out into the open room. "There has to be an explanation for this, Iz. One we're just not seeing. As grumpy as he is, Rico wouldn't kill anyone. And why? He'd have no reason."

"Cass is right," Nell said. "It's certainly not because a party in the murdered man's honor was too loud." She brought out the ridiculous because there was nothing else there, no motive for Rico violently pushing someone down deadly steps.

At least none they knew about.

"We like Rico," Cass said. "But we don't know much about him, except that he amassed a fortune and his wife left him. And he and the mayor don't much like each other."

"Rico hasn't exactly been nice to people," Izzy said. "There are probably others on his bad list."

"True. If he was the victim, the police would have their hands full deciding who *didn't* murder him," Cass said.

That lightened the mood slightly.

"I think Cass is right—we need to find out more about Rico," Birdie said. "About why he was upset that there was going to be a reception for a photographer close to his house. Disturbing his peace."

"I was going to check on Frodo, anyway," Izzy said. "Make sure the veterinarian was able to give him some antibiotics. Maybe I can talk to him again."

"In the meantime, there's probably no need to give the police a reason to disturb the man and take them away from finding the true murderer. They have their hands full. The flyer probably means nothing. Maybe Rico spilled ink on it, or the dog messed it up," Birdie said. But even Birdie knew that markers didn't spill ink and old inkwells were no longer household staples.

"It's the motive part of all this that puts up a roadblock,"

Nell said. "It's difficult to find one when no one in town knew the man."

"Except for Sam," Izzy said sadly.

Birdie sat up straight, her perfectly knit rows spread across her lap as she examined the square. She was knitting a supersoft blanket in shades of yellow, blue, and green. Sixteen squares, and each one bearing a heart, a flower, a bear. A quilt in knit form to warm a special baby.

But she was thinking about Izzy, not her blanket. And of Sam, her dear friends the Brewsters. And old Rico. A dear man under that thick layer of grumpiness. And all of them living beneath the cloud of murder. And perhaps living down the street or across town from the person who committed it.

"All right, then," she said in a tone they all recognized. Her get-down-to-business voice. "We often say, 'As far as I know,' when we're talking about this murder. So clearly, we don't know as much as we sometimes think we do. Not us. Not the town or the police. So we need to find out what we don't know." She took a sip of water and went on. "The person who is dead was a stranger to us. The murderer may not be. Considering that, 'not knowing' is a frightening thought."

Birdie realized she was close to lecturing, so she quickly got up and fetched the pot of coffee that was perking on a side shelf. Izzy brought mugs and cream to the table. Lecture or not, they were all mulling over Birdie's words.

Nell pulled out a soft ball of yarn. Long stretches of marled colors that blended into each other, self-striping in sea-glass colors and as soft as a baby's skin. But it was for Cass, not the baby. A warm cashmere shawl to wrap around her as she nursed sweet baby Brandley in the middle of the night.

Comfort, she thought, then looked up as Birdie offered her a mug of coffee and warned her not to let a drop of it touch the beautiful shawl.

Nell looked up, her fingers and needles still moving, magically casting on a row. "So Rico's name has to stay up there, a credible suspect, though we hate admitting that. He was yards away when Harrison was killed. We need to know if he knew him. We need to know more about a messed-up flyer. We need to know more about Rico."

"And why he might have had bad feelings about him," Izzy added.

They nodded.

"Rico has been such a recluse over these past years," Birdie said. "One of my mah-jongg friends lives near him. I wonder if she remembers anything about his early days in Sea Harbor. I shall ask." She closed her eyes for a second, as if writing herself a note inside her head. Then she opened them again and smiled. "Done."

Nell looked at Cass. "And then there's Deb, Eddie's friend. You saw her with Harrison that night."

"Up close. It was just the three of us talking for a few minutes. She liked him. And he didn't object to how close she was standing or to the come-hither dress she was wearing. The pregnant lady—that would be me—was soon no longer a part of their conversation. They walked off together, went somewhere, deep in conversation."

Deb. Nell began piecing some things together, thinking more clearly. She thought back to Eddie's face, his puppy-dog adoration of the beautiful young caretaker. And Deb's look when she met Harrison on Friday.

"Deb met Harrison hours before the reception," Nell said out loud. She explained about Harrison's arrival. "According to Eddie, Deb took his car that day, and she went off with Harrison. Showed him around town, apparently."

"Dear Eddie," Birdie said. "He has an oversized crush on the young lady."

"I wonder if Eddie saw them go off during the reception," Cass said. "He's a good kid, but he sometimes seems younger than his years. He has had a hard time finding his place in life, I think."

"He has some trouble controlling his temper, too." Nell told them about the gnome that Eddie said he had tripped over and broken while parking cars. "He was embarrassed when I came out to see what had happened, and made up a story. It wasn't an accidental trip. Shards of the poor gnome's head were on the other side of the drive, and his shattered hat was in another direction. Eddie threw it. And Eddie is very strong."

Strong enough to push a man down a flight of dangerous steps. Deadly steps.

And it had been at about the same time Jane was calling Harrison's name inside, inviting him up to the microphone to greet their guests.

Their imagination saw Deb and Harrison walking off, Eddie standing in the dark, along a line of cars, watching them.

Eddie. Rico.

"What about Deb? She's one strong lady," Izzy said. "Physically, I mean, though maybe the other way, too. I've seen her running, and a couple of times at the Y. She spent time with him that day, and later, at the party. What if she thought she and Harrison might have a go at it, and he rejected her? I'm pulling at straws here, but people have killed for less."

"It's enough to put her on the suspect list," Cass said.

There was something else about Deb that was niggling at Nell. And then she remembered. The odd visit to the Brewsters' to return Harrison's keys. The keys that should have been on Harrison's body and instead were found . . . But she couldn't remember where. She pushed the thought to the back of her head. She'd ask Jane.

"The thing is," Izzy said to no one in particular, "we know these people whom we're connecting to the murdered man. But we don't know *him*, except maybe through newspaper clippings and the little Sam knows from being in his class." She got up and refilled her coffee, then stood near Birdie's chair. "Who is he? Who *was* Harrison Grant? How can we suspect people of killing him if we don't know who he was?"

Her questions settled into each of them. They were good ones. How could they come up with motives for killing a man if they didn't know what he was like? Honest and up front? A liar? Compassionate? Or did he use people? All four of them had thought Harrison Grant a nice, gracious man when they met him. Sam had a different take on it. But where was the truth?

Birdie was looking into the fire, the light reflecting off her lined face. Listening and thinking. Her thoughts going in different directions.

Nell sat back in her chair, wrapping her fingers around her coffee mug. She looked at Izzy. "That's what's missing, Izzy. You're right. Birdie's right. We need to walk in his shoes. The problem is he didn't walk in Sea Harbor. At least not until Friday. That makes it more difficult."

Izzy's face brightened. "But he did, Aunt Nell."

"Of course he did," Birdie said, realizing where Izzy was going. "The affair that Liz Santos told us about. Harrison *was* in Sea Harbor before."

Nell scolded herself for not remembering it sooner. Somehow, the thought of a long-ago affair was easier to consider, to think about. Above all, it removed suspicion from people they cared about.

"But motive," Cass said. "Okay, Harrison had an affair with a married woman who lived around here. Then he moved on, leaving her behind. He comes back last week. She's still here and decides she finally has a chance to get revenge."

"Or the woman's husband?" Izzy said. "Maybe he knew. Maybe . . ."

They had seen enough movies to fill in the last "maybe" easily.

"The bigger problem is we don't know who the woman or her husband is," Cass said.

"But at least we can try to walk around Sea Harbor with Harrison. Where he might have walked those years ago, and then on Friday, when he went off with Deb," Birdie said. "Who knows where his fine Italian shoes will take us? Maybe we'll find everything we're looking for. Walks have always served us well."

And in the process, perhaps their friends and neighbors, people they cared deeply about, could go back to leading their decent lives.

Izzy was nodding, feeling more confident. "I think we've all been in hiding. A couple days ago we couldn't imagine anyone who would have wanted Harrison Grant dead. Now look." Izzy's hand swept the air, as if the names were all there, written across the empty space like something out of *The Hunger Games*. *Rico. Deb. Eddie Porter.* And now these unknown people, not yet with names. A jealous husband. A woman who had an affair . . .

And among suspects, there was one they latched on to most tightly, one they liked more than the others. Because it wasn't a proper name at all. It belonged to no one they knew. A nameless woman who had an affair. A long time ago. A motive, too. It was perfect.

Feeling some sort of direction, they allowed the knitting to take over, let thoughts of murder suspects settle, along with Nell's mushroom casserole and the wine. Talk turned to the baby shower that was taking a hold of Sea Harbor knitters. A welcome diversion. Life instead of death.

"Mae told me that even people who aren't coming to the shower are bringing in hats and sweaters and baby blankets for the hospital, the shelters," Birdie said. "It's good timing, according to Mae. Right before cold weather hits."

"Oh, Cass, I almost forgot," Izzy said, watching her friend

put aside her oversized bonnet. "Those needles I ordered for you are up on Mae's counter."

Birdie and Nell glanced over at the growing bonnet. New needles were sometimes an incentive to start over. Or so they hoped.

Cass abandoned her knitting, suspecting her baby hat was doomed. She went up the steps to the semi-dark room, found the needles, then yelped as she collided with something hiding in the shadows. She leaned down and rubbed her ankle, looking at her assailant. A plastic storage container. An old one, from what she could see. She leaned in closer, checking it out more carefully.

"What's this Iz?" she called out, but her words were lost in the music and crackling fire and conversation coming from below.

A piece of old wrapping tape held the lid in place. She turned on her phone flashlight and peered through the sides of the box. Newspaper articles?

More curious now, she used the flashlight to highlight items inside the box. As if drawn to the colors, the bright light focused on a small brochure, wedged up against the side of the box by the rest of the contents. An advertisement, it appeared, for a photography exhibit. She looked closer, straining to keep her balance. Was it Sam? In his youthful days? And then she saw the name on the brochure.

Cass picked up the box and balanced it against her round belly, then carried it down the steps to the knitting room.

The others looked up as she moved over to the fire. "I didn't mean to be a snoop, Iz. Well, yeah, maybe I did." She set the box down on the table. "What's this?"

Izzy looked at the box, then laughed. "It's nothing. No hidden treasure, Cass, sorry. It's Abby's smelly beach toys from last summer, probably wrapped in seaweed. Shelby Pickard found it in Sam's trunk and thought Sam might need it. I was about to throw it out. "

Cass directed her cell phone light on the box again, first the lid, and then moved it over the side. "I don't think your box has smelly toys in it, Iz. Take a closer look."

Izzy stood and looked.

She looked again.

And then she sat back down.

Hard.

Chapter 21

The name *Sam Perry* was scrawled on the side of the plastic storage box with a marker. Small and faint, but visible.

But what had caused Cass to bring the box down to the knitting room was someone else's name. The name on a brochure wedged against the side of the box. The advertising piece was small, pamphlet size, and looked to be old and smudged. But what was clearly visible on the advertising piece was the name of an acclaimed photographer, one who was now dead.

Izzy's first thought was to put the box in the car and take it home to Sam. It was taped shut, and his name was on it, written in a handwriting she didn't recognize. It was clearly intended for Sam.

Izzy fingered the dry strip of tape. It was brown and curled at one end, added to keep the old lid from popping up—not necessarily to keep people out. It was loose, about to fall apart. Izzy looked at the others, then back to the box.

She ripped off the tape and lifted the lid.

Dust wafted up from the box. The contents were messy and appeared to have been haphazardly tossed inside. It reminded

Izzy of a drawer in her house, filled with random things she didn't want to throw away but wasn't sure what to do with. Abby's baby cards, photos, sweet notes from friends.

At closer glance, she could see that some of the papers were actually photos, old photos, like the kind someone had developed in a dark room. Not clear and crisp, but like the ones Izzy remembered from a photography class she'd taken in high school.

But on top of the messy heap was a cream-colored envelope that stood out—a clean, crisp envelope of good quality, the kind used for wedding invitations or elegant events. It looked new, and printed on the envelope's left corner was an elegant logo and a name—*Harrison Grant Photography*. And in the center of it was a scribbled note:

Give to Sam Perry—old workshop photos, etc.

Izzy took it out and stared at it.

By now the coffee table had been cleared of mugs and knitting needles, and the box sat open and exposed, the envelope resting in Izzy's palm. It was sealed.

"Iz, where did Sam say he got this?" Cass asked, looking at the box.

Izzy tried to think back. "He never mentioned it. Shelby found it in his trunk. That's all I know. I didn't give it much thought. I figured Sam must have forgotten to take the beach toys out of his trunk."

"Sam had Harrison's things in his trunk on Friday," Nell said, thinking back to their arrival at Art Haven that morning. Sam had brought some things inside. She remembered seeing them in the foyer—photographic equipment, a briefcase, a suitcase and computer case. Deb Carpenter had shown up, too, and had helped carry things upstairs.

"Hmm," Cass said, reaching into the box and pulling out the brochure she'd seen on the side of the box earlier. "It's an old brochure of his." She tossed it back in the box.

The "his" no longer needed a name. Harrison Grant was in the center of their thoughts. And Sam wasn't far behind.

It was the envelope in Izzy's hand that drew their attention. It was clearly Grant's professional stationery—and intended for Sam. It had rested on a jumble of pictures, notebooks, some magazines, all seemingly thrown together. Random things.

Izzy carefully set the envelope aside. It had been sealed shut. Opening a sealed envelope with someone else's name on it still made her feel that the United States Post Office would be after her, and her face would soon appear on one of those wanted posters on the post office wall. It was definitely private.

Nell pulled out a photo near the top of the box. It was large and protected in a clear plastic sleeve. A black-and-white close-up of three men coming out of a coal mine, their faces hardened and blackened with dust, their eyes old. Stark and arresting. "This is beautiful. And awful."

Birdie took the photo from Nell and held it up. She slipped her glasses out of her hair and put them on. "This is quite amazing. Truly fine work. It reminds me of Dorothea Lange."

Izzy looked over at it. "Sam and I went to an exhibit of Lange's photographs at the MFA a few years ago. He admires her work greatly."

She took the photo and looked at it again, touched it gently with the tip of a finger, then turned it over. *Sam Perry* was written in pencil at the bottom of the print in his familiar scrawl. A number. And a date.

Izzy took a deep breath. "This is Sam's. Of course it is. He took this photo. It's amazing." She passed it around.

"Maybe the guy was cleaning house and found these," Cass said.

Nell nodded. "And wanted Sam to have them. A gracious gesture."

Izzy took the photo from Nell and looked at it again. "It's an amazing photo. But why do I think—"

"Think what?" Nell asked.

"I don't know. It's just that the workshop was a long time ago. Why would Grant have these photos? This seems odd to me."

"Well, even if it was a long time ago, it's a lovely photo to have," Birdie said. "I've been wanting to buy one of Sam's photographs for a long time. I shall remind him of that. Although, this kind of photo belongs in an exhibit somewhere, for people to stop and ponder, to learn from."

Izzy smiled. She set the photo aside and looked back into the box, fingering through it carefully. And wondering. Sam was a saver—had old college notes, silly things Izzy had given him before they got married. Why wouldn't he have saved a photo that was clearly above the norm, a quite incredible photo?

There were smaller photos in the box, too, all in black and white and covering all categories: clouds, single objects, faces. A photo of a park bench against a sunset. A rusted-out car in a junkyard, a bare tree against a stark sky, a child's face shown only in gray and black shadows. On the back of some of the photos was Sam's name, and on some he'd simply put SP, scrawled in pencil, along with the date and number, the class. A younger Sam. But already filled with talent.

"Sam will be so happy to have these," Nell said. "It was considerate of Harrison to bring them."

Izzy nodded. "But I wonder why Sam didn't keep these when the class ended? I still have some of my law journal articles, and I no longer practice law. Sam's still a photographer—and these are amazing photos."

She pulled a notebook out of the box. It was a black-and-white class book, the kind she'd used in college, even when most things were put on the computer. The workshop name was on the outside: The Art of Black-and-White Photography. Harrison's name was written below. She flipped through it. It was his instructor's class book, with the students' names listed alphabetically, each with her or his own page. Some with notes scribbled on the side. Izzy flipped through it until she found Sam's name. And there was a list of his photographs. Numbered and named and dated. She held it up for the others to see. "It's a trip back in time."

"We'll have to put everything back in the box so Sam can have the pleasure of going through the photos himself, seeing his beginnings from this side of the fence," Birdie said. "He will enjoy it. It's a fine gift from his teacher, and perhaps will be the thing that eliminates any uncomfortable feelings Sam has about the man."

Izzy continued to pull out photos. It was clear the box had been put together hurriedly and things had ended up in it by mistake. Random brochures and a scribbled reminder list of meetings, a restaurant take-out menu, notes to his assistant, and a heap of airline boarding passes with a rubber band around them. Izzy pushed those items aside, separating the trash from Sam's wonderful photos.

"What is that, Izzy?" Birdie asked, looking over Izzy's shoulder as she pulled out another photo.

"It's another shot of the mining town. I think Sam must have done a series." She handed the photo to Birdie.

"No, not the photo. There's something stuck on the back." A white edge stuck out beyond the photo. Birdie turned the photo over. It was a smaller photo, its face stuck to the back of the other, larger one and barely visible. Gently, trying not to tear it or damage the image, Birdie pried off the small photo and turned it over. It was a black-and-white image of a woman, mostly of her face.

"This doesn't look like Sam's work," Birdie said. She frowned and looked closer, then handed it to Izzy.

Izzy's eyes opened wide. "Wow. It's gorgeous. Well, *she's* gorgeous, at least as best you can tell from this old shot."

The photo was slightly smudged from being stuck to the other one, probably for a long time. But not enough that the subject's beauty didn't show through. They all agreed that it was the subject's eyes that filled the photo.

Birdie looked at it again. "This reminds me of portraits I saw in a book Archie Brandley carries in the bookstore. It's a collection of Harrison Grant's portraits. Archie said no one looked at the book before, but there's a recent demand. Some think it may be valuable now."

"There's money in murder, I guess," Cass said.

"Jane Brewster has a copy of that book. She said Grant did portraits early on and was actually quite good at it," Nell said. "Did you look through the one in the bookstore, Birdie?"

"I did. They were all portraits. What I'd call fireplace portraits. This one looks like it might be a sample, so to speak. Maybe a small shot taken to decide what the real portrait should be."

Izzy looked at the photograph more closely. "Sam used to do something like this when he was asked to photograph friends' families. If they were wanting a certain setting, he'd take a bunch of snaps, then study them until he decided the right angle, light, shadows, all those things we mortals don't think about. But he didn't take this one. It's too . . . too something. Formal, maybe?"

"I agree," Birdie said. "But it is lovely, even in this small, old, and smudged state. But it might well be the subject who's lovely. She has a Mona Lisa–type smile, which is captured even in this small print."

They all looked at the young woman. Her smile enigmatic. Her dark eyes large and arresting.

"Birdie and I are right. This isn't a photo Sam took," Izzy said, although the others weren't sure Izzy wished that or knew it to be true. But they agreed. It wasn't like anything else they had seen of Sam's. Even the photos he took of his own family captured movement and life, not a formal pose.

Izzy turned the photograph over. *HG* was written on the back in black. "We're right. It's Grant's. Funny that he initialed a little snapshot like this."

"I wonder why it's with the others," Nell asked.

Izzy looked at the back of the larger photo again. "I think it was a mistake. It was stuck to the other, probably from moisture and heat. And hidden there."

After going through more photos in the box, they determined Nell was right. Harrison had clearly put the box together in a rush. Most of the photos were Sam's, but an occasional misfit had been added in.

They were still rummaging through the plastic container when Izzy finally had a niggling feeling that they might be invading her husband's space, looking at a chapter of his life without him being there to have his own say. She lifted the lid from the floor.

"Hey, wait a minute. What are these?" Cass said. She pulled out several magazines. "Danny collects old *Mad* magazines. There might be a find in here."

She pulled out a couple more—*A New York Today* magazine with a photo of Harrison Grant on the cover, smiling, handsome. An article inside about celebrity photographers. Another was creased open to a page in *Vanity Fair* filled with party photos. The largest photo was of a group of well-known photographers at some event. Harrison was in the center, holding a glass plaque of some sort.

"It looks like a teaching award in his hand," Nell said, pointing to it. "If Sam is any example, he deserved it."

Then Cass pulled out a heavier publication, a British periodical of photography, yellowed slightly in spite of the fine quality of paper it was printed on.

On the cover was the winning photograph of the coveted International Photography Award for that year. A stark and arresting black-and-white photograph.

A familiar photograph simply titled *Three Men and a Mine*.

And inside was a picture of Harrison Grant accepting his fifty-thousand-dollar award and an article applauding his winning black-and-white photograph. And heralding the photographer's entry into the elite Society of International Photographers.

Chapter 22

"Did you know?" Izzy asked. She and Sam sat across from one another at the kitchen table.

Sam hesitated, his eyes on the photos spread on the table. The prestigious British journal with his photo—his *Three Men and a Mine*—on the cover looked up at him, as if daring him to answer.

He looked at Izzy. "Did I know that he used my photo as his own? Yes, I knew. Not right away. But yes."

"You never once mentioned it to me." Izzy knew her husband so well, everything about him. They had no secrets. But they did. She wouldn't let herself wonder if there were more.

"Harrison was smart," Sam said. "Everyone in the workshop signed agreements that our photos could be used as examples in his other workshops. Or brochures. That sort of thing. Or that's what we assumed it meant. Who looks at those agreements when you're feeling special just to be in this guy's class? He kept whatever he wanted, prints and negatives. Few objected. People thought somehow it might benefit their career.

"Harrison had a slow start to fame as compared to some

celebrity photographers. But he had the looks, the charisma, and the ambition. He wanted it so badly. We all could see that. If it meant using others to get there, he would do it."

"But you let it be," Izzy said. "Your photo won a prestigious competition. It put Harrison Grant on a career path he might never have traveled. And you never said a word. Not to anyone. At least that's what I'm assuming . . ." The thin layer of anger and hurt she felt at being left out of a piece of Sam's life was real, but mostly, it was a coating for a deeper, more painful emotion. Anger and hurt were easier to handle than worry for someone she loved deeply.

Sam drained the beer and set it down, his fingers squeezing the can. Izzy had come home early from the knitting group, had given sleeping Abby a kiss, and only then had put the storage box on the kitchen table. And emptied it.

Sam had looked at it as if he'd never seen it before, at first unsure of why the box elicited the expression he was seeing on his wife's face.

He vaguely remembered putting a box in the trunk of his car at the hotel when he'd picked up Grant on Friday. He must have missed it when unloading Grant's things at the house. He had had no idea his name was on it.

And now it was in his kitchen, on his table, disturbing the night.

"Your photograph is so amazing, Sam. So very special," Izzy looked down at the three miners. She touched the photo lightly. "Why? That's what I don't understand. Why did you let him get away with it?" The fact that fifty thousand dollars was also an issue was almost irrelevant to Izzy. Sam's art being credited to Harrison Grant was the crime. A terrible one.

"I was on my way to finding my own professional path when I found out what he'd done. I didn't pay much attention to awards and foreign publications back then. I was deep into my own career, doing the best job I could, trying to improve my techniques. Find my niche. And I did. I had taken that workshop from Grant in New York, through NYU. It was a great course, hard to get into. And I learned a lot. Afterward, I traveled around, doing a little Ansel Adams kind of photography in California, some Stieglitz other places. Experimenting. I did some portrait work in between to make money—most of us did—and then I moved on to doing 'art,' as some called it."

"And it is that," Izzy whispered, looking again at the photograph of the three miners.

Sam continued as if he hadn't heard. "But I always went back to what I loved. People. Life. What a person told me through his eyes and the wrinkles on his face. The tilt of his head. What he or she let me see."

Izzy retrieved another beer for Sam, some bedtime tea for herself. Trying to be patient. But always listening.

"Okay, Iz. You ask why. That's why. I was happy with my life. I was getting better and more experienced as a photographer, making contacts, getting some attention for my own work, and I didn't want to bring something like an unethical teacher into my life. I didn't want to go to a lawyer or to the news. I didn't want to be connected to a guy who had the morality of a slug. At least he did back then. So I exed the whole thing out of my life and moved on. And until Jane Brewster asked me to invite him to Sea Harbor, I rarely thought of it again. That's the truth."

Izzy knew it *was* the truth. Because it was so Sam. No matter that fifty thousand dollars would have been like five hundred thousand to him back then.

"So that's why you argued with Jane . . ."

"Actually, it wasn't the first thing I thought about when Jane brought Grant's name up. It was his treatment of women. He treated women like . . . like things. Things to be used and thrown away. There were two very good-looking women in our class, and that's how he treated them, using them. A lot of us students, men and women, could see it. Years after that, I'd hear rumors here and there that he had perfected his awful manner with women as he grew older. I didn't want him bringing that to Sea Harbor."

Izzy reached out and touched his hand. "Hey, you . . ."

Sam managed a smile. "I knew I'd win you back."

"Don't be so fast. You're not quite there yet."

Izzy pushed the sealed envelope his way. "A love letter?"

Sam tore it open and pulled out a folded piece of stationery. A check fell onto the table. Izzy knew before looking at it what it was. Sam did, too. *Fifty thousand dollars. Payable to Sam Perry.*

Izzy wondered which arts group or nonprofit Sam would sign the check over to. Using Harrison Grant's money on a pony for Abby or equipment for his sailboat or a fancy vacation for all of them wouldn't bring any pleasure to the Perry clan.

But her most fervent wish was that they wouldn't need it for legal fees.

And she wondered if that had yet dawned on Sam.

Sam unfolded the sheet of paper, revealed the message, written by the same hand that had scrawled his name on the outside of the envelope. It was a quote from Benjamin Franklin: "Never ruin an apology with an excuse."

And Harrison Grant hadn't.

They sat in the quiet for a while, absorbing and sorting and straightening out the evening as best they could—the discussion, and the contents of an old box. Old photos. An old life.

And a dead man's attempt, in maybe the best way he was able, to say he was sorry.

He hadn't asked for forgiveness. Maybe he would have eventually, but Izzy suspected not. And that was as it should be. She knew that forgiveness was really for the other person to do, the person harmed. Something the person wronged could do for himself—a way to release anger or resentment and make oneself move on.

And her Sam had done that a long, long time ago.

She stood and walked back to the oven, thinking of the Harrison Grant she had talked to at the reception. The man who seemed to have apologized to Sam from the dead. The man she'd liked, an interesting, thoughtful man. Not the man represented by the cover of the photography journal. A thief.

She warmed up two blueberry scones and brought them back to the table, along with the teapot and sugar bowl. A late-night snack. Something her aunt Nell would do. Scones and sugared tea. A spoonful of sugar to make the medicine go down . . .

She sat back down, stirred her tea, wondering who would bring it up first—the elephant still hanging out in their small kitchen.

Sam finally addressed it. "I know what this is doing to you, Iz. I know what the police will ask me tomorrow. They'll want to know why I didn't much like the guy."

Izzy nodded. Waited.

"And I'll tell them. Everything."

And you will be handing them a perfect motive for murder.

But neither of them would say that out loud.

"Were you planning on telling the police before we knew about this box? About the secrets inside?" She jabbed the journal's cover, which she was beginning to dislike intensely.

Sam looked at it and saw the mark she'd made on the journal with her fingernail. "I don't know," he said. "It was so long ago. It hasn't been a part of my life, not in any way."

Izzy looked at him hard.

"Well, okay," he said. "I would have told them, yes."

Izzy didn't ask if he'd have told her first.

Some things were best left unsaid.

Chapter 23

Nell had worried about Izzy going off alone that night, with a box of her husband's past sitting beside her in her car. But Izzy needed to be with Sam, not with her aunt. Not with Birdie and Cass.

And Nell needed Ben.

They sat together on the comfortable couch, Nell's soft robe and Ben's arm wrapped around her as she detailed the evening of knitting. The evening that had ended with more loose pieces of yarn than Cass's first attempt at a beanie.

Ben listened carefully. Both surprise and concern in his voice when he asked an occasional question. Sam's connection to Harrison Grant was revealing, and far more than that of a student in a workshop. But Ben was confident that what had happened years before would not come back to haunt a good man, a man who was like a son to them.

"Sam probably did know about Harrison's plagiarism," Ben said. "It would certainly explain his feelings about Harrison Grant, and his reluctance to let the man back into his life. Into any of our lives." And then he added what Nell was thinking.

"Sam Perry doesn't have a revengeful bone in his body. Everyone in Sea Harbor knows that. This will all work out."

Nell knew that Ben's words were more for her benefit and were fueled by Ben's own beliefs that our legal system was good, the best in the world, and that truth mattered.

All true, things Nell believed in with her whole heart and soul. Motive wasn't all that mattered in finding a murderer, although it could complicate lives while the other things were put in place. But suddenly the urgency to find that person had increased a hundredfold.

Danny picked up Cass from the yarn shop just as the others drove off. He was surprised they had ended earlier than usual. "That's a first," he said, starting his car and pulling away from the shop.

"Here's another first. We forgot about dessert. There's a full plate of brownies hidden somewhere in Izzy's back room."

Danny laughed, then looked over at his wife's sober face. "Hey, did something go wrong tonight? Or is it that you didn't get a brownie?"

Cass laughed lightly, unconvincingly.

Danny looked at Cass again, and then he checked in the rearview mirror and made an abrupt U-turn at the end of Harbor Road.

"The Ocean's Edge is open. Their brownie dessert is better than anything you knitters could have concocted. It's calling us, Cass."

The restaurant was a quiet place at this hour, the busiest dining crowd finished. Peaceful, with a beautiful view of the water to calm spirits. Danny knew that.

Cass looked over at Danny. His eyes were on the road; his face was relaxed. But there was a look behind those glasses, a look that she saw there when she knew he was thinking only of her. Not of how tired he was, or of a book that had a deadline soon. A look that warmed her inside and out, even on very cold days.

She touched his arm, squeezed it lightly, while silently giving thanks for the gazillionth time that this amazing man had let her talk him into marrying her.

Danny growled at her, his smile growing.

Don Wooten, owner of the Ocean's Edge, welcomed his friends, wrapping Cass in a hug as best he could, and wisely refraining from saying a word about her due date. Instead, he smiled broadly and said he had a wicked brownie delight with her name on it. "On the house," he added.

They sat at a favorite table near the lounge, tucked in a corner behind several ficus trees with tiny lights wrapped around them. They looked out windows and doors that stretched across the back of the restaurant and opened to the deck in warm weather and to the ocean beyond. In one direction the view spanned the water and moved up to the Ravenswood neighborhood and Birdie's estate, high on the hill.

Cass looked in that direction, then smiled as she thought of her close friend, home by now and probably already tucked into her high bed, dreaming of her Sonny. But were she standing in the den at that moment, she'd be able to aim her telescope and check out their dessert. In the other direction the inner harbor slowly curved around for as far as they could see. The shore bending past the fishing piers and the green space where Santa would arrive in his lobster boat in a couple of months, the Harbor Road shops and restaurants, the museum and the corner park near Izzy's shop, until it slowly wound along the sea to the Halloran Lobster Company offices and the Canary Cove Art Colony, and all the way to the cozy neighborhood beyond it, where she and Danny—and soon their baby—lived.

"A peaceful night," Cass said, settling back in her chair.

"But not so peaceful in Izzy's yarn shop tonight, I'm guessing." Danny turned his head, then motioned to the waitress for a beer and a pot of tea.

"Nope. Heavy discussion. But you brought it back, Brandley. Peace, I mean." For a few minutes, anyway. After the waitress brought the tea for Cass and a beer for Danny, the peace gave way to talk of a plastic box containing a piece of their friend Sam Perry's life.

After Cass had told Danny about the award-winning photo that had been stolen from Sam—which was how Cass thought of it—and the photo of a mysterious gorgeous woman, the waitress brought to their table a mountain of chocolate: a thick, moist brownie covered with caramel fudge sauce, strawberries, and mounds of whipped cream. Two spoons were set beside the gigantic crystal bowl.

Danny hadn't said much but had listened intently as he always did, his mind absorbing, thinking things through. "How was Izzy when she left the shop?"

"Anxious to see Sam. Needing to see Sam."

Danny nodded. "Sam knew what Harrison did."

Danny wasn't asking, Cass knew. And Sam hadn't shared this truth with him. But Danny was one of Sam's closest friends, and he knew the way Sam's mind worked, in a way that maybe even Izzy didn't. It always amazed Cass how perceptive her husband was. She had decided years before never to throw the man a surprise party. He would know about it before the planning ever began. And he wouldn't like it.

"We all suspected that he knew, I think. Even Izzy. Though no one said it out loud. Mostly because we wished he hadn't known. There are way too many questions for him to answer if he'd known."

"Sam can answer questions. What you were really worried

about is that if he knew about the plagiarism, there would be a giant motive for murder jumping right out of that box."

"Something like that." Telling Danny that Sam could no more have killed the photographer than sung *Aida* was meaningless. Danny knew that. And as she looked over at his intelligent eyes, knowing his mind was processing everything they'd talked about, she had a sudden realization that none of what they'd talked about surprised Danny in the way it had all of them. Maybe it came from living in the world of fiction. Or maybe it was just Danny. Calmly taking it all in. Then making sense out of it.

Danny picked up his spoon and took a huge mouthful of the brownie dessert.

"It's going to melt, Cass," he said.

Cass nodded.

And picked up her spoon.

A vibration from her phone interrupted her first spoonful of ice cream. She dug in her purse, while Danny continued making a dent in the rich mountain of chocolate and cream. Cass gave him a look, then looked down at the text message.

Where is she?

That was it. Cass frowned. No name, but she knew whom it was from. No employee escaped Cass's contact list, much to their chagrin.

She texted Marco Costa back.

I don't know, Marco.

She slipped her phone back into her purse and vied with Danny for the next scoop. She briefly wondered where Elena could be. She didn't drive, and the night was pleasant enough. She loved to walk along the water, she'd told Cass. And sometimes into town. But she was pregnant. And Marco would worry if he didn't know where she was, just like Danny would.

The dessert soon worked its magic, and Danny called for the

check. "You're bushed, Cass. I'm getting you home before you fall asleep on me."

He paid the check and helped Cass into her coat. "I'll bring the car around. Don't run off on me."

Cass picked up her purse and walked along the window side of the restaurant, watching the tide move in, the waves grow, light from the moon catching the frothy caps that crashed against the granite wall. *Awesome*, she said silently, opening herself to the calm that the sea brought to her. It was especially welcome tonight.

Cass joked with her mother sometimes that the ocean was her church, that watching the tides, the movement of the water, sinking into the simple sounds of the sea, was a spiritual experience for her. Calming.

"I read somewhere that I have a blue mind," she'd told Mary Halloran.

"A blue mind is a mindful one, a spiritual one," her mother had said.

Cass had only scanned the article and wasn't sure what it meant, just that it had felt right to her. But her mother had walked off with a pleased smile on her face.

She turned away from the windows now, looked back at the dining area. A few tables were being served dessert; a few people were in the lounge, near the water, listening to a string trio. Cass made her way toward the entrance, her thoughts turning back to the day, to knitting, to friends.

She waved at a waiter who lived down the street from her, then paused as she heard a familiar voice coming from one of the booths tucked behind a row of potted plants. She looked over,

Harmony Fairchild was resting her head against the high-backed booth, a smile on her face, as a waiter refilled her wineglass. A half-eaten piece of pie sat on the table in front of her. It wasn't until the waiter moved away that Cass was able to see the yoga teacher's companion.

Elena Costa was nearly dwarfed by the large red-leather booth, but her smile matched its size.

Cass stood for a minute, watching the two women, considering walking over to say hello. But they were having a good time. *Like friends*—a thought she had had in the yoga studio, too. She stood to the side as several people walked by. Then moved a step closer and stood in the shadow of one of the plants.

Friendship . . . yet it didn't look exactly like that. Something was slightly off. She certainly knew from her own life that the least important things in friendship were age and age differences. That wasn't it. It was something she couldn't put her finger on. Harmony seemed a bit more solicitous, maybe.

But whatever the *it* was, it wasn't preventing them from enjoying being together tonight, and that was nice to see.

A waitress hovered near their booth, a coffeepot in her hands. Harmony smiled up at her. A pleasant, happy look on her face.

As Cass watched, Harmony took out her camera and handed it to the waitress. Then she moved around to the other side of the table and sat down next to Elena. The waitress took a photo of the two women.

A wave from the restaurant owner pulled Cass's attention away. Don Wooten nodded toward the front door, beyond which she could see Danny waiting in the car. She glanced once more at the two women in the booth. Harmony had moved back to her side of the booth and was leaning in to hear something Elena was saying. They looked comfortable and happy in each other's company.

She remembered Marco's text. For one minute she considered answering it. No, less than a minute. She was not about to insert herself in Marco and Elena's life. Not in that way, anyway.

Then she turned away and hurried outside to a waiting Danny. To home. And to bed, with Danny beside her, helping her feel the world would soon be back on its axis. It had to be. Didn't the world know it needed to welcome a new baby Brandley into its fold?

Chapter 24

Sam's meeting at the police station wasn't until midmorning, and no, he didn't want Izzy to go with him. When he'd been called to the principal's office in high school, he'd always gone alone. No need to change the pattern now.

But he did volunteer to get Abby to preschool so Izzy could get in an early morning run. "A run would be good today," he said to her.

Sam was right. She needed that time to be alone, to let her head clear and her emotions reset.

By the time she and Sam had finally gone to bed the night before, Izzy had felt some sense of peace and calm. Sam had held her close and made her feel that way, convincing her he was fine. And she and Abby were fine, too. Everyone they loved and cared about was fine. Things would be fine.

But along with being calm, Izzy's resolve had deepened into a force, like a seed inside her, growing mightily. Everyone needed a clean bill of health, and that would happen only when Harrison Grant, whoever he was, was out of their lives for good. *And it would be soon*, she had promised herself.

She and Sam had talked for a long time, trying to put themselves in Harrison Grant's head. Wondering who he was when he came back to Sea Harbor, carrying a box from years ago that revealed a dishonorable man. Was he the same man that Sam had known those years ago?

Sam had said he and Harrison hadn't talked much on the short drive from the Gloucester hotel. But Grant had said he'd like some time with Sam while he was in Sea Harbor. Maybe during the week to follow. There were some things he'd like to talk to him about.

At the time, Sam had told Izzy he had thought little of the comment. It could have simply been a polite gesture, since they'd known each other way back when. Or maybe it had had something to do with photography, with the lecture series. And if it, whatever *it* was, had been something that would be helpful to Jane and Ham and Canary Cove, Sam would have helped as best he could.

But in hindsight, both Izzy and Sam suspected those weren't the issues Grant wanted to talk about. A plastic storage box that held the past had changed Sam's perspective.

Izzy went alone on her run, leaving Red behind, her head filled with thoughts of a long-ago affair, a jealous Eddie Porter. A beautiful young woman rejected? Or an old man who had eliminated Harrison Grant's face from a brochure? Or from his life . . . ?

But once she hit the smooth sand on the beach, she settled into her run and tugged the thoughts from her head, then threw them out to the ocean breeze, where they were caught and pulled apart like tissue. Until they disappeared.

She picked up her speed, enjoying the nearly empty beach. She felt the rush of the run, her body and spirit lifted. A dozen gulls foraging for food along the water's edge caught her attention; then she looked over at the rise in the road that led to the mansions on the hill. She half expected to see Rico and Frodo lumbering toward her. Although she wasn't sure what she would say if she met them. She and Sam had agreed that it would be better not to mention the flyer. It didn't mean much all by itself. And they hadn't been able to come up with any good that would come from it, at least not now. *But an explanation would be nice*, Izzy had thought.

Thoughts of Rico and Frodo made her slow down near the end of the sand, where the ocean's edge curved around.

She wasn't ready yet to run around that bend, along the narrow beach and the many hillside steps that led up to the beautiful cliffside homes. She wasn't ready to come face-to-face with images of a dead body staring up at the blue sky.

Eventually, she would, but not today.

She looked up the road again and thought again about Rico and her resolve the night before to talk to him again. She thought of Frodo, too. Had his wound healed? Had Rico done what the veterinarian recommended? And then she wondered if he had even followed through and called the veterinarian.

With that thought in mind, and without a real plan except to avoid the place where she had so recently found a dead body, Izzy started running again, a slow gait that took her away from the beach. She headed up the road to the Cliffside neighborhood.

She had no idea if Rico would let her in, but somehow it didn't matter. When she made it to his driveway, she stopped, leaned down, her hands on her knees, and took deep breaths. She looked up at the house for signs of life but realized that was foolish. Rico's house never changed, day or night, summer or winter. It always looked empty. And sad.

The slight tap of a horn behind her caused her to back to one side of the drive. She smiled in surprise at Tegan Johnson, the new veterinarian in town. Tegan was a pretty, cheerful woman and had already made a name for herself in Sea Harbor. She got out of the car and greeted Izzy warmly.

"Thanks for the new client recommendation, Izzy. Frodo is a sweet dog."

Izzy laughed. "I noticed you didn't say that about Frodo's master."

Tegan chuckled. "Rico's an interesting man. Reminds me of my grandpa. But he truly loves Frodo, and in my book, that means there's good behind that crusty exterior. And by the way, he said some nice things about you."

"No he didn't," Izzy laughed.

Tegan smiled. "Well, maybe it was about your dog, Red. But truly, he was grateful, in a slightly belligerent way, that you suggested I come to see Frodo. You were correct that the wound might well have gotten infected. He said you liked Frodo. And the tone in his voice told me that meant you were okay. He even mentioned your friends, especially Birdie Favazza."

"I know Rico likes me underneath it all. And my friends, too. It's just that these past few days he's been under some kind of pressure. Maybe it's Frodo." But Izzy didn't really think that Frodo was the cause of it. Nor did she want to talk about it with his dog's vet. Rico had been unusually bothered days before Frodo met up with the motorcycle.

The veterinarian began walking toward the front door, and Izzy followed.

"I was coming over to check on Frodo myself," Izzy said. "I think I'll have a better chance of getting past the front door if I'm with you."

Tegan nodded and knocked on the door.

Much to Izzy's amazement, it opened an inch on the first knock. "A miracle," Izzy whispered. "He probably didn't see me through the side window."

Then the door opened wider. Rico Silva stood in the space,

his feet firmly planted at the door. He looked at Tegan, then at Izzy, then back again. Then he nodded and, with a wave of his hand, ushered both women inside.

Frodo was waiting for them, too. In the kitchen, on his bed, his tail wagging so hard that clouds of dust floated up into the air.

It took just a few minutes for Izzy to greet Frodo and see that he was doing better and would soon be joining Red on the beach. She offered Rico a smile to that effect, and he nodded again. *In an almost pleasant way*, she thought. *Relieved* was probably closer to the truth. His dog seemed to be his life these days.

She stepped back, and the older man took his place right behind Tegan, who was now crouched down beside Frodo, speaking softly to the dog. Rico watched the veterinarian's every movement, her fingers gently probing, then rubbing a salve around the shaved wound. Rico nodded as Tegan worked, as if giving her permission.

"Let's see how he does outside," she said to Rico, then looked over at Izzy. "I forgot some sample ointments in my car. I wanted to leave them with Rico. Could you please get them? You might have to rummage through a bag in the back. They have Frodo's name on them."

Izzy dashed out to Tegan's car and found the medicine almost immediately, then quickly came back inside. From the foyer she heard Tegan and Rico talking and then the kitchen door opening and closing as they took Frodo outside for a short walk around the yard.

Izzy closed the front door softly and lingered in the entry, looking around more carefully this time. The foyer was round, with a sweeping staircase curving up and up, until she couldn't see it anymore. The walls were painted a warm yellow, and the dark hardwood floor was softened by a round rug of rich rusts, light greens, and yellows. The decor looked like it had been influenced by an interior designer with a definite feminine touch, but the mood had probably been dictated by the owner, which surprised Izzy. The colors were rich but warming, and the area was cozy in spite of its size and without the formal feeling of large homes like this. She tried, and failed, to imagine Rico planning the decorations.

Then she remembered that Rico wasn't always alone in the big house. A woman had lived in it with him.

Several rooms spun off from the foyer, one with glass panes in the door revealing a large dining-room table in the middle of a lovely room. A Persian rug lay on the floor, and a chandelier hung from the tall molded ceiling. Much to Izzy's surprise, the table was set with porcelain dishes and silver, as if it had been prepared for a dinner party. The table and the plates were covered with a layer of dust; the silver nearly black with tarnish.

On the other side of the hallway, the double doors were solid, intricately carved. One was open a crack, as if the wind might have blown it open.

Izzy walked over to it and opened the door an inch more. And then another.

And then she tiptoed into a perfect room.

It was beautifully decorated, with fine wooden chairs upholstered in soft sea-green and yellow fabric. The walls held paintings, watercolors of the sea. Izzy recognized several well-known watercolorists and for a moment stood in awe, as if in a museum. But a comfortable one, inviting.

A curved sofa, big enough for a whole family, faced the focal spot in the room. A wall of warm textured stone, with a unique fireplace in the center. Izzy could almost imagine it lit, warming the room, people laughing and talking in front of it, children running around.

And then she looked above it, at a large portrait of a woman, amazing in its detail.

She stood still on the soft carpet, stunned.

The woman was beautiful. Exquisite, really. The portrait was perfect, the lighting exact and highlighting high cheekbones, the tilt of her chin. The subject was probably sitting on a chair when the photo was taken, but the camera's lens had focused on the waist up, filling the ebony and gold frame fully.

Izzy examined the woman's expression. It was controlled. Her dark eyes looking directly at the camera. Almost as if speaking to it, caressing it.

Izzy's breath caught tightly in her chest, her fingers squeezing the medicine tubes in her hand.

Rico's wife.

It had to be. Who else would be holding court over this amazing fireplace and room in this huge home? Izzy had never tried to picture the wife who had run off, leaving Rico alone in their mansion. But if she had, she suspected it wouldn't be this woman.

It had happened over twenty years ago, people said. What was Rico like back then, when he had a wife? And this woman . . . What was she like *now*? Where was she?

And why had she left this amazing place?

Izzy shivered, suddenly feeling like she was in the middle of a Daphne du Maurier novel. And Mrs. Danvers was about to walk in on her and expel her from Manderley.

She took a step closer to the portrait, then stepped back again, trying to put the woman over the fireplace into proper perspective. Trying to fit her into Rico Silva's life.

Noises coming from the back of the house startled her. And then came the sound of Tegan's voice calling her name.

She spun around and headed toward the door. Then looked back once at the portrait, feeling its eyes on her, saying something.

Izzy looked into them, wondering,

Who are you? Where have we met before, Mrs. Silva? Somewhere. Someplace.

But before an answer came, Tegan's voice drew Izzy out of the room. She closed the door softly behind her and hurried down the hall.

Chapter 25

Nell stepped out of the shower to find her phone vibrating with a voice message, along with nearly vibrating words from Izzy, asking if she'd be out shopping for Friday night's dinner. If so, could she stop by the shop? And if not, could she stop by the shop, anyway? She had a morning class first thing but would be there most of the day.

Nell sent back a quick reply. **Of course. I'll come by late morning.**

She would have stopped in no matter what her schedule was like. Izzy and Sam had had a lot to unravel the night before. And she'd be there to listen, to be a shoulder, if that's what Izzy needed. Nell loved Sam, too.

Ben had left the house early that morning, leaving Nell a note on the kitchen counter saying he'd pick up cheese and wine for tonight. Nell answered him with a text.

Sounds good. But where are you?

His reply was quick.

Early meeting, then coffee with Sam. Didn't want to wake you.

Of course. She should have known Ben would touch base with Sam. See if he could help. Offer advice.

It would be an unpleasant morning for Sam, and Ben would lessen the discomfort. Others often referred to Ben and Sam's relationship as similar to that of a father and son, but in fact, they had their own special kind of bond. A hybrid, and unique in some ways. But whatever it was, it filled a void in both men, a sturdy relationship, and loving to the core.

After coffee and a quick check of kitchen staples, Nell tapped her to-do list into her phone and headed out to Art Haven to meet with Jane. She'd promised to finally pick up the copper and steel wind spinner that Ben had purchased the night of the reception. Nell knew it was taking up space that might be needed for other art.

The spinner was shaped like a flower, Ben had said, perfect for their garden.

Nell had refrained from reminding Ben that their garden was small and that they already had two of Jane's small statues guarding it. The truth was, it wouldn't have mattered. Ben loved Canary Cove art in all shapes and forms, and he loved supporting the artists who worked so passionately at their artistry. Ben joked that one day there'd be no room in their house left for them, that they'd move into a condo and plant a sign in their front yard that read CANARY COVE MUSEUM. COME IN. ENJOY.

Ben joked, but his wife suspected that might be exactly what would someday happen.

Jane had coffee on in the large kitchen when Nell arrived. And a change of plans regarding the wind spinner.

She motioned for Nell to join her at the long chef's table. It made Nell feel like she was chatting with staff in the *Downton Abbey* kitchen.

Sunshine poured in the many windows along the back, making the kitchen cheery and hospitable.

"The sculpture Ben bought is heavier than it looks," Jane said. "So I asked Eddie Porter and his friend to transport it to your backyard. They're doing some work at Rico's and will be by shortly."

"That's perfect," Nell said, relieved she wouldn't be running errands with it in her CR-V. And that Ben wouldn't be breaking his back trying to get it in the perfect spot. "What is Eddie doing at Rico's?"

"Some odd jobs. I'm not sure of the whole story but somehow the mayor was involved." She laughed.

Nell remembered the story and laughed along with Jane. "It's small town living at its finest."

"But, anyway, I wanted you to be here when they pick it up," Jane said, pouring Nell a cup of coffee. "It's not that I don't trust Eddie, but he's been distracted lately."

"Because of his friend?"

Jane smiled. "Deb, yes. You caught that vibe, too? But it's also the investigation. The fact that they were both here that day and both had contact with Grant. Deb, especially, seems even more remote than usual."

"Is she around? I remember her saying she didn't have class on Friday."

"She is."

Nell glanced at a brass ring of keys sitting on the kitchen table. "Have you asked her about the keys? Where they found them? It was a little vague."

A shadow behind them drew their attention away from the keys and to the small butler's pantry off the kitchen. Deb Carpenter stood in the doorway, her forehead and running gear damp, her cheeks red.

Nell wasn't sure if the flush was from hearing them talking about her or from the exertion. But either way, Deb looked prepared to handle it.

"What would you like to know about the keys?" she asked, walking into the kitchen.

"These keys were on Harrison Grant's key chain," Jane said.

Her voice was calm, not accusatory. "But they weren't found on his body. Yet you and Eddie—"

"Had them," Deb finished. "Or at least I had them. Poor insecure Eddie went through my purse and found them. And then he insisted on taking them over to your house, which made little sense to me. But I figured out what he was thinking. That it would give him some leverage over me, knowing where he found the keys and not telling you or the police. Like maybe I would owe him something. He's sweet but so young."

Part of the explanation actually made sense to Nell. Eddie *was* so young, emotionally far younger than Deb. And he was probably in love with her. He thought she might be guilty of something, and keeping her secret might stand him in good stead with her.

"What had you planned to do with the room keys?" Jane asked.

"Before or after Grant was murdered?" she asked. Then she answered her own question as if it should have been obvious to Jane. "After I found out what happened to him, I was going to leave them in his suite. The police, you, everyone would have assumed he forgot them there. And he wouldn't be around to ask. I don't need the distraction of being mixed up in this. My classes are hard this semester."

Nell and Jane looked at each other. Deb spoke as calmly and matter-of-factly as if she were telling them she'd made eggs for breakfast.

"All right, then," Jane said. "What were you going to do with them *before* he was murdered? Why did you have them?"

Jane was trying to match the mundane tone Deb had set, although Nell could tell she was becoming frustrated with the young woman. Deb's cushy job at Art Haven might be short lived. Nell picked up her coffee mug, listening to the conversation and feeling a kind of generation gap she rarely felt with people of any age. But having a nonchalant discussion about a dead man and a murder with this young woman bordered on surreal.

Deb wiped her forehead with the edge of a towel looped around her neck. "I had them because Harrison Grant unhooked them from his belt and gave them to me. I needed to study, and he said I could use his suite if it was quieter, since it was at the front of the house, away from the partyers. He said he'd meet me there later." Her brows lifted, as if the questions seemed foolish to her, but were they now satisfied?

Jane took a deep breath as Deb started to walk toward the refrigerator. She stopped her with another question, her voice no longer as quiet. "And why was that? Why were you meeting him later?"

Deb stopped and faced Jane. "The man had a terrible back problem. Didn't you notice? I could tell by the way he walked. Photographers often have back problems, though that might not have been the cause of his. I don't know. But in any case, I know what to do about things like that. It's one of the things I'm learning in my program. So I told him I'd meet him after the reception and massage the muscles to make it feel better."

A ruckus in the hallway brought Eddie Porter into the kitchen. He was followed by a large, swarthy man in jeans and a puffy vest, slightly older than Eddie.

Eddie glanced at Deb in surprise, as if she didn't quite fit in the same room with Nell and Jane. Then he gave her a tenuous smile.

Deb shrugged, answering with a half smile, then took a bottle of water from the refrigerator. She waved good-bye to anyone in the room who happened to be looking at her—which was everyone—and headed through the butler's pantry to the back staircase.

Jane looked over at the boys and broke the silence left in Deb's wake. "Muffins?" she asked with a smile, motioning toward a box on the counter.

Eddie moved toward the muffins.

"It's Marco, right?" Nell asked, looking at the muscular man.

"Right. Hey, we've met. I remember," Marco said. "You've been down to the wharf a few times hanging with my cool boss. Ms. Endicott, right?"

"Nell works fine, Marco." She introduced him to Jane, along with the fact that Marco's wife, Elena, was pregnant—and lovely—and was taking yoga with Cass. "We're teaching her to knit," Nell added.

"Man, Elena is something, right?" Marco said. "She's the most beautiful woman in the whole world." In that moment, the big, robust fisherman looked like a young boy after meeting his first princess.

Beside him, Eddie gave a laugh, which was muffled by a mouthful of muffin.

"Hey, it's true, Porter. You know that. Elena is great." He punched Eddie's shoulder playfully, then looked at Jane and Nell and explained that Elena was a great cook, too. Farm food, the kind that was good for you. And she could garden good as a farmer. And she was a great wife. Also, the smartest woman he'd ever met. "She's everything. And now she's a yoga expert, too. Can you believe it? She wants me to go and do those things they do. She says it will make me calm. Her instructor is wicked good, she says. Kinda weird, I think. I mean, who would want to spend all her time doing that? But Elena, I mean, she can do about anything, anywhere."

Nell was smiling, knowing that if she or Jane didn't break into the conversation soon, Marco was likely to tell them things about Elena that his wife might prefer remained private. But she was happy to hear the accolades and see the love that filled his tanned face when he talked about his wife. She suspected Cass, as his boss, didn't hear those things and worried about the kind of father Marco would make. *He'd be just fine*, Nell thought. A tough guy who would turn into a marshmallow when he held his new baby in his arms.

"So you two are friends?" she asked, looking at Eddie.

Marco answered. "Played football in high school. Best team that school ever had. Eddie was a shrimp, younger than me, but we pumped him up. Look at him now. He's one strong dude, right, Ed?"

Eddie shrugged.

Thinking Marco the leader of the duo and the one with the truck, Jane asked if he'd follow her to the patio area so she could show him the sculpture and explain what she needed.

Left alone with Eddie, Nell suggested he sit down with her for a minute. There were plenty of muffins left, and there was something she wanted to talk to him about.

Eddie sat and slumped down in the chair. He stretched his legs out beneath the table, then finally looked up at Nell. "It's about Deb."

"Well, I don't know if it's about Deb. It's more about you, I think."

"I didn't do anything, Nell."

"I don't think you did. But I know how angry you were last Friday night—"

Eddie interrupted. "When she went off with him, yah. She'd done it earlier in the day, too. Just took my car keys and left. And that night . . . I mean, did you see the way she was dressed? And then they went off again. I was parking cars, and I saw them come out from the back patio, where the crowds were, then walk down the drive toward the street." Eddie stopped speaking long enough to claim another muffin.

"I was mad. Really mad. I know, I get mad too easily. My brother, my ma, they all tell me that. But Deb, she just brings that out in me. It shoulda been me, not Grant, she was walking off with. We were okay until he came along."

Nell listened carefully.

"But I didn't kill the guy, if that's what you're thinking," Eddie said vehemently. "If I killed people, maybe I would have. But all I killed was that stupid-looking gnome." He looked down at his hands, played with his fingers. "And yah, I shouldn't have done it."

"Sometimes anger gets the best of us, Eddie, and you have to let it out. Better a gnome than some other ways. But deep breaths and a long run or swim might be another choice. A chance to save the gnomes of the world."

Eddie managed a half smile. "Sure. I was still mad, even after the guy was killed. Deb was acting weird. So when I found the keys, I hung on to them. I knew it would look bad for her if the police knew she had them."

Nell sat back, drank her coffee, letting Eddie get it out.

"You know, it was like I was being her protector."

"Did you see Deb again that night, the night of the murder?" she finally asked.

Eddie said that he had. "They weren't gone long. Ten minutes maybe. When they came back, Grant was sort of nice, actually. Kind of tipped his head that way he did, thanked Deb, though I didn't know for what. 'Course, I imagined all sorts of things. But I think it was what she told me, that she was going to loosen his muscles, make his back feel better or something. I know she had done it for other people. Even me once. She's learning all about those things. I had to stay with the cars, but she said she'd had enough walking around and looking fancy, so she was heading upstairs to get in her sweats and study."

"Did she say where she and Harrison had been?"

"Just that he had wanted to know about the houses on the block. Who lived in them. Which ones. Like maybe he wanted to buy one or something, she thought, and he'd go back later."

"And where did Harrison go after Deb went upstairs?"

"I don't know. He stood with me for a minute, looking around. Checking his watch. Like he was checking the time or looking for someone? But I didn't see anyone. Then I got busy with a couple cars coming in, and I called to Marco to help. We were parking them down the road, in an empty lot. I suppose he went back out to the patio or wherever. Or was still on the driveway, by the garage maybe. And then, I guess, he disappeared."

"Do you believe Deb about the keys?"

Eddie started to laugh. Then he said, "Believe her? Deb doesn't know how to lie. It's like a sickness with her. She even does hard truths, like, I'd say, 'Hey, did you like that poem I wrote you?' and she says, 'No. It's silly.' Or 'Did you like dinner with my family?' And she says, 'No, your mom sucks as a cook.' Sometimes I wish she would lie."

Nell looked over at him. "You wish she would lie? Why, Eddie?"

He took a long breath, then released it slowly. "Because it'd hurt a lot less. You know?"

Chapter 26

Nell had stayed longer than she intended to. It was already late morning. She texted Izzy that she was still coming by the shop but was meeting Birdie at Garozzo's deli first. Could she bring her anything?

Garozzo's was all Izzy needed to hear. It was an anxious day. The class had been chaotic, she told Nell. She'd meet them there. A Garozzo special—even a Harry hug—would calm her down.

Birdie and Izzy were already there when Nell arrived. They were standing in the deli section, talking to Harry, the beefy owner, who was touting the merits of a soup they were featuring that day. "*Stracciatella*," he was saying, "the perfect remedy when you're a little achy, a little grumpy. It's like a warm blanket. Only tastes better."

"You think we're grumpy, Harry?" Birdie said, smiling up at her old friend.

Harry's guffaw filled the deli section and startled some folks waiting in line for take-out sandwiches. "Bernadette, my sweet, you are always a ray of sunshine. But the whole town is grumpy.

And it will be until this"—Harry covered his mouth, as if muffling the words—"*murder* is solved. But this egg soup will help. You will love it. Light and delicious, just like my mama's, only with my special broth. Perfect egg drops, a handful of spinach strips, a little fresh Parmesan." He pinched his fingers together and squeezed his eyes closed, as if he were tasting the soup in the air.

Harry finally stopped when he realized Nell was standing behind him, listening. He swiveled his large body, then embraced her fully.

"I will take exactly whatever you're describing, Harry. But I would prefer it at a table and in a bowl." Nell smiled.

Harry grabbed menus out of habit and led his ladies through the dining area and to the table he had labeled as their own. The table was big enough for six, but Harry put them there no matter if it was just Birdie who had come in to read the paper and have a cup of tea or the four of them, along with bags and packages. "A little bit of privacy," he would say, "for those deep conversations you ladies have."

The women loved the table for its wide window, which often hosted gulls on the ledge outside and offered views of sailboats and fishing trawlers going out to sea. Today there was a sunny blue sky and a calm sea to enjoy. And the truth was, they *did* like the privacy, even when their conversations weren't deep or private. Talk in Garozzo's deli sometimes spread like melted butter through the town, becoming rich fodder for the day's rumor mill. With a murder investigation going on, privacy was preferable.

Nell sat across from Izzy, waited a moment for Harry to disappear, and then asked her about Sam.

Although it had taken Izzy and Sam hours to sort through the box and the emotions it had dredged up, she was able to relate it to her friends in minutes. Birdie and Nell could easily fill in any gaps that occurred.

"Sam is a rock," Izzy said finally. She wrapped her fingers around a cup of honey-lemon tea Harry had set in front of each of them. "He has a way of calming me before I become anxious."

Birdie and Nell were relieved. It had been emotional in the knitting room the night before, as pieces of Sam's past were laid out on the table. They could only imagine how it had been for the two of them.

"But something urgent is on your mind," Nell said. "I could tell from your message."

"It's not about Sam. It's about Rico."

Nell and Birdie waited.

"Well, not Rico, really. It's about a portrait I saw in his house, hanging above his fireplace." She explained briefly about how she'd ended up in his living room. "The woman in the picture is absolutely amazing, bigger than life. It must be his wife."

"His wife," Birdie said slowly. "Oh my. It's been so many years."

"It's like a shrine, Birdie. The room is spacious and very beautiful, but it's clearly not used. It's like a beautiful church that no one ever goes into, but it still holds something sacred."

"Imagine living all these years with a memory. With a reminder of a painful loss."

"Living with a wife who disappeared would be difficult," Birdie said. She had done her own homework on Rico's wife, and she filled them in on what she knew. "I had breakfast with a lady in my mah-jongg group who lives down the street from Rico. She remembers his wife. They shared a housekeeper. His wife's name was Martina. She was young and very beautiful. Years younger than Rico."

"I'm sure there were rumors about that, too. Why they married, I mean," Izzy said.

"Of course. It was speculation, but Rico was very rich. And she was very beautiful. So people talk, no matter what the truth might be."

"How long were they married?" Izzy asked.

"According to my friend, they may still be married. No one knows that. But they were here together for a couple years before she left. Maybe even three."

"Did she know how they met?" Izzy asked.

"No. But she thought Martina waitressed at one of the bars around here. Maybe Jake Risso's. That was frowned upon by some of the neighbors."

"Jake's," Nell repeated. "That's interesting. I wonder what Jake remembers about the whole thing."

"It was a while ago, but I wondered that, too," Birdie said. "My friend says memories are dim not just because it was a long time ago but because people didn't know either of them well. But they were aware that after two or three years, Rico's wife was gone. It was sudden. Cleaning ladies may have had a role in passing the news. The disappearance was described as eerie. She was there, and then she wasn't."

Izzy thought for a minute, as if looking at an invisible timeline. "Is it for sure that she never came back?"

"That's what I've heard," Birdie said. "Why?"

"Because I think I've seen that woman somewhere."

"In town?" Birdie asked.

"I don't know. Looking at her portrait made my head all fuzzy."

"Fuzzy? You, Iz?" It was Cass's voice, breaking into the conversation.

They looked up to see Cass standing at the end of the table, her face smiling in the way of the cat that ate the canary. Standing next to her was a woman they had never seen before. Someone who looked nothing like a canary.

Nell looked up at the woman as one did with a stranger, about to offer a polite smile. And then her smile broadened as if somehow greeting an old friend.

The woman was about her age, with a long, plain face. A familiar face. And then the memory came into focus, why she felt she knew this woman. The memory of her favorite childhood doll. That was it. No, that was her, this woman standing in front of her. Poor Pitiful Pearl. with her oval face, her pug nose, and her wistful smile. The doll had arrived one Christmas, wearing a Nikita Khrushchev–style head scarf and packed in a plain brown box.

And Nell had loved her. Fiercely. Caroline Chambers, Nell's sister and Izzy's mom, would have nothing to do with Pearl, preferring to spend her time with Barbie and Ken. But to Nell, Pearl was a forever friend.

And now, here she was, grown up and standing next to Cass, but bearing the same nose, the same plain face, and the endearing wistful smile.

"I went to the yarn shop to bring you chocolate, Iz," Cass explained, holding up a bag from Annie's Sweetshop. "Mae sent me here, and on the way, I met this nice lady who was looking for a place to eat. Ladies, meet Charlotte Simpson."

She then introduced Izzy, Nell, and Birdie and nudged Izzy over, suggesting they make room for both of them. Charlotte was in town for the day and in need of Italian food. "Finding you three here is karma." Cass smiled.

Birdie patted the seat next to her and settled in.

"So, Charlotte," Birdie said pleasantly, wondering what Cass was up to. They were a welcoming group, but Cass was acting strangely. "I don't think we've met. Are you new in town? Tell us about yourself."

Charlotte listened to Birdie's request, then nodded, and did exactly that. In detail. She began slowly, methodically, by explaining how she'd flown to Logan from LaGuardia, then taken the train up to Sea Harbor because she didn't drive. Never had, she said. Never wanted to, although she was often teased about that. She said she loved Italian food, and described for them a favorite restaurant in New York, where she often ate on Wednesdays because they had a special. And she was hoping there would be an Italian restaurant in this little town. So she had checked the Yelp app on her cell phone, and then . . .

Cass saw that Charlotte might need some help in getting to the interesting part of why she was in Sea Harbor. She stepped into the monologue and explained to the others that Charlotte had come to town because her employer had died. Harrison Grant. And the police had asked her to come to go over some things.

Izzy, Birdie, and Nell sat up straighter.

"Oh?" Birdie said pleasantly, her gentle tone telling Charlotte she was among friends, not strangers.

"Mr. Grant died tragically, as you probably know," Charlotte said.

"Yes," Nell said. "We were with him that night. This must have been horrible news for you. I'm so sorry for your loss."

Charlotte nodded. "Working for Mr. Grant is the only real job I've ever had in my life, other than babysitting and college waitressing jobs. Over thirty years. I think I will retire now, a little earlier than I had wanted to. I'll miss going to work every day."

"He was your only employer?" Izzy asked.

"Yes. A cousin who was also a photographer suggested me for the position not too long after I graduated from college."

"You were his agent, is that right?" Birdie asked.

Again, Charlotte thought about the question. "*Agent*," she repeated. "Well, to be truthful, Mr. Grant was his own agent, although he did refer to me that way on paper sometimes. But it wasn't accurate." Then she rattled off her duties, smiling a little at the length of the list. "I did the paperwork, arranged appointments with dentist, doctors, contacted and scheduled clients, set up shoots. And then there was the accounting—which is what I studied in college. The payroll. Plane and hotel tickets, quiet payments—"

Cass interrupted. "Quiet payments?"

"Mr. Grant didn't always behave. Or so it seemed. Hush payments sounds so crass."

Nell smiled. She knew in her mind that her own Poor, Pitiful Pearl doll had had a sense of humor. And she suspected Charlotte Simpson did, too. Maybe rusty from disuse, but it was there.

Charlotte went on. "Sometimes his actions required money to take care of things and make problems go away. I should be more discreet and not call them cover-ups, but truthfully, I think that's what they were." Charlotte Simpson's voice was neutral, not assigning blame, simply reciting the facts.

"It sounds like you were a full-time office staff all by yourself," Nell said.

"Yes I was. But I'm very capable. Methodical and precise, my mother always said. Financially and legally proficient. I learn things easily. So I could adequately do everything and anything Mr. Grant needed done."

"What was he like?" Nell asked. "We knew him only for one short evening. But we found him charming and gracious."

"Quite honestly, I really don't know what he was like. Your social evening with him was more than what I had. I managed the office, which also had his photography studio and a waiting room. But we had little personal contact. I know plenty about him from numbers—from all those things I told you about. Schedules, appointments, checks I wrote, plane tickets I arranged. I can tell you how many cavities he had, that sort of thing. But not if he laughed a lot or told jokes or was emotional. I didn't see that person, only what could be recorded and scheduled."

"So no wild office parties," Cass joked.

The others were trying to process the notion of working for a man for over thirty years and not knowing whether he conversed easily or was gracious or helped the elderly across streets.

"It was a peculiar arrangement, I admit that. But I liked it. He paid me generously. I don't think the police found it particularly interesting, though, and I know the fact that he had no family was disappointing to them. Although he appeared in magazines, at parties, and attended many shows, I couldn't give them the names of any friends. Or enemies. I simply don't know if he had any."

A waitress appeared with a loaded tray. She set soup bowls on the table. "Harry said to bring two extras," she said. She added a basket of warm sourdough rolls, small pots of butter, and more cups of tea, then disappeared.

"But you would know the clients he was with the most, say, during this past year, or years before, that sort of thing?" Nell asked.

"By name and check, yes. But this past year there were few photo shoots or client meetings. I had stopped booking sessions, and he wasn't accepting the pile of invitations to parties and things like that."

"What was he doing?" Nell asked.

"Traveling." Charlotte took a pair of rimless glasses from her pocket and put them on.

"For pleasure?"

"I don't think so. But I don't know. He was quite methodical about it, whatever it was. Mostly short trips." She reached into her bag and pulled out a slim iPad, brought it to life and then turned it so the others could see it. In seconds a series of dates filled the small screen. "It's a little obsessive of me, but this is an example of how I organized Mr. Grant's life. These are months of travel. I also have airline tickets, hotels, contact numbers for everything. I can tell you where he was nearly every day. I have the same for appointments, photo shoots, parties."

"You've kept records like this ever since you started working for him?" Cass asked.

"Oh, yes." Charlotte nodded, clearly proud of her work. "It's what I do," she said, turning off her iPad. "What I'm good at. Keeping a log filled with numbers. And it served Mr. Grant well. I was surprised sometimes at the authority he granted to me. Especially since we rarely even saw each other. I even bought a condo for him once. Not for him, really. But can you imagine that? Buying a condo without seeing it?"

"It's quite remarkable," Birdie said. "You would be in demand, Charlotte, should you decide to continue working. I would love such a record of my life. I forgot what I had for breakfast today. You would be able to tell me."

Charlotte smiled, pleased. She removed her glasses and tasted a spoonful of the soup. "Stracciatella," she said excitedly, then declared it as good as her mother's. She seemed to relax a little more with every spoonful of the soup.

"Why do you suppose Harrison had pulled back on his photography this past year?" Nell asked.

Charlotte looked surprised at the question. "Why?"

"Well, yes. Why? He was successful . . ."

Charlotte took another spoonful of soup, as if considering her answer while she savored Harry Garozzo's Stracciatella. Finally, she looked up at the four women watching her.

"Because he was dying."

Chapter 27

Cass's spoon slipped into her soup bowl.

Charlotte looked slightly flustered. "You didn't know that," she said.

"No. If the police have that information, it hasn't been released," Birdie explained. "Or maybe the full autopsy may not be back yet."

"It was a rare kind of cancer and difficult to detect. Of course, Mr. Grant never talked to me about it. I know only because the reports came to me. For some reason, perhaps because our relationship was so impersonal, he allowed that to happen. My niece once teased me that I was my boss's robot. But that was just fine with me. As for his health, I even received messages on the phone from his doctor. I must have been on some kind of HIPAA-approved form."

"He seemed healthy," Nell said, still trying to reconcile the image of the man they'd met with Charlotte's news.

"Yes, as best I could tell, he was reasonably pain free. He certainly managed to travel with ease, at least it seemed that way. I assumed he wanted to use the time he had in personal ways.

But please understand that is my assumption, not what he told me. He never told me why he was making all these short trips, nor would I have expected him to."

"Where did he go?" Cass asked.

Charlotte returned her glasses to her small nose and touched the iPad screen again. Another chart came up, filled with cities and airports, phone numbers and contacts. At the bottom was a flight to Boston Logan. His last trip. Flight number. Hotel. Phone numbers.

"So there's nothing after his trip here?" Cass asked.

"That's right. I thought that odd, too, because he liked to plan ahead. But it looks like Sea Harbor was his last stop for now."

The unintended significance of her words brought a cloud of quiet over their table.

Finally, Birdie asked, "I wonder, Charlotte, might it be possible for me to copy down some of the recent travel cities?"

Coming from someone else, the request might have seemed intrusive or inappropriate or an invasion of privacy. But coming from Birdie, it sounded like she might be asking for a favorite recipe. Intrusive to the cook, maybe, but a compliment, too. Charlotte suggested that emails were more efficient, and within a minute, she had emailed Birdie a page out of her file. "Flights. Dates. Phone numbers," she said. It would all be there.

Izzy fiddled with her spoon, stirred her soup, feeling uncomfortable about asking another personal question. But Charlotte's attitude seemed to allow it. Harrison Grant was dead. And what she had to offer was mostly numbers and dates. Something outside the realm of the personal, it seemed. "We think Mr. Grant may have been on Cape Ann before. Is that something you might have a record of?" she asked.

"Yes. I should have that. When do you think he was here? I don't always remember specific places, because I have my files to remind me. It's best not to clutter the mind with details that don't need to be there," she said with a smile.

Now Izzy looked embarrassed. "Well, that's what we don't know. When. Probably about twenty years ago. That was way before you started keeping these kinds of computer records, I suppose."

"Yes, back then I used a ledger," Charlotte said. "I had good handwriting then, but it's gone now. A bit of rheumatism. So eventually I inputted all those old records into my computer. It seemed incomplete without them and disturbed me. I have this insane sense of order, you see. I even make it a habit of checking phone numbers over the years in case they've changed. Updating them. Maybe it's a touch of OCD."

"Well, it has served you well." Birdie smiled.

Charlotte took off her glasses and focused on what little remained of the egg drop soup in her bowl. Finally, she broke off a piece of bread and cleaned the bottom. "Please don't think me inappropriate. This truly is delicious." She looked up from her bowl. "Both the soup and chatting with all of you. You are rather remarkable, sharing your table with a stranger. This is a nice place, your Sea Harbor. And you are all quite lovely."

"Somehow you don't seem like a stranger, Charlotte," Nell said. "We're happy to share this place with you. It's a favorite. And our town, too. Maybe you'll come back to visit us for pure pleasure, and not because the police asked you to come."

Charlotte smiled.

"I hope we haven't imposed on you with our questions about Harrison Grant," Birdie said. "It's such a small town, and everyone's been affected by his murder. We're anxious to bring peace back to this special place."

"Of course you are. I'm sorry I can't be of more help. As I told the police, I simply can't imagine who would want to kill Harrison Grant. And that was true because figures and dates don't kill people. And that's what I knew. Not a person. And somehow—maybe it's because I'm here with you nice ladies—that strikes me now as enormously sad." She took a drink of tea, then wrinkled her forehead. "But there was something else you asked me. What am I forgetting?" She looked over at Izzy.

But before Izzy could reply, Charlotte remembered. She asked Izzy for her email, too, then put her glasses back on and began searching on the iPad with great efficiency. She seemed most in charge when she was moving numbers around. "I don't need the time frame," she said. "Just the name of your town." She smiled as she explored different screens on her device. "And I know that name. Sea Harbor. It's so lovely. Yes. I believe it is a place I will return to sometime."

Her fingers, slightly bent, moved like magic, touching the screen here and there. Then she pressed a button, and the screen went black. She looked again at her watch, then back at the women sitting at the table. She smiled at Izzy. "The dates, the information you wanted, are now on your device."

Izzy started to thank her, but Charlotte had already gotten up. She slipped on her plain nubby tan coat and retrieved her lumpy bag, slipping the iPad inside. "I must be off to catch my ride to Logan Airport and to my home." Her smile was broader, a little more relaxed than an hour before. "But I shall be back, I hope. Thank you."

Nell watched her walk off through the now-crowded deli, her coat bearing a slight resemblance to the burlap bag her Poor Pitiful Pearl doll had come in.

And this grown-up Pearl was every bit as wonderful as the one whom she had cherished all throughout her childhood.

The four women stayed on at the deli for a while, revisiting Charlotte Simpson's information in her absence. They wondered about her life with Grant, and about a personal life now that he was gone. But even more they wondered about the information she had left with them. A man informed not by flesh and blood, by personality and emotions, but by numbers: dates, phone numbers, addresses.

"She didn't seem to be grieving her boss," Izzy said.

"But I don't think she disliked him," Cass said. "I think it's just difficult to mourn numbers, and that seemed to be the substance of their relationship."

An odd one, they all decided. But somehow it seemed to have worked for both of them.

Nell sat back and put her napkin on the table. "I think those numbers are curious. They may be helpful in getting to know the man better. At the least they'll tell us where he went. And the phone numbers go to someone, hopefully."

Birdie agreed. "We may not be walking in our Mr. Grant's shoes exactly, but I will be willing to try flying in his first-class airline seats."

The others laughed, unsure of what Charlotte's numbers and Harrison's travels would tell them, but it would be more than they knew about the man before they had met his kind assistant, the plain woman with an amazing record-keeping habit.

Homework. That was how Birdie looked at it. She stood up, put on her coat, and told the others she was going home to Sonny's den and her computer, where she would spend some time telecommuting. "Isn't that what it's called? But no matter, I don't like to fly these days. It will be far nicer following the man around this way."

They watched Birdie walk away, returning waves of greeting to nearly every table in the deli as she made her way to the door.

As they waited for the waitress to bring the check, Nell brought up Eddie Porter. "He didn't kill Harrison Grant. I feel fairly certain of it. Nor did Deb Carpenter. Although I didn't ask about specific timing, they probably could be alibis for one another. Without trying to, Eddie already verified Deb's version of seeing Harrison that night, including where and when she went after leaving him. It wasn't practiced. I don't think either of them could make up stories well. And what they said separately about that night makes logical sense, so it's something I don't think Eddie could make up."

"Which takes us back to Rico," Izzy said. "And I hate that. I wish I hadn't seen the flyer."

"But that still doesn't give him a motive," Nell said. "I think we need to push this as hard as we can, learn everything we can about Grant—and about Rico, too. And then we can see if the pieces fit. Try as I might, I cannot imagine Rico standing at the top of his steps and pushing a man to the bottom."

"But the fact that Rico and Frodo didn't come down those steps the next day . . . He used the road. For the first time . . ." Izzy held her head. "I'm not liking this at all."

Izzy couldn't let Rico go, and Nell knew it was because she wanted so desperately for him to be cleared. And he was becoming increasingly difficult to ignore as a suspect.

The police were looking into Rico, too, but so far they had found little, Ben had said. But the fact that Harrison Grant had left a lovely party, one at which he was a special guest, to walk down to Rico's home and then be pushed down his back steps was worse than puzzling.

"All right," Izzy said, her voice lighter and more determined. "I'm going to check out the dates on which Harrison visited the area before. The *when* and *why*. We'll check into Liz Santos's story. An affair. A married woman. The pieces kind of fit together."

"The mysterious woman who may have met him here. Yes. We need to know more about her," Cass said. She looked at Izzy, who finally gave a nod.

They all agreed. Even though they weren't sure they'd like what they found, they needed to follow the tracks.

As they started to collect their things, Harry walked over to their table and hovered. "Was everything okay, ladies?" he asked.

"Fine, Harry," Nell said. "It was wonderful soup."

He looked at Cass. "And your friend? She liked it, too?"

"She loved it. The best she's ever had."

They all knew where Harry was headed. *Who is she, and why is she here?*

But he had to settle for a less satisfying reply.

"She's a friend from New York," Cass said with a smile.

Harry humphed. "At least she liked my soup, so that's good. But I like to know people's names, you know?"

"It's Charlotte, Harry. Her name is Charlotte."

"Okay, thanks. It's good for business, you know. I need to know. Like who's that guy over there with Harmony? He's eaten in here before, but no one has ever introduced us, so I just listen, and then I can say, 'Enjoy your meal, Gustaf, or whatever.' "

"With Harmony, my yoga teacher?" Cass asked. "Where?"

Harry pointed across the room to a table near the windows facing Harbor Road.

They looked over. Harmony Fairchild sat across from a man about her own age, nice looking, with a short, neatly trimmed beard. He was nicely dressed, his khaki slacks neat and the button-down shirt pressed.

"I know him," Cass said. "He's a photographer. Name's Frank. See, Harry? Just ask me."

"A photographer?" Harry asked.

"He took some photos of our yoga class. Well, of Elena, actually. Harmony wanted them for a marketing brochure."

"He looks more like a close friend than a photographer," Nell said. "Look at Harmony's face."

"Hmm," Izzy said. "She looks very happy."

Harry laughed. "So you think he's okay. Then I do, too. I guess I'm just too suspicious. Harmony is a good customer and a nice lady. I guess she wouldn't be cavorting with bad guys."

Harry was called away, and they looked back at Harmony, seemingly happy and animated as she and the man talked.

"A close friend," Nell said again. "Look at her face. Must be."

"It looks like it," Cass said. "She never mentioned one, but then, why would she?"

Outside the deli, they stood together for a few minutes, talking about the week's Friday night dinner at the Endicotts'. About what they could bring. Who was coming. For Cass, it would have to be something ready made. A loaf of bread was assigned, and Izzy volunteered a salad. Nell wasn't sure who was coming, she said, but as usual, it would be just the right number and exactly the right people. It always was.

They looked through the window before parting company and noticed that Harmony was now alone at the table, enjoying her soup. She looked up, spotted them, and waved. Then she smiled broadly. Her face bright. Clearly, a happy face. And they suspected it wasn't just because of Harry's *stracciatella*.

The happiness was contagious, and they all smiled back.

"So what is it? She won the lottery? The power of yoga? Or . . . ?" Izzy asked as they began to walk away, the feeling created by Harmony's happy smile staying with them.

They glanced back once more. Harmony was still smiling.

"Nah, that isn't money or yoga," Cass said. "Yoga brings a quiet smile. That one looks like the lady's in love."

Chapter 28

Nell waved Izzy and Cass off and walked in the opposite direction on Harbor Road, heading toward the small corner market next to Jake Risso's tavern. The market had things she couldn't find in the larger grocery stores and would probably have the apple mint she needed for the couscous tonight.

Jake was standing outside his bar when she approached, and waved her over.

"Nellie, come say hello," he hollered, loud enough to turn some heads. He was standing with another man, and for a minute, Nell hesitated, not wanting to intrude or get involved in a longer conversation, which she didn't have time for. Then she looked again and realized who Jake was talking to. Curiosity lured her over. The pleasant-looking man who had been enjoying soup with Harmony Fairchild greeted her with a smile.

Frank, Nell remembered. She smiled at him, then greeted Jake with a hug.

Jake turned to his friend and introduced him. "Frank Ames, meet Nell Endicott," he said, then followed it up with a description of what a great friend of his Nell was, what a leader she was in the community.

Nell laughed off Jake's exaggerated introduction. She furrowed her brow to soften her look as she tried to make sure it was the man she'd just seen across the street. "You're a photographer, right?"

"Photographer?" Frank laughed and pulled out his cell phone. "This kind maybe. But no, not so anyone would notice."

"But Frank has excellent taste in beer," Jake said, not wanting the conversation to get away from him.

Frank laughed. "I don't live too far from here. I'm in and out of Sea Harbor often and always make a stop at Jake's place. Best beer selection on Cape Ann."

"Frank's a good man," Jake said, slapping him on the shoulder. "Man's got good taste."

"Speaking of taste," Nell said, "I saw you over at Garozzo's deli, enjoying his soup."

"Great soup," Frank said enthusiastically, his smile broadening. "And that explains the photography thing. You probably saw a camera on the table."

Nell didn't remember a camera, but she let it drop. "We noticed you because some of my friends take yoga from Harmony Fairchild."

"Oh, that's it. Sure. We always stop in at that place for soup when I'm in town. The *stracciatella* is amazing. And I hear Harmony's a pretty good teacher."

Nell couldn't tell if it was Harmony or the soup he was most enthusiastic about.

He looked down at the slight bulge above his belt, laughed, and looked at Jake. "Harmony suggested yoga to me. It's how she got so calm, she said. I'll give it a try if you do."

The two men laughed at the improbable thought. Then Frank Ames shook Nell's hand again and said he was off. "Busy day. Another meeting," he said, then headed down Harbor Road, his long, purposeful strides getting him wherever he was going in a hurry.

"Frank's a good guy," Jake said, then dismissed talk of his acquaintance, canceling Nell's opportunity to find out more about the man.

Instead, Jake wanted to talk about Sea Harbor itself. "So, Nellie, what's going on? Surely something. Some good news. What do you know?"

"Well, what's the word in the bar?" Nell asked, looking through the front door. The place looked empty. "Aren't bartenders in the know?"

"I wish. I wish I could solve this whole thing. It's empty around here. There's usually a group of old-timers who come in to watch an afternoon game, but it's a slow time. People are sticking closer to home, maybe. Even my regular guy is home today. Nursing his dog, I hear."

"You mean Rico, " Nell said, seeing the concern on his weathered face.

"Yeah. I'm worried about him. Poor guy has had it rough this week. Dead guy in his backyard and now an injured dog."

"Izzy went by today and says Frodo's up and walking. I'm sure they'll be over to see you soon."

"Hope so. I miss the old guy. He's usually in here like clockwork, soon's I unlock the place. Frodo too."

"Speaking of Rico, Izzy said she saw a portrait of his wife. Or at least she presumed it was his wife. Izzy and I didn't live here while they were married, so it was a surprise."

"He still has that thing up?" Jake snapped. "I told him to burn it."

"Izzy said she was beautiful."

Jake looked off toward the sea, his wrinkles deepening, his cheeks sagging. "She was that, sure. They met right in there, him sitting at the bar, her serving him a beer. Never forgave myself for it."

"So she worked for you?"

"Yeah. Martina. That was her name. Yes, she did. A decent waitress, always got the biggest tips. The most attention. There was something about her, though. Mood swings, I guess you'd call it. And then she set her sights on Rico. And when she decided on something, there wasn't much that could stop her. A little obsessive, that one."

Nell was quiet. It wouldn't explain things, maybe, but she half wished Jake would say Martina had fallen head over heels in love with Rico. Had loved him madly. That they had been blissfully happy together. Even if it had been for a short period of time, she wished that Rico had experienced joy.

But that wasn't the look she saw shadowing Jake's face. Nor did it fit with the town's old, dust-heavy rumors.

"Rico's a good man," Jake said. "Always was. Even had a sense of humor in those old days, like telling jokes, cracking us up. We'd go out on the boat together. Caught some whoppers, and when we didn't, we'd tell people we did." Jake chuckled at his own memories. "And then Martina came into the picture. She was a puzzle, that one. She didn't make many friends while she was here, but the staff liked her enough, I guess. She gave them tips on being better at what they did, on how to get bigger tips. She bewitched the men. And Rico fell hard."

"What about the other guys?"

Jake shrugged. "They liked her. Sure, she was gorgeous. There was one guy—kind of a ladies' man, but not a bad guy. Good looking. Hung out here a lot. People talked about seeing him and Martina together different places, and there was talk because the guy was married."

Nell listened carefully.

"Does he still live around here?"

"Over in Rockport. And he's still married. Nice wife, with the patience of a saint, some say, though those playboy days are behind the guy I suspect. Four kids'll do that. But that fling or affair or whatever you call it was before she and Rico hooked up. And it ended. But, hey, that was long ago. Who remembers?"

Nell was processing it all in her head as Jake talked. The affair rumor that Liz Santos had talked about. But the pieces, the people, didn't fit together. A married man in Rockport was definitely not Harrison Grant.

"Although he never looked like it," Jake was saying, "but Rico was kind of debonair back then, not to mention being filthy rich. Everyone knew it because he wasn't shy about talking about it. Some patent, he told me. He gave a ton of his money away to good places. Martina heard the rumors about his wealth, made sure they were true. And that was that."

Again, Nell waited for the love part, but it didn't come. "So Rico married her?"

Jake nodded. His eyes were still looking far off toward the ocean, as if he was trying to rewrite the story that had unfolded in his bar. Giving it a different ending. Not one with a lonely man and his dog coming in each day.

"We all hoped for the best, all my regulars," he said. "We liked the guy. Still do. It just didn't look to us like this thing with Martina would work."

"What happened? Did Rico ever say?"

"Never. Not a word. And I knew not to ask. All's we knew was that she disappeared. No one seemed to know why. There was always talk, sure, but nothing that was concrete, no other names thrown about, none of that. And there didn't seem to be any missing men around, so we figured she went off alone. Most folks decided she had just got tired of being married to him. Or who knows? Maybe she had someone waiting for her somewhere else. Someone suggested maybe she even had a husband somewhere else, that this thing with Rico was all a lark for her. Stranger things have happened, I suppose."

"But if she married him for his money . . . ," Nell began.

"Right? We all thought so, too. That's the puzzle. She got nothing. Nada. Not once she left. She probably spent a share of his money while she lived with him, a lot of it on making the house a showpiece. But then, poof. She was simply gone." He paused. "And along with it, my buddy's life."

Sonny's den was always warmed by his presence. Birdie felt it every time she walked into the room. Her friends felt it, too, but not in the way she did. Only Birdie felt his arms around her, heard the love in his voice. And though Nell, Izzy, and Cass professed that they detected the faint odor of Sonny's cherry pipe tobacco in the room, Birdie knew she was the only one who really did.

She sat at the old high-backed desk that Sonny had brought back from a trip to South America. Wood inlaid with leather strips and marked with the years. Birdie set her cell phone beside her and turned on her computer.

Then she said to the air, "All right, Sonny, let's see what we have here."

The screen filled with Charlotte's organized chart. Neat columns of cities and dates, flight and contact numbers looked back at her.

"Harrison Grant. Famous photographer. Who was he?" she asked Sonny.

And then she studied the days he had traveled in the past few months, and noticed something curious. All the recent trips were one-day trips. In and out.

Odd. And a good place to begin following Harrison Grant around, she thought.

When she clicked on those same cities for a past history, she discovered Harrison Grant had been to each of them over the years, but for longer periods of time, for photo shoots or gallery shows or longer business trips.

She scrolled through the cities. "Walking in his shoes," she told Sonny. She stopped at Pennsylvania.

Philadelphia. City of Brotherly Love. Perhaps a good place to start. She scanned the columns. Harrison had done a long photo shoot there eight years before. A shoot lasting several days. And one or two repeat trips. Charlotte had listed the studio, the address.

A month ago he had retraced his steps. This time a one-day trip. And a phone number.

Birdie dialed it. A woman answered, a firm, self-possessed voice on a recording, asking her to leave a message. Birdie hung up.

After getting several more voice messages in Seattle and San Francisco, all women's voices, Birdie finally heard a real voice at the end of the line. A cultured voice belonging to a woman who lived in Chicago.

When Birdie mentioned Harrison Grant's name, the woman's voice grew so cold, Birdie wondered if it was snowing outside. She explained the call by fudging the truth. But not much. She thought, judging by Harrison Grant's office papers, that the woman might be an associate of his, and wanted to let her know of the accident.

The woman seemed to object to being called an associate. And then to being called at all. Harrison Grant was a black mark on her soul, she said dramatically. But then she asked, her voice dropping slightly, what Birdie was talking about. "An accident?" she asked.

Birdie took a deep breath, sensing the woman hadn't heard about the murder. Perhaps Harrison Grant wasn't as well known in the Midwest. "He fell down a flight of stairs and died," she said.

There was a sound of surprise on the other end. Then silence.

Birdie knew she was going out on a limb, but she told the woman they were trying to trace Harrison's final days, to make sense of the tragedy, and knew he had come to see her recently. Was it possibly a meeting she could share?

The woman seemed to recover from the news of his death quickly, as her voice was once again strong. *And with a touch of haughtiness*, Birdie thought.

"He came to apologize to me," she said. Birdie could tell from her voice that she was saying far more. It was telling Birdie that Grant's words had meant nothing to the woman. And that he might have deserved his flight down the stairs. Aloud, the woman expanded on why he had apologized. He had pursued her, photographed her on a set, done damage to her reputation, before he threw her away like trash.

Birdie was quiet.

The woman continued, telling Birdie that his apology was an empty gesture, and that she hoped the door she slammed in his face had broken his nose. And perhaps more.

In a little more than three hours, Birdie had listened to several women's recorded voices, polite and professional, asking her to leave a name and number and telling her they would call her back. And to an equal number of women who picked up the phone, then didn't hang up when Birdie explained her reason for calling.

Those who had spoken with Birdie had similar stories. Harrison Grant had apologized to each woman for wrongs he had done to them, for the lies he had told, and for the lives he had disturbed and harmed. Marriages had suffered. And the women had suffered gravely.

Some of the woman had said they had accepted the apology, then had told him never, ever to darken their doorway again. Others had had similar reactions to the woman in Chicago.

Sam Perry was right. Harrison Grant hadn't been nice to women.

Chapter 29

"Grilled lamb chops, couscous with apple mint, and whatever Birdie brings for dessert." Nell named off the evening's dinner as Izzy walked into the kitchen, carrying a wooden salad bowl filled to the brim with torn lettuce, sweet pears, and toasted pecans.

Sam came up behind her and gave Nell a quick hug, then followed a racing Abby and Red outside, where they had spotted Uncle Ben near the grill. Nell watched as Abby bypassed Ben when she spotted the small rope swing her great-uncle had hung from the maple tree growing directly through the floor of the deck. Izzy and Nell could hear Abby's delighted shrieks through the thick glass doors.

"Sam looks good," Nell said, watching him as he lifted Abby onto the swing. "I can tell a lot from that man's hug." She pulled out a cutting board and handed Izzy a knife, along with a handful of mint and some scallions.

"He's okay, but I don't think he'd let me know if he wasn't. Sam is such a protector. The police asked a lot of questions today, he said, especially when Sam told them about the plagiarized miners photo. Apparently, even the chief was amazed at the way Sam had handled it back then. It did make a revenge motive all these years later look a little flimsy."

Nell agreed that it diluted any motive he'd have to hurt Harrison all these years later. But nevertheless, it was still a motive. And Sam had also made it known he didn't like Grant and didn't want him coming to Sea Harbor. He was also among those who had gone around looking for Grant that night, and he could possibly have gone off without someone seeing him. Nell knew with absolutely certainty that Sam didn't kill him. But that was because she knew and loved Sam, something that wasn't true of investigators on the case.

"The thing is," Izzy was saying, her knife making quick clicks on the cutting board, "Sam makes the story so simple, so easy to understand. The whole story about what Harrison Grant did with his photo, claiming it was his own. What Sam did when he found out about it. Which was nothing. I know Jerry Thompson believes him. How could you not?"

"How did Sam find out about the plagiarism?"

"Apparently a guy he knew from the workshop had done some work with Grant in Europe later, and he suspected the photo that won the award was Sam's, not Grant's. He remembered Sam doing a similar series, but he wasn't sure. Sam didn't confirm or deny it to the guy who told him about it. He probably just nodded in that way he has and went about his business and his life."

Nell nodded, pushing her worries to the back of her head. She added couscous to a pot of broth and stirred it lightly, then put a lid on top and turned the heat down. Yes, that was their Sam. Nell could tell from Izzy's manner that she was proud of her husband for walking away from what Grant had done, instead of challenging it legally. Even though his reasons were simply that he liked the life he had and wanted to move ahead with it, it was also true that he would have become known as the guy whose photo Harrison Grant plagiarized. Not Sam Perry, the amazing photographer who chronicled life as it is.

As Izzy chopped and Nell pulled out plates and napkins, Nell told her about her conversation with Jake Risso.

"We have heard most of what he told me about Rico. Although when it comes to reasons why Rico's wife left him, it's a collection of what people pulled together because they wanted an explanation. So they came up with their own reasons. I suppose we all do that sometimes. People demand reasons. But made-up reasons are rarely credible. The fact that Martina married a man for his money was probably true, Jake said. But then she left town all by herself, without getting any of it. The reasons for that are thin. It wasn't that she was running off with someone's husband. She simply disappeared. If only we could find her—"

"You're right. It doesn't make sense," Izzy said. "But who knows what life with Rico was like? And maybe there was a prenup or—"

Footsteps, many of them, brought Jane Brewster across the family room, followed closely by Birdie, Cass, and Danny.

Jane carried a beautiful stoneware bowl she had made and fired in her studio. It was a shallow piece with raised leaves winding around the perimeter. Fresh grapes, pineapple chunks, and blueberries were heaped in the center. "Ham is at a gallery opening," she explained. "But I needed to be here."

While coats were hung up, Birdie walked over to the bookcase and noticed the plastic storage container they'd gone through the night before.

Cass stopped, too, then looked over at Izzy, standing at the kitchen island. "What's up? Why is that here?"

"Sam took it to the police station," Izzy said. "A show-and-tell, I guess. It went along with his story. He and Uncle Ben ended up here afterward, and so did the box."

"I dreamed about it last night," Cass said. "I kept thinking of all those old photos. And I woke up thinking the box had more to tell us than that Harrison Grant was a despicable person."

Izzy and Nell looked at her, waiting for more.

Jane was standing on the other side of the island. Listening. Nell had told her about the photos, about Sam's role. She had felt Jane's sadness about the whole long saga, one that had been brought to a head by Jane urging Sam to invite the man to the Canary Cove lecture series.

"I don't know if Grant's murderer is somewhere in that box," Cass said, "but I think there are more answers in it than we saw last night. I feel it pretty strongly." Cass walked over to the island and broke off the end of a baguette, smearing it with the tapenade Nell had put out.

"You could be right," Birdie said. "I think our surprise last night clouded our perspective. We were expecting Abby's beach toys and found a plagiarized photo instead."

Nell agreed. "And even though it's Sam's name on the box, it may hold other secrets that have nothing to do with him."

"Another look at the contents can't hurt anything," Birdie said.

Nell handed Birdie a glass of wine and looked out toward the deck. The sound of the men's voices as they prepared the grill blended with Abby's sounds of pure delight as Sam pushed her on the new swing. Happy sounds.

Birdie turned and followed her gaze. She smiled, then turned back to the women standing around the island. "I spent the afternoon on my computer and phone. I was trying to walk in Harrison's footsteps, albeit electronically. Trying to find out who that man was who had stolen photos from our Sam, who had deceived an honorable profession. That is a sad way to live. What kind of a person would do that?"

"I've been thinking about it, too," Nell said. "It didn't match the man we met here last Friday night. I consider us good judges of character, all of us. Things didn't match up when we met Harrison Grant."

"Exactly. So I looked a little into what he was up to before he came to us. Harrison Grant was on a journey of apology."

For a moment no one said anything.

Finally, Jane spoke. "To whom? I know about the box, the photo." She shook her head, as if scolding herself. "I still can't quite believe I forced Sam to bring this man to town, someone who had committed the ultimate artist's sin."

"I wonder if he'd done to others what he'd done to Sam?" Nell asked.

"I don't know if he had plagiarized again," Birdie said. "But he probably didn't need to. What he'd done with Sam's photo had achieved what he needed. Recognition and entry into the elite photographers' circle."

Jane thought about that. "That's true, Birdie. Once he was sanctioned by the photography community, he could enhance his reputation on his own. And he *was* a good photographer—somehow that can get forgotten in this mess. But like so many people in the arts, you sometimes need a lucky break to be recognized. Harrison made his own. Sam, on the other hand, didn't need the lucky break. His talent and patience got him to the top of the documentary photographers."

"So, what about the apologies?" Cass asked. "What's that about?"

"From what I found out about his actions during his career, Grant made repeat short trips back to cities where he'd conducted photography business over the years," Birdie explained. "Harrison Grant liked women, and he met lots of them while doing his advertising and celebrity shoots—and in other situations, too. But 'liking women' and respecting them didn't mean the same thing to him. It seems he used his power to treat women badly. Fast-forward to the one-day trips he made to those same cities during the past year. But this time he wasn't on professional business. It seems he revisited these women to apologize. Not to seek forgiveness, but simply to apologize to the women he had hurt. As he said in his note to Sam—forgiveness wasn't what he was seeking. He just wanted to apologize. Some women told me they accepted it. Some didn't."

"I wonder if his apologizing was to make himself feel better," Nell said. "Or was it for the women's sake? I think maybe he was doing it for the women, not to ease his own conscience. Sometimes a simple apology can matter greatly to the person wronged. Maybe the thought of dying made Grant realize that. Maybe he finally did something for someone else—the women he'd hurt."

"That image fits better with the man we all met that night," Izzy said.

"So . . ." Jane frowned as she collected her thoughts. "Are you saying Harrison accepted the invitation to the lecture series to apologize to Sam?" She looked at Birdie. Then at Nell and Izzy.

No one was sure, but Nell had an opinion.

"I don't think so. He could have mailed the box to Sam. He also had time alone with Sam, when he could have apologized. I think his apology to Sam was separate. Also, we know from Eddie Porter that Harrison was looking around for someone that night. He had a piece of paper in his hand, Eddie thought. Like a name or something."

"A piece of paper?" Birdie asked.

"Eddie thought that's what it was," Nell said. "But it might have been nothing. What he was sure of was that Grant was looking for someone."

"Beatrice Scaglia told us the same thing," Birdie said. "She was sure he had come to Sea Harbor for reasons other than the lecture series. She insisted he was looking for something. Or someone."

"This piece of paper is interesting," Cass said. "He had something in his hand when I was talking to him. I thought it was a drink napkin."

"Yes," Birdie said, perking up, her voice animated. "It looked like he had something in his hand in the photo the newspaper printed. Not readable, of course, just a fleck of white. It might have been nothing, or something?"

"And it fits in with Harrison looking for someone that night," Cass said.

Nell thought about that. She hadn't noticed Harrison looking around. But it seemed others had. He had talked to Deb. And had seen all of them, those who had planned the event. And certainly had spent time with Sam. Who else did he know in Sea Harbor?

"Imagine that the woman he was looking for was similar to those I called today," Birdie said. "Women who slammed the door in his face, who were angry and hurt by this man. Perhaps he was looking for someone in Sea Harbor, a woman with whom he had had an affair—and had hurt deeply. And he had come back to find her, and to apologize."

"That fits with Liz Santos's recollection and the rumors. Harrison Grant was having an affair with a married woman in Sea Harbor," Nell said.

"Maybe," Izzy said. "Or maybe it wasn't about that at all." She slowly chewed on a carrot stick, her forehead wrinkled, sorting through her "devil's advocate" kind of thoughts. Then she said, "Or maybe he was looking for a man."

Chapter 30

Friday night dinner wound down as the wind picked up outside and talk of rain was discussed. Inside all was warm and dry. As the candles flickered on the long wooden table, the grilled Moroccan lamb chops were anointed as a new favorite. The spicy yogurt marinade kept them so moist, Danny had trouble resisting a third. So he didn't.

"And he stays skinny," Cass complained. "How is that fair?"

The minty couscous with toasted pine nuts was also on the "make again" list, but maybe with a tad more lemon zest and a handful of Italian parsley. Nell mentally recorded comments to scribble down in her recipe book later. Who liked it. Who didn't. And who ate it when.

"Someday Abby will inherit Aunt Nell's cookbooks," Izzy laughed, "and she'll rub her finger over the smudges and the butter stains, the blobs of panko crumbs, the notes to add more butter or wine or more cream in the steak soup—and she'll wonder if we were all huge and unhealthy, with muffin tops and flabby chins."

"But if there's a shortage of food," Danny said, "she can just eat the book."

Everyone laughed.

Danny pushed himself from the table, forcing himself away from the remnants of lamb. "I need to move this body." He began collecting plates and carrying them into the kitchen.

Nell followed close behind. The others shuffled chairs, wiped tables, checked sports scores. Sam disappeared up the back stairs to check on a sleeping Abby.

"Hey, everyone," Cass announced, looking at a text on her phone, "don't forget that the best mystery writer in the universe has a gig over at the Bookstore of Gloucester tomorrow night."

"Tomorrow?" Nell said, surprised, then checked her phone. "Of course. I have it right here. Sunday. My days are confused right now. Somehow, your book event seemed far in the future, Danny."

The others agreed. Murder had taken a toll on orderly, pleasant days. Parties and dinners and going to work or play. Suddenly none of it was orderly . . . or ordinary.

"That's what having a baby seemed like a while ago," Cass said. "Far in the future. But it's not. So I hope at least one of you shows up at Danny's talk, just in case baby Brandley needs a ride to the hospital in the middle of a juicy part of the book."

Danny walked over and gave his unborn baby and his wife a hug. "Fat chance I'd miss out on that," he said, his voice with a strange catch in it.

"This baby won't come during his father's talk," Birdie said. "Our newest baby has good sense. This baby wants the town back on its axis before she or he makes an appearance. Once that's done, once Sea Harbor is a safe harbor again, we'll start the welcome festivities."

Danny moved from Cass to Birdie and gave her a hug, too. Then quickly followed Ben outside to check the grill embers.

Birdie's prediction had quieted the room. *Safe harbor.* Every baby deserved one.

Then Cass, as if Birdie's words were a call to action, walked over to Sam's box, sitting on the bookcase.

"Let's look again," she said, picking it up and carrying it back to the kitchen island. Izzy and Nell cleaned off a space.

"Speaking of photographs," Nell said, "remember the man we saw with Harmony today?"

Cass looked up. "Frank, right?"

"Yes. I ran into him later. He's not a photographer."

"Sure he is," Cass said.

"Well, he doesn't admit to it." Nell repeated her conversation.

"That's weird," Cass said. "Harmony said that's why he was there that day, to take photos for her brochure." She frowned.

"Maybe she didn't want to pay for a professional one," Nell said.

"For a brochure?" Izzy said. "That wouldn't make good sense."

Nell looked at Cass. "I agree, Cass. It's strange. But maybe there's an easy explanation." Maybe, she thought to herself, it was just another example of ordinary things becoming ominous when a murderer was in their thoughts and lives and neighborhoods. Nothing seemed quite what it was. Or what it should be.

Sam came down the back steps and into the kitchen and changed the subject by announcing that Abby was making "dream" sounds.

"Happy giggles and sounds," he said. "Mostly, words like 'swing,' 'push,' 'higher,' and of course, the usual 'I love my dad very, very much.'"

"And we do, too," Nell said.

Sam glanced at the box. "I hope that thing isn't just a boondoggle, isn't causing more trouble."

"I think it's the opposite," Cass said. "I'm not even sure the things in here we assumed were meant for the trash are really trash."

"What do you mean?" Izzy said.

Cass thought for a minute, then shrugged. "I don't have the faintest idea. But there's only one way to find out."

Sam stood watching for a minute, seeing some of his photos from the long-ago workshop being pulled out and lined up along the island.

"So what's with the dates on the back of these?" Cass asked him, flapping one in the air.

"That was a Grant thing. Assignment dates, student initials, workshop name or number. It's how things were kept straight."

Sam picked one photograph up and looked at it closely. He turned it over, then back, a crooked smile softening his face.

"Does it bring back memories?" Nell asked.

"Yep. And some good ones. It was the beginning of a life that turned out to be a great one. If I hadn't decided to really give this profession my all, hadn't had some success at it, hadn't been invited by Jane, here, to visit Canary Cove a few years ago . . . If all those things hadn't happened—even that infamous workshop—then I might never have met all you pretty terrific folks, and then met, again, this quite amazing woman here. In this very house." He moved over to Izzy's side and pulled her close, then rubbed his cheek against her hair.

Nell could feel the emotion in his voice—for the little girl a floor above, for this woman he loved deeply—and she also heard his message.

It's going to be okay, Izzy, he was telling her. *Life is good. We're good. And this man from my past is not going to change our life in the slightest. We won't allow it.*

"Aww," Izzy said, taking the photo from his hand and looking at it again, hiding the feelings that shadowed her face.

"Hey," Sam said, lightening the mood. "Here's something about Grant we used to laugh about."

Jane looked up from the sink, her lower arms deep in suds. "Laughter is good," she said. "Lay it on us."

"You probably know this fact, Jane. Portraitists—painters, I mean—sign their works either on the front or the back, but more frequently on the back. Either a full name or initials."

Jane concurred.

"But usually photographers doing portraits don't do that. I'm not sure why. Maybe the clients don't want it. When I did a few family photos, I never considered putting my name on them. It'd be a little bit like inserting myself in that family's life. But, anyway, Grant did. Always signed them somewhere. He used to tell us it was for the family's benefit. The portraits would be more valuable that way. His ego was intact, a giant-sized one, even back then."

They laughed, but not heartily. Harrison Grant wasn't generating many laughs. The man had done something bad. To someone. Something that was bad enough that someone had murdered him for it. And now it was messing up the lives of people they all cared about.

"So it went okay today, Sam?" Jane asked. "With the police, I mean."

"Sure. They're good guys doing their job." He chuckled again, gave the kind of half laugh Izzy knew he used when he wanted to make other people feel better. And he was concerned that Jane was putting too much blame on herself for unintentionally getting her closest friends involved in a murder.

"But here's another thing that shows I'm not always living in the present. I realized as the police were asking me things that I had screwed up one thing. Unintentionally. They wanted to know when I'd seen Grant last, before I picked him up for the reception."

"It was a few years ago, right? At some conference you told me about?" Izzy said.

"Right. That's what I told them. But later today I was thinking about it and remembered that I had seen him more recently. Last week, that night we went to dinner in Gloucester?" He looked at Cass and Izzy. "I left you guys at the Franklin and went to get the car. I'm pretty sure—no, I'm positive—I saw Grant near the parking lot, talking to someone in a doorway."

"You didn't say anything about that when you picked us up," Izzy said.

"I know. I'd been bothering you guys enough about the moon and the man coming to town. You were tired of my talk and besides, it didn't seem important. So he'd come to town a day or two early, but that was his business. Right?"

"Who was he talking to?" Cass asked.

"I don't know. A stranger, maybe. Someone who lived in those condos above that new coffee place. He looked like he was asking directions. Next time I looked, he was heading back to the Beauport Hotel. No big deal."

Sam shrugged, confirming to himself that it wasn't anything, then grabbed his jacket and a mug of coffee and headed toward the deck doors. "Man talk time," he said with a pretend tip of a pretend hat.

"Maybe we were all seeing Harrison Grant in odd places, especially Sam," Izzy said. "If I remember right, Sam was also seeing things in the moon that night."

They laughed, and the mood lifted briefly. Jane went back to the dishes, and Birdie poured more coffee.

Nell looked over at Cass. She was already digging around, looking for more in the box, for those secret clues that she was sure Harrison Grant had left for them. Every now and then, her body would stiffen, as if she'd felt a bump or a kick, and her hand would move from the box to her belly, which she would pat gently, then let her hand rest there a bit.

Nell felt dampness in her eyes and grabbed a tissue. In the middle of the mess, there was joy. And she reminded herself not to forget it.

Izzy helped herself to a glass of wine, then moved back to Cass's side and watched her check the notes and photos in the box. "You won't find that photography journal or Sam's *Three Men and a Mine p*hoto in there," Izzy said, trying to sound nonchalant. "The police kept them."

"Kept them?" Nell said, her brows lifting. "Sam's photo? Why?"

"Jerry promised he'd keep the photos safe," Izzy assured her aunt quickly. "We'll get the photo back. The chief even talked to Sam about an app that can help restore old photos. Did you know Jerry Thompson's an amateur photographer in his spare time?"

Nell managed a smile, feeling that the roles had changed. She should be keeping Izzy feeling safe, and telling her that everything would be fine. Now Izzy was talking too fast, trying to put her mind at ease. And not about photos. About lives. "I know, Izzy," she said, tucking her own worry away. "It will be okay."

They began passing around some of the photos again, ones familiar to them now, the search lacking the surprise of the night before. And the clues they were seeking hidden somewhere out of sight in the now familiar plastic box.

Cass picked up a black and white photo, another pose of the young woman they'd seen the night before. She held it up, her eyes squinting to see the features more clearly, wondering if it looked familiar because they'd looked at it the night before.

Beside her, Nell was hiding a yawn behind her hand, and Jane had folded up the dish towel and was checking her messages. Ham was back from the gallery show, she said. It was time for her to head home.

Outside, the wind was picking up, slapping branches against the kitchen windows.

As if on cue, the French doors opened, bringing in a gust of cold air, along with Danny, his collar up and his car keys in hand. Sam and Ben followed, carrying in the grilling tools.

"The witching hour," Danny said to Cass and Birdie. "I'm getting you two ladies home before they come out."

While Nell and Ben walked friends to the door, Sam went upstairs to bundle up a sleeping Abby, leaving Izzy sitting on an island stool, picking through the box, resenting its presence in her life.

Mindlessly, she pushed aside photos and papers with the tip of her finger, as if pushing them out of her life and back to the past where they belonged. *Enough*, she said to herself and reached for the lid. A small photo sat beside it, one Cass had been holding earlier. Izzy picked it up and recognized the young woman they'd noticed the night before. It was faded like the other, slightly yellowed and cracked. Not clear, but familiar.

Izzy held it up to the low-hanging island lights and looked at it more closely. Then she squinted, trying to bring the image into focus.

It was then, as Ben was calling to her, telling her that her family was waiting in the car, that her breath caught tightly in her chest.

But it wasn't the woman in the photo that held her in a painful grip.

It was what was behind the woman.

She slipped the photo into her purse, grabbed her jacket, and followed Ben's voice out to the waiting car.

Chapter 31

The meteorologist was right. Saturday brought a chilly rain to Sea Harbor, plastering fallen leaves to the gutters and sidewalks. Causing traffic in town to slow down. A lazy indoor Saturday.

"Not a good day to run, Izzy," Sam announced as Izzy came into the kitchen. He was standing barefoot at the stove, flipping pancakes. Abby was already at the table, begging Sam to make her next pancake look like Wilbur, her favorite pig.

Izzy stood near the cupboard for a minute, looking at them. Loving them.

And then she announced she was going out anyway. Errands. A whole slew of them. And she'd never once melted when she got wet. She kissed Abby on the top of her head, gave Sam a hug, and headed out into the wet morning.

Rico's house was dark, as always, and the gate hung loose. Leaves were scattered across the drive and sidewalk, and wet windblown piles had formed beneath the trees and along the fence. The familiarity brought her a small amount of comfort, even if she was finding it in Rico's messy yard. She sat in the car for a minute, the only sound that of the wipers swishing back and forth. Finally, she pulled up the hood of her rain jacket, got out, and ran for the front door.

She wasn't surprised or bothered when Rico kept her waiting, the rain pouring over her hood and streaming down her face. It wasn't as cold as she'd expected, and the rain was almost refreshing in a peculiar way. She lifted her head and breathed in deeply through her nose, then released the air slowly through her mouth. "Ha," she breathed. Her yoga "ha." Then she closed her eyes and her mouth and inhaled again.

"What are you? Wicked crazy?" Rico yelled.

Izzy's eyes shot open.

Rico stood beside the partially opened door, the gap just wide enough for him to stare at his drenched visitor. "You're a drowned rat, you crazy woman," he said.

Frodo stood on the doormat behind his master. His tail was welcoming, and he ignored his master's rant.

Izzy felt water running down her nose, onto her jacket, soaking her jeans, and gathering around her boots. But the door didn't close. Finally, she squeezed through the opening, then stood still on the mat beside Frodo.

Rico stared at her, then watched her carefully as she leaned over and tugged off her rain boots, trying to keep the water off the hardwood floor.

Izzy felt his look, but he wasn't pushing her out. That was a good sign.

"You're a damn pest, you know that?" Rico said.

Izzy nodded, standing up straight now, staring back at him. She glanced over at the closed doors to the living room. Then she looked back at Rico. Finally, she pulled out the photo that she'd protected in a plastic sandwich bag, and handed it to him.

Rico stared at it, every inch of his face frozen except for his eyes.

"I knew you went in there when you were here before," he said finally, his voice so low and unfamiliar that Frodo looked up, his head cocked to one side.

Then Rico, still holding the photo in his hand, walked over to the heavy wooden doors and opened them.

Izzy followed.

The room was dark, like the day outside, gray and unwelcoming. At first, all Izzy could see were shadows. Once Rico flipped a switch beside the door, small ceiling lights near the sitting area turned on.

Above the fireplace, against the distinctive hand-carved granite wall, which was visible in the black-and-white photo, a single light illuminated a woman. It made her almost as real as if she were sitting there in front of them. They walked over, stood before her. The woman's eyes seemed to focus directly on Rico.

"It looks like she's looking at me. But she's not, you know. She was looking at him," he said.

Izzy felt sure he was right. It was an intimate gaze looking directly at the camera. With Harrison Grant behind it.

Izzy scanned the whole photo, down to a black smudge, no bigger than a thumbprint, in the right-hand corner. A name erased, nearly hidden in the shadows. The date still visible. One of the dates Izzy had found in Charlotte's email to her. Harrison's travel dates.

She had awakened in the middle of the night and hadn't been able to get back to sleep, so she'd checked the email again. Looking for Harrison's trips to Sea Harbor. And there they were, just as Liz Santos had said.

She looked up into the large dark eyes and thought of Charlotte's files. Of Harrison's life in numbers. But it wasn't numbers she saw when she looked at Rico and then at the photograph. It was people.

Rico followed her gaze to the corner of the frame. "He put himself in the photo. I took him out."

I took him out.

Izzy took in a sharp breath, then let it out slowly. The connection between her and this man standing next to her, shorter by a foot, was an unexplainable bond. Strange, but real. And whether Rico wanted her to or not, needed her or not, she'd be there for him. Even if he yelled at her and ordered her to go away.

"Martina wanted her portrait painted. And she wanted it hung right up there, above the fireplace. I was happy about it. It was so permanent, you know? But I wanted it to be of *her*, not something a painter would paint, bringing his own ideas to it, painting his interpretation of her, all those tones and things they add and subtract. Instead, I wanted a photograph, something that would catch her spirit, those incredible eyes exactly as they were. Depict what was there. I checked it out and found a photographer who had won some big award in Europe. I figured he must be good, so I offered him big bucks if he'd come to Sea Harbor and paint my wife. The money was big, so he agreed."

Izzy was surprised, although she wasn't sure why. But the fact that Rico himself had brought Harrison Grant into his wife's life added a terrible irony to it all.

"That photo you have there, that little one . . . I was here in this room when he took it. A bunch of them. 'Testing the light and angles,' he said. And testing her. I could tell. That very first day, I could tell."

Rico was rambling some, but Izzy listened as carefully as she could, pulling out the time frame, the few days it took for his wife to fall in love with her photographer.

"While he was in Sea Harbor, Grant picked up a few other high-paying jobs," Rico said, "which brought him back to town."

"So you knew about his affair?"

"I never saw them together, if that's what you're getting at. No one did. Jake would have told me if he suspected it. But I knew Martina. I knew. Grant came to Cape Ann, and they met somewhere. Who knows where? She musta had a friend around here somewhere, a place she could go. Once or twice a buddy would think he saw her around Cape Ann, Gloucester, maybe over in Rockport, times when she'd told me she was looking for antiques or meeting her friend for some shopping spree. It didn't matter. I'd hear the guy was around, and I suspected something. But I thought it'd all go away. 'Some spouses stray,' my tavern buddies would say. But they knew where their homes were, where their real life was, and it was just a passing thing. 'A woman like Martina?' they'd say. 'She has everything. Don't worry about her. If there's anything there, it'll pass.' "

Izzy tried to take his words in, to feel what he had felt those years ago. And all the years since. The sound of his sadness was raw, as if it were yesterday.

"And it did pass. I knew it was over. Martina acted strangely, distant, but at least she wasn't seeing him. For a few weeks, things were almost normal. There might have been something going on in her head, but I let it be. I was crazy with relief that she wasn't going off. About a month or two later, I had a business trip to Italy. I wanted it to be like a honeymoon, to erase the taste of those bad times. Forgive and forget.

"Martina said she wasn't feeling so good, but I should go on the trip without her. 'Go to the doctor,' I said. 'Take care of yourself.' She told me she'd travel with me next time. So I went. And then I came back. To an empty house."

Izzy could feel the emptiness, the air being sucked out of the room. Out of his house.

He looked around the room. "I didn't change a thing in here. Martina loved this room."

"But you must have thought she'd come back, right?"

"Yeah. I thought that for a long time. A lifetime, maybe. She didn't take much with her. A few clothes. Some money from the checking account, but not a lot. None of the valuable doodads she had bought for the house. She was impulsive. I thought that's what this was."

Izzy hesitated but finally asked, "Did you assume she had run off with Harrison Grant?"

He sighed. A long and painful sound. Frodo licked his hand.

"I wasn't sure. But that seemed logical, right? I tried to call her but got no answer. I even had a guy go look for her in New York, but he found nothin'. Like I said, she did impulsive things. Highs and lows. It drove me crazy sometimes. But in the end, I loved her, you know? I could wait. What else did I have to do?"

"Did you contact Grant yourself?"

Rico was quiet for a moment, as if thinking about Harrison Grant was too painful. Finally, he said, "Yeah. I was going a little crazy and imagined maybe he was making her promises or holding her hostage or all kinds of crazy things. So I finally went there myself. I thought I might find her, too, but at least I'd know she was safe, and she could tell me herself it was over. At least I'd know.

"But I couldn't get within a city block of the guy at first. I finally found him in a fancy bar. He was a little tipsy, and I confronted him. He knew right away who I was. At first, he acted like a guy like me should expect a wife like her to have affairs. What was the big deal? He was an arrogant you-know-what.

"Then he told me he didn't have a clue in hades where my wife was. And he added that Martina's brains didn't match her beauty. She begged him to take her back, he said. To marry her. She tried to trick him, blackmail him, making ultimatums. She was crazy, he said, but he took care of it. It didn't take much to convince her to never, ever contact him again, he said. *Or else*. Women were easy to scare. *Young* and *stupid* were the nicer of the words he used. He made it clear that she'd be sorry if he ever saw her again. And then he turned on me, said he had some pictures of Martina. Ones I might not like to get around. And he suggested strongly that I never contact him again, either."

Rico's voice was harsh and furious as he repeated Grant's words. If Harrison Grant were to walk into the Silva house in that instant, Izzy was absolutely sure Rico would kill him.

He finally paused, took a deep breath, trying to collect himself.

He hadn't once looked at Izzy as he talked. She remembered going to confession when she was young, with an unseen priest listening behind a screen. She felt like that now, standing with this man, who might have done nothing but love a woman who didn't love him back. At least not enough.

"Did you look for her after that?"

"For a while," he said. "But then I stopped. It was clear Martina didn't want to be found. I'd call her, but she never answered her phone. Except for one time, but it was almost a year after she left. Someone answered, an older voice. She said Martina couldn't come to the phone and hung up on me. Then, a few days after that, I tried again, and the number had been discontinued. Shut off. Just like that. And I stopped looking, hoping she had found peace."

Rico finally looked away from the portrait and walked across Martina's room and into the foyer. Izzy followed. They stood side by side on the wet doormat while Izzy pulled on her rain boots. Outside, she could hear the rain lightening up, now more of a patter on the windows and steps.

She zipped up her jacket and looked at him again. His face was unreadable. But he didn't turn away.

"Rico, that night at the reception for Grant, I thought I saw you coming up the beach steps over at the Art Haven place."

She waited.

He scratched his scruffy beard, then looked at her. "No problem with your eyes. I saw the flyer for that thing you were doing, so I knew he was there somewhere."

"So you were coming over to talk to him?"

"Maybe. Don't know for sure. Then I remembered what he'd said those years ago, that he had pictures of Martina. I didn't know what he had meant back then, didn't want to know. Maybe he was lyin', anyway. But maybe not. Besides, what would I say to the guy with all those people around, anyway?"

Izzy was quiet, not wanting to go any further, not wanting Rico to say things to her she didn't want to hear. But finally, she did.

"Okay, Rico, then that next morning, when we met on the beach . . ."

Rico stared at her, as if daring Izzy to take back the question she was forming in her mind. But Izzy held her ground. She stared back, knowing he already knew what she was going to ask.

Finally, he said, "Frodo and I headed down my back steps that morning, going to Paley's Cove, like always. We saw him lying there at the foot of my steps. Right there on my property, dead as a beached tuna. Frodo turned away, headed back up the stairs like it was the thing to do, and I followed him. Then we walked out to the road and down to the beach. Just like you hollered at me to do forever."

Izzy tried to process her thoughts about what had happened that day, to move on. But to what? To ask what?

At that moment, the sound of a car in the circle drive interrupted her thoughts and sent Rico to the small windows bordering the door.

The look on his face caused her to move to his side.

She and Rico stared through the light rain at a familiar car.

As they watched, Detective Tommy Porter and a policewoman stepped out of the car and looked up at the house, then walked up to the door.

Chapter 32

Cass and Elena waddled through the rain and into the Y, leaving wet puddles along the way. Soft music welcomed them into the yoga studio at the end of the hallway.

When she had pulled up in front of the Costa home to pick up Elena, Cass was surprised to see Marco at the door, holding an umbrella, and then ushering his wife to the car.

"He finished the fatherhood book," Elena had whispered to Cass as she climbed into the front seat. And then she'd added, "He's a good man, Cass."

Cass was beginning to believe it. Maybe scrappy young Marco was growing up.

The Saturday yoga class was almost always full, but Harmony spotted the two stragglers coming down the hallway. Her face brightened, and she cleared places in the front row.

With a shake of her head, Cass nixed the idea for herself, claiming with hand signals that she needed back-row privacy today. *Just in case*, she thought, although she was unsure of what "just in case" referred to. It could easily mean her own private, modified version of the child pose that allowed for a ten-minute nap. Danny's baby was a night owl.

Looking over heads and bodies, Cass could see that Elena had already unrolled her mat and was sitting cross-legged in a quiet pose, eyes closed, collecting herself.

Libby, a longtime waitress at Garozzo's deli and a neighbor of Cass's, lowered herself down next to Cass, grinning at her and patting her barely visible bump. "The third. Can you believe it?"

Cass laughed. Libby was at least five or six years older than her. She gave her a high five. "A surprise?" she asked.

"*Huge* surprise," Libby said.

"So you're an elderly multigravida. I've got these terms down pat, Lib."

Libby's laugh was loud and, in the quiet of the yoga studio, slightly raucous. She covered her mouth.

"Me too," Cass said. "But I'm a primigravida."

"You're a babe compared to me. Don't try to one-up me."

"So what does this do to your waitressing job?"

Libby laughed. "Easy. I'll ask for more hours. Waitressing and people are my therapy. And my older kids are babysitting age. Besides, hubby Joe is thrilled with this surprise. He loves babies. So he can babysit, too. And I will happily toddle off to work. I love Harry's deli. Keeps me alive and a better mom. I meet all sorts of people there. Including that lady up front."

"Harmony?"

"Yeah. She eats at the deli a lot these days. Has business meetings there. Cheap office rent." Libby laughed. "That's how I heard about this class. But actually, I met her, heck, a couple dozen years ago maybe? A long time. Another life, as we call it. Pre-yoga. Pre-kids. Pre-life.'"

"Harmony has kids?"

"No, I was talking about me. But the rest of it was Harmony, no yoga back then and not much of a life. We met in a Gloucester bar, down near the harbor. There was a group of us. Accidental friends, we called ourselves. I was the youngest, I think. We were all down and out on our luck—lost jobs, messed-up relationships, all of us having a hard time in life and trying to figure a way out. Harmony was a real mess back then. She had just gone through a hard time, lots of losses. A divorce maybe but she never said. Something had happened that put her over the edge, and she acted a little crazy, angry, not always thinking clearly, you know? We weren't sure if it was just the things that had colored her life or if it was her.

"But, anyway, she was in a dark place. Most of us moved on, pulled ourselves together, like you do at that age, and I lost track of her, until years later, when she showed up in Harry's one day. I didn't recognize her at first. She had pulled herself up. It was nice to see. And surprising."

Cass listened with interest. At first, in the warmth of the yoga room, surrounded by the mats and peaceful women, the Harmony that Libby was describing didn't fit.

She looked toward the front of the room, where Harmony was talking to Elena, looking motherly. She wondered if Elena and other young moms in the class were somehow filling a void in Harmony.

As she watched her now, calm and in control, she realized that it wasn't a total surprise that Harmony had had a tough life. She had hinted at it that day in the Virgilio clinic. But she had stopped short of any details. And now here she was, in front of this class. Smiling. Calm. Not looking like the woman Libby had described, or the one who had started to let Cass see what was beneath that smiling facade. She seemed to have her life together.

Good to see, Cass thought. *Sometimes things work out like they should.*

She hoped this was one of those times.

An hour later, Cass rolled up her mat and joined Elena. Harmony stood with several of the women from the class and smiled over at them.

"Harmony, a quick question before we go?" Cass said, suddenly realizing she was about to lie—and she hadn't planned for it. "I need contact information for that photographer who took pictures for your brochure. I'm collecting names in case Danny and I want some taken of junior here, once he's ready."

"Photographer?"

"The one who took photos of Elena. His name was Frank, I think."

"Oh, sure. That one. Sure, well, I'll ask him. I'm not sure he does babies, but I'll let you know."

"How did the photos turn out? Were you happy with them?"

"The photos?"

"Of Elena. For the brochure."

"Oh, those. He still has them. They're good. But how can you go wrong with Elena, right?"

Cass wondered if her cheeks were as red as they felt as she thanked Harmony. Probably more profusely than necessary. Lying wasn't her game, hard as she sometimes tried. Her next thought was of her mother. Mary Halloran wouldn't have liked that show at all. Why hadn't she just asked Harmony why she'd said Frank what's-his-name was a photographer? And what did it matter, anyway? And a third thought was the fact that she'd asked Harmony about the photos the last time she'd seen her. And Harmony's first reaction had also been confusion. As if she didn't really know Frank at all. Or remember a picture being taken until Cass had jogged her memory.

And finally, she wondered why she, Cass Halloran, was letting herself be obsessed with the whole thing.

She dismissed her thoughts and hurried after Elena. They picked up two juice drinks from the bar and headed out to her car, their heads ducked against the rain.

"That's a good idea, Cass. Baby pictures," Elena said.

"So, do you think the photographer is good? Have you seen his photos?" Cass asked, getting into the car.

"No. But he was very nice."

Cass realized she hadn't dismissed the thoughts completely, after all. "Frank was his name. You were a photographer's dream that day. Did you sign the release papers Harmony mentioned?"

"Papers?" Elena shook her head. "I guess I forgot. I'll ask Harmony about it. But it's not important, Cass. It's only for a brochure."

Cass nodded and moved to a safer topic, one removed from what she was now considering her own paranoia. "Have you had your photograph taken before? You're a good subject. So at ease."

"Oh, sure. My parents loved taking my picture when I was little. I was an only child, and I think they poured all the love they had for the large family they wanted into me. And some friend of Marco's took a photo at our wedding."

"No, I mean for magazines. Or ads. Professional. Like a model. Maybe I've seen one of you."

Elena laughed, slightly embarrassed, as she assured Cass she'd never been a model. Nor would she want to be one. And unless Cass knew the family she had au paired for in Boston, they'd probably never met in person either, because she hadn't gone out much while she was working there.

And then she told Cass her big news. News that was far more important than photography or modeling. Or even yoga.

Marco was waiting for her at home to take her to the mall to get a crib for the baby.

"A crib?" Cass said.

"Yes, Cass, a crib." Elena laughed at Cass's surprise. "A baby crib."

They pulled away from the curb and headed north. Then Elena went on to talk about crib safety requirements, in case Cass hadn't read the articles yet. Compliant cribs, she said. And she talked about the danger of blankets in the crib and how close together the slats needed to be.

Slats? Cass needed to talk to Danny about that. They'd need a crib, too. One with slats that were close together. She mentally recorded the list in her head but was mostly reassured by the fact that she planned on borrowing everything she needed from Izzy—and surely Abby's crib had the right kind of slats.

"So, Elena, am I correct in thinking you probably have the nursery all ready?" She turned off Harbor Road, heading toward the Costas' neighborhood.

"We do. Marco painted it a gentle green. It reminds me of new gardens and spring, new life."

Cass imagined it. She looked over at Elena and saw that she was thinking about it, too, and its future resident.

"I was inspired by photographs of my nursery, the one my parents decorated for me," Elena said. "My mom and dad weren't rich, but my nursery was filled with unimaginable love. From that very first day. My parents told me often about how they were in my life from the very beginning, coming to the hospital as soon as they heard I was on the way. Staying there all night. I was born early, was a little sickly, they said, but a week later they took me home to their small rural house. My father said they turned me from pale to pink in a heartbeat. It just took love, he said."

"I almost forgot that you were adopted. But how great that your parents didn't miss any of your life."

"That's what they thought, too. They were right there, waiting for me to pop out, my dad said. All the papers had been signed. 'Every *t* crossed,' my mother would say. The woman who birthed me told them she wanted me to have a happy home. And that's what I got."

"Do you think about her? Your birth mother?"

Elena looked slightly surprised, then thoughtful. "Well, I think about her in a kind of universal way, like we're all connected somehow. But have I ever thought about her as my mother. No. My mother was Greta Abrams. She mothered me."

Cass glanced over at Elena. *Amazing*, she thought, not sure she had any other words.

Elena settled into quiet memories then, ones that made her face light up.

She was young, Cass thought. She definitely wasn't naïve. Her youth was deceiving. Inside that youthful woman, Cass was discovering traces of an old soul. "Sea Harbor must be very different for you. It's nothing like rural Pennsylvania," Cass said.

"But it has the ocean, and it has Marco. My garden. It has you, Cass. I'm happy here."

"Speaking of nice people, Danny and I were at the Ocean's Edge the other night, and I saw you and Harmony having dinner. I would have said hi, but you were having a good time and I didn't want to interrupt. It was nice to see that. I sometimes wonder about Harmony's life outside of yoga."

Elena didn't respond, and Cass drove on, slowing the windshield wipers when the rain turned into a light drizzle.

Finally, Elena said, "It's a nice restaurant. She came by my house that day and knocked, invited me to join her for dinner. I was surprised. It was kind of like seeing a teacher outside of school, you know? But she was sweet, and I read into her voice that she needed company. Marco was out helping Eddie with a moving job to make some extra money for the baby. So I went. I'd never been to that restaurant before. Marco isn't crazy about white tablecloths." She smiled.

Cass chuckled. "I get it. So Harmony picked the restaurant?"

"Yes, she said I'd like it. And it was really nice." Her words were hesitant. Sincere, but layered with another emotion. Then she said quickly, "The food was wonderful. I took a big doggie bag home for Marco, and he was happy. He even forgave me for not telling him, though I'm sure I left a note before Harmony and I walked out of the house. Right on the refrigerator, where we leave things. He sometimes has trouble finding things."

"I think Harmony has this motherly thing going on."

"Yes, maybe that's it," Elena said, her voice lifting, as if Cass had reached in and pulled out her thought. "I don't mean to sound ungrateful—Harmony is a sweet, generous lady. A great yoga teacher. But she seems needy."

"Needy?" Cass said.

"Yes . . . but I'm not sure why I think that."

"I think you have a good take on people, Elena."

"It's what you said, that motherly instinct. Maybe I remind her of a daughter she never had. But she wants to guide me, offer me advice, like she wants to counsel me."

"About your life?"

"Sort of, yes. I don't want her to feel bad, Cass, but I don't need that kind of advice. And I don't want it. My parents gave me that. They guided me. People think I'm naïve because I look so young, but my parents were strong and caring and compassionate. That's how they were, and that's what they guided me to be."

"Your parents sound like good folks. My dad was like that while he was alive, making sure Pete and I were 'ready to walk and wield a good life,' as he used to say. And my mother is wise beyond belief."

Elena seemed pleased to find a kindred spirit. "What our parents gave us will make both of us wonderful mothers," she said. "It's their gift to us."

Cass rounded the corner with Elena's words in her head. She slowed down in front of the well-kept house. Even in the rain, it looked cheery, or maybe it was Marco, standing just inside the door, waving.

Wonderful moms. A challenge, and one Cass had struggled with for nine months now. Would she be a wonderful mom? But Cass figured Elena was right. And partly because neither young Elena nor older primigravida Cass would be doing it alone. There'd be wonderful dads in these babies' lives, too. And a whole village ready to pitch in to help.

Elena opened the car door and stepped down. Then turned back to get her bag. "I hope you understand what I said about Harmony being needy. I appreciate her efforts and the way she helps others in the class. Maybe getting involved in others' lives helps fill her own needs, whatever they may be. I think some people are like that. I hope she'll find a life for herself."

"Maybe," Cass said. She could tell that for a strong woman like Elena, that kind of attention could be smothering. And although Elena wasn't the shy, introverted woman Cass had first pegged her to be, she was too nice, too kind, to completely back away from it.

Elena started to close the car door, then looked in once more. "Speaking of Harmony, did you hear her mention the extra class she's having Monday? Or maybe it was an email or text . . ."

Cass didn't remember. Or quite possibly had blocked it out. But somehow her body was telling her that relaxing with a book might suit her better on her day off. "I don't think I can make it Monday, Elena."

Elena stood still for a moment, thinking, ignoring the sprinkles gathering on her jacket. Then she said, "I don't think I will, either. But I'll see you next week." She waved happily and nearly skipped up the steps to a waiting Marco.

Cass drove slowly down the block, through the small neighborhood of houses, one after another after another. Was it her imagination, or did they look a little better than they had the last time she looked? A little neater, bushes trimmed and grass mowed, piles of leaves raked to the curb. *The Elena effect*, she thought with a smile, feeling almost sure she was right.

She glanced over at a small park on the corner. FISHERMEN'S VILLAGE PARK, a sign read. The small green space had swings and a slide. There was an old gazebo, where, she remembered,

Pete and some of the fishing crew had played music during a picnic with the whole crew last summer. Families in the neighborhood came to the park, put down blankets, threw frisbees. It was a perfect neighborhood place for Elena and Marco to take a bundled-up baby Costa for a walk in the weeks to come.

A smooth dirt walking path around the park's perimeter already hosted a few toddlers on big wheels, a man jogging. She recognized the man as someone she and Pete had recently hired. Hardworking, a good fisherman and a nice guy. A teenager was walking a dog. A young couple strolling.

Cass slowed down, pulled over to the curb, and watched the activity. And then she put the car in park and leaned across the passenger seat for a closer look. A familiar figure was walking through the park, a dreamy kind of walk. She wore yoga pants and a windbreaker, her hands loose at her sides. A smile on her face.

Cass shifted back behind the wheel.

And then she drove on, slowly, wondering why Harmony Fairchild was walking through a park in the small fishermen's neighborhood. Across town from her yoga studio. And miles from her condo in a nearby town.

Chapter 33

The four women were sitting on the rooftop of Jake's tavern, while Danny, Sam, Ben, and some of Jake's regulars watched a college football game downstairs at the bar.

Once the rain had stopped, a surprising temperate breeze had started blowing across town, allowing Jake to open the door to the roof. The rooftop heat lamps, coupled with the unusual autumn temperatures, created an atmosphere perfect for sitting on the old couches and chairs, away from televisions, noise, and people.

It was one of Nell's favorite views in all of Sea Harbor, sitting in the quiet beneath the night sky, above the town. The harbor lights rippling on the water in the distance. It wasn't a manicured or high-end real estate kind of place. Just plain weathered couches on a rooftop, with peanut shells on the floor, a deep sky above. And heaven close by. Somewhere.

She looked over at Izzy, slumped on one of the wide couches. As soon as they were settled, the door to the roof partially closed, the whole of Izzy's morning with Rico had come out in a rush, as if she might not be able to finish if she paused too long. The barrage of questions that followed filled in any small cracks.

"The police were there for an hour or more," Izzy said. "They told Rico he can't leave town. Not that he had planned to. But just the words being said out loud put a big exclamation point to the reason they were there."

She'd dialed her uncle while the police were getting out of the car. An impulse, she'd said, as she'd thought Uncle Ben would hear things Rico wouldn't. He had driven right over. And his quiet, wise presence was what both she and Rico had needed.

Rico had allowed Ben inside, then told her to leave. Had commanded her to, actually.

She'd refused.

"So why had the police shown up in the first place?" Cass asked. "They couldn't have heard what he was pouring out to you while the two of you stood in front of that woman's photo."

"They'd received an anonymous tip."

"Anonymous?" Birdie asked. Her tone spoke clearly to what she thought of anonymous tips. "What kind of tip?"

"It said that years ago Rico Silva's beautiful young wife ran off."

"That says nothing," Cass said. "Everyone knew that."

"The anonymous tipper added that she had run off with a well-known photographer."

There was a pause. Then Cass said, "Well, everyone's a photographer these days."

Birdie and Nell listened as the two younger women worked to vindicate this man—to punch holes in logic and common sense. To protect someone they'd all taken into their lives.

"It's been a week since they found Grant," Nell said, resisting the impulse to concentrate on the stars and forget about murder. But she knew that wasn't going to happen. "'Nothing' can easily become 'something' in a lagging murder investigation. They'd have to pay attention to a tip like that, anonymous or not."

Izzy and Cass knew that, too. They all did. But somehow saying it out loud moved them along to a realistic discussion, hopefully one that would truly help Rico.

"Sure, you're right," Izzy said. "It *is* something if you're the police trying to find a murderer. The anonymous tip was a fact, and Rico confirmed it readily. He even told them about looking for her, about talking to Grant, and how Grant had said Martina begged him to take her back. Tricking him. Blackmail or something."

"Which didn't work, apparently," Birdie said. "He did to Martina what he did to those nice women I spoke with. He threw her away, because that's what he did."

Izzy nodded. "But the worst part about this being out in the open is that Rico's confession allows the police to check off important boxes—motive, opportunity, proximity."

Nell saw the look of regret on Izzy's face. As if she had somehow contributed to all of this.

"When Tommy Porter told Rico about the tip, Rico did nothing to help himself," Izzy added. "In fact, he did the opposite."

"How?" Nell asked.

"He filled in missing pieces, as if he'd sent the anonymous tip himself. He admitted knowing about the affair, going after Grant."

"But he didn't confess to a murder," Birdie said softly, not knowing if that was the case, but believing with her whole heart that the Rico she had known all these years was not a murderer.

"No, he didn't," Izzy admitted. "And the police didn't ask. They just took down the story as he told it. Word for word. I watched Rico as he was talking. He was like a deflating balloon as he relived that awful time in his life. He was devastatingly sad."

Birdie looked at Izzy. "Did the police have any idea who sent the tip?"

"I don't think so. But I don't think that was important to them."

"Maybe they know more than they said," Nell began. "But I think it might be important. The tip had to have been sent by someone who knows what was going on with Martina."

"Someone who is either on the sidelines, a fly on the wall, or a confidant," Izzy said.

"But why?" Birdie asked. "Why would someone send a tip like that, instead of just going to the police and pointing figures, giving them more solid information, if he thought there was some?"

Nell poured glasses of wine and seltzer and passed them around. *Why and who?* "I wonder if Martina had any friends," she said.

"Rico mentioned there might have been someone she saw occasionally, although he didn't have any names," Izzy said. "Maybe not close friends."

"I know she didn't have friends in the Cliffside neighborhood," Birdie said. "There was no one her age, and she didn't seem interested. My friend tried. She had a welcome coffee for her. Martina came into her lovely home, looked around at the circle of neighbors, at their wrinkles and salt-and-pepper hair. And then she left. Just turned around and walked out." Birdie chuckled at the story. One that had probably been embellished over the years, but no matter: there were usually bits of insight in embellished old stories.

"But I still think she had to have had a friend," Izzy said. "Or an acquaintance. Cape Ann is too small to keep something like that so secret."

"Probably not an acquaintance. It would have to be someone she trusted," Nell said.

"So a friend, or someone who thought he or she was a trustworthy friend," Cass said.

"But why after all these years?" Izzy asked. "Martina has been gone a long time, is probably living a decent life somewhere. She seems to be resourceful. Even Rico finally let it go. He'd somehow accepted that he'd been rejected and she wasn't coming back."

A waiter appeared at the rooftop doorway with a basket of calamari, a platter of grilled shrimp and sauces, and another bottle of wine. "From your men friends," he said, setting it down on the large table.

But the women barely heard, their thoughts on the barrage of questions crowding the rooftop.

"So Grant's motive in coming back here may have been to apologize to Martina," Cass said. "He probably thought she'd come back to Rico. And maybe he was looking around for her at the reception."

"Or to apologize to Rico?" Izzy suggested, but her voice lacked conviction.

"Harrison's apology pilgrimage didn't seem to include men," Birdie said. "At least not according to the women I talked with. Which makes me think it wasn't Rico he had come to see. His travels were focused on women."

"Charlotte mentioned Sea Harbor was his last stop," Cass said.

The irony of Charlotte's comment kept them silent for a minute.

"*Last stop*," Izzy said. "I wonder if he saved the hardest for last. Did he hurt Martina more than the others? Did he regret it the most? And where would he have gone from here?"

Cass piled calamari on her small plate. "I think we're missing something. Grant got all the way through that long list of apologies without any of the women killing him. Why did it happen here in Sea Harbor? And if he was here to find Martina, well . . ." Cass stopped. It was like a hitting a stone wall. And yet it wasn't.

Izzy rummaged around in her bag and pulled out the black-and-white photo of Martina that she'd taken to Rico's house that morning. It was still in the plastic sandwich bag, still a little worse for wear. She set it next to the bottle of wine for them all to see. As if Martina herself might speak up, tell them who she had left behind in Sea Harbor. Or who might have wanted her lover dead. Or if she herself had snuck in that night and gotten revenge.

Cass stared at the photo, picked it up, set it down again. She frowned.

"Cass is right," Izzy said. "I think we have all the facts that we need. But we haven't put them together in the right way."

Birdie and Nell were quiet, pulling threads together in their heads, taking them apart.

Birdie had finished with her shrimp, wiped her hands off, and taken out her knitting. "It will help me think," she said and began working on a half-finished baby hat for what Mae was now calling the community baby shower. The soft green hat was a basic baby hat pattern, but Birdie had changed "basic" to unique by knitting a baby lobster that she'd attach to the rim at the end.

"Birdie, this is amazing," Izzy said in awe. She touched the claw of the crustacean, tiny and fanciful.

Birdie smiled a thank-you, her fingers moving continuously, and then she pulled the women's attention away from sweet baby beanies and back to business. "We know that Harrison came to Sea Harbor to apologize. I think that's a given. And from everything else we know, I think it was to Martina. It fits too neatly in his list of travel dates. I looked at them carefully, and they were meticulous. Methodical."

"So he was looking for Martina," Izzy said. "Rico's would have been the logical place to look, but he could easily have found out that Rico lived alone, so he wouldn't find her there. Where else would he look?"

"Sam saw him in Gloucester that night. Earlier than expected," Cass said.

"Maybe that's why he came early, to apologize before the series began. Knock on the door, apologize, and then move on," Birdie suggested.

It made sense. But not completely.

"So did Harrison find her? Did he get to apologize?" Izzy asked. She looked at Birdie, excited, her brows lifting with the sudden thought. "*Numbers*, Birdie. You have Charlotte's file full of numbers."

Birdie's face lit up. "Numbers. Of course! That's how Harrison knew where to go. Where to call. And that's how I found each of those lovely women." Birdie took a sip of wine, her brows lifting in delight. "Homework," she said.

"Homework?" Sam said, climbing the last step to the rooftop deck. "I'll have none of it. But I will have my wife, please. You may all be wide awake up here, but the guys downstairs are falling asleep in their beer. It's not a pretty sight."

Nell checked her watch.

Sam nodded. "Time to call it a day."

"Until tomorrow," Birdie said with a smile as she put her knitting away. "Tomorrow is another day." She smiled at Sam, then at her friends.

It was a hopeful smile. Hugs were passed around, and thoughts pulled together. They were ready to unravel and knit together, again, to find the dropped stitches and pick them up. Until it was all smooth.

Nell picked up the photo still lying on the table and looked at it again. It seemed to have grounded them, as if Martina were leading them along.

"She looks familiar," Nell murmured. "I think I've seen her before."

"It's those dark eyes," Izzy said, looking over her aunt's shoulder. "They're haunting."

Nell kept looking. It was more than her eyes.

She held the photo closer, then handed it to Birdie, then Cass.

Cass held it for a long time. She narrowed her eyes as she tried to see beyond the aging of the photo, the plastic baggie. Her breath caught in her chest. Then she looked again.

Izzy looked at it from a distance. "There's something mesmerizing about her," Izzy said. "She takes over the room in Rico's house."

Nell took the photo back, looked at it a final time. She'd seen it before, but clearly not in Rico's living room.

But where?

Nell leaned back and looked up into the deep night as the others headed to the staircase.

It was in that quiet moment, when she looked up at the blanket of stars, that she finally remembered where.

Chapter 34

Sleep for Nell had come in starts and stops. Her head filled with a map that had too many roads crossing each other. She thought of the Robert Frost poem, the roads in the woods, the one less traveled. And a beautiful woman in an old black-and-white photo.

She and her friends had stumbled on the road, but a simple nice woman had helped them continue on their way. A woman who looked like one of Nell's favorite trusted childhood dolls.

Perhaps it was the "slowness" on that road that had caused the sleeplessness. And the pieces that looked right, until they looked closer and saw a dropped stitch. A missed yarn over.

Ben had told her that the police were close to arresting Rico for suspicion of murder. The motive was strong, but things were missing. No prints in the right places. His and Frodo's footprints were all over the yard and steps—but they lived there, and so did their footprints. Probable cause loomed large, Jerry had said. And Rico's belligerent personality made it difficult, too. People didn't like him. But more importantly, Rico didn't like people.

And Harrison Grant was at the top of that list.

But he didn't murder the man, he had said simply.

And at least four Sea Harbor women believed him. They just needed to walk faster along that road less traveled, the one filled with holes and ruts and muddy soil.

Cass hadn't slept easily, either. And she couldn't blame it on baby Brandley this time. It was thoughts and impressions and feelings that had become tangled in her mind, as if tossed in a blender, along with bits and pieces of the evening's rooftop discussion, murders and motives and disappearances. Like a bad dream that pulled out disparate fears and fused them all together uncomfortably.

By the time the sun had come up and she had had her coffee and Danny's cinnamon French toast, the thoughts were settling, becoming less tangled. Less disparate.

She thought about how initial impressions about people in her life could change when you peeled off a layer, went a step deeper.

And she thought about Harrison Grant's murder.

Then she called Izzy Perry and asked her what she was up to that day, other than making herself gorgeous for Danny's book event that night in Gloucester.

A brisk Sunday walk was Izzy's plan, and not only because of Cass's cryptic phone call. She needed the walk to think clearly. And she needed her friends.

The far shore, Birdie had suggested, with the yacht club beach their destination. She knew the terrace and the beach would be empty on a crisp October Sunday, and there'd be coffee, patio chairs, and a quiet beach to help them gather their thoughts. The sea air to clean out the cobwebs.

The plan had taken no convincing. It seemed no one had slept well the night before.

"I found phone numbers for Harrison's trip to Cape Ann the first time he was here," Birdie said now, sliding back into the large Adirondack chair. The semicircle of chairs faced the sea, their backs to the yacht club terrace. "I also found numbers for his trip last week. I recognized a few of them—the Beauport Hotel's, the Canary Cove Art Association number. There was another. It was the same one listed on trips twenty years ago, and also on the list Charlotte gave him for his recent trip. It was also a local area code. I tried it. It was out of service."

Liz Santos, the yacht club manager, had spotted the women down on the lower beach terrace and sent staff people down with an armful of Hudson's Bay blankets, a carafe of coffee, and a plate of warm blueberry scones. "Liz said she knows you women are hale and hearty, but she sent these down just in case," one of the young waitresses said.

"You are all quite wonderful," Birdie said, smiling up at them as she immediately tucked one of the multi-striped blankets over her legs.

Izzy pulled a blanket around her shoulders, then reached for a coffee mug. She wrapped her cold fingers around the steaming mug and took the conversation away from the yacht club's famous Scottish scones. "So it was probably Martina's," she said, and then repeated details they now knew, as if in doing so, they'd come together more quickly. "Rico tried to call Martina, too, after she left. Probably that same number. He just wanted to hear her voice, he said. But she never answered. Months later, he tried again, and the phone was picked up by someone else who said Martina couldn't come to the phone. And when he tried again a day or two later, the number was no longer in service. That was when he knew that Martina had wiped him out of her life forever, plain and simple."

"If that's what happened," Cass said.

"What do you mean?" Nell asked.

"How do we know what Martina did or why? The whole

mystery of her disappearing like that doesn't feel right to me. She had married Rico. Why didn't she come back to him when Grant rejected her?" Cass took a deep breath. "I think Martina had other reasons."

Nell thought about Cass's words, wondering if there was more to them than she was saying. She looked at Cass closely, trying to read her expression. There was clearly something on Cass's mind, and she had a suspicion it fed into her own thoughts. Maybe they needed to let some thoughts simmer first, get other things out of the way, then see if the suspicions came together in a less fragmented way.

"Cass's right," Nell said out loud. "We're trying to make her actions simple. Logical. One man rejects you, so you go back to the first. But is that what everyone would do? Is that what you'd do?"

The "you" was universal, but the question was a good one, and they thought about it, admitted the difficulty in presuming what another person would do in any given circumstance. What rules of logic or morality or desire would that person follow? It was especially difficult to figure out the answer when they were talking about someone they had never met. And when they had no idea what had gone on in her head.

"Martina was erratic," Izzy said. "I don't think Rico was completely surprised that she didn't come back. And maybe it would have happened eventually, with or without Harrison Grant in the picture."

"One of the women I called said Harrison didn't take nicely to anyone putting demands on him. Didn't Harrison tell Rico his wife was devious or was tricking him?"

Nell sat up, listened. "Why?" she asked, holding on to the thought. "Or maybe more importantly, how?"

The thought simmered, gaining some strength, as they sat in their chairs, facing the view spread out in front of them for as far as they could see.

A few sailboats bobbed in the still waters, trying to catch a stray ocean breeze but content with the stillness, with the water, the world. A scene of calm and beauty. Quiet.

Behind them was the silent churning unrest that murder was wrapping around a town.

They refilled their mugs, drank the hot coffee, and replayed what they knew.

Someone in Sea Harbor hated Harrison Grant enough to kill him.

Someone who was hurt by him or knew he was having an affair. . . .

Then Nell pulled out the photo that she had taken home with her the night before. She set it on the small beach table, leaned it against the coffee carafe, and told them she had figured out where she had seen Martina Silva before.

The group fell silent.

And then the voices picked up in rapid fire as pieces of the puzzle fell in place, as bits of conversation took on new meaning. Separate encounters during the past days that had been tucked into shadowy parts of memories were given life, until a picture was visible, ragged and fuzzy, but revealing the beginning of an end.

And then Cass leaned slightly forward and laid out in the sand why she hadn't been able to sleep the night before.

Chapter 35

When they finally made their way back to their homes, their minds were spent, and their emotions reduced to puddles. A conclusion was what they were looking for, at least what they rationally wanted. All the pieces of yarn knit neatly in place. Smooth rows. A paint by number with almost every number painted.

But the knit piece had holes, and the unpainted numbers glared at them. *Paint me in*, they said.

They were almost there, ready to finish it all and yet hesitant to move forward. The last steps that would change someone's life forever. Murders left no one unscathed, not even the innocent.

But for now, brief moments of quiet, showers, and time to dress for Danny Brandley's book event were what they needed to think about.

Cass insisted on driving everyone to the book signing that evening. "I need more practice operating these wheels before there's a real baby in the backseat," she said, holding the door open for Birdie, telling her she got to ride shotgun again. "Pete and I used to kill for shotgun when we were kids."

Birdie chuckled, letting Cass help her into the car. "Is it a dangerous seat when the driver is practicing?" she asked. Once she was in, she twisted in the seat to greet Nell and Izzy, who were sitting in the back, then snapped her seat belt into place.

"This buggy even has cup holders that warm up baby bottles," Cass said, amazed at the conveniences afforded such tiny beings.

"It's a great car," Nell said, smiling distractedly from the back.

They all lapsed into silence then, as if they were all talked out, as if chitchat took too much effort, or maybe they had decided that sorting through things in their heads would be more helpful.

Cass drove the winding road over to Gloucester carefully, although it was almost empty on a Sunday night.

Nell's thoughts turned to Harrison Grant, and she wondered if he'd noticed the glimpses of the sea as he traveled this same road with Sam such a short time ago. What had he been thinking?

One more apology. One more thing to check off a list. And then what was next for him? A better life with the time he had left?

Or was it exactly what he'd planned?

The four women walked into a busy, noisy bookstore when they arrived a half hour early for Danny's event. They dodged a man carrying a box of wine and looked over at the stacks of Danny's books filling a table near the window.

Nell waved at the Bookstore of Gloucester owner and gave her a thumbs-up at the wonderful job she'd done in making Danny's event a festive one. It wasn't just Sea Harbor that was affected by a murder, and it was nice when the larger Cape Ann community came together for an enjoyable evening.

A staff member was arranging small cakes from Sandpiper Bakery on a narrow table near the wall, along with glasses for wine and soft drinks. Nell spotted Ben and Sam near the back of the store and headed toward them to see if they could help with anything.

Izzy looked around, spotted Sam, and waved. Then saw Cass heading out the door they'd just come in. Izzy followed.

"Fresh air," Cass said, wiping her forehead.

"Cass, it's cold out."

"I think my thermometer is broken. Or maybe it's being boxed in. Weird things bother me these days. Like I actually wanted to make cookies yesterday."

"Uh-oh," Izzy said. They started to walk away from the bookstore entrance, out of the way of people carrying things in and out. "That's a sign, Cass. Nesting. Have you seen Dr. Virgilio recently?"

"Oh, practically hourly. I asked her if she'd like to move in with me and Danny." She laughed as they continued to walk. "But don't worry. Danny took over and made the cookies. I fixed the broken faucet in the bathroom. That's not nesting. Right?"

Izzy shook her head, giving up, then glanced at Cass's profile. The baby had definitely dropped. Her concern soon became a smile that she couldn't control. *A baby. Cass's baby. Impossible. But real—and soon.*

But there were things to do before that baby could come. And it was becoming clearer by the hour what those things were.

Cass was looking at her watch. "We're early. Danny doesn't always start on time, anyway. He gets too busy talking to his adoring readers. So, what do you think?"

"I think we're starting to be like Birdie and Aunt Nell, crawling into each other's heads and thinking the same thoughts."

"That wouldn't be all bad. Just keep yours clean, okay?"

Izzy laughed. "And yes, to what you're thinking." She paused at a corner store. To the right was an alley leading down to Rogers Street. Izzy looked across the street the other way, then pointed toward the Franklin restaurant in the next block. "So that's where we ate that night . . ."

"And around here somewhere is where Sam saw Grant, right?"

"Yes. He was going to get the car in that parking lot on Rogers Street. He said he passed a coffee shop down an alley somewhere around here. There were apartments or condos near it. Maybe above it, and he thought—no, he was sure—he saw Grant talking to someone in the entrance to the apartments."

"So should we do a Birdie and walk in the guy's shoes?" Cass asked.

"This time we actually know where he walked." Izzy turned down the alley. "Maybe the person Grant was talking to can tell us exactly who he was looking for. But if he was trying to find Martina, why here?"

"Something must have directed him to those apartments. I can't imagine he was randomly knocking on doors," Cass said. "He was looking for something here. Maybe we'll get lucky and find out what."

They spotted the small parking lot in front of the coffee shop building, then walked around a few cars parked in the lot and saw an entrance to the coffee shop, and another one that looked like it led to apartments above.

Cass pointed above the shop. "There are lights on in all those windows up there. Let's give it a try."

A glass door, the apparent entry, was unlocked, and they walked into a dimly lit area with a bench on one side. Built into the opposite wall were three mailboxes, a buzzer next to each.

Izzy took out her phone and turned on the flashlight, then tried to read the names. "James Aisles," she read. "C. J. Newton. LTG Services." She straightened up.

"Let's try C. J." Cass said. "It's likely a woman. They use initials."

Izzy pressed the buzzer, and a male voice answered, clearly irritated at being interrupted. In the distance a television blared, some announcer screaming about a football fumble. Izzy apologized quickly, just in time for the man to hang up on her.

"Maybe 'James' is for Jamie?" Cass suggested.

Izzy gave it a try, and another man's voice answered, friendlier than the first. She explained they were looking for a woman who lived in one of the apartments, but they weren't sure which one. "She left something on the train, and we'd like to return it."

Cass gave Izzy a look of surprise and amusement. She whispered, "That was smooth, Iz. You lie well."

"Woman?" the man said.

"We thought it might be C. J. Newton," Izzy suggested. "But a man answered. Does he have a wife?"

"Nah. No one would marry that guy. No wives around here. Only woman is the one in number three. Did you try that one? The name on the mailbox is something weird, like a company."

"Do you know her name?" Cass piped up from behind Izzy.

"No. It's the condo right above the lobby. Right next to mine. I know she's home because I heard her come in. Music's playing, too. She must be cleaning or something."

"You said these are condos?" Cass asked.

"Right. We each own it. Why? Are you looking for a condo?"

"No, just curious. But thanks."

Izzy pressed the buzzer.

They waited a few minutes, now hearing the music above their heads.

Izzy buzzed again.

The music stopped.

After the third try and a long wait, Cass looked up at the ceiling. "I think I hear footsteps."

Izzy shrugged. They walked outside and looked back up at the windows. The middle apartment was now dark.

"Strange," Izzy said. She checked the address on the building.

They turned and walked back toward the alley, taking a shortcut between two parked SUVs. Cass noticed a familiar parking sticker in the window of one of them. She stopped, looked again, then cupped her hands and tried to see inside the car. It was a green CR-V, several years old and well taken care of. It looked familiar to Cass, but it also looked like every third or fourth car in Sea Harbor. The only difference was that this one looked like it was packed for a trip. And there was another difference, too.

"Cass." Izzy nudged her lightly, pulling her attention away from the car. She pointed up at the middle condo. "Look."

Cass looked up, just in time to see the window curtains drop back into place. Behind them, a shadow moved away.

Chapter 36

Nell had found a parking place near Pelican Pier. She and Birdie bundled up against the late morning breeze and started down Harbor Road to meet Cass in Coffee's, the Harbor Road coffee shop she frequented. The owner had started giving Cass free lattes on Mondays, celebrating the ten years in which Cass had rarely wavered from starting her day off at Coffee's. It came along with the expectation of complimentary lobsters on the owner's birthday, and Cass complied.

"I talked to Cass briefly. She's concerned," Nell said. The statement was worse than redundant. It was empty. All of them were concerned—and sad and hopeful and slightly fearful, all at once. Emotions that didn't live together comfortably.

"Is Izzy coming?" Birdie asked.

"As soon as she goes over the shop schedule with Mae."

They pulled up their collars against the wind and crossed the street, hurrying into Coffee's where the fire would feel especially good today.

"Crazy weather," the owner called out. "Winter, summer, spring, and fall all in one week."

Birdie chuckled, then ordered three coffees and followed Nell to the table near the fireplace. It was where they expected to find Cass, her feet propped up on the stone hearth and a book in her hand. A coveted quiet spot that Cass claimed as her own.

But they were wrong. Cass was sitting close to the crackling fire, but straight up, her feet planted beneath a low table. She was doodling on a coffee-stained napkin as she held her cell phone to her ear with the other hand.

She spoke a few more words before ending the conversation, then put the cell phone on the table and smiled at her friends.

"Are you all right?" Birdie asked, unbuttoning her coat and sitting down next to Cass.

"Not really," Cass said.

Nell managed a smile and pulled up a chair. "No, of course not. It's not an 'all right' kind of day, is it?"

"Was that Izzy on the phone?" Birdie asked.

Cass looked down. "No, I was talking to Elena. She mentioned to me this weekend that there's an impromptu yoga class today. We had both decided not to go, but I wanted to check to be sure she didn't go." Cass managed a half smile. "She's baking bread and cleaning the basement. She thought her washing machine was dirty. Now, how can a washing machine get dirty?"

They chuckled.

"And, yes, I reminded her about nesting. Who made up those fairy tales for pregnant women, anyway? I will never have this baby if I have to find a nest first."

Birdie patted her hand, and Nell smiled, neither woman having given birth, but both of them thinking they would have nested beautifully if it had happened. And Cass would, too, either before or after.

"But you look worried, Cass. You're concerned about Elena," Birdie said softly.

Cass looked at her meaningless scribblings. Then smiled at Birdie. "So, did you hear? They sold a lot of Danny's books last night," she said, knowing Birdie wouldn't answer.

"It was a nice evening. And I don't think Danny even noticed that you and Izzy missed most of his reading and talk," Nell said.

"He knows I could give it for him," Cass said, looking toward the door as Izzy's bright orange jacket came into view.

She headed their way, bringing the chilly air along with her. "Sorry I'm late. I stopped by city hall." She pointed to the large tote bag slung over her shoulder and settled down in a chair.

Nell had brought the old photo again, as if Martina was now a part of the group, helping them bring the tumultuous days to rest. They knew her more intimately and read things in her face that weren't there just days ago. Today they passed the photo around more slowly, looking at her more carefully, trying to read emotion in her face.

Once Martina's image was back on the table, they focused on the flames leaping in the grate and thought about the power of anger, so strong it could kill a man.

Then Izzy leaned down and pulled out the copies she'd made at the register of deeds office.

"The woman Harrison Grant talked to at the condo—or whoever was there last night—didn't want to talk to us, but we learned it was a condo, not an apartment rental, so I thought the property deeds might help us out," Izzy said.

She laid the papers on the table and highlighted the names on the top sheet. It had been bought under a corporation name. But had changed hands. Two owners. First one. Then deeding it to another.

They read the names, the transactions, then looked at the photo of Martina.

Cass swore she nodded at them.

Another piece of the puzzle, a big one this time—missing for a long time—fell into place. *Clunk.* The sound was real, at least to each of the women who heard it.

"Are you ladies meditating or what?" Jake Risso's loud voice jarred them out of their thoughts, startling Izzy into spilling coffee onto the table. A brown circle meandered near Martina Silva's photo. Izzy soaked it up quickly with a napkin.

"Hey, sorry there. I didn't mean to scare you."

Cass pulled herself to attention. "You're just a scary dude, Jake. What're you doing in here? Did you finally figure out that brown swill you perk in your bar isn't real coffee?"

Jake's laugh was hearty, and they all managed to smile. "Coffee's and I have our own private liquid exchange," Jake said. "It's a free market kind of deal." He laughed again.

Nell spoke up. "Not to change this intriguing subject, but, Jake, there's something I've been meaning to ask you. That nice fellow you introduced me to a few days ago, Frank . . ."

"Oh, sure, Nellie. Frank Ames. Nicest guy in the world."

"For some reason, we thought he was a photographer," Nell said.

"Yeah, you said that. But he's not, at least not a professional one. Lots of people are photographers, even if they're not, you know what I mean?"

"Okay, so he's not a photographer, then, but does he have another job here?" Cass asked. "Besides being the nicest guy in the world."

"Sure he does. And I hear he's good at it. He's a . . ." And then he paused, grinning down at the four women who were waiting for the sentence to end. "Tell you what, let him tell you himself. He'll get a kick out of it. I just saw him. He was headed across the street to Garozzo's deli. He can't pass up that soup Harry makes."

They all looked in the direction of Garozzo's, although a windowless wall, a fireplace, and a city block marred their view.

When they looked back, Jake was headed toward the door, where a new crowd of customers was streaming in.

"It's not as quiet in here as I thought it'd be," Cass said. "Maybe a take-out order of Garozzo's sandwiches and Izzy's back room would be better."

"A good plan, Cass dear, but before we go," Birdie said, "I have my own show-and-tell. It goes right along with Izzy's findings." She pulled a small iPad from her tote and touched it a few times until a screen of numbers appeared.

"You're getting to be quite a techie, Birdie Favazza," Cass said.

"Yes, I am. Now, it occurred to me that the file Charlotte sent to me with Harrison's travels included addresses he'd need as well as phone numbers. I didn't pay attention to them, because we knew where he'd be, what the addresses would be—the hotel, the Art Haven home, Canary Cove. But when I looked last night, there was one that wasn't connected to the art colony activities."

She enlarged the numbers until one stood out. A now-familiar address.

Nell caught a glimpse of Frank Ames as they walked into the deli. He was sitting toward the back of the restaurant area, partially hidden behind a table of ladies in purple hats who were celebrating someone's birthday. It was difficult to see who was with him. Nell stepped closer to the entrance. Just then he stood up, grabbed a jacket from his chair, and seemed to smile at someone. But when he walked around the purple hats, he was alone.

Frank strode through the restaurant, smiling at folks, and then saw Nell standing in the deli. "It's nice to see you again. Nell, right?"

"That's right. You have a good memory," she said, then introduced him to Birdie and Izzy. She pointed over to the counter, where Cass was placing their sandwich order. "I think you've met Cass Halloran, too?"

Cass walked over, smiling. "Hi again."

"Well, sure. Good to see you. We met at Harmony's yoga place."

"That's right," Cass said. "And at the risk of seeming to be stalking you, Jake Risso sent us over. We have this little thing going on. He seems to disagree with us that you're a photographer . . ."

Frank laughed. "Now I remember. Because of that day at Harmony's."

"Right."

"And that's why you thought I was a photographer."

And a close friend of Harmony's, Nell thought, remembering the day they'd seen Harmony and Frank together in the deli. The enormous smile on Harmony's face. But she was beginning to wonder if they'd jumped to all sorts of conclusions about Frank Ames's relationship with the yoga instructor, conclusions based solely on what they'd seen: a pleasant man and an obviously happy woman. But not on what they had known or even what they had felt.

"So no, I'm not a photographer. I'm a PI. Frank Ames, private investigator, at your service, ma'am." He did a comical bow, along with giving them a wide, friendly smile.

"A PI," Cass said, surprised. "So you were working with Harmony . . . not, well . . . whatever."

Frank nodded in response to Cass's statement, looked around, and then lowered his head, as if about to speak to Cass in a more confidential way.

The others took the cue and walked over to the counter to check on the sandwiches.

The two moved away from the line and to a quieter corner of the deli, away from the crowd waiting for orders.

"That's right," Frank said. "Working *for* her, actually. The job is over now, but you probably know that."

Cass started to ask why she would know that, but Frank continued. "We met here a few days ago with my report. It was a hard case with a happy ending. I like that kind. Much better than the ones where the husband really did have five wives and fifteen kids . . ." He laughed again. "Joking about that, of course. Most cases are pretty mundane. But this one, well, for the most part, had a good conclusion. The news seemed to bring great relief to Harmony. Made her one happy customer. I hope you felt the same way."

"Me?" Cass asked.

Frank's tone was quiet and discreet. "I know, I might have given you both the report, but Harmony said you were busy, and she was paying the bills, so I assumed it was all right. You and Elena Costa are close, right?"

"Well, yes, I suppose you could say that."

Frank looked relieved. "Harmony had explained to me that you had taken Elena and her husband under your wing, employing her husband, watching over her, and that you were also concerned about the need to trace her background, with her having a baby and all. She said both of you felt the need for the Costas to have some certainty. So I took the case. Glad to help. It wasn't that difficult finding out about the birth. Harmony had a suspicion about who her birth mother was, and she was right. Adoption cases used to be difficult, but these days it's easier. Organizations seem to understand the importance of kids knowing their history, especially medical."

"You said the case had a good conclusion for the most part? What was the part that wasn't so good?"

"Well, that was devastating to Harmony, I'm sure. It's always difficult to find out news like that. Elena's mother died soon after childbirth."

Chapter 37

Elena Costa kissed her husband good-bye, then told him he was starting to be a worrywart. Where was the carefree Marco she'd married? Harmony had explained that at Elena's stage, it'd be very helpful to squeeze this class in. Her muscles needed to be prepared to help that amazing baby come into the world. Then Elena grinned and said, "Who knows? It might be my last class for a few weeks, Daddy."

Harmony was waiting in the car. She leaned over, opened the passenger door, and helped Elena inside.

"I hope you don't mind that I came early."

Elena was checking her phone—Marco had already sent an emoji message filled with hearts. She grinned at the phone and set it down on the console. "I'm sorry, Harmony. That was rude of me. Sometimes I think Marco is pregnant. He's so very excited. What did you say?"

"It's nothing." Harmony smiled over at Elena and drove out of the small neighborhood. "It's such a beautiful day."

Elena looked out the window at the bending trees. It was cold and windy, but nice that Harmony saw another side to the day.

They drove through Canary Cove, then toward town. Elena wondered about her decision to go to the extra class. Cass hadn't thought it was a great idea and had seemed relieved when Elena said she was going to pass it up, too. She continued to look out the window, enjoying the quiet, her mind turning to the new baby crib, to Cass, her wise mentor. Even Marco had admitted Cass was a good lady. Tough sometimes. But fair. All the guys thought so, even though they liked giving her a hard time. Then Elena closed her eyes for a minute, her forehead resting on the glass, and imagined the first time she and Marco would hold their baby. A strong pull inside her brought her eyes wide open. She took a breath, then slowly released it, her body relaxing.

She settled back in the seat and finally turned her head to look over at Harmony, apologizing for ignoring her.

"You're just having delicious baby thoughts, I can tell. And quiet is good. It will help you be ready. But I need to tell you something." Harmony turned another corner, then passed a wooded stretch of land along the road. "I got a message on my way to your house that there is a leak in the pipes at the Y. The class is postponed. But you were already ready, and it's such a beautiful day, so I thought a ride would be good for you. For both of us."

Elena again looked out the window. They were crossing the bridge, heading toward the highway. She turned back. "That's nice of you, Harmony, but I'm feeling strange. I don't want to hurt your feelings, but I'd like to go back to my house, to Marco. He worries. I think I need to be home." Elena's voice was calm. She'd seen the baby seat and the bottles and blankets in the back of the car when she'd climbed in. *Donations for somewhere*, she'd thought then. *Harmony was generous*. Now they frightened her.

"I have a cabin in Maine," Harmony was saying, as if Elena hadn't spoken. "It's beautiful up there this time of year. Well, all year, really."

Elena forced a smile, feeling a new cramping in her lower abdomen. "It would be nice to see it someday. Marco and I . . ." She breathed in, letting it out slowly. "Marco and I and the baby will drive up, and you can show us around."

"It's such a lovely place. I do yoga every morning, out on a small dock I have." Harmony smiled, her eyes on the road.

Elena bit down on her lip, holding back the tears and the discomfort. "Harmony, I think I'm going to have this baby soon."

Harmony's expression didn't change as she picked up speed. "I told your mother I would raise you the way she would want. I begged her to let me do that. And now there's a new baby to care for . . ."

Elena tried to force a calm into her voice. "You're a good person, Harmony. You've been kind to me. Could we please stop here for a while, just until—" She paused as her breath caught, the pull inside her body strong and jarring. She waited, breathed, then spoke again. "Could we pull over so I can find my phone? It must have fallen on the floor. I hear it. Marco's calling. And Cass will be checking in—"

Harmony's voice was smooth and even, as if guiding Elena into a yoga pose. But talking to someone who wasn't there. Her smile never changed, even when she spoke. "Don't you worry, sweet Martina," she said. "I will take care of your baby."

Elena felt a dampness beneath her legs. Harmony looked over, smiled, then looked back to the road.

"Everything will be perfect. Marco and Cass don't understand things like I do. There are pine trees everywhere. Wild berries to pick. And we can plant a garden."

Elena began to breathe, slowly, carefully, while the tears ran freely down her cheeks and the car picked up speed.

Chapter 38

Cass related her conversation to the others, including the inaccuracies Harmony had used when hiring Frank. "Maybe she thought having both of us concerned about finding Elena's mother made it more urgent."

"Or maybe she was just lying," Izzy said, carrying the bag of sandwiches into the yarn shop.

Birdie had called Charlotte Simpson as soon as they left the deli. She'd answered on the first ring. And of course, she had the information Birdie needed at her fingertips. Yes, she remembered the condominium. She had arranged the sale herself. For the company. And then put it in someone else's name a short while later. She had done it all over the phone. And yes, she knew where it was.

Ben hadn't answered Nell's call, and then she'd remembered his city council meeting. And that he'd be seeing the chief, too. She and Ben had talked for a long time that morning. The holes were there. They both could see that. But the direction was clear. But some holes loomed larger for Ben, his cautious side weighing in. A murder conviction labeled one for life, even if one was proven innocent, he'd reminded her.

But now the holes were filled, even if questions remained.

The back room was empty.

"A slow day," Mae said. "You all look tired. Go on down to the knitting room and enjoy your lunch."

Izzy took the wrapped sandwiches out of the bag and put them on a tray, but for the first time in any of their memories, Cass didn't take the first one. Or any.

She sat at the end of the library table and called Elena. When there was no answer, she tried Marco. The conversation was brief, but the women listening in saw concern flood Cass's face.

She hung up and repeated the conversation. "Apparently, Harmony called Elena and suggested she take today's class, that it would help her prepare for the delivery. Marco tried to talk her out of it, because Elena had had some pains during the night. Cramping, he said."

Cass made another call. The YMCA confirmed her fears. There wasn't a pregnant mom's yoga class scheduled for that day. The receptionist said that maybe it was a private class. But Harmony's car wasn't there so she couldn't imagine who'd be teaching it.

"The green CR-V?" Cass asked, and the receptionist said yes.

The CR-V with the Y parking sticker that Cass had seen in the Gloucester parking lot the night before. The one packed to the gills with baby equipment.

Nell finally reached Ben and relayed what they'd discovered, the urgency, the fact that Elena Costa might be in danger. And a description of Harmony Fairchild's car.

Cass looked around the table. Without a word, they put their jackets back on and piled in Izzy's car, not sure where it would take them.

They were driving in circles—over to Gloucester to the condos, to the Y, the Ocean's Edge, and around the small park near the Costas' home. Marco's truck was gone from the drive beside the house, and Cass wondered if he'd gone to the yoga studio to look. She tried Elena again. And then again and again.

It seemed like a lifetime later when Cass's phone finally rang.

It was her doctor. And Elena's. Dr. Lily Virgilio.

Relief flooded Izzy's car as Cass clicked her phone on speaker and held it out.

Elena was in labor at the birthing center, Dr. Virgilio said. A woman had dropped her off at the door and sped away, so fast she had almost hit an attendant, a bystander had reported. Elena was concentrating on having a baby, as she should, and didn't have much of an explanation of who the woman was.

"Marco is on his way over," Lily added. "But Elena wanted me to let you know, too. She said to tell you that everything is going to be fine."

It was one of the few times Cass's closest friends had seen her cry. Simple, slow tears streaming down her face.

Just before Lily hung up—she had a baby to help deliver, she said happily—she added, "Elena did manage to say something about a yoga class or something, although the conversation was interrupted by contractions and didn't make complete sense. But she wanted you to know that the teacher might be in distress—and maybe in danger."

Cass hung up her phone, wiped the tears with her sleeve. "It sounds like Elena thinks Harmony is going to harm herself."

Izzy had pulled over to the curb while Cass was talking. Then she turned toward the others. "I think I know where she'd go."

It didn't take Izzy long to find the lost cove, but only because she had been there before—the day Harmony had had a birthday yoga class for her and her friends. And it was where Beatrice Scaglia had gotten sand in her tights.

But where Harmony Fairchild found peace.

It was so hidden that Izzy had dared Sam to find it one lazy Saturday. They'd packed up Abby and a picnic lunch and tried, just for the adventure of it. It had taken over two hours of wrong turns and hidden roads, but finally they'd found it. Today, with a sense of urgency fine-tuning her sense of direction, Izzy found it again. Quickly.

Once necessary calls had been made, including to Sam, who would head over to guide the police to the hidden beach, Izzy had concentrated on the road, and they had all fallen into silence, the only sounds the bumping of the car along the deeply rutted road. Branches from wild bushes had crowded their way, brushing against Izzy's car. Overgrown trees, eerily twisted from nor'easters, had blocked out the sunlight, until finally the narrow passage had given way to an open space and to the ocean.

And to a single green CR-V parked in a gravelly spot at its edge.

They got out of the car and walked closer to the sea, across a rocky stretch, and around a bend, where a small sweep of sand was spread out like a blanket.

A lone figure was sitting Padmasana in the middle of it, her eyes closed, her breathing slow, and her face enormously sad.

Cass led the way across the sand. She stopped a few feet away, and her shadow fell across Harmony.

"Elena and her baby are going to be fine, Harmony," she said quietly. "Thank you for taking her to the hospital."

Harmony didn't look up. "When she cried like that, in pain, I couldn't stand the sound. It was wrenching, making me dizzy. I needed it to stop. I needed to make it stop."

She fell silent again, as if communing with someone they couldn't see. Or going back in time. Another life.

Finally, she opened her eyes.

"Martina called me. One time. I learned she was about to have a baby and was giving it away. I begged her to give it to me. I loved Martina. The baby was a part of her. How could I not want it? She owed me that baby. And then a miracle happened. Elena came into my class that day, looking exactly like her mother. I knew it even before Frank confirmed it for me. Martina had finally given her baby to me."

Cass rubbed away the chills on her arms. "So you were in touch with Martina after she left Rico? All those years ago? She told you she was pregnant?" Cass said.

"I knew she was pregnant when she left Sea Harbor. She wasn't sure who the father was, but she didn't care. She would use it to get Harrison Grant. I knew that wouldn't work—I knew what he was like—but I thought she'd come home then. Go back to Silva and all his money. Be there for me. My one true friend. She had become everything to me. And she cared for me, too, or maybe I was just useful to her. I don't know. But she needed me to be able to keep things from Rico, and that was enough. When she left, I was nothing. She never answered my calls. And then that one day, she called me. But it wasn't because she was coming back. It was something else."

"She was giving you the condo that Grant had bought for her. A place for them to meet," Nell said gently.

Harmony nodded. "Yeah. That's why she called. To tell me that she had changed the deed. It was right before she had the baby. She was staying with an old aunt for those months. Never coming back."

Harmony's voice turned hard. "But strangers got the baby. All I got was that condo. She wanted neither of them. And she especially didn't want Rico. She mentioned complications in her pregnancy. High blood pressure or something. Said that she'd already signed the child away. That's how she put it. Signed the child away."

Harmony's head tilted back as she looked up at the sun. Then she lowered it again. "I begged her to let me have the baby. I would love the child."

Tears ran down Harmony's face, but her body was composed and relaxed. In touch with something none of them could feel.

"Martina hung up on me that day," she said. "When I called back, there was no answer. The next time I tried, a few days later, when I thought the baby would have arrived and she'd have changed her mind, the line was dead. And so was she."

There was no feeling in Harmony's voice when she told the rest of the story.

She had seen Grant in the bar at the Beauport Hotel when he came for the lecture series. Seeing him there had been an accident, although she'd known he was coming to town. The posters had been everywhere.

But that same night he'd suddenly shown up at her door. It had shocked her, but she had realized soon that he had no idea who she was. All he wanted was to find someone named Martina.

"I told him I had never heard of anyone named Martina. But after he left that night, all that anger came back. Over twenty years of anger. How he had broken Martina as surely as if she'd been a porcelain doll. And all those awful months of not knowing where Martina was, the pain of losing her. The years after, feeling abandoned. So I left a note for him that I had news about Martina and would meet him that night."

"But why at Rico's?" Cass asked.

"It seemed the right place," Harmony said. "Irony maybe. He wanted to know about Martina. That big house was Martina's. And he came."

In the distance, sirens filled the air. Harmony didn't move.

"He told me he had come to apologize to Martina for the pain he had caused her. And then . . . and then he apologized to me."

"Did it help?" Cass asked gently, as if somehow asking the question might change the ending.

"Of course it didn't help. Why would I accept an apology from him? You can't apologize for destroying someone. Harrison Grant destroyed me. And he threw away my Martina, destroying her. You can't apologize for killing someone. He couldn't . . . and I won't."

Finally, Harmony stood up, as if lifted up by the air, and smiled at Cass. Then she walked slowly past the women, across the sand, toward the spinning lights and the waiting police.

Chapter 39

They had gathered together at Ben and Nell's for soup, courtesy of Garozzo's deli, before a short visit to the birthing center to welcome a new baby.

Jerry Thompson had suggested he drop in, too, rather than bringing them down to the station to smooth out some details. And there was also Garozzo's soup, his second-best favorite, after Nell's.

"It's clear Harmony needs help," Jerry said, wiping the last bit of Tuscan chicken soup from the bottom of his bowl. He stretched his long legs out beneath the dining table. "And she'll get it. But it's also a fact that she had decided to murder Harrison Grant that night. It wasn't good planning. She could have failed had Grant not been ill. But unfortunately, she was successful. Anger is a powerful weapon."

"This is jarring for Rico. It's so much to take in." Nell stood and began to clear the empty soup bowls.

"He's mourning Martina," Izzy said. She looked at the police chief. "I went over to be with him after Tommy had told him about Martina's death and about Grant's murderer. About

Harmony, this woman he'd never met and the enormous role she had had in his life."

The silence that filled the room was heavy with thoughts of how a man's life had been shaken to the core. In tragic and hopeful ways at once.

The question of Elena's paternity hung in the air, but Izzy addressed it before it was brought up.

"Rico says the issue of Elena's biological father is of no consequence to him, not now. Maybe never. He is just celebrating her. The news that Martina's daughter has been living here in Sea Harbor, just miles away, is truly mind boggling to him. And joyous. It's awesome. And I swear that big old house of his looks brighter already."

The thought of the Cliffside neighborhood grouch going soft made all of them smile.

"Harmony Fairchild had been in trouble with the law a few other times," Jerry said. "But years ago. Mostly for anger and other emotional issues. People had seen her at the Beauport that night Grant was there, and the bartender mentioned her staring at Grant. They knew her over there because she teaches a yoga class for guests occasionally. So we talked to her. But we couldn't make a connection to Grant."

Cass stood and suggested those going over to welcome baby Costa should head out before it got too late. Izzy, Birdie, and Nell were ready with baby books, stuffed animals and several soft, snuggly knit baby blankets. All machine washable and ready for baby burps.

Danny stood, too. "Hey, how about I chauffeur you ladies over in our baby bus?"

"Are you sure?" Cass said, surprised. "That's nice of you, but we won't be long."

"Yeah, I'm sure," he said with a smile. "I need another look at that place, that birthing center."

"Why? Are you changing your mind about this whole thing?" Cass asked.

They all laughed, but Danny held his ground. "I figure a trial run can't hurt. Maybe Marco can give me some tips. Besides, you are all masters at listening to your feelings. I *feel* like it'd be a good idea for me to go. Intuition."

"Well, then, you should come with us," Nell said, holding out his jacket.

It was an hour later that Ben got the call from Nell, telling him not to have a nightcap. They might need a ride home. And then she explained why.

Danny Brandley's intuition was almost as sophisticated as that of the four special women he'd driven to the birthing center. Cass Halloran Brandley was about to have a baby. Danny had felt it. And had even had her suitcase ready in the back of the baby bus.

Chapter 40

"It takes a village to have a baby shower. At least here in Sea Harbor," Mae Anderson said, bossing people around the room.

Once it was clear Izzy's yarn shop wasn't big enough to hold both the participants and the knitted baby clothes and blankets—hundreds of them, at last count—Jane Brewster had suggested another venue. Art Haven, a chance to fill the mansion's rooms and hallways with good feelings, good spirits, great vibes, the kind that celebrating new life can create.

Mae had agreed and had taken to directing the Canary Cove artists, who had taken on the project with unexpected fervor, designing huge handwoven baskets for donated baby hats, a cardboard train car to take blankets and hats and onesies to Children's Hospital. Clotheslines hung from one wooden ceiling beam to the next all around the great room and filled with hanging baby clothes in every color of an artist's palette. No baby on the North Shore would have a bare head or a blanketless bed this coming winter.

And, of course, there were balloons hanging inside and out, with hand-painted fish and bunnies and bears circling around each one.

Mae was pleased. "Well, what do you think?" she asked Nell and Birdie. They were standing on the sidelines, watching friends and neighbors stream into the room—women of all shapes and sizes, babies, and a larger than expected scattering of men. All smiling.

"It's perfect," Birdie said. "Amazing."

"And happy," Nell added. She waved to Mary Halloran, Cass's mother, who was coming in with a trayful of cupcakes. And beaming.

"How many novenas do you think it took Mary to get this grandbaby?" Izzy wondered aloud as she walked up to Nell and Birdie. She was fiddling with music on her phone, finally finding the Pharrell Williams song and playlist that seemed to be the theme of the day. "Happy." In minutes she sent the song's contagious lyrics pulsing through the sound system.

Nell laughed at the noticeable upbeat in people's footsteps, especially in those of her grandniece, Abby, who was twirling in the center of the room, clapping her hands to the catchy vibe.

People wandered around, touching the piles of soft yarn, finding the right needles in the wicker baskets. Sinking into the comfortable chairs, placing yarn on their laps. The gathering was informal, no presents to unwrap, no presentations.

Just friendship and knitting. And thoughts of new life.

Ben walked over with Sam, admiring his twirling grandniece. "Where're the Brandleys?" he asked Izzy. "Danny's folks just walked in."

"They're on their way. Danny just called," Izzy said.

Nell walked into the foyer and looked out the door. More people, more sweaters and blankets and food. And then she stopped and looked again when Danny and Cass's baby bus pulled in.

She hurried outside to welcome Elena and Marco, Danny and Cass, all arriving in the Brandleys' new car. It pulled up, and they piled out.

Along with two special infants. James Enrico Costa and Joseph Archibald Brandley. Dressed to the nines in hand-knit lobster-themed sweaters and hats. They were robust month-old boys, healthy and strong, with vigorous lungs. And destined to be friends for the rest of their lives.

"These guys wanted to come, too," a voice beside Nell said.

She turned.

Rico Silva stood beside her, clean and almost shaven, with Frodo and Red in front of him.

"Izzy dropped off Red earlier for a bath. I give good baths. They look good, right?" he said.

The two dogs thumped their tails.

Before Nell could concur, Izzy came up behind Rico and Nell. "Well, clean at least," she said. She gave Rico a hug. It was Izzy's claim to fame that in one month she'd gotten Rico to accept hugs without a single twinge.

Elena walked over to the threesome, smiling at Rico. "Just who I was looking for. Going in?" she asked him, tucking her arm in his. Behind her, Marco swung baby James Enrico's carrier to the music that was pouring out the open door.

Nell watched them all walk inside and began to feel the tears swell as she looked at the lives that had been changed and toyed with and upended in the past weeks and had ended up on top. Whole. And happy.

Two hours later the crowd thinned out, and the baskets and cardboard train were filled with baby clothes and readied for delivery to hospitals and shelters.

Izzy was standing alone in the foyer, feeling the weary satisfaction of a wonderful event, when she spotted Rico alone on the front steps.

She walked outside and stood beside him, breathing in the fresh air and watching Frodo and Red chasing each other around the circle drive. Rico was silent, content, and aware of Izzy at his side,

On the other side of the drive, Marco and Danny were packing up the car, ready to take their families home.

Rico turned to watch the babies disappear inside the large SUV.

"They are lucky babies," Izzy said. "Much loved."

"Miracles," he said, his voice gruff. "That's what those babies are." His brows pulled together, as if tugging at thoughts that had been percolating in his head. He took a deep breath and spoke softly, his eyes still on the car, his words aimed at Izzy.

"Truth is, missy, I think I knew Martina was dead. People thought I was grieving all those years, but I think I knew she was gone. I knew it somewhere inside me. Right here." He made a fist and thumped his chest. "I think what I really was, was lonely."

Just then Danny drove slowly around the circle drive and pulled to a stop in front of them. The back window rolled down, and Elena's head popped out. "James Enrico needs a good-bye hug," she said. "Come, Papa Rico."

Izzy watched the flush climb up Rico's neck and touch his cheeks. He walked over to the window and followed orders, the baby's round head almost the size of his own.

Finally he stepped back and the car began to drive away, with Danny beeping a good-bye on the horn and Elena's face at the back window waving at Rico.

He walked back to Izzy's side. "Ya know, I don't give a tinker's damn about a paternity test. I told you that, right?"

Izzy nodded. She did know it. He'd told her several times. But she knew from her uncle Ben that for legal reasons, he probably should have one. She also suspected his reasons for not pushing it were out of love.

As if reading her thoughts, Rico went on. "I'll do it if Elena wants me to. Sure I will. But it doesn't make any difference to anything. She and James Enrico are my family. I'm telling you right now, missy, it's all right here in my heart. How much I love those two. She's my daughter. He's my grandson. That will never change, no matter what some piddly lab tests show. She's my daughter until hell freezes over and for as long as this body holds out, I'll be there for both of them. And maybe after that too."

Izzy put an arm through Rico's, and they watched together as Frodo and Red continued their circle runs, tails wagging and heads moving in the wind.

Rico tilted his head back, the few hairs left on his head flying in the breeze, and laughed. "And believe it or not, missy, I'm even beginning to like that goofy Marco."

Izzy's head went back, too, her laughter blending with the old man's.

Then they turned together, arms still linked, and walked back into the house.

Acknowledgments

I am grateful for those who helped me in the writing of this book, both by touching it with ideas and inspiration, and by being in my life as I wrote it. During its inception and growth, my husband and I closed up our longtime family home in Prairie Village, Kansas, and moved to Gloucester, Massachusetts, to a new town and into a small condo, close to family and the most welcoming people on earth, who made this life change a true gift. I am grateful to all those dear friends from Kansas to Massachusetts who helped us on that journey emotionally and practically and inspirationally. And continue to do so.

And my thanks go to the many others who helped me through the days, the months, of writing this book~

To my friend Nancy Pickard, who brainstormed the original idea for *A Crime of a Different Stripe* with me, then helped me pull the story together during a mini writers' retreat on Folly Island, South Carolina.

To Wendy McCurdy, my editor, for her patience and help; to Lauren Jernigan, for her social media expertise; to Elizabeth Trout; Michelle Addo to the production team, the layout and copy editors, and to the whole Kensington family, which supports authors completely, making us feel a part of this great book-loving company.

To Christina Hogrebe and Andrea Cirillo and the entire JRA family, for more years than I can count of encouragement and support.

To my very own "idea board"—Sr. Rosemary Flanigan and Mary Bednarowski, who are always there to play with the vague ideas I throw at them, and then magically take them to new places. And to my amazing, deeply missed PV (and Fairway and Leawood and KC!) friends, who put up with a writer friend whose book signings were often on inconvenient nights, and they came, anyway.

To Muffy White, a good friend and gifted photographer, who has deepened my appreciation of the art of photography through her own work, which, in turn, helped me write about it in *A Crime of a Different Stripe.*

To Arwen Severance, owner of the Bookstore of Gloucester, for all her help and support with the Seaside Knitters Society Mysteries, from ordering to selling to sending signed books to readers, and most especially, for keeping this wonderful, much-loved independent bookstore vital in our town.

To Memory Lane, an amazing and talented social media guru, who helps me navigate the mysterious world of social media and connect with readers in new and exciting ways.

To my husband, Don, and to Todd, Danny, and Aria, our three grown-up kids, who always, but especially this year, have been a true inspiration to me in my writing and in my life.

And to my amazing readers, without whom there would be no Nell, Birdie, Izzy, and Cass. I love your emails and messages and notes and all of you. You inspire me every single day.

Little Waves Baby Hat Pattern

Designed for *A Crime of a Different Stripe* by Jessica Gingerich*

Birdie knit this simple baby hat for Cass's baby and added her own special touch by adding a tiny knit lobster to the rim.

Materials

1 skein of Starbright Muse Fibers Elementary Worsted (208 yards/ 115 grams per skein, 100 percent superwash merino wool) *or* about 75 yards (90, 110) of worsted-weight yarn

US size 7, 12-inch circular needles and a set of size 7 DPNs or a needle for magic loop for decreasing the top of the hat. (Or US size 7 circular needles, 32 inches or longer for magic loop method.) Needle sizes may differ; make sure to get gauge.

One stitch marker

One of the following: a length of ribbon about 12 inches long *or* a size G crochet hook for making a crochet chain *or* size 5 knitting needles for making an I cord.

Gauge: 20 stitches and 30 rows = 4 inches in stockinette stitch

Sizes: To fit preemie/newborn (infant/toddler, small child) About 11 inches (14.5, 18) around, or 5.5 inches (7.25, 9) when laid flat

Directions

Cast on 54 (72, 90) stitches and join to work in the round. Place a marker to keep track of the beginning of the round.

Garter brim:
Round 1: k around.
Round 2: p around.
Round 3: k around.
Round 4: p around.

Proceed to Little Waves Baby Hat Pattern.

Little Waves pattern:
Rounds 1 and 2: k around.
Round 3: *(k2tog) three times, (yo, k1) six times, (k2tog) three times* around.
Round 4: p around.

Work rounds 1–4 of Little Waves pattern 3 (4, 6) times total. Now knit all stitches around in every round until the hat measures about 3.5 inches (4, 5.25) or the desired length from cast-on edge when measured from the shortest part of brim.

Decreases:
Round 1: *k7, k2tog* around. 48 (64, 80) sts remain.
Round 2 and all even rounds until round 14: k around.
Round 3: *k6, k2tog* around. 42 (56, 70) sts remain.
Round 5: *k5, k2tog* around. 36 (48, 60) sts remain.
Round 7: *k4, k2tog* around. 30 (40, 50) sts remain.
Round 9: *k3, k2tog* around. 24 (32, 40) sts remain.
Round 11: *k2, k2tog* around. 18 (24, 30) sts remain.
Round 13: *k1, k2tog* around. 12 (16, 20) sts remain.
Round 14: *k2tog* around. 6 (8, 10) sts remain.

Cut your yarn, leaving an 8 inch tail. Thread it through a yarn needle, and run it through the remaining stitches. Cinch them in and gather the top of the hat. Weave in the ends, and block if desired.

FINISHING:

For a bow embellishment, you have the option to create an I cord, cut a length of coordinating ribbon, or crochet a chain about 12 inches long.

The designer recommends using size 5 needles (or two sizes below whatever you knit the hat in) to create the I cord, or a size G crochet hook for the crochet chain, so that the yarn is a bit denser.

Once you have the desired length of I cord, ribbon, or crocheted chain, weave it through one of the groups of 6 eyelet stitches closest to the brim of the hat. Leave the two tails of the cord/ribbon/chain hanging outward toward you, and then tie them into a neat little bow.

*My thanks to Jessica Gingerich for designing this baby hat for the Seaside Knitters, and to Susan Hancox, owner of YarnSong, a wonderful shop in Plaistow, New Hampshire. Jessica designs for YarnSong and has patterns on Ravelry, along with an Etsy shop called Starbright Muse.

Read on for a preview of the next Seaside Knitters Society mystery . . .

A DARK AND SNOWY NIGHT

The Christmas trees are up, the Seaside Knitters are crafting warm and beautiful gifts for the holidays, and friends and families are gathering in picturesque Sea Harbor, Massachusetts—a place where traditions run deep, but so do some treacherous family secrets . . .

Winter in Sea Harbor is a feast for the senses—crackling bonfires, the scent of snow in the salty air, carols ringing out on the village green. This year, the Seaside Knitters have a sackful of obligations in addition to their usual Christmas preparations. Izzy is so overloaded with knitting classes that she hires an extra salesperson, but the new addition has trouble fitting into the yarn shop's holiday spirit. Cass, juggling the stresses of running her lobster fishery, has finally found a nanny for her active toddler. Molly Flanigan seems practically perfect in every way—until she suddenly disappears, taking Cass's beloved rescue mutt with her . . .

Meanwhile, the holidays are kicking off in style at Mayor Beatrice Scaglia's holiday party, where a well-dressed crowd admires the mayor's sumptuous new home and the celebrity chef catering the event. An additional treat for Ben and Nell Endicott at the festive affair is reconnecting with a dear college friend, Oliver Bishop. But it's not just reunions and the appetizers that are to die for. Before the party-goers can toast the beginning of Sea Harbor's festive season, the chef—and young wife of the Endicott's old Harvard friend—is found dead beneath the mistletoe . . .

Izzy, Birdie, Nell, and Cass must uncover the pattern to these mysteries to remove suspicion from those they love, bring a murderer to justice—and keep Sea Harbor's holiday magic from vanishing into the chill winter air . . .

Available from Kensington Publishing Corp. in Fall 2022

Chapter 1

Wednesday night before the snow

Nell Endicott and Oliver Bishop's whirlwind college romance had lasted three days and two sessions of Lit 201. It ended by mutual relief, and was happily replaced by a friendship that deepened through college courses, graduations, marriages, careers and life changes. And one devastating death.

"The years slid right by us, Nell Endicott. Gone in a heartbeat. How did that happen?" Oliver leaned forward in the leather lounge chair, his elbows on his knees and his eyes on the woman sitting across from him.

Nell took the glass of wine Ollie handed her across the small table. She drank some and sat quietly, thinking about his words. *It was life*, she thought. *And it was Maddie's death. That's how it had happened*.

She looked back at Ollie, his face lined with the years, but still handsome. His prominent cheekbones were flushed from the flames crackling in the fireplace beside them, or maybe the Scotch, Nell wasn't sure. He cocked his head to one side, a trace of a smile appearing as he looked across the room at a long-haired guitar player singing mellow cover songs, as if he somehow knew the older crowd that night was deep into the past. Or wanted to be.

Ollie picked up his glass and stared at the liquid, as if surprised to see it, then tilted his head back and drained the glass. "Being here like this, it all comes back. Lots of years."

Across the lounge, along a long bar, the decibel level rose where a younger group gathered to watch the final plays of a Patriots game, and Nell leaned closer to be heard.

"We've known each other nearly half our lives, Ollie. Complicated and simple times, happy and sad ones. That doesn't go away easily."

Nell watched the lines in her friend's face deepen. She could see him touching on memories, lingering there.

"I miss her, too, Ollie," Nell said. "I'll always miss her. She was your wife. And she was the closest friend I ever had. Maddie's death hollowed out a part of me."

"I know that. Sometimes I was jealous of whatever it was you two had. It was so . . . I don't know, intimate, like the two of you wrapped yourself in a bubble and no one else could get in."

Nell smiled. "But I introduced you to each other, don't forget that. I found you the most amazing wife. So our bubble wasn't ironclad. It had a hole in it. Ben found a way in there, too."

Ollie settled back and stretched out his legs, a long swatch of graying hair falling over his forehead. He lifted his glass toward her. "Thanks for letting me in. We had some good times, the four of us."

They did have good times. And Ollie was right, too, about her friendship with Maddie. The two of them were soul sisters, almost from the first moment they met that gray September day all those years ago. She sat back in the chair, took a drink of her wine and slipped back into time remembering that day, climbing the steep stairs in the old dorm building. The creak of the steps, the musty smell in the old wood floors.

She found a closed door with a brass number nailed to it. She was *here*. Eighteen years old and excited and nervous in such huge waves she thought she might be sick. *Harvard*. This Kansas girl's dream. Finally, she took a deep breath, released it slowly, and opened the door to her assigned room.

There, tan legs folded into a pretzel, sat a girl in a torn sweatshirt and shorts, her hands dotted with neon green paint and hair pulled back into a ponytail. When she looked up, her entire face opened in a smile. On her lap and bed were scattered the makings of a collage, a sort of Welcome sign. Somewhere in the mess Nell spotted the letters of her name.

A voice lifted from the bed.

"You're finally here. I'm Maddie. Welcome to our suite."

Nell stared as words tumbled out of the woman's perfect mouth, her face spirited and happy and blotting out every bit of gray from the thick September sky.

Before Nell could answer, the woman was off the bed and wrapping the much taller Nell in a hug.

Madeline Solomon. Her first roommate. And her last. It took fifteen minutes, or maybe less, for the two young women to know they were destined to be together in one way or another through the arduous, thrilling, enormously life-changing roller-coaster ride of college.

Nell shook herself free of the memories and brought her thoughts back to the man in front of her. The sadness in Ollie's eyes, the grief etched into the lines of his face, were still fresh and new all these years after Maddie's death.

Sounds picked up in the distance as the lounge became more crowded and Ollie motioned for another Scotch.

Nell wondered briefly if she should have come. It was supposed to be a happy reunion with an old friend. An old friend with an exciting new life.

"Enough about the past, Ollie," she said lightly. "Tell me about your restaurants in New York, Ollie. And your wife. I'm looking forward to meeting her."

Ollie's body seemed to relax as he shifted back into the present. "Rachel. Well, how much time do you have? For starters, she's supremely talented. A fine chef. Not as good as I once was, but almost—" He chuckled softly.

"No one will ever be as good as you, Ollie. The cause of our 'freshmen fifteen,' plus how many more pounds? All those meals cooked up in that dingy Somerset place you lived in."

"Those were the days. Rachel would have come with me tonight, but she had to do some interviews in Boston. But you'll meet her soon enough. You'll like her, Nell. Everyone likes her. Unless they don't." He took a long drink.

"I read somewhere that she gives you credit for her success, for giving her a start."

"I suppose you could say that. Although Rachel isn't the kind of person people actually give things to. She decides what she wants, and then she takes it. People think they're offering her things, but that's because Rachel makes them feel that way."

Ollie's face and tone of voice gave Nell few clues as to whether that was a good thing or a bad thing. She took a drink and listened.

"Rachel came into the restaurant on a particularly bad day. Maddie was already in hospice, I was distracted, the restaurant was suffering. And there she was at the alley door. She stepped inside, looking around, almost as if she'd cased the place first. I watched her from the glass window in my office, slightly wary, although I couldn't tell you why. She walked around, waving steam from soup pots toward her face, checking out the combination of spices. I even saw her stick a finger in a pot of thick sauce and was about to charge out of the office and send her back out the door.

"But then one of the guys washing dishes pointed her toward my office and she headed over and walked in, as if I had been waiting for her. She checked out the mess of papers on my desk, a couple of crates on the floor, a dirty coffee cup. The expression on her face as she looked around was pure disdain. But when she looked at me it disappeared. I couldn't quite read whatever the look was that that took its place. It was businesslike, I remember, not flirtatious. She announced that she was there to work. She could start right away.

"I thought she was on something, but she went on, telling me she knew kitchens, and mine clearly needed her. It was a mess, but she'd straighten it out. Prep chef, fry chef, expediter, on and on, naming a half dozen positions. She'd take any job. Then she added that it didn't really matter where I assigned her. She'd do whatever needed to be done, and from what she could see, that was nearly everything."

Ollie shrugged, then chuckled at the memory.

"That didn't unhinge you? You never liked people telling you what to do, especially when it had anything to do with cooking," Nell said. "You were one scary cook if anyone got in your way."

Ollie laughed. "You'll get what I mean when you meet her. Besides, she was dead right. The restaurant was failing financially, although the news of that hadn't quite leaked out. I wasn't handling things well back then—"

Nell glanced at his large left hand, its veins prominent, strong fingers that once whisked butter and wine and fresh herbs into award-winning sauces. But it was the angry scar across it that stood out. She took a breath and looked up quickly. "So, did she? Did she straighten things out?"

"Yep. She did. I was mostly absent, being with Maddie, trying to make her live."

Nell looked at her old friend, then fell into the sad, shared silence. In the distance, the old Al Green song, "Let's Stay Together," filled the bar, as if the woman on the tall stool knew it fit into their memories.

As the song ended Ollie picked up the conversation again.

"Things calmed down at the restaurant without me. Rachel fired and hired people right and left. Paid off old debts, unpaid bills. She just did it, going way beyond any authority she had—which was basically none. But I could have cared less. Besides, in the end, her decisions were all smart, effective, all on target. Visionary, almost. She was a stranger. Thinking back, it was eerie that she dropped into my life that way."

"But. . . ?"

"But? No buts. It's a good thing." Ollie stretched out his legs and looked into the flames. "She's an unusual person. She knew worlds I knew little about, even though I was an established, accepted restaurateur. But Rachel—she could talk to everyone—suppliers, printers, neighbors, food writers. Not to mention a layer of society Maddie and I didn't rub shoulders with. She somehow managed to pull critics back to my tables, the ones I'd lost when Maddie got sick. Rachel charmed the heck out of them. Brought things back to life."

Nell listened quietly, trying to imagine that world. She had flown to New York to sit with Maddie shortly before she died. Ollie had stayed away that day, giving the two of them space. Maddie talked very little. Nell had held her hand, their love passing wordlessly through the gentle clasp. Nell knew when she left that day that she wouldn't see Maddie again. Not in New York. Not on this planet. But neither woman said goodbye. Their embrace was enough to cement that they would carry one another with them, wherever they were.

And now there was a Rachel, replacing Maddie in Oliver's life.

She looked over at Ollie, suddenly grateful for this woman

whom she'd not met, but who had given her friend another chance to be happy. "It sounds like Rachel is a gift. An angel," Nell said. "Who knows how it all works? Maybe Maddie had a role in this so you wouldn't completely screw up the magnificent restaurant she'd supported you in building, the one you both put your heart and soul into."

Ollie shrugged. "Maybe. Or maybe she sent her to rescue me from myself. I was pretty screwed up. Rachel helped, that's for sure. And in these years since. Things aren't always smooth, but it works out. She's a superb chef with a head for business. She thinks big, always planning for the next thing. Half the time she forgets to tell me about the newest grand plan until I see proposals, whatever. But her sense of what will work is pretty impeccable. The success of the restaurants is proof of that. She's got some new plan going on now, in fact. It's really what brought us up here."

"Catering Sea Harbor's mayor's annual holiday party?" Nell chuckled. "That's 'big' for Sea Harbor, maybe. Beatrice Scaglia is sure she won the lottery, having a famous New York chef cater her annual event. But big for Oliver Bishop? For his famous wife?"

Now it was Ollie's turn to laugh. "No, not the mayor, although she's a character, that one. She came to New York to charm us. Dressed to the nines and flirting with me shamelessly, not realizing that it was Rachel she should have been impressing. But the catering was calculated, something Rachel is very good at. She wanted to get a feel for the town so that she could—"

Nell lifted one hand, interrupting his sentence. She leaned forward and half stood, looking beyond Ollie to a tall man coming in from the dining area. She waved to get his attention, then glanced at Ollie and pointed across the room. "I'm sorry to interrupt you, but I just spotted a good friend that I want you to should meet. You have much in common."

Don Wooten spotted Nell at the same time. The owner of the Ocean's Edge restaurant and lounge smiled and waved back, raising one finger that he'd be over in a minute, and then continued toward the bar where a bartender was gesturing for the boss's attention.

"Wooten?" Ollie said, his forehead wrinkling, straining to see where Nell was looking.

"Yes. Don owns this restaurant," Nell said.

"The Ocean's Edge?" Ollie glanced back into the tasteful restaurant area, then around the comfortable lounge.

Nell sat back down. "Yes, I'm sorry. He looks busy right now. I'll introduce you later. You'll like Don."

But Ollie had stopped listening, his attention focused on the large television set above the bar, a half smile creasing his face.

He pointed to the screen. "You asked about meeting my wife. Nell, meet Rachel Fontaine."

Nell looked up at an attractive woman with pitch-black hair, pulled back into a knot. The television camera highlighted a narrow face, high cheekbones, a polished smile. Rachel Fontaine was sitting across from the evening newscaster, a popular interviewer who was guiding viewers' attention to an architect's rendering of a nearly all-glass restaurant and an attractive woman smiling at it.

Nell smiled. "She's lovely, Ollie."

But before she could comment further, the large screen suddenly went black.

For a brief second, the bar noise was muted, too.

And then, another sound.

Behind the bar, Don Wooten slammed the remote control device down on the bar surface, shattering it to pieces. Batteries skittered across the polished teak. Next to him, the young bartender squeezed a towel in his hand as if for protection, his eyes wide. Several bar regulars sitting close to the usually easy-going restaurant owner teased him for his bum choice of a remote.

Others pitied the bartender who may have caused the commotion.

But all were happy the television hadn't failed them earlier during the game.

Laughter and voices picked up almost immediately and drinks were slid across the bar surface as the guitarist packed up for the night and recorded hits filled the restaurant lounge, bringing the area back to its after-dinner spirit.

But what Nell felt wasn't the crowd's spirit, and what she saw wasn't a room of happy revelers.

What Nell saw was her good friend Don Wooten, his face darker than the wintry night, moving around the bar's end with great urgency, then disappearing through a service door and onto the cold, wave-soaked deck.